INTEGRITY

Integrity

First published in English in 2016 by
New Internationalist Publications Ltd
The Old Music Hall
106-108 Cowley Road
Oxford
OX4 1JE, UK
newint.org

Originally published in Sweden as *Tunna Väggar* by Pärspektiv Förlag in 2013.

Translated by Cindy Kite

Translation editor: Jo Lateu

Edited by Chris Brazier

Front cover design: Andrew Smith

Design: New Internationalist

Lyric to 'Fix You' by Coldplay © Universal Music Publishing Ngb Ltd.

Printed by TJ International Limited, Cornwall, UK
who hold environmental accreditation ISO 14001.

MIX
Paper from
responsible sources
FSC
www.fsc.org   FSC® C013056

British Library Cataloguing-in-Publication Data.
A catalogue record for this book is available from the British Library.

Library of Congress Cataloging-in-Publication Data.
A catalog for this book is available from the Library of Congress.

ISBN 978-1-78026-235-2

INTEGRITY

Anna Borgeryd

New Internationalist

*To Emma, Nina
and all the others
who are going to grow up.*

Mayday

'*Confianza.*' That's what he had said. He who wanted to be called Juan.

She lay awake in the darkness and felt the breeze from the northern Colombian rainforest blowing through the mosquito net. The scent of vegetation and life blended with more pungent fumes reminiscent of death. The singing of the cicadas didn't disturb the calm breathing of her colleagues. They usually fell into bed and slept deeply, exhausted from their long workdays. But tonight she lay fully awake. Memories of the last 33 hours played like a film in her head.

The blindfold had prevented her from seeing where he was taking her. First towards the northeast, she guessed, down into the lush ravine where the leaves steamed and the birdsong was most intense, but then south again along meandering paths, upwards. She had understood that they were in a real hurry. But when he had removed the blindfold from her eyes, he had nonetheless taken the time to look at her with respect: 'Your trust is good.'

Yes, that's probably true. She had been rewarded with hours during which she had felt extraordinarily alive. That passion for life and the adrenaline kick that comes just when you need to fight for it. Anxiety that her efforts wouldn't be enough. Would she be able to stop it – would Juan's trust in her prove to be well founded? Or would the newborn baby boy's mother die from blood loss despite her efforts? What had he really meant, the new grandfather who anxiously gesticulated towards the fantastic view? And who were these people – the white-clad indigenous group who had built tidy stone roads and steps that crisscrossed the steep mountainsides in the jungle?

Their huts and gardens; their respectfully offered, peculiar food and unfamiliar language; last night in a surprisingly comfortable hammock – everything spun around in her head until her thoughts returned to the most important question: would the patient survive the difficult birth? She thought so. She had had the presence of mind to take the station's best flashlight and a broad-spectrum penicillin in addition to the standard equipment. She had needed to use 27 stitches. They were not as perfect as if Adam had done them, but they were properly placed and, judging from the flow of blood, she had done them in the right order.

Now she was back in her bed in the greying wooden building that housed the aid organization's maternity clinic. She ought to be dead tired, but the life-affirming experience of having felt so fully giving and receiving pulsated through her body. Such a beautiful world, and, strangely enough, she had fitted in, had been filled with purpose.

Unforgettable, she thought, smiling, yet at the same time irritated because she couldn't sleep, couldn't get the rest she so desperately needed. *Because who knows what I might be needed for tomorrow?*

Suddenly, threatening male voices broke through the chorus of insects outside. They weren't speaking loudly, so they must be close! She sat up in an instant, filled with a chilling feeling of danger. She had just put her feet down on the old missionary station's worn wooden floor when she heard Pierre trip up the stairs. His usually calm eyes were round with fear when he rushed in among the bunks in the women's dormitory. 'They come! You run!'

Footsteps on the stairs – heavy boots – blocked the escape route. She ran to the window, ripped off the ramshackle frame with the mosquito net that blocked her way, and, with a pounding heart, looked down into the darkness. *Maybe the tall grass below would cushion the fall. But it must be at least four meters!*

She swung one of her bare legs smoothly over the window frame and hesitated. She caught a glimpse of Pierre's pajama-creased back when he bravely turned back towards the strangers. She heard the dull thud of a rifle butt hitting a cheek and how her boss tumbled heavily to the floor.

Jump or die flashed through her mind as she pulled her right leg sharply over the wood. She left blood on the frame, but didn't notice the scratch as she fell from the second floor into the darkness. When she landed, the only thing she could feel was a stabbing pain in her left knee. She fell helplessly backwards and everything mercifully went black.

June 2007

1

People do not decide to become extraordinary.
They decide to accomplish extraordinary things.

Sir Edmund Hillary

Peter saw the ad for the first time on a flight home from London. A handsomely styled picture of Lennart Stavenius advertising an exclusive brand of watch. Tall, with stylishly greying hair and dressed like some kind of Indiana Jones, he stood in front of his Cessna Skyhawk on a pontoon, with the Himalayas bathed in golden evening sunlight in the background. The caption said:

People do not decide to become extraordinary. They decide to accomplish extraordinary things.

Something beyond the ordinary.
Peter felt pride flood through his body like an adrenaline kick. Not everybody had a father like his! He was filled with a desire to be in an ad like that himself when he was 54. He reclined his wide, business class seat all the way back and put his hands behind his head. The likelihood that he would get the chance was good, because the family business was a recognized export success. The idea of following in his father's footsteps was agreeable and filled him with a pleasant feeling of going from one success to another. He shifted his gaze and looked out the airplane window at the sunlit clouds. He could see a long way in the beautiful, light blue world.

2

Vera sat in the university teacher's office. She maneuvered her crutches so that they supported her left leg at the one, slightly bent, angle that didn't hurt and wondered nervously what the red-haired woman would say.

'Your request isn't unusual.' Åström was a graduate student, and she was in charge of the summer course that Vera really wanted to take. She turned towards her computer screen and clicked on an email. '*The Development of the Discipline of Economics* isn't full... but we haven't contacted everyone on the reserve list. We can't let you in ahead of people who applied before the deadline.'

She must be the university's dream employee, thought Vera. Calm and matter-of-fact, groomed like an old-school movie star and with a bookcase stuffed with knowledge behind her.

Åström glanced at Vera with a slight smile. 'But there's nothing more boring than calling and fussing with half-hearted types... Have you any particular reason for thinking you should attend the sign-on lecture? That would give you a good chance of being admitted.'

Cecilia Åström's blazer was exactly the same color as her light, grey-blue eyes. Vera looked down at her not entirely clean khaki pants and tucked her sandaled foot with the dirty big-toe nail under her damaged leg. But she had no trouble answering the question. 'Yes, and it's a reason I'm sure you haven't heard before.'

✹

Two weeks later, Vera sat on the bus on the way to campus. The sun shone and she looked out of the window, gazing in wonder at the dripping from the birch trees onto the warm asphalt. Raised in a village in the northern Swedish forest, she usually took them for granted, but now she saw the trees with fresh eyes. *Givers of life. Brilliant sun-catchers.*

Up at the front of the bus, a turquoise, dolphin-shaped balloon on a thin string floated in the air. The balloon consistently moved in the wrong direction. Vera noticed it immediately – the dolphin went forward when the bus accelerated, backwards when the driver braked. On the roundabout, when centrifugal force pushed everybody to the right, the balloon went left.

Just like me, she thought. Starting over at 30, when everyone else is settling down. *A new chance? A new life?* She considered the strange phenomenon until she understood what she was seeing. The law of inertia also influenced the air molecules in the bus! *They move backwards exactly like the rest of us when the bus increases speed, forcing the balloon forward.*

The abnormal behavior of the dolphin was understandable. *But what's my excuse?* Tears burned behind her eyelids. Vera looked out of the window and forced herself to stop by taking a deep breath. She discreetly dried her tears and told herself that her knee would soon heal, and that everything else would too. She thought about midsummer, at home by the river. How many magical nights like that would she get to experience in her life; shouldn't she be living as intensely as possible?

Since her teens Vera had felt like she had an antenna tuned in to the universe. It sat in the middle of her body, right in front of her backbone, and it picked up a unique signal from somewhere. The result was a life guided by a warm feeling of self-evident direction. But the antenna wasn't the same after everything that had happened in Colombia; it disappeared, flickered only for short periods, pointed her in an entirely different direction. There was nothing secure and consistent about it any more. It was like a dying person with regrets, who wanted to tell a secret that would change everything. And huge questions were the only thing she carried inside herself now. *What are we doing?* What science can explain why it doesn't help to try to save the world with your own two hands?

She was pulled back into the summer day by the braking of the bus as it reached the university. With small drops of tears dried on the inside of her glasses, in cut-off jeans, grey hoodie and backpack, she raised herself up with the help of her strong right leg. The rings on Vera's left hand twisted and chafed against the crutch. If someone had noticed her make-up free face, they would have seen rounded features accentuated by bushy eyebrows and protruding ears.

It was the beginning of the second week of the summer course, and they were going to study the classics. She eased herself off the bus with her bandaged left leg, her messy brown braid swaying. She hadn't understood it, but she had followed her dying antenna just the same and was now on her way towards the unknown.

Because this – the world as it is – surely this can't be the best we can do?

3

Peter didn't know what it was down to. Was it the summer day, calling to him to throw down the chalk and go to the beach? Was it Sandra's distracting glances and embarrassingly flirty comments during the break? Or maybe the lecture wasn't going too well because of that grey girl on crutches and her irritating questions. It was true that he hadn't been teaching very long, but even so. He had never even *heard* of anyone questioning *The Wealth of Nations* before!

He had just explained Adam Smith's classic theory about the Invisible Hand – how acting in one's own interest actually promoted the common interest – when she started in. She was already asking the question as she raised her hand.

'Why did Smith think that?'

Peter said something about England in the 1700s and how industrialization increased the speed of exploitation, which suddenly created great prosperity.

'What great prosperity?'

A few people in the class giggled, but the grey girl with the crutches just waited for an answer. He had never seen anything like it: an inconspicuous person who boldly maintained eye contact for so long. It was as if she had a firm sense of self that was completely independent of what he thought of her or how she looked. She waited to hear what he would say, and he looked away with an unpleasant feeling of responsibility.

Before his first lecture, Professor Överlind had given him some advice about what to do if he got a question he couldn't answer. 'Just say, "I don't know but I can find out and let you know during the next lecture if you want".' Professor Sturesson added, 'Say, "you find out and tell us next time," and then they'll stop asking such questions!'

And that worked fine, as long as the student asked about the size of Peru's GDP last year. Not even a university teacher could be a walking encyclopedia.

But the girl on crutches wanted something else. After his short capitulation, Peter looked up again. Her dark blue gaze passed through her irritatingly smudged glasses and forced its way right into his skull. She demanded that he understand what he was talking about. Peter was struck by a naked feeling that he didn't.

Fortunately, endless hours hanging out in bars had taught him what to do if a girl asked an uncomfortable question. Deflect with a counter-question, preferably a charming one that got the girl talking about herself

'What do you mean?' he managed to say. *Maybe not the smartest riposte, but at least it was something.*

'Prosperity measured in terms of return on investment or how many people's basic needs are met or what? What did Adam Smith mean?' was her immediate response, and her gaze remained stubbornly focused on Peter's.

The silence became embarrassing. The girl with crutches shifted in her seat. 'How about I phrase it like this, instead: what is all this based on?' She pointed at the book in front of her. Her voice was soft, but her eyes were unrelentingly penetrating. 'Why is this a good idea?'

Are her eyes blue? Can she even see through those dirty glasses? Peter said something half coherent about how profit is presumably necessary in order to meet human needs, but that the pioneering economist from the 1700s perhaps wasn't so precise on that point.

Sandra looked up from her French manicure, a shadow of worry on her attractive face. 'Will this be in the test?'

Peter noticed the look that the girl with crutches gave Sandra. Fortunately the lecture was over – time was up. He wondered if she had done it on purpose when one of the crutches slid into the aisle just as Sandra passed. She tripped, and – damn! – succeeded in showing a little too much of the tattoo on her lower back.

Afterwards, Peter and Cissi Åström went for coffee. Cissi was the only one in the department on this fantastic summer day. She glanced at him. A critical observer might have seen a thoughtless youth with cocky posture and a slightly crooked mouth suggesting unreliability. But, like most people, Cissi only saw 184 centimeters of effortless beauty under his sun-bleached surfer hair.

'Debriefing?' The question came immediately. Apparently he was giving off stress vibes, and maybe Cissi remembered how a group of demanding students could annihilate you. Half numb, Peter followed his red-haired colleague.

'Was it her, that Sandra?' Cissi asked, smiling knowingly as they sat down at the table. Peter stiffened uncomfortably.

'Do you know what she said to me? "I don't have time for the test, because I have to write my blog!" Apparently she has thousands of readers just waiting to hear her creative twist on the fashion of the day, so I need to understand that she can't prioritize a take-home test for one measly reader!' Cissi snorted. 'I mean, sure, I'm the first to agree that fashion is fun, but I wonder why some people even go to college!'

Peter was silent. He knew that starting an intimate relationship with a student was against the rules. It didn't seem like a big deal if Sandra turned out to be uninterested in her summer class. It wouldn't be the first time; girls often took circuitous routes to get close to Peter.

He wondered if Cissi had noticed anything, if this seemingly well-meaning pep talk was actually an effort to get him to admit, and end, his little adventure with the class's curvaceous blonde.

'But I'm only guessing! How did it go today?' Cissi looked at him with interest.

'Not so well. I was going to bike to the lake and swim, but I feel completely wiped out.'

Cissi supported her chin with her hand, and Peter saw that she thought she understood exactly what he meant.

'It's a strange feeling to stand in front of people your own age who are gawping like baby birds.' She changed her voice, mimicking something Peter sensed was still Sandra. 'Feed me knowledge! Give me my credits so I can get my grant! But, by the way, I only have time to study three hours a week!'

14

Peter looked out of the window at the fine summer weather. It didn't really matter; a career in academia was nothing he had ever considered. He felt sorry for the poor bastards who spent their lives trying to get people to understand economics. He had only accepted the department's job offer because Lennart was going to force him to spend his summer doing currency hedging and other administrative crap.

His father had a habit of making unpleasant demands on him, and lately it had increased. In June, just after Peter had come home from a party weekend in London with his cousin Charlie, Lennart had confronted him and given him a choice – no money or a job at the office. Peter didn't like being dependent on his father and his company, so it had felt completely right to take an unpredictable path just to feel like he had a little freedom. He couldn't help smiling in satisfaction when he thought about how he had been able to decline Lennart's job proposal because he had been asked to teach a course at the university.

Not everybody thinks I'm a disappointment, was the satisfying underlying message. Of course, it was Professor Sturesson, an old acquaintance of his father, who had offered him the job. Like Peter's dad, Åke Sturesson had come from humble but character-building circumstances. Both men had succeeded in making something of themselves, and they liked to congratulate each other for belonging to 'Stockholm Business School's most noble graduating class, the most successful class in history.' Peter knew that the low status of teaching wasn't something people in academic circles spoke openly about. In other words, there was very little risk that his dad would find out that summer teaching was shunned by exhausted assistant professors, that professors basically never bothered with undergraduate teaching, and that summer courses were taught by impoverished graduate students and semi-gifted undergraduates like himself.

'Of course,' Cissi continued, 'fortunately, some students are interested. They're the ones who give you an energy boost. Which reminds me! What do you think of her – Lundberg?'

Cissi's round face radiated with something that most resembled enthusiasm. Not that he was in any way interested in Cissi. He looked at her, a well-dressed pencil pusher who couldn't quite hide her hippie nature. Because he wasn't opposed to making even ordinary, older women happier, Peter now turned on his charm offensive: 'What do you think is so good about "her – Lundberg"?'

The answer was a crazy story more unbelievable than any pick-up line Peter had ever used. Peter didn't really listen very carefully, so he didn't know quite how it happened. Somehow, before he had finished his coffee he had promised Cissi that he would check with Kalle, who lived in his dormitory, whether the room he was looking to sublet was still available. Apparently Cissi knew some super-gifted but wretched Vera Lundberg who had a cosmic right to a bit of luck. And she – Lundberg – needed a place to live.

4

'Are you starting to figure out how money works?' Cissi asked. They were lunching on baguettes at the only campus coffee shop that was open during the summer.

Vera hesitated. In truth, Cissi was one of the best teachers Vera had ever had, but it felt weird to say so. Instead she said: 'Definitely more than before, in any case. It's really interesting. It's always good to know the history of things.'

Cissi smiled. 'Well, you're definitely taking the right course, then. But now you need to tell me why a nurse would suddenly start studying economics.'

Vera looked at Cissi. 'The short or long version?'

'The long one, I guess.'

'I was a volunteer with Basic Needs, in two of the wealthiest countries in the world if you measure wealth in terms of natural resources. The Congo is as big as Western Europe and has huge reserves of minerals, especially the kinds that we need to make computers and other modern electronics. Colombia's natural environment is fantastic, and they export a huge amount of biomass. Unfortunately, the resources are worth an enormous amount of money.'

'Huh? What do you mean, 'unfortunately'?'

'Because of the market value of the resources, people are willing to use violence to get control of them. I think there are four factions in the Congo, five in Colombia. Ordinary people who just want to live in peace are exposed to violence and suffer from shortages of everything – clean water, food, shelter, healthcare... Those are the people we try to help. In the Congo a lot of people suffer from cholera and are victims of sexual violence. Ironically, we were transferred to Colombia because it became too dangerous to be in the Congo.'

Cissi watched as Vera gently rested her leg on the sofa next to her. 'Is that where you hurt yourself?'

'Yeah, but I'm glad I got to see northern Colombia; that's where we were. It's so unbelievably beautiful! Have you ever heard of Sierra Nevada de Santa Marta, the world's highest coastal mountain?'

'No.'

'Imagine an area of a few thousand square kilometers that contains all the world's climates. From coral reefs in the Caribbean to mangrove swamps and rainforests, deserts, steppes and tundra – all because the mountain rises out of the sea to a height of 5,700 meters. The mountaintops are always covered with snow; at the top it is -20 all year round.'

'Sounds gorgeous!'

'Yeah, what an experience it was! A completely unique people lives there… Kogi, the only indigenous civilization that still lives as it did before Christopher Columbus.'

'There are people left that still live like that?'

'The Kogi have lived on agriculture for thousands of years. They moved higher up into the mountains when the conquistadors came.'

'And that allowed them to survive?'

Vera heard doubt in Cissi's voice, and a feeling of sorrow arose in her as she admitted, 'Many of them died.' Vera stared down at her tea, remembering. 'And I got to visit them. It was unreal, because they usually keep to themselves, and it is difficult to find them.'

'So how did you get to them?'

'The other people on my team were away doing vaccinations. I was doing inventory in the room where we kept the medicines. Suddenly he just appeared – a long-haired Kogi man dressed in white. He said: "We are in need of you. Can you trust me, please?" I just stared at him. As it turned out, I was forced to wear a blindfold when I went with him.'

The corner of Cissi's mouth twitched and she mumbled, 'Secret dream number… 86?'

'What?'

'No, but I mean, blindfolded… why?'

'They don't want people to be able to find them,' Vera said simply.

'But weren't you scared?'

'Yes, there was one thing I was afraid of... I usually don't go out alone on difficult deliveries, and I was afraid that things would go so badly that I would be forced to do a fetal dismemberment.'

'What? Is that what it sounds like?' asked Cissi with a grimace.

'Yeah. I still remember in Kivu, when Pierre had to crush the little head of a fetus that was stuck. But sometimes you have to do it, for everybody involved. I was usually the one who talked to the relatives, and when I had to tell the grandmother... oh, how I cried when I told her...'

'What?'

'That the baby was dead and would be buried with his mother, unless we tried to save the mother by breaking the baby's skull. I can barely even manage to talk about it, and I was afraid that I might also be forced to do it.'

Cissi was pale. 'I understand. It was the best thing to do given the situation. So it got... stuck to death?'

'Yeah. But afraid... in Colombia there are lots of things to be afraid of, but I was never afraid of the Kogi. And the man who came to get me because his woman needed help, he was calm, despite the fact that it was urgent. He said he was named "Juan", which I don't believe for a second. Juan is a Spanish name, you know, but I just said... "Okay, where are we going, Juan?" And he said, "Al Corazón del Mundo".'

'The heart of the world... How lovely; he meant his wife?'

'Actually, that's what I thought too, but it wasn't. I rode for what must have been an hour, blindfolded, on a bony donkey that climbed upwards though the jungle. I was glad when we got to a suspension bridge where he took off the blindfold and let me get off.' Vera stopped talking and smiled inwardly at the memory. There was a long silence.

'What are you thinking about?' asked Cissi and looked at her, curious.

'"Your trust is good," he said. "That is good. Without it, you are alone and an easy target."' Vera took a bite of her baguette. After a while she continued. 'From the bridge I was allowed to walk; we continued upwards until we got to a village with round huts. We ran the last bit.'

Cissi swallowed the last bite of her baguette. 'How were they?'

'The village midwives had just got the boy out, feet first, just using their hands. It was fantastic.'

'Was he alive?'

'Yes, the son was okay. But the mother was bleeding a lot.'

'Uh-oh... not good...'

'No, you could say that I got there just in time. Juan translated what I said for the midwives, told them what I wanted to do to save her. They knew what stitches were, and they let me give her anesthesia and stitch her up where she had torn.'

Cissi squirmed like a worm on a hook; her sharp inward breath whistled between her teeth. 'Did it work?'

'I managed to stop the bleeding. She survived the evening and the night anyway, and I gave her our best antibiotics. I think she will have survived, so long as nothing unexpected happened.'

She had barely eaten anything and Cissi was finished. Vera took another bite and waved her baguette in the air. 'This is what happens if you talk all the time!'

'But the things you've gone through! What happened after that?'

'They were very kind. The next morning Juan came and woke me up; I was supposed to go with his father-in-law. Later, when I got home to Sweden and searched online for information about the Kogi people, I understood that he was their Kogi Mama, shaman and leader. The old man took me to a lookout point and pointed and talked. I stood there – I had just woken up; the sunrise was fantastic... The jungle spread out over majestic mountains, crops far down in the valley and the turquoise ocean all the way at the bottom. And yet, what I remember most is his face... completely lined. You know, beautifully old and dignified, but worried like a child. And I tried to listen. "This is our work, our responsibility," I think I got about half of what he said, but later I saw a film on the internet, and I understood what he was talking about – *From the Heart of the World, The Elder Brothers' Warning*.'

'El Corazón del Mundo was actually the place?'

'Yeah. The Kogi say that their Sierra Nevada is the heart of the world, that they are older brothers and the rest of us are ignorant little brothers and sisters. They feel a responsibility to maintain the balance in the world and... protect the river of life, but now they can't do it alone any more. El corazón enfermo, the mountain that is the heart of the world, is sick. What he pointed at wasn't the beauty that I first saw; it was spots of bare earth at the foot of the mountain and clear-cut areas that were like sores on the side of the mountain. Since ancient times the Kogi have lived in balance with Mother Earth, but we little brothers and sisters don't understand anything; we dig her to pieces and destroy her. He said that we live in a new time. And if the mountain dies, then the whole world will die. And she is critically ill; the river of life is weak.'

'River of life? What was he talking about? Something spiritual?' Cissi's big eyes shone.

'Maybe, but I think he was mainly talking about the water; that's how I understood it later. When the water doesn't flow like it should...'

'I get it,' Cissi said and looked worried. 'Climate change. The glaciers are melting; the tundra is drying out, too little water in the rivers.'

'Yes. Kogi Mama described it as Mother Earth is sick and the world is out of balance. "When death comes to the top of the world, it continues downward too." And it isn't just superstition. They have problems with their harvests; they're finding it harder and harder to feed everyone.'

'Yeah, it's scary how dependent we are on one another, how much we influence one other. And them too, even though they've tried to hide themselves on a mountain,' said Cissi thoughtfully.

'Mmm... When I did some more online research I found a coalition of Indigenous Americans. There was stuff about

Koyaanisqatsi, and then everything fell into place. I understood that I had been given a task that morning with the Kogi Mama.'

'Koyanis… what did you say?'

'Koyaanisqatsi. It's a word in Hopi that means life out of balance – an insane, unsustainable lifestyle.'

Cissi considered Vera over her teacup. 'Oh. You think you got an assignment, a mission?'

'Kogi Mama asked me, "Little brothers and sisters, what are you doing?"'

Cissi looked quietly at Vera, thinking, before she finally said, 'A big question.'

'Yes. And what we're doing has to do with money, so now I need to study economics.'

Cissi smiled crookedly, 'But that clear-cut area he asked about, maybe it was to grow drugs?'

'Yeah, most likely. Forty years of war, millions of refugees, everything seems to be about controlling the drug trade.'

'Listen, that guerrilla attack, how did you manage to survive it?'

Vera felt a tingling sensation through her body. How many times had she brooded over all those questions. *Did anyone survive? Eliza? Pierre? Stuart? Camilla? Was it a difficult end? Why was I spared? How can I repay the debt?*

Vera swallowed. 'Pure luck. I was in bed, but awake. We girls slept upstairs, and that gave me a little time. I jumped out of the window, hurt my knee, hit my head on the side of the building and fainted. I was found later by some colleagues from town who came when they couldn't contact us.' She shivered again, down to the bone. Violent strangers had kidnapped the people who had become her closest friends, and she had lain there, injured and helpless, in the dark, protected by a small tuft of grass.

'What about the others?'

'The guerrillas took them. They're still missing. Maybe dead in the jungle? I don't know.' Vera looked down.

Pure luck. And of course Pierre.

✖

22

Seven weeks after she had come home to Sweden, it was time for a follow-up appointment with the orthopedic specialist. Vera lay barelegged and freezing on the paper-covered bed in the doctor's office. She looked down at her stiff left leg and then up at the doctor in the white coat.

'Yes, it's still quite swollen...' The 60-year-old man's hairy fingers squeezed her left knee in practised fashion. He shifted his hands quickly to the right knee, squeezing and comparing it with the left. Then he tried pushing her left knee downwards towards the bed. The pain caused Vera to jerk her right foot beneath her other leg to protect it.

'Ouch!'

'Okay, okay. Take it easy. It's going to be difficult if you don't let me examine you properly.'

He pulled her right foot out and moved the healthy leg out of the way. 'What about this direction?' More carefully this time, he tried to bend Vera's knee by pushing her lower left leg backwards. That didn't work either. 'Are you sure you can't straighten out your leg or bend it either?' The doctor looked at her in concern and felt the fluid-filled joint yet again.

'No, I can't.'

'And you're still using crutches.' He turned towards the computer screen and read from it. 'After almost eight weeks?'

Vera heard the doubt in his voice. 'Yeah, I know, it's strange. But it's healing really slowly.'

'You can stand up. Show me. What happens when you try to walk on it?'

'I can support myself on it a little bit, like this.' She stepped cautiously and fumblingly forward on her bent, stiff leg. 'But I know that it isn't normal; maybe we need to do an MRI to find out what's wrong?'

The doctor looked disapprovingly at her.

'Or maybe laparoscopic surgery?' she tried, but she could tell by his body language that this wasn't the right thing to say either. Vera suddenly remembered a messy situation that had occurred about six months ago. The team had been faced with several difficult-to-diagnose patients who had fled from the South.

Camilla had pulled her off to the side and warned her against drawing too many of her own conclusions around the doctors. 'You take care of anesthetics; let them do the diagnosing.' Then Camilla had whispered kindly, 'Not because you can't, but they'll soon figure it out for themselves; you'll see.'

'No, an additional examination is not appropriate at the moment,' said the doctor firmly.

'But there's something wrong, isn't there?' pleaded Vera.

He told her to get dressed and turned towards the computer. She wondered what he was writing in her medical records. He ended the appointment with a quick handshake, and his white coat rose on his chest as he sighed. 'Once the swelling has gone down you'll be able to move it. You'll see. I'll put you down for another visit on November 5th, but my guess is that you won't need it. I suspect that by then you will have trained the knee and regained stability on your own.'

Vera understood that the doctor was trying to cheer her up. Or, as Pierre used to say in his charming French accent, 'The foremost duty of a *médecin*, is to *amuse* the patient, while she will naturally heal herself.'

But Vera was not amused. The doctor's decision gave her a sick feeling in her stomach. The fifth of November! She left obediently, staring down at the yellow tape on the vinyl floor that led her to the next stopping point, the well-meaning physical therapist. She gave Vera a sheet of paper containing pedagogically illustrated exercises to do. Vera knew that she couldn't even do half of them.

✹

Vera was surprised. Her mother usually slept late after a night shift at the nursing home. But today Gunilla had set the table with four kinds of bread, three different sandwich fillings, tea, yoghurt and cereal.

'How did it go at the psychologist's?' asked Gunilla.

'Oh,' Vera said evasively, 'I'm finished with that. Finished working through the trauma.'

'Are you sure? I agree with Erika. You aren't yourself at all!'

Erika, Vera's athletic best friend since school, had graduated from college with a degree in information technology and moved to Sydney. She had come home over the summer with some guy named Tom whom she'd met when she was surfing in the South Pacific. But Vera and Erika had only seen each other twice...

Vera put down her teacup. The memory of her friend's uncomprehending effort to help her – 'Come on now! You're usually bursting with energy!' – left her with a feeling of emptiness. Vera had thought a lot about the last thing Erika said before she left: 'Where's the old Vera?'

'I noticed that you've hardly touched your medicines,' her mother continued, pushing away her yoghurt bowl. 'Not the Stilnoct or the one that helps against depression.' Gunilla sounded reproachful.

Vera sighed. 'It was nice of you to... get all that stuff for me, but I listen to music to help me sleep.' *They ought to prescribe Fleetwood Mac and Debussy*, she thought and continued, 'I've almost stopped having nightmares.'

'You and your father and your music!' Gunilla looked at her uncomprehendingly.

I don't know what I would have done without it.

They were quiet for a minute, then Gunilla asked: 'What about that course you're taking? What is it about?'

'I guess you could say it's about the development of the modern economy and how to understand it,' Vera said as she put a piece of bread in the toaster.

'Economics? Not medicine?'

Vera sighed and refrained from trying to explain, something she had become quite practised at.

Gunilla looked at her daughter. 'How are you? Are you at least eating enough?'

Vera nodded.

'This studying, you aren't borrowing money to finance it, are you?'

Vera shook her head.

'Well, then you're going to have to work in the fall, aren't you?'

'I'm going to take Economics I in the fall.'

A deep frown formed between Gunilla's eyebrows, and Vera quickly added, 'But I'm happy to work extra in the evenings and on weekends.' She had been planning to do that anyway. Even if she usually didn't need much money, you couldn't live on nothing, and she hated being financially dependent on other people.

'Uh-huh. Since you're going to be in town anyway, do you want me to check if they need help at Solbacka?' Gunilla wondered.

'Yeah, sure, do that. But don't promise anything, because what if I'm not better in the fall?' She gently felt her left knee.

'Of course you'll be fine in the fall! If your knee were really that bad then they would have operated on it right away; you know that! You just have to stick it out, and then you can start working, and well... everything will go back to normal. You'll see.'

Vera was almost finished eating when Gunilla finally forced out the question that she badly wanted answered. 'What really happened between you and Adam when you came home in May?'

The food in her mouth seemed to expand; Vera caught her breath and couldn't look up.

Gunilla gripped her hand comfortingly. 'You know, Eva and Krister were down visiting him, and he is really sad. Eva called just to say that he really misses you. He wants everything to be back to normal again.' Gunilla tried to catch Vera's eye. 'Just remember, however bleak things seem, he loves you.'

Vera took a deep breath. Yes, that felt like the truth. Despite everything that had happened, she knew that Adam loved her.

But what she said each time he contacted her was the only thing that she was sure she felt: I just don't have the energy to see you at the moment.

5

Peter forgot the promise he made to Cecilia Åström. He didn't do it on purpose; it was just that living up to other women's expectations of him took all his time. But in August, when Kalle unexpectedly showed up in the otherwise empty dormitory to move out of his room, which was next to Peter's, Peter suddenly remembered the crazy story.

'You know your room is hard currency, don't you?' he said happily as they clapped one another on the back. 'I heard the most exaggerated sob story, cooked up by somebody desperate to get their hands on these cleverly designed square meters.' Peter made an elegant gesture, as if he were a well-paid real estate agent showing a luxury condo.

'Oh, knock it off!' Kalle looked up from his removal boxes. He was on his way to Kalmar to take a substitute teaching job, and he was thinking hard about where to put what.

Peter continued, inspired. 'Imagine a nurse who could have been living a life of leisure as a rich man's wife. But she travels the world instead, working for Doctors without Borders. She's somewhere in South America for a few months, saving lives. Then some armed guerrillas invade the camp and kidnap everybody they can find, including a colleague, an older Swede!'

'Shit!' Kalle said. He straightened up, pulled up his shorts and dried the sweat off his forehead with the arm of his faded Greenpeace t-shirt.

Peter smiled at his friend, who, at that moment, looked more than ever like Fred Flintstone – thick hair sticking up in all directions, grey five o'clock shadow around his chin and hairy, stocky legs.

'I know! Creative, right?' Peter was always fascinated by elaborate fantasies. 'But wait! There's more! This girl got away, barely, but she hurt herself, broke her arm or something, and got sent home. There's something wrong, though; the arm won't heal. She goes home and lives with her mother and then walks straight into the Economics Department and says, like, "How does money work?" Can you believe it?!'

'Yeah, good question,' Kalle mumbled from inside a removal box.

'And now she apparently needs to live here, if you're not opposed to renting out your room to a one-armed mythomaniac?' Peter grinned and helped Kalle with the last pile of books about animal behavior and micro-organisms in water.

Kalle wrinkled his brow and actually looked almost sad.

Peter's smile faded. 'What the hell, Kalle; don't you have a sense of humor? Can't you appreciate a good backstory when you hear one? And think of me who has to live here; what if the girl is half as good-looking as she is creative? Maybe she's both a damn good storyteller and an SHB 10?

Kalle took a step forward and pushed his index finger into Peter's chest. 'I gave you that book to… Do you understand the risks of acting like you do? Of all of this…'

'What risks?' Peter asked, interrupting him.

'You know, different girls all the time.'

'Oh, you take it much too seriously!'

'It wasn't to teach you new sexist expressions,' concluded Kalle stubbornly.

Kalle was somewhat unusual as a biologist who, in addition to his courses in high-school pedagogy, had taken 15 credits in Women's Studies. It was actually a little suspicious, but Peter was willing to overlook it. Kalle had been a good dormitory neighbor, and Peter hoped he would come back when his substitute teaching position ended.

'What?' grinned Peter. 'SHB 10? Abbreviations are so practical! "Super-hot babe 10 points" takes so long to say.'

'And you sound like an idiot,' muttered Kalle.

'What…?' Peter thought he knew what the problem was. 'If you need a few tips about how to pick up girls, then you can read *The Game* yourself.'

'I have read it,' said Kalle and blushed under his stubble. 'It

28

gets good at the end, but I guess you haven't read that part?'

'Song lyrics. You can listen to them from beginning to end. Somebody cared enough to summarize the most important stuff. But books... ' *How in the hell would I have managed to read* Lord of the Rings *if I hadn't skipped over all the language Tolkien tried to construct?* he thought. 'You only read as much of a book as you need to in order to get the main point.' Peter was never one to work unnecessarily. There were easier ways to get ahead.

'But that's what I'm saying. The point comes at the end.' Fred Flintstone looked irritated.

'Doesn't seem so to me. Isn't it an instruction book for repressed unfortunates? "Here's what all you frustrated nerds should do if you want to have sex with gorgeous girls".' Peter made quotation marks in the air. 'But those tricks... never needed 'em.' He looked frankly at Kalle.

Kalle sighed, 'But what if it's all true?'

'What?'

'Just because you sometimes tell huge lies doesn't mean that she, that girl, is lying,' continued Kalle as he closed the last jam-packed box. 'I actually read something about Red Cross workers being kidnapped somewhere in the spring.'

He went over to his desk and turned on his laptop. 'Have you checked it out? What's her name?'

Peter couldn't remember her name, but after another conversation with Cissi and a few clever white lies, he reappeared in Kalle's room. 'Vera... what a strange name, sounds like an old woman. Vera Lundberg, and apparently she took the course I taught in the summer. In which case she's no ten-pointer anyway, the best looking girl in the class was Sandra, SB 8.5,' continued Peter teasingly.

'God you're sick! Incurable,' Kalle muttered kindly and typed 'Vera Lundberg' into the search bar.

'Thanks. You too,' smiled Peter.

Six minutes later, the internet had given them the following information:

Vera Magdalena Lundberg turns 30 on January 26. She is

the only child of Sven-Erik and Gunilla and lives at the same address – Lingongatan 9, Vindeln. In the summer of 1999 she married a doctor, the now 32-year-old plastic surgeon Adam Henningsson. 'The couple are keeping their own last names,' Kalle read out loud from the wedding announcement in the newspaper.

'Then why the hell does she live with her mother?' Peter looked at Kalle in bemusement.

'How do we know? Something temporary. Or something serious. Plastics guy maybe hit her? Wife-beating is a lot more common than people think,' said Kalle grimly. He got up and stretched his aching shoulders.

Peter sank down into the chair that Kalle had vacated and clicked some more: 'Look at this!' He read out loud from an article in the country's most widely read daily paper. 'Vera Lundberg is the Swedish nurse who narrowly escaped being kidnapped by a splinter group of FARC guerrillas on the fifteenth of May. The Marxist branch of Fuerzas Armadas Revolucionarias de Colombia...'

Peter had traveled in the Caribbean enough for his Spanish accent to be pretty good, but he still went too slowly for Kalle, who put his arms on the table to support himself and continued reading on his own, '...demanded a sum equal to 30 million kronor in exchange for releasing four European doctors and nurses, who, it is now feared, have been executed in the jungle.'

'Yeah, apparently it takes real Marxists to demand a hefty sum of capital,' grinned Peter.

Kalle eagerly read on, 'Lundberg has criticized the freeing of Ingrid Betancourt by the military under false pretenses. The immunity and security of volunteers is now under greater threat... She wonders what has really been done to try to free her imprisoned colleagues.'

'So what does she want?' Peter interjected. 'Does she want the military to undertake a rescue mission or not?'

Kalle studied the picture of a pale, serious girl with her leg in a bandage. 'Isn't she more like a ... lame Florence Nightingale?'

When Peter looked more closely at the grainy photograph

he realized: Vera Lundberg was the maddening, grey girl on crutches! But it was too late now. Do-gooder Kalle was determined to have her as 'the world's coolest and most worthy' subletter and had already written down her telephone number. *Damn!* How the hell could he have known that her unbelievable sob story was actually true? Seriously, sometimes he talked before he had thought things through. He was filled with vague discomfort, as if an important test were approaching that he knew he wasn't ready for.

6

Vera was surprised at how quickly she got back into the old routines. Morning meetings, care schedules, feeding, personal hygiene and the all-important 'List', which, if not properly filled out, could mean unnecessary enemas for the elderly residents. 'Well, Ulrik hasn't pooped for a week now.' If it wasn't written on the 'List', it made no difference what poor Ulrik tried to say about what he had actually produced.

Vera understood the importance of structure, rules and sticking to schedules. But rationalizing to the point where it felt like the people you were supposed to be helping were unhappy, that was where she drew the line. It was partly for that reason that she had quit her job at Solbacka the last time.

But it was mostly because something else had tempted her. She smiled at the happy memory of her life with Adam during their college years. Life was simple and full of meaning; they were on their way. His journey: first medical school and then training to become a surgeon. Hers: four years to become a nurse anesthetist.

They went home together in the late afternoons. They usually slipped into the supermarket to buy something for dinner, unabashedly discussing surgical alternatives in the fruit department. An endless number of solutions had been debated at the stove in their small, well-designed two-room apartment. They used to go to the movies, spend time with friends and go to church once in a while.

It was Adam who had first suggested that they go abroad after graduation – to help take care of people and contribute to the church's mission by using their medical training to do volunteer work. His faith had always been stronger than hers, but Gunilla belonged to the same evangelical church, and she had made sure that her daughter attended revivals and bible study like the church's other teenagers.

But the truth was that everyone involved had quickly realized that Vera wasn't an ordinary child of the congregation. Her questions had stopped being harmlessly cute, like they had been in Sunday school, when she asked about something she thought was obviously wrong: 'Why does it say that Abraham gave birth to Isaac? Everybody knows that mummies give birth to babies!'

When she got older she asked questions about morality. How could God become so angry at Pharaoh that he hardened his heart? When Pharaoh refused to let Moses and the Jews leave, why did God bring down plagues on all Egyptians? Isn't it more like a human sin to be so vengeful, to want to punish an entire people?

And if you went to heaven if you were a good-hearted heathen who had never heard of Jesus – but not if you had heard of him, but hadn't become Christian – didn't you expose people to risks if you went out evangelizing? 'I mean,' Vera had asked, 'if a stranger came along, someone who also took people from our country and enslaved them, how likely is it that we would want to believe in their God? What if the good heathens would have gone to heaven if only we had left them alone? What would Jesus have said about that?'

Someone in the congregation had eventually talked to Gunilla, who, ashamed of her daughter's deviant behavior, took her out of bible school. When Gunilla got home she yelled at Sven-Erik because she blamed his Social Democratic atheism for Vera's embarrassing defect – the endless questioning! It had always been important to Gunilla to fit in with her childhood congregation. She was anxious that no-one should ever whisper anything negative about her or her family.

Quitting bible study didn't bother Vera. She genuinely wanted her questions answered, but she had pretty quickly figured out that the standard answer to the most interesting ones was: 'If we had answers to all our questions, then we would be like God, and of course it is only God who is God.' Why then did God give me a brain that wonders about all these things? thought Vera, but she kept her mouth shut.

Since childhood, Vera had been most interested in the practical question of how you can live a good life, and the best answer she had come upon was the golden rule: *Do unto others as you would have them do unto you.* That was something in the bible that rang true for her.

So the idea of doing volunteer relief work stuck with Vera and, over the years, grew into a decision. Obviously she would go with Adam and help where they were most needed. Every day, every page she read and practical exercise she completed was meaningful because it helped her develop the skills that would heal, ease and prevent illness somewhere out in the world. She had been proud of herself, and even prouder of Adam, who, thanks to a combination of skillful hands, mental acuity and perseverance, had developed into a surgeon with God-given talent. His incisions and stitches were so precise that the scars from his operations were barely visible on his patients' skin.

The workday was over and Vera had only one errand left to do before going home. She walked through the hallways of the nursing home, no longer noticing how the fluorescent light reflected off the apricot-painted wallpaper, the practical and protective wall molding wisely placed at wheelchair level, the horrible silk flowers and the solitary, scrawny yucca plant. Filled with the memory of what had been a self-evident 'we', of Adam and her, she knocked on the door to Solveig Marklund's room.

Solveig opened the door, saw Vera's introspective, slightly sad smile, and asked kindly, 'So how is Vera doing today?'

Vera looked at her favorite patient. Solveig was sitting in her wheelchair. She had been forced to move to Solbacka when her husband Gustav had died two years earlier, because she had been deemed too physically weak to take care of herself. But there was nothing wrong with her mind, and the walls in her little two-room suite were covered with photographs, paintings, colorful bits of fabric, buttons, ribbons and unusual souvenirs that testified to an unusually creative life.

'I'm fine,' said Vera, but realized instantly that Solveig's gentle observation of her would reveal a more truthful answer. 'Well, my knee isn't better yet,' she quickly added, pointing at her thin left leg, still stuck in a slightly bent position.

'But you can manage working here?'

'Yes, a few evenings and weekends. And this is important!' said Vera, and from her backpack she pulled out a little fruit, bread and cheese and a tin of crackers that she had bought for Solveig.

Solveig smiled gratefully and maneuvered her wheelchair back into the room to get her wallet.

But, as always, Vera refused. 'We can take care of that later; it's just so nice to talk to you. I know that you're an evening snacker, and I don't want you to starve because of Solbacka's schedules. And you sleep so much better if you aren't hungry.'

Solveig rolled herself back towards the door, smiled with her lovely, wrinkled face and took Vera's hands in her own soft, liver-spotted ones. 'Thank you, you kind person.'

Kind person, thought Vera as she carefully hobbled toward the bus stop. It's kind people who make life bearable. Like that guy who called and offered her his dorm room, at least for a year, just when she had started to realize that she couldn't live much longer under the same roof as her mother. In spite of everything, she could actually afford a room in a dormitory!

He said his name was Kalle, and he sounded confident, if a little shy. At first Vera was convinced that he had made some kind of mistake, but then he said that Cecilia Åström had mentioned her. Cissi, she's also a kind person, Vera thought. Sometimes you're lucky in the people you meet.

It was a friendly dormitory. She had felt the good atmosphere as soon as Kalle opened the door. He had looked just like she expected: broad and furry like a teddy bear. A young English guy named Matt had immediately turned up and introduced himself. There was some kind of little brother charm in his friendliness as he stood there peering out from under his hair in a much-too-big cardigan.

She had been surprised to discover that Peter Stavenius – that young, unimpressive lecturer from the summer course who had spent most of his time hitting on one of the students – lived in the room next to hers. But there was probably nothing really wrong with him either. What were you supposed to do if you happened to meet 'the one' in a strange setting? They seemed like they were a good match, he and Sandra – two blond, pretty-people types. 'Ken and Barbie,' the other students in the class had called them when they snuck away, thinking they were unobserved, and cuddled during the breaks. In Peter's defense, it wasn't easy to be compared to Cissi, who was a real superstar teacher.

On her way home to Ålidhem, Vera thought about how differently she looked at the world now. It was the same town, the same student neighborhood and the same university. But it wasn't the same Vera. And not the same Adam... she almost added. But the pain caused by that line of thinking hit her full in the stomach and the analogy ended abruptly in a fuzzy haze. She remembered the trauma psychologist's choice of words. Here was a 'destructive spiral' that her psyche blocked entirely.

✷

The semester began and the city started crawling with students. Life in the dorm was congenial, and Thursday evenings were especially enjoyable. Those who felt like it got together to cook dinner and, for the third Thursday in a row, Vera and Matt joined in. Lotten, who was studying gastronomy, showed them little tricks with the confident authority of someone who knows what she's doing. Lotten came from the far south of Sweden, and it struck Vera that the tall, fair-skinned woman reminded her of Camilla in many ways.

Matt was another story altogether, a young guy from Sheffield with loose body language and overgrown brown hair that was constantly dishevelled. He had begun his second year at the School of Design down near the river. Matt had spent a few summers in Sweden when he was a child and had studied Swedish the previous year. He already spoke it incredibly well, thought Vera, glancing over at his distinctive profile. His forehead stuck out almost as far as his nose, giving him a rough, caveman-like appearance that contrasted with his mild personality. It was mainly the small Swedish words that gave him trouble. Vera smiled inwardly at today's incident as she stood slicing onions for the paella. Lotten had shown her how to first make a horizontal cut and then to slice the onion half in a fan shape before chopping it. That way, the thin pieces stayed attached to the root until vertical slices made straight across the onion detached them in small bits.

'So how did the first years' initiation go?' asked Lotten, raising her light eyebrows without lifting her eyes from the neatly lined-up ingredients – a fresh raw chicken, rice, tomatoes, tarragon, bayleaf... Lotten's fiancé Noel ran a trendy Spanish restaurant in Dublin, and tonight they were cooking the specialty of the house: Nueva Casa's famous paella. She poured oil into her large, heavy-bottomed pan, which she kept in her room when she wasn't using it, along with her cherished knives.

'Fine. It was fun.' Matt's job was to peel the shrimp at the sink, and he carried out the task with almost meditative concentration.

Vera had bought dessert from the chocolate aficionados at the Fruit Corner, and on her way back to the bus she happened to run into the Industrial Design department's initiation rite. The Matt she had seen there was completely different from the ordinary one. 'He was dressed as a police officer, and the first-years were in striped clothes like prisoners wear. They were supposed to carry people cross the street...'

'Oh, right,' said Lotten, with the soft diphthongs characteristic of the Skåne dialect. 'Was it Toby's uniform?' Toby, one of the more reserved dorm residents, was studying to become a police officer. He was in his last year of studies, and he went home to Skellefteå as often as he could.

'Yeah.' Matt continued to focus on the work his hands were doing.

'An old woman aged about 75 came along, pushing her husband in a wheelchair...' Vera began to giggle. 'So imagine a couple of two-meter tall ... well... giants lifting the woman up and carrying her away. And you know what she says?'

Smiling, Lotten looked up from the saffron just as the oil began spreading a delicious scent through the kitchen. She tilted the pan skillfully, stirred and added finely minced garlic. Matt glanced at Vera from the sink and prompted, in unison with her, 'It's OK, Theodore, it's just that time of year!'

Vera laughed so hard that tears ran down her cheeks, and she felt the tension that she had been living with for months recede into the background. Lotten and Matt smiled at her. She put down the knife, pushed the chopped onions towards the stove, took off her glasses and dried her eyes with her right arm.

'But I managed to scare old Theodore anyway,' said Matt glumly.

'Yeah, hahaha...!' Now Vera was laughing so hard she was doubled over. 'Sorry Matt, I don't mean to, but...'

'I was only trying to say, "Sorry, sir, let me push you",' said Matt, turning towards them. 'So I said: *jag skjuter på dig.*' His messy hair and innocently twinkling eyes made him look like an angel-faced boxer in an apron. Vera's laughing had now infected Lotten.

'I know, I know! The poor guy looked completely terrified.' Teary-eyed, Vera patted herself like she was looking for something in her pockets. 'He went like this, looking for his nitroglycerin, so I had to get involved.'

Lotten's pale skin was beetroot-red from laughing. 'Wha... what did you do?' she stuttered.

'I said uh...' Vera got her breathing under control and steadied her voice. ' It's okay! He just has a little trouble remembering which words to emphasize. He means *skjuter på.*' And I wheeled him to the other side of the street.'

Matt mumbled from the sink: '*Skjuter på, skjuter på, skjuter på.*' He looked up and shook his head glumly. 'Swedish! How are you supposed to remember what means "I'm going to shoot you," and what means "I'm going to push you???"'

Peter and Sandra came into the kitchen. She was carrying the latest Louis Vuitton bag in a tight grip.

'Sounds like a party in here!' Peter smiled inquisitively at the laughing, rosy-cheeked cooks. 'I'm not sure if you've met before; this is Sandra,' he continued. 'Eh...'

'Peter's girlfriend,' said Sandra and offered Vera her

manicured hand.

'Yeah... Hi, Sandra.' Vera dried her hands on a kitchen towel and took her hand. 'Yeah, we were on the same summer course.'

Sandra looked blank. A long, embarrassing silence.

'And I recognize your voice, of course,' continued Vera thoughtlessly. Realizing what she had said, Vera reddened and hoped that no-one would ask why.

Peter looked around enthusiastically. 'Boy does it smell good in here! What's for dinner?'

'La Paella Suprema,' said Matt, not without some pride.

'La Paella Nueva Casa!' smiled Lotten.

'Is it okay if Sandra eats with us too?' Peter looked around hopefully.

'Yeah, there should be enough for her too,' said Lotten. 'Peter's girls don't usually eat much,' she whispered to Vera. 'But you know the rules,' she said sternly to Peter.

'No, what?'

'No Great Escapes here!' Lotten looked meaningfully at Peter. That was the name of Peter's family's company, and Vera wondered if Peter got it. She went over to where Matt was standing by the sink and pointed at the note over the *Your mother doesn't live here* sign: 'Do the dishes or DIE!'

'I prefer not to do dishes,' said Sandra and looked worriedly at her fake nails.

'Okay, no problem; Toby and I can do it,' said Peter. 'He's usually late too. Mmmm, it smells fantastic!'

7

Outside it was raining, but the atmosphere in the Department of Economics was celebratory. Peter refrained from sipping champagne out of his plastic glass during Professor Åke Sturesson's long-winded speech. The greying 60-year-old with glasses and a goatee beard spoke before an audience of around 30 exuberant colleagues, who politely broke off their mingling to listen.

'So we are going to be the core recipient of the Swedish Research Council's new funding for *Future Wealth and Welfare*. Entirely in line with the Lisbon Strategy, the goal is to create a distinguished center of research...'

Peter suppressed a yawn, drew a deep breath and lost his concentration because of a small, blond woman. She was really pretty, that new graduate student, Jeanette with the upturned nose... And what great breasts! He had always been attracted to women with good posture and suitably deep décolletage; it radiated self-confidence and sent a look-at-me message that he knew he wasn't alone in appreciating. He fired a small, playful smile her way. She smiled blushingly back at him.

He hadn't exaggerated. If there was anyone who didn't need to read about how to become a pick-up expert, it was Peter Stavenius. Peter was quite sure that he knew what the secret was. First, he simply liked people in general and beautiful women in particular. Second, he didn't care that much. 'If you don't get one, there are a thousand others waiting,' his grandmother used to say, and it was really true for him. Every flirt and new contact was an exciting exploration of possibilities. But there wasn't really anything at stake; it didn't really matter whether this girl liked him or not.

Matt, the exchange student who lived in the dorm, was impressed and claimed that Peter hypnotized most women within a radius of about 10 meters. Peter smiled, flattered at the memory of how thankful Matt had been just to borrow that book, *The Game*, that Kalle had given him. Matt had acted like he had been given a love bible directly from the hands of the Master.

The department secretary, Lilian Blom, was one of the countless women who appreciated young Peter, but when Sturesson's speech was over she turned her attention to Cissi. 'Many of the applicants had promising research strategies, but we think that...'

The end of the sentence disappeared in a buzz of excited voices. Cissi leaned toward the well-dressed 55-year-old with her hand cupped around her ear, 'What?'

'The rumor is that we won because of your idea, that students and people from disciplines other than economics should be invited to participate!' Lilian strained to make herself heard.

Cissi smiled with pride. 'Yes, I think it will be good. Welfare isn't just about economics.'

'Indeed!' Lilian gave her a loaded paper plate. 'Perhaps happiness is also a little bit about raspberry cake! Yes?'

Sturesson appeared behind Peter and eagerly put his arm over his shoulder. 'I talked to your father about the good news. You're a third-year student now, right?' Peter barely had time to nod before the Professor continued, 'Yes, I told Lennart; in the application we promised to include students in the project, and of course you are a given.' He slapped Peter lightly on the shoulder before he let go.

It was obvious that Peter was expected to be grateful. He hesitated; in all honesty he wasn't really sure what he was being offered. That was one problem with his masterly contact with women: it meant that he often failed to pay attention to other things. Now he risked looking like a complete idiot if he asked about something the Professor had just explained at length.

'I'm not really sure...' Peter searched his memory, frantically looking for an abbreviation he had heard somewhere in the speech. 'Eh, yeah, I wonder what OMC really means?' Peter quaked at the thought of the reaction he might get. The last thing he wanted was for Åke to call his dad and say that his son was completely uneducable. It seemed like Lennart was constantly getting information that supported that conclusion anyway.

Fortunately, Åke's florid face showed no sign of surprise or disappointment. Peter now concentrated on what Sturesson had to say, despite the fact that Jeanette was standing at the door trying to catch his eye.

'Yes, it refers to the open method of co-ordination. So the member states' welfare systems will become more similar, because nobody wants to be the worst. You know, the Third Pillar!' The man with the goatee smiled sunnily at his chosen rising star.

Peter's smile was stiff and fake, 'But how is it supposed to work in practice?'

Now the Professor's face darkened, 'That's exactly what I just said!'

Damn! thought Peter. *Silence is golden.*

'And besides you, we are going to choose two more students,' continued Sturesson, 'a graduate student and a first-year economics student. We are going to begin by getting the public on board, so the first publication will be directed at a wide audience, not academics, and one of the chapters will be yours! So young man, now all you have to do is roll up your shirtsleeves and make history!'

Not just incomprehensible, but deadly boring, too. A bunch of demands and expectations already communicated to his father. But Sturesson didn't know who he was dealing with. Peter knew all there was to know about graceful exits and he shook his head. He arranged his face in a flattered but regretful expression. 'Oh, I am really grateful for the offer, but unfortunately I can't accept it.'

Sturesson looked disappointed, but nodded. 'I understand. Pity. I thought you might be able to do it as your senior thesis, but of course you're also very busy with the family business, aren't you?'

Peter nodded. Letting someone guess incorrectly was, after all, the most convenient of white lies.

✷

When the celebration was over, Sturesson found Cissi and stuck a stack of papers in her hand. It was the printed copy of the department's winning application. Cissi looked questioningly at her advisor.

'Read here,' he muttered and pointed to a particular passage of the text.

'Um... fresh perspectives measuring up to the challenges of our time. New interdisciplinary perspectives... students and practitioners from different walks of life.' They had taken her ideas word-for-word! Cissi was warm with pride.

'Wow, that's great... that you're working from that perspective and it succeeded! Congratulations!' Cissi chose her words carefully. She smiled and gave the application back to him.

The Professor squirmed and pulled at the collar of his jacket, as if it were suddenly too warm and he needed air. 'Yes, so, we must promote mobility in research and such... but there are some problems with this, because now we're really in a hurry. I can recruit a third-year student, but this multi-disciplinary and "different walks of life" stuff... I don't know, maybe I went a little overboard?'

He scratched his neck irresolutely. 'You teach a lot; can you find some undergraduate who has been a mechanic or something, who can do some kind of first publication in the spring, someone we don't have to be ashamed of?'

'Yeah, okay, I understand. When do you need a name?' wondered Cissi carefully.

'Now.'

Cissi was filled with strong, mixed feelings when she walked home, umbrella up to protect her from the rain. When she worked on the application it was understood that she would be part of the project; it was so close to her own research focus – *Welfare in a Globalized World.* And now they had won! She looked longingly at an appropriate lamppost, but restrained her happy impulse to swing around it theatrically, hollering 'I'm Singing in the Rain!'

At the same time, she was angry. It was the impossible deadline that irritated her. It wasn't the first time that graduate students had been forced to step in and cover for Sturesson's shortcuts. But it was the first time it had affected her. He had written something that sounded good, without actually being prepared to do it. It was her idea, and she had nothing against helping to get it done, but he could have said something a few months ago, so she wouldn't have to pull a rabbit out of her hat.

Luckily, she had a really good idea. She smiled inwardly at the puddle in front of her. And she stamped like Gene Kelly, so that water splashed in all directions. Cecilia Åström had just turned 35, but a stuffy grown-up was something she would never be!

8

Economics (from the Greek *oikos*, house and *nomos*, law) focuses on the husbanding of resources under conditions of scarcity. Scarcity is defined as a condition in which available resources are limited in relation to the total demand and need for them.

Cecilia Åström's introduction to 'The Development of the Discipline of Economics'

Vera was dissatisfied after the first few weeks of the semester. It felt more like she was studying mathematics than economics. She was supposed to accept some assumptions and then do calculations. The latter was no problem. It was also important to keep track of decimals when administering anesthesia, otherwise the patient might die or wake up in the middle of the operation, and that wasn't exactly a situation you could just shrug off with an 'ooops'.

Musing about whether or not her studies would turn out to be meaningful wasn't the only thing that distracted her as she sat studying in her dorm room in the evenings. Stavenius was another distraction. It wasn't so easy to concentrate on calculating marginal productivity curves when rhythmic bumping and ecstatic cries leaked through what seemed to be a paper-thin wall.

At first she mainly felt embarrassment and a little curious fascination that she dared not acknowledge. But that was before she realized that the sounds came from dealings with multiple women, not just his blonde girlfriend. It upset her, and suddenly she felt torn about how to respond. Should she pick up the phone and call her old classmate, even if she actually didn't know Sandra at all? Or maybe not. It was absolutely clear that this was something Al Gore would call *An Inconvenient Truth*. And faced with inconvenient truths, people react differently. Vera knew that if it were her, she would absolutely want to know, regardless of the unpleasant consequences. But what did Barbie with the expensive handbags want? Vera decided not to say anything, but she wasn't satisfied. Despite the fact that she had a hard time imagining a woman more different from herself than Sandra, Vera felt like she had let herself down.

The noise from the next room forced Vera to develop a routine. When it was really intrusive she usually banged the wall with the heel of her hand. But once, when the sound came through the bathroom wall, she couldn't bring herself to do it. It was some new voice that sounded like Meg Ryan in the famous fake-orgasm scene in *When Harry Met Sally*. Assuming that this girl wasn't faking as skillfully as Meg, Vera felt like she didn't have the heart to interrupt her during what was apparently a fantastic experience. And, based on her observations of Peter's recent behavior towards a whole line of different women, it wouldn't surprise Vera in the least if the woman in question imagined a future life together with him.

Vera was at least learning new words, and she tried to comfort herself with that. It was 'homogeneous goods' and 'perfect competition' and 'marginal revenues,' and she did the calculations correctly and passed her first test. But she was not at all convinced that it was really going to help her understand what was happening in the world. Furthermore, she had very palpable economic problems of her own. The rent for the dormatory was certainly affordable, but she also needed money for food, her student loans and the bus. Vera agreed with her mother that additional student loans were unthinkable, but working part-time at Solbacka didn't even pay enough to cover her modest expenses.

The time Adam called and she actually managed to collect herself enough to answer, he had sounded strangely brisk, and she had become nauseated and tongue-tied. Later she would realize that the few things she had managed to say had been lies. *Yes, she was fine. Everything would work out, as long as*

*he stopped apologizing all the time. Yes, she looked forward to
seeing him; maybe next month? And no, no, she didn't need any
money.* In fact, she had already been forced to borrow a little
from her dad, Sven-Erik, which was definitely a short-term,
emergency measure. She just needed to admit it: She was poor.

✖

It was Tuesday when Cissi Åström called. She wanted to invite
Vera to lunch after Wednesday's lecture. They met in one of the
stairwells in a corner of the large student cafeteria.

'Hi. You sounded surprised when I called,' smiled Cissi.

'Surprised? I… guess maybe I don't expect you to remember
all the students you meet,' Vera said.

'A jungle midwife, the star of the summer course? That you
remember.'

Vera smiled as they went slowly up the stairs. 'Oh. Thanks.
Otherwise I felt like I mainly just asked irritating questions. I
think I made Stavenius go haywire.'

'No, he appreciated your interest,' said Cissi, thinking she
was speaking the truth. 'And such students are in short supply.
By the way, you know that it was Peter who fixed the dorm room
for you?'

'I thought it was you and Kalle.' Vera suddenly felt a little
discomfort in her stomach.

'No, I don't know Kalle; it was Peter who talked to him.'

Vera couldn't understand why he, of all people, would
have done anything for her, but she pushed the question away.
Once they had settled themselves in a quiet corner with their
vegetarian pasta Vera said: 'Now it's my turn to listen to you.
Who is Cecilia Åström?'

Cissi cocked her head and observed Vera as she took her
first bite. She started to talk about her childhood in a village
a little to the south, about her parents' passion for dressing
unique individuals. How she and her older sister had grown up
in the family's stylish clothing store, which people from the
city flocked to because of the exceptional service. There was
something about Vera's quiet openness that led Cissi to tell her

things that she didn't mention to many people. For example, the sad ending to the story of the family clothing store. When Vera asked why they were forced to close, Cissi shrugged her shoulders and said, 'Increased competition and new shopping habits.'

Nonetheless, Vera could see that something important lived on, because when Cissi talked about things that 'really fit', her eyes shone with enthusiasm. 'It's all about starting from what you've got. And paying attention to detail and how things go together. It's hard to explain. I still think like that, even in this job.'

'Yeah, it can be like that,' answered Vera. 'Me, I think that health and economics are connected.'

'Yes, right... speaking of that. The thing is, the department has won a contest.'

'Oh?' said Vera and put down her knife and fork.

'It is a big research project about securing future well-being and welfare. The first thing we're going to do is write a book, with different authors for each chapter.'

Vera listened thoughtfully, heard Cissi talk about 'multi-disciplinary' and 'alternative perspectives,' but didn't understand why she was telling her all this. Not until Cissi came right out and said, 'We want you to be involved and describe the landscape.'

'What?'

'Yeah, we want you to write one of the chapters. Well, you have to do an interview first, and show the old guard in the department that you aren't completely clueless about economics, but I can help you prepare.'

Vera's heart pounded and Cissi continued enthusiastically. 'The goal is to help create conditions that secure people's future, in Sweden and Europe. It's actually an opportunity to make a difference!'

Is it possible? That influential people will listen to what a nurse has to say about welfare?

For a dizzying instant, Vera strongly felt the antenna that, for so long, had connected her to the meaning of the universe. It was a glittering second, but then the force that called itself realism spoke instead.

'You know... my mother told me that a full-time, temporary position at the geriatric home where I work is probably going to become available. Somebody has a chronic shoulder problem. If so, I'll probably take it.'

Cissi stared at Vera. 'I thought... I thought you if anyone... Didn't you say you wanted to do something for the world? You realized that the economic system has such an impact on the world that you would be able to do more if you understood how it worked? And answer that question: "Little brothers and sisters, what are you doing?"'

'Yeah.' Vera's heart beat harder. Her brain felt like mush, her thoughts slow and elusive. She was reminded of Pierre's words... What was it he used to say with that accent that made his words feel like butterflies? *Be careful what you wish for. It may come true.* Wasn't this one of those times? What was keeping Vera from accepting the peculiar mission that had kept her afloat in recent months? Wasn't it a miraculous coincidence that she had been sustained by what most people would call an unrealistic ambition and then suddenly been offered a chance to pursue it? A chance to give it a try in reality?

It was the word 'reality' that made Vera see the obstacle so clearly. She said, 'but I need a job because, to be honest, I'm... insolvent.' It was a new word for broke that she had learned. 'I mean, I don't even know if I can continue taking the introductory course.'

Cissi saw that the solution was right in front of her. She didn't feel the same spontaneous happiness about it, but she was supposed to work a miracle. 'If it's money you need then we can fix it. You get a stipend of 40,000 kronor this semester and the same amount in the spring if you write a chapter.'

Vera stared at Cissi as if she were offering manna from heaven. Now there was nothing else to blame it on. Now it was only courage that she needed. And her urge to take on the task was so strong that she would just have to develop courage along the way. 'Oh!... Thanks! I mean, yes, thanks! I'd love to write a chapter!'

✳

49

Almost all of Vera's things were at Adam's, in the apartment in Stockholm. She really needed to go there, if for no other reason than to retrieve most of her clothes. After five weeks in the dorm, when the fall chill began to come, she particularly missed her dark jeans and forest-green wool sweater with the large, cozy collar.

It was strange. She could no longer bring herself to entertain the thought of *going home*. But a trip to Stockholm. It would have to be at the weekend, in two weeks: the beginning of October. She took a deep breath. Then perhaps her mother and Eva would also stop asking. In recent weeks her mother had started talking about 'for better or worse', and Vera knew very well what she was referring to. It wasn't always a matter of doing what you felt like. She had made a promise.

Besides, she had basically already told Adam that she would come.

9

Peter's fall semester was exciting. Maybe a little too exciting, he found himself thinking. It was damned good luck that he hadn't agreed to participate in that strange welfare project. His active social life hardly left him time to study and go to jujutsu.

He often went out with friends, and he frequently took some girl home with him. Sandra was kind of half-steady, even if he had never promised her anything. Linda called quite often, and she was always fun to be with. And then there was that pretty, new graduate student, the little blonde, Jeanette. That had also become a little too exciting. Peter had only just turned 24, but he still wondered if he was starting to get old, if he worried about such a trifle when the girl didn't seem to care.

To say that Jeanette had been eager was an understatement. Single-minded didn't do her justice! She had suggested that they meet at the gym, and after a workout at the palace-like training complex on campus, they walked the short distance home to Stipend Lane. Once he had shut the door to his dorm room, very few minutes passed before she wanted to do it in the shower, and Peter wasn't the type who refused. He had definitely been right... She had glorious, firm, almost swollen, natural breasts, and she was uncomplicatedly turned on. Simply put, it was good sex. Unusually good for a first time, Peter noted. But they didn't notice until afterwards that the condom had broken. Peter got a cold lump in his stomach. Jeanette, on the other hand, took it remarkably calmly. She showered, dried herself off on his only clean towel, dropped it on the floor, got dressed and left with a smiling, 'See you!'

Peter didn't really know what was worrying him. When he was younger he would never even have thought about the minimal risk that Jeanette might, for example, have HIV. It was true that he had had to take a chlamydia test once, when one of his one-night stands had turned out to be infected. That had been no fun at all. He had imagined what it would be like if he were forced to call, say, five girls he had been with since then, and say that he had probably given them a venereal disease. But he had listened to his dad, who during an unusually intimate exchange had told him, 'Sow your wild oats, but make sure you have a condom!' and the test had been negative. What a relief that had been! Maybe he should get himself tested again, just to be on the safe side?

What a drag I'm becoming, thought Peter. *If I don't watch out I'll become like Vera, who hobbles around in her baggy clothes and looks crabby all the time.* Her biggest evening pleasure seemed to be sitting in her room eavesdropping and then banging on the wall and disrupting. He could have sworn that Vera considered it a sport to identify absolutely the least appropriate moment to bring out the heavy artillery.

Just because she didn't seem to be getting any, that was no excuse to be so damned snippy to others.

✳

It was time for the fall board meeting. Peter sat on the flight home to Stockholm and read *Fortune* magazine to get into the right mood for Great Escape. You needed to 'know your target group', as his dad used to say. And he wasn't so dumb that he didn't realize by the time he was 20 that in order to meet 'the most well-to-do one per cent of the population, which engages in conspicuous consumption,' you needed to hang around Stureplan and do exactly that, engage in conspicuous consumption.

Peter remembered as if it were yesterday the very rewarding conversation he had had with his father, which had resulted in him getting a corporate American Express card, and the many hysterical party nights and high-status contacts that the card had financed. Not to mention all the girls he had raked in – good-looking, young, rich and generous, he could pick and choose among hundreds of Stureplan wannabes.

Then things had got a little out of hand. When Peter started racking up charges in excess of 300,000 kronor but only delivering a few vague contacts, Lennart immediately pulled the credit card, thus ending his triumphal march among the cream of Stureplan. Peter had always suspected that it was his Uncle Ernst, finance officer at a large bank and chair of the board of his father's company, who had called his little brother's attention to the cost of Peter's networking. Ernst talked all the time about what the accountants would say. But it didn't feel completely wrong to give up the slicked-back hairstyle and expensive clothes and move up to northern Sweden to study. Peter had honestly begun to tire of spraying girls with 10,000-kronor bottles of champagne. Been there, done that, Peter thought. The feeling was just, 'Yeah, okay, now what?' In any case, he thought it was more fun with girls who found him attractive regardless of his father's money.

For a while Lennart had been furious. Now it had faded into a permanent disappointment, and Peter only got paid for his participation on the Board or if he did other work. In Umeå Peter tried to show that he was a Stavenius – damned right he could also finish a 'character-building period of studies' in a crowded dormitory with poorly installed vinyl flooring, furniture that was both old and disgusting, and a shared kitchen in which people warmed all kinds of stuff in the toaster. But compared to Charlie, Ernst's son, who was independent and earned big bucks in finance, Peter fell short. These days Lennart had a skeptical attitude to his son's merits, and he didn't hesitate to tell Peter all about cousin Charlie's success in London. And Charlie was only five years older than Peter. The latest was that Charlie seemed to be on his way to earning a bonus this year that was as big as Great Escape's entire profit. The jealousy was never expressed, but it was palpable, a restless dissatisfaction. Peter didn't know if it was because Lennart felt himself inappropriately outdistanced by his young nephew, or if it was simply a disappointment to have the less successful offspring. Whatever its cause, the situation hurt Peter more than he was willing to admit.

Peter flipped distractedly through *Fortune* and suddenly saw Lennart in the ad for Rolex watches again. *'To accomplish extraordinary things.'* Perhaps it wasn't as easy as Peter used to think? Lennart made it clear to Peter that he shouldn't count on being supported, that he needed to get serious and do something sensible with his life. 'Do something sensible' was code for following in Lennart's footsteps – get a degree in economics, enter the labor market and start making good business deals. By the time cousin Charlie was 25 years old, he had already made his first million, entirely on his own.

When he arrived at Strand Street, Peter entered the code and stepped into the office. He no longer noticed the beautiful vaulted ceiling and the row of crystal chandeliers. He greeted Barbro, Lennart's proper secretary, who had worked for the family since they had been in the interiors business. He walked across designer carpets and passed racks with exclusively designed Great Escape catalogues. At the far end of the office was the boardroom, with its thick wall-to-wall carpeting, large oval mahogany table and gold-framed diplomas that the company and Lennart had received over the years – 'Exporter of the Year,' 'Businessman of the Year' and 'Sweden's Super Gazelle 2005'.

As Peter greeted all the dark-suited men, he suddenly felt out of place in his grey blazer. Strangely, back at the dorm it had made him feel too dressed up. Dark suit, he thought: I need to get one. He discreetly wrote a note to himself on the yellow notepad in his board-meeting file folder, while the introductory formalities went on in the background – approval of the agenda, minutes from the last meeting... He woke up a bit during the quarterly report and concurred when the board members noted with satisfaction that the company was growing well in the US; their recruitments seemed to have been successful, and the New York office was proving to be a profitable investment.

The next agenda item was about a proposed investment. Lennart went through the travel company's current destinations before quickly getting to the point. He wanted to purchase two Eurocopter Dauphins – monster helicopters that could carry up to 12 passengers at high speeds. Peter knew that under the existing investment ceiling set by the board of directors, the CEO could unilaterally approve expenditures up to 10 million. So that meant that these machines went for more than that.

Uncle Ernst, the chairman of the board, asked why their

regular, one-motor helicopters weren't sufficient. Did the company really need all five of them in Europe? Couldn't a couple be transferred to New York? Ernst was always careful that the company's fixed assets were being put to work; he had seen too many companies fail due to exorbitant capital costs. He referred to it as being 'weighed down'.

Peter thought that Uncle Ernst and his boring questions probably had something to do with Great Escape's success, even if it was the charismatic little brother who drove the company's development and stood in the spotlight. Because it was now that Lennart was most alive; Peter saw the fire in his father's eyes when he talked inspiringly about Great Escape's new offer – a grizzly bear hunt with a private helicopter direct from Manhattan! The latest market survey from New York had shown that people were willing to pay a lot for that type of exclusive trip, and advance sales had been fantastic. These two-motored behemoths could fly sufficiently fast and safely in all weathers so the Wall Street elite could get to Alaska for a long weekend to hunt 'one of the world's most formidable predators'.

Not as formidable as the Wall Street elite, Peter thought with a grin.

'What do you say, Peter?' Lennart looked at his son as if he had just made a statement.

'What is all this based on?' Peter looked almost dazedly at the CEO and Board in front of him. A feeling of déjà vu crept up on him from somewhere.

'Uh?' Lennart looked at him as if he had said *staphylococcus.*

'Why is this a good idea?' continued Peter, now completely engulfed in a time-bridging Matrix feeling.

The chair of the board glanced approvingly at his nephew. This was actually an Ernst-type question.

Lennart irritatedly noted his older brother's expression and answered sharply, '18,000 dollars per paying customer, and demand exists!'

Peter was pulled out of the odd, unfamiliar mood and he smiled crookedly, 'Oh, right – why didn't you say so?'

✳

55

The meeting broke for coffee. As they were standing beside the trolley with refreshments, Lennart passed his son a cup and whispered, displeased: 'Nice that you finally show a little interest in Escape, but damn it! You can at least ask sensible questions, can't you? I have enough trouble with people who don't get the genius of these trips. Just the messing around about landing rights is...'

Peter sipped the hot coffee.

'Don't slurp!' his father shot immediately, and Peter put down the cup, his lightly burnt tongue mumbling something that was supposed to resemble an apology.

'We've hardly done any marketing, but we already have three fully booked weekends in March. And then suddenly everything comes to a dead stop. I don't get how the *land of opportunity* can be such a bureaucratic nightmare all of a sudden. They completely reject the Wall Street landing pad and are hesitant about giving approval for West 30th. Can you believe it?'

'No, why?' wondered Peter.

Lennart shrugged his shoulders. 'The usual, too close to the limit. They drone on about rotor diameter and noise, but, damn it, the latest Dauphin is quieter than those tin cans that are constantly flying tourists around the city!'

Peter's curiosity grew. 'Do you mean that we have already sold direct helicopter trips to Alaska?'

'Yes, the Ultimate Adventure. Expensive. Exclusive. Half-crazy, but still possible.'

'How is it possible?'

'If you're interested, Barbro has all the information,' said Lennart, and they returned to the meeting.

The question about the investment decision had been tabled, and the meeting moved on to other matters, but Peter continued thinking about Wall Street-Alaska. It would undoubtedly look good alongside the company's other destinations, and he believed his father: it would be a profitable sales success. He skipped lunch with the Board, choosing instead to eat a chicken salad in Barbro's room while working on an exciting idea. Was there some way to reconcile 'the Ultimate Adventure' with the pile of rejection letters from everybody from the Federal Aviation Administration to the City of New York? Peter had actually negotiated for the family business in some small matters, but this time his social skills and charm were hardly enough. He read the reasons for the negative decisions. He looked things up in files and surfed the internet and determined that it was definitely a crazy idea – it would take 16 hours' flying time plus five fueling stops to get the grizzly-bear-hungry finance yuppies to Alaska. Was there some other solution?

When the meeting resumed after lunch he said that he had something he wanted to say about the issue that they had tabled, and the Chair said he could have time at the end, during the agenda item 'other matters'. He had two hours of waiting, and he discreetly prepared before finally getting the opportunity to talk.

'13 million dollars is a lot of money.' He felt Lennart's cautious gaze resting on him. 'But we have a large demand at a price that is clearly profitable. Wall Street-Alaska is too good an idea not to implement!' Peter had turned toward the rest of the Board, but he was intensely aware of his father, just beyond his line of sight.

'But we don't know if it's a flash in the pan or if demand will last long enough to pay for the investment,' objected Ernst from the short side of the table, spinning the Chair's gavel with his long fingers.

'Exactly!' said Peter. He saw his father's face darken in response to his brother's boring common sense. 'So I have the following proposal...' *For that reason, and because we don't actually have landing rights*, he tried to signal to Lennart with his gaze. 'We take a regular Raven to Manhattan, paint it for "the Ultimate Adventure" and make sure that we get the Wall Street landing pad for it. That way, the target group will see an advertisement for it outside their office windows every Friday. And then it can fly to Newark or...'

Lennart shook his head. 'No, our customers don't want that. Time is money.'

'Exactly. Time is money.' Assume that we have our own theme-park hangar in Newark where we directly outfit the guys for the trip. After they have the necessary gear they immediately board a comfortable private jet to Alaska! Then we don't need to settle for Admiralty Island; we can get all the way to Fort Yukon in six hours. No refuelling stop.'

'Yes, but the Eurocopter has an entirely different mobility and provides a completely different experience,' said Ernst, suddenly on his little brother's side.

'Yeah, of course, but we rent that in Alaska from some search-and-rescue firm. The guests are just going to sleep on the long trip anyway.' *It's over 5,000 kilometers, gentlemen,* Peter thought, but instead he said: 'It will still be seen as super exclusive and half impossible. And, of course, it's a helicopter at the beginning and at the end, where it will be seen. Their pals will think they flew the chopper to the wilderness, because those are the only kind of pictures on Facebook.'

Ernst smiled broadly at his nephew. 'No big investments necessary, we focus on concept and packaging. And the Newark hangar with add-on sales possibilities… The New York office can set this up. What do you say, Lennart?' He held his pen, ready to cross out the decision to table the matter.

Lennart's mouth formed a minimal smile, and he gave a little nod. A pleasant warmth spread in Peter's chest.

✖

When Peter came home late on Thursday he heard confidential voices from the communal kitchen. He went straight there and was surprised to discover Matt and grey Vera curled up on the sofa drinking tea. Could she actually be that social?

'Don't let this kind of stuff ruin you,' she said, critically thumbing through a black book. 'You are much better than this.'

Peter saw that it was *The Game* that she was talking about, the pick-up manual that he had loaned to Matt. It looked like it had been read a lot. For some strange reason, Peter felt challenged to defend it. That he had barely read it himself was suddenly unimportant. 'There are actually things in there that are appreciated and work, at least on real women.'

'Real men don't need to lie and play-act.' The retort came lightning fast.

'Yeah, right, like your husband, that plastics guy. Is he a real man? Why are you living here, anyway?' countered Peter.

Vera flinched as if she had been slapped in the face, got up and hobbled away. At the door she stopped, turning around and saying in a strangely trembling voice, 'Not that it's any of your business, but I am going to Stockholm on Saturday... to him.'

In the empty kitchen, Matt threw up his hands in irritation. 'What's your problem? Why are you on her case all the time?'

10

Fight the feeling, leave it alone.
Cause if it ain't love, it just ain't enough to leave
a happy home.

Pussycat Dolls, 'Don't Cha', 2005

Vera felt strangely nervous. It was only Adam she was going to see – her husband, who loved her. Yet since the spring, he had also become a hurtful stranger. This duality tore at her, and when she met his eagerly searching eyes at the Arlanda airport arrivals gate, she was immediately forced to look away, to redirect her gaze to the floor.

This is where it can all fall apart, she thought as she looked at the tracks of thousands of travellers' feet. Feet that were hurrying home to where they belonged. For her, it wasn't that easy. She observed the distance to the floor, how far she would fall if she collapsed, and felt an inner trembling in her chest. He had reached her now and gave her a hug. Passively, she lifted her arms and lightly touched his back, recognized his familiar scent.

He was the same as ever: dark and slender. A restrained way of moving. But he looked older, more haggard and worried. Had he lost weight? His shoulders were more angular than usual. He had let his stubble grow, so his beard was no longer rough, but felt soft against her cheek. He was still strikingly handsome, with his dark hair, clear blue eyes and fine features. And the beard suited him, she thought. Yet he was no longer her Adam.

He had stopped asking for forgiveness. He talked about the weather. After a couple of hours at their favorite pub on Söder, the atmosphere was better and there were glimpses of how they used to be. In those moments, Adam's face lit up like a 100-

watt bulb. When they talked about her knee, he agreed that it sounded like something wasn't right.

'Unfortunately, it's probably the cruciate ligament. I'm also guessing there is a meniscus splinter stuck here.' With practised fingers, he pushed carefully on Vera's joint.

'I think so too, I've said so, but...'

'You have very little thigh muscle left to stabilize it.' He felt her left leg without embarrassment and looked concerned, 'You *are* being really careful, aren't you? You can easily twist it so it rips even more. It wouldn't take much external force at this point.'

'I know. I have a doctor's appointment again in a month, so they'll have to come up with a solution then.' Vera shifted position, uncomfortable with Adam's touching her.

'Västerbotten County government,' sighed Adam and removed his hands. 'Pity I'm not an orthopaedic surgeon. I would have gone in and fixed it right away.'

'Yes, you would have,' Vera admitted.

'And we would have done the ears too,' smiled Adam as he stroked one of Vera's ears.

It had been a standing joke between them, that he would remove some of the cartilage that made her ears stick out unusually far from her head. And she usually joked back that it would have been a good idea, if it wasn't such a waste of resources. Because seriously, although it was tiresome that the priest at their confirmation classes had called her 'You there, with the ears', there was nothing really wrong with them. They didn't hurt and her hearing was good. There were lots of people with real problems who didn't get the surgical help they needed. Like her knee right now. Or the people with burn injuries in Colombia whom Adam could have given new faces, if only he had been there. But this time she couldn't make jokes about her protruding ears. It was like something was stuck in her throat.

They sat close together on the bus home to the apartment on Liljeholmen, trapped in the moisture and heat with strangers who politely avoided each other's eyes by looking out at the city, which was cloaked in a grey drizzle. Vera realized that she felt terribly lonely sitting beside her husband and all these people. When the radio station blaring forth from the driver's seat switched pop songs, it hit Vera all at once. As soon as she heard '*I know you want it, it's easy to see,*' her breathing became uneven and she realized helplessly that it was going to get worse. She stared at the floor of the bus, at the black and yellow striped tape warning passengers to be cautious. She tried in vain to get her lungs to work normally.

Pitiful. That is what she had become. She – who used to dare to do everything she wanted to do. She had dared to work at a field hospital, in the midst of communicable diseases, mere kilometers from the war. But now she couldn't even deal with the sound of a little dance music. Vera felt a rising pressure in her chest and her hands tingled and started to go numb. In the end, she made a decision. Panic-stricken, she pushed the stop button, got up and stumbled off the bus as soon as it stopped. Full of questions, Adam grabbed her backpack and followed her.

'I feel sick,' was all Vera managed to say as she hobbled anxiously along the edge of the park, looking for an undisturbed corner. There was no tree cover, no dense vegetation, no big rocks. At last, in desperation, she lifted the lid of a dog-waste bin. There was a pile of black plastic bags inside, and the stench overwhelmed her. She vomited on the disgusting pile of plastic and closed the lid. Her delicious lunch – thrown up on the park's collected dog shit. She dried her mouth on a wet hazel leaf that nature had kindly provided. Weakly, she sank down on a wet park bench. Adam dried off a patch of the bench with his gloves and, pale, sat down beside her. Awkwardly, he put his arm on her shoulder.

'Darling Vera… I'll call a taxi.' He got out his mobile phone and began pressing buttons.

Ominous thoughts came into Vera's head. *'Darling Vera'? What do you mean by that?* Unspoken questions filled her whole world. She noticed that he was worriedly seeking eye contact with her, but she continued to watch the rain hitting the grass. All she could think was, *you have to stop saying that!*

'How do you feel?' he asked when he opened the door of the taxi for her.

She was wet; she was shivering, but at least the empty, hard knot that was her stomach felt calmer. 'Better, I guess.'

He stroked her hand as, in silence, they travelled the short distance to the three-room apartment that they had renovated together.

'Maybe you'd like to take a warm bath?' he asked in the elevator, and tears formed in her eyes at the familiarity of his thoughtfulness.

'Maybe,' she managed to say before turning to face the corner and pretending to look for something in her backpack so he wouldn't see her tears. She shuddered in the face of what she now knew. *If I just go inside it will be better*, she promised herself. *Come home? Come... in.*

But the metallic click of the key in the lock released a seeping anxiety. Adam went straight into the bathroom and began to fill the bathtub. Vera stepped hesitantly into what had been her home. She went into the half-renovated kitchen and ran her hand over the tiling that they had chosen together. She was listening to the second hand moving with precision around the face of the kitchen clock when she caught sight of something in the dish drainer – my cup! *At least it's washed now. Was that what he had planned to do with himself too... And then just act like normal again, clinically correct, as if nothing had happened?* The sound of running water stopped.

'I did the laundry; I'll just run down and get it so you have clean towels.'

She heard Adam's happy voice disappear out into the stairwell. His light steps on the stairs were a cruel contrast to what was going on inside her.

She walked around in the apartment, her eyes wandering. She remembered that the only thing she had thought about when she had been rescued was coming home here and seeking protection. On the painful trip over the Atlantic she had pictured how Adam would build a fire in the fireplace, sit on the sofa with her in his arms and soothingly stroke her back. And everything would heal. But it hadn't turned out that way at all. The coffee table caught her attention and something inside her protested violently: *I don't like surprises any more than you do!* And once again it was as if she were lying defenseless and the only thing between her and the guerrilla was the darkness and a little downy grass.

She knew that a bus would be arriving at the stop across the street in about three minutes. If she could just keep out of sight so that he didn't see her... She grabbed her backpack and left.

✳

Cissi kept her promise. Vera accompanied her back to her office after her lectures, and Cissi explained what *Future Wealth and Welfare* involved. Vera was given tomes and compendiums to read through, and then Friday came, the day she was to be interviewed by the department's executive board. The board members would decide if she was a suitable representative of 'the common people', yet also capable of saying something of interest about future welfare.

On the way down the hall, Vera whispered, 'What do you think they're sitting there hoping for?'

Cissi grinned crookedly. 'They probably want a car mechanic with a burning interest in financial derivatives. Unfortunately, I don't know any, and I think it would be hard to find one given the time constraints we've been working under...'

It wasn't an answer to lessen Vera's nerves.

Aware of the seriousness of the situation, Vera was pale-faced as she entered the seminar room. Its walls were decorated with portraits of straight-backed men, each one bearing a plaque engraved with the date of their promotion to professor. The executive board members, all of whom were over 50, sat with their backs to the sun: tall Professor Överlind, with bushy, greying hair; department head Marianne Lange, a small, tough lady; Professor Sparre, with his dark, sharp eyes; and, of course, the day's main protagonist, Professor Åke Sturesson. Secretary Lilian Blom sat a bit off to the side in a flawlessly ironed white blouse, ready to take notes. A blazer was completely appropriate for the situation, Vera noted with relief, stroking her arms lightly.

After a few polite introductory comments, including an invitation to Cissi to join them, they began to question Vera about her background. Vera felt like she was at a job interview. They seemed particularly interested in her years as a thoracic anesthesiology nurse, when Adam had been training to become a surgeon.

'So then, opened chest cavities are bread and butter to you?' Överlind touched his breastbone.

'Well, I don't know if I would say that,' Vera answered, smiling tentatively towards their silhouettes in the backlight, 'but, yes, I have participated in a number of heart and lung operations.'

'Why don't you still work there?' Sparre sounded suspicious.

Why do you ask that? Vera wondered as she tried to answer. 'I was waiting for... I was going to go with...' She stopped and looked down at the table. 'I had planned to work as a volunteer, so I went abroad last year, first to the Congo and then Colombia...'

'And now you are back in town,' Sparre persisted, 'but not at the hospital?'

'No, I have actually applied for a part-time position in anesthesiology, but...' Vera wondered if she should mention all the complications with her knee and the discussions with the unemployment office about her degree of disability. She opted instead for the more impersonal reason why she was not, at the moment, doing the thing she was trained to do.

'You know how the labor market is for college graduates in this town.'

They nodded; this was a well-known problem. The unemployment office in Umeå struggled with the country's, if not the world's, best-educated group of unemployed people. Who wanted to employ someone with a PhD in physics to work in a grocery store? He would probably be Einstein-eccentric and give customers the wrong change because he was busy daydreaming about formulas. Vera knew someone with a pure physics PhD who started playing online poker and now earned

65

three times as much as he had earned as a graduate student, just by 'reading the board' – code for systematically winning money from people who couldn't count the odds, but humbly folding when the opposition was superior.

'You know about these things; is it true that you can perform a heart massage directly with your hands?' asked Överlind, as he squeezed his left hand lightly in front of his chest.

'Yes, it is. I've done it myself.' From the corner of her eye, Vera saw Cissi looking at her in surprise.

'In other words, you can hold a heart in your hands and get it to start pumping again?'

Överlind's interest made Vera wonder if he felt himself in need of such help. 'As the anesthesiology nurse, my clothes aren't usually sterile. I stand behind a cloth sheet. It is my responsibility to make sure the patient is properly anesthetized, and only the surgeon touches the patient.'

'But you said that you have held a living heart in your hands...' said Sparre with a critical tone.

'Yes. We had an emergency situation on the ward once – a patient who had been operated on to repair a coronary artery went into cardiac arrest. You are not supposed to compress the thoracic region of a person who has just been through an operation. In that case you open the sternum wire.' Vera saw that nobody understood, so she explained: 'That's the steel wire that holds the chest cavity together after the operation.'

'Why can't you apply compression from the outside to get the heart started again?' asked a pale but fascinated Överlind.

'When you attach a new coronary artery to a heart, *one* possible reason for cardiac arrest is that a stitch is leaking. In that case, applying pressure will just make it worse.'

All eyes in the sunny room were on Vera. She didn't understand. She had studied economics and read about welfare, and they were asking questions as if she were applying for a job with an air-ambulance team and they suspected her of pretending to be an anesthesiology nurse.

It was Lilian Blom who finally broke the silence. 'Was it leaking?'

'No. It was a ventricular fibrillation – the heart hops and shakes, but it doesn't pump. I lifted the heart out of the pericardium and touched it really gently until they came with the... well, they're like small metal spoons that are used to shock the heart and synchronize the electrical impulses.'

'Did it work?' asked Överlind.

'Yes, he survived. In fact, it's surprising how often things turn out well. Even if it was tense at the time.'

'And now you are... one of our first-year students?' Marianne Lange sounded surprised when she consulted her papers.

'Yes.'

'Why is that?' Sturesson and the others looked searchingly at Vera.

She fell silent. *I have been sent by what remains of the aboriginal people... because everything we have the power to take, is not actually ours for the taking.* She looked at the group in front of her. *No.* She could not say *'Koyaanisqatsi: little brothers and sisters, what are you doing?'* Instead she said, 'Because I want to understand, to know more about how the economy functions and the ideas behind how we use our resources.'

'And what are you going to do with that knowledge?' wondered Lange kindly.

Suddenly, Vera saw the connection. Perhaps the antenna that flickered like an electric field around her spine had not taken a strange, 90-degree turn after all? In the academic world, it was two different disciplines, but for her it was the essence of what had always been her calling. 'I want to help. To ease, to heal, to prevent. I want to... save the world.'

She shrugged her shoulders in embarrassment and, as soon as she had said it, she realized how silly it sounded. Words were insufficient to explain the cluster of characteristics and life experiences that motivated her. What could she say about those chaotic months in Kivu when she tried to help victims of rape and people infected with cholera in the middle of a merciless war? Or about her time in Colombia? How could she explain that four volunteer workers being kidnapped had been the last straw that had forced her onto a new path?

The senior academics chuckled and exchanged amused glances. Vera blushed, and rushed to correct herself, even though she felt that the essence of what she had said was true.

'I mean, I want to participate and contribute… to something that can change the world for the better.' *That's the way it is*, Vera thought, almost defiantly. Now she sat before them, her life's goal on display, like a throat exposed for a flock of predators. She had assumed – wrongly it seemed – that the interview would be an economics test. A rejection now would sting much more than if she had failed that kind of test. On the other hand, she thought, *if they don't want me now, then the project isn't for me anyway.* But then, despite the strong backlighting, she thought she saw that Sturesson actually looked flattered.

'Yes, our investigation definitely has a chance to change EU member states' welfare systems for the better. And that's as good a start as any other, right?' said Sturesson, and he winked at Överlind and Sparre on his right. Överlind smiled, but Sparre did not look amused.

'Do you know anything about economics, then? For example, can you explain Pareto optimality?' Sparre's dark, close-set eyes bored into her.

'Well, I've only been studing economics for six weeks…' Vera began.

'And *The Development of the Discipline of Economics* during the summer,' added Cissi.

'Perhaps it is not necessary to conduct a direct interrogation here,' said Överlind, looking around. 'Didn't the application say that the point of the last place was to have someone who *isn't* an economist?'

But Vera did not want to avoid the question. 'Yes, I am a beginner, but as I understand it, it means that resources are optimally distributed; at Pareto optimality it is impossible to make any individual better off without making at least one other person at least equally worse off.'

They looked at her. Överlind amused, Sturesson, Lange and Lilian kindly, and Sparre with a hard-set expression on his face.

Vera continued: 'Based on that, the first theorem of welfare was formulated, which states that welfare is optimized when the production of goods and services takes place in a completely free market.'

Överlind pushed his chair back and put his hands behind his head.

But Vera was not finished. 'It's like we vote with our money about what should be produced. Whatever people are most willing to pay for is assumed to give us the most welfare. But...'

Vera was just about to bring up what she saw as problems with a blind faith in 'the invisible hand' of the market, when she suddenly felt a sharp pain in her right ankle. She turned her head and looked at Cissi. Vera realized that Cissi thought she should keep quiet.

The atmosphere became more disorganized and relaxed. Sturesson wondered about formalities. Vera answered that she could begin right away and that she would gladly accept Cissi as her advisor.

Cissi looked happy and held up the compendium that had been put together for the project. She asked, 'Just a detail – in my chapter, how much attention do you want me to pay to the question of the share of GDP that goes to the public sector?'

Sparre quickly asked, 'Yes, what was Sweden's GDP last year?'

Vera's hand leafed distractedly through the folder as she glanced at Cissi. But Sparre pointed sternly at Vera. 'No, no. I am asking you. And I don't want you to look up the answer.'

Vera saw in the backlight that everyone was looking at her and waiting. It became embarrassingly quiet. She took her hand off the compendium. 'Sweden's GDP last year was 2,995 billion kronor.'

Lange and Överlind exchanged a satisfied glance. Lilian put down her pen. Vera's cheeks had turned red, but she couldn't stop herself. She held up the folder and said, 'But that information isn't in here.'

Sparre twisted irritably, looked at the clock, mumbled something about how they had gone on longer than planned and got up to leave the room. Sturesson glared at Sparre as if he had just scored an own goal.

Vera felt like she had been interrogated for 24 hours. Her hands were cold as ice and her pulse was racing. She and Cissi waited alone in the corridor outside the room. All the members of the department's executive committee remained inside, except for the one who had departed hastily.

'Don't worry about Sparre,' Cissi whispered. 'He's against the whole idea; it has nothing to do with you. He thinks that if you don't have a PhD in economics you can't contribute anything of interest. But I think you disproved that.' Cissi looked proud.

Vera wondered for a second whether or not she dared speak up; then she said: 'But why did you kick me just when I was getting to the most interesting part?'

Cissi looked down and said, 'I just thought… it was really just a factual question, and you had already answered it correctly. Sometimes it's just as well to save the objections for later.'

Suddenly the door opened and they streamed out.

'So, we have made a decision. Welcome on board!' said Sturesson and shook Vera's hand. Överlind and Lange did the same. Lilian was carrying so many binders and papers that her hands were full, but she smiled and told Vera that she should come to her office to complete 'a little paperwork, signatures and suchlike'.

When the group wandered off, Cissi dropped her papers and threw her arms around Vera: 'Congratulations, research colleague!'

With her free arm, Vera hugged her back. Even if she had failed today, it would still have been worth it, she thought warmly, because she had spent time with Cissi and learned so much. 'Thanks for all your help! And you were right; they did ask about Pareto optimality. Not to be confused with the Pareto *principle*, which states that 20% of the time we talked about what was 80% important – namely economics,' Vera said smiling.

'I think they just wanted to know a bit about your background and stuff. But somebody who has literally held a heart in her hand – that's somebody you should be able to trust, right?' Cissi looked appreciatively at her.

Just before Sturesson disappeared he stopped so suddenly that Lilian almost ran into him with her pile of binders. He called Cissi from the far end of the long, empty corridor. 'You... um... Ågren?'

Cissi winced and began to pick up her papers, which were spread all over the floor. 'Mmmm?'

Vera thought it was strange. Hadn't Åke Sturesson been Cissi's dissertation advisor for three years? 'Her name is Åstr...'

Cissi stood up abruptly and the elbow she drove into Vera's side was enough to silence her.

Sturesson's voice sounded authoritative: 'The banquet. Formal attire. At minimum!' He nodded distractedly at Vera. 'Yes, that includes you too, of course.'

11

Linda had called, sounding secretive. She and Peter had agreed to meet at the city's biggest shopping mall. He had combed his hair back and put on the preppy cap that he knew Linda thought he looked good in. He saw her familiar shiny black hair a long way off. As usual, he felt relaxed in the company of the fun-loving girl he had studied business administration with two years ago. They had also enjoyed quite a bit of sex together, and that was what she seemed to have in mind when she dragged him off to the women's underwear department of the big clothing store chain.

Peter had always felt uncomfortable in the presence of all these intimate women's garments. So when Linda turned and went further into the underwear section he stayed close to the demure nightgowns and pretended to look for something in comfortable cotton for his mother. He was standing right outside the women's changing rooms and could see the feet of two girls under the swing doors.

Piles of clothes that they had already tried on were draped over the doors. Peter sighed. They seemed to have spent hours in the changing room. A poor kid of about 15 sat outside, exhausted and gloomy, his schoolbag thrown on the floor and his jacket open. He had baggy jeans, headphones around his neck and big, unruly hair. Maybe a son or a little brother, thought Peter, sharing in his suffering.

He heard a vaguely familiar female voice from inside the changing room on the left. 'We can fix this relationship crisis.'

What relationship crisis? thought Peter curiously. Whose? The boy's? The other participant in this marathon session of trying on clothes? Then Linda suddenly appeared, holding up a bra in front of her.

'Peter, what do you think of this red lace?'

He barely had time to look around in embarrassment before Linda disappeared again into the vast array of merchandise. Peter tuned in again to what the girl in the left-hand changing room was saying.

'Okay, but you need to ask yourself: what *is* love?'

Nobody answered. The item of clothing being tried on in the right-hand changing room seemed to be causing a problem, because a pair of gloved hands was stretched upwards in an effort to get something rust-red and shiny to slide on. The girl on the left continued, 'This is what love is: it's when you don't need to say anything. When you just... when you just know. What do you think about then?'

It was the boy outside who answered: 'I think about football.'

Peter smiled. Linda appeared again and Peter glanced at her, embarrassed by a leopard-patterned thong.

'Yeah, I don't know,' he said uncertainly and pulled his cap further down on his forehead. Linda giggled and turned back to the merchandise.

That was when he saw her. She suddenly stepped out of the changing room on the right wearing a long, red dress that accentuated her slim, hourglass figure. She held up her dark, curly hair, looked down and smiled confidently, waiting for the girl in the changing room on the left to zip her up at the back. It was as if he saw everything in slow motion.

His mouth was suddenly dry, his hands were sweaty, and he could only stare, caught in a strong feeling of being in the wrong place. She was a complete stranger, and yet he was filled with a strange feeling of togetherness. Seeing her felt like coming home. Peter couldn't help it. His whole being glowed and he felt intensely that *I should be the one standing behind her.* His pulse raced at the sight of the small, clean lines of her face, her warm complexion and her dimples. She let go of her hair and twirled around once.

When she backed in between the swing doors to her own changing room, she looked up, into his eyes, and it was like an electric shock went through his body. He felt completely defenseless: it was his own happy future he thought he saw in her eyes. She had stopped halfway into the changing room, and he was sure that she also felt that the contact between them was full of meaning. He was enjoying trying to figure out what that meaning was, when the beauty shuddered and the inscrutable gaze transformed into something that looked like fear – or was it distaste? – before she quickly backed into the changing room and the doors cut off their eye contact. The magic was broken.

Peter looked around in a daze, and realized what had happened. The girl in the changing room had seen Linda! She stood smiling beside him with a black corset with stocking-fasteners pressed against her body.

'Peter. You and me... tonight?' she said quietly and tried to make eye contact with him through his tunnel vision. Linda's forthright flirting was something he had always appreciated, but now it felt cheap and tasteless compared to the feelings that still pounded through his body.

He realized that he hadn't made a particularly good impression. He understood how it had looked, but what could he say? *Noooo, this isn't my wife, just my old fuck buddy.* It didn't really feel like a successful opening line, and there was nothing Peter could do except quickly and discreetly grab Linda and get out of there. Averting her plans for tonight was something he would have to do elsewhere.

His heart pounded disagreeably, stressed by new, uncomfortable feelings, and every step away from the girl in the changing room added to a strange weight in his chest. He didn't recognize himself. He felt uneasy and his footsteps were unsure, as if he were about to lose something immeasurably precious.

12

Be proud of who you are.

Vera's teabag

Vera had persuaded Adam to send her favorite jeans, her green sweater and her fall jacket. She thought she had enough clothes, but now there was that banquet. 'Formal attire, at minimum.' What on earth did that mean? Vera felt lost. When Cissi offered to help her, she accepted gratefully and went over to Cissi's apartment on a Thursday morning.

Vera looked out through the bus window at the people out in the fall sunshine. It was windy, and on the long, curved pedestrian bridge she saw a woman in a beret lose her balance as she pushed her overloaded bike up the steep slope. She fell, along with the bike, her grocery bags, and everything. Two teenage boys in baggy-crotched jeans hurried forward to help her. The shorter one helped her up and out of the path of a middle-aged man with a briefcase and a knitted hat who was braking as he biked downhill. The tall one ran after three oranges that were playfully rolling away down the bridge. Vera smiled. She had retreated home to Västerbotten because she hadn't felt that she had anywhere else to go. Now she realized that if you had doubts about your faith in humanity, this was a place where you just might get it back.

Cissi lived in an attic apartment just east of downtown. Vera had to climb all the steps with her healthy right leg, stamping like a child learning to use the stairs. Three flights up in the old wooden house there was a large studio apartment with dormer windows and mismatched furniture, spiced with a new-age aesthetic. When Vera saw the batik throw and the waterfall with the rotating stone, she felt like the only thing missing was the scent of incense. Otherwise, books, clothes and shoes dominated the apartment. It was messy and cozy, both foreign and homely at the same time. Next to one of the windows there was an old-fashioned make-up table with a mirror and, in Vera's eyes, an unbelievable amount of cosmetics.

Cissi offered her Ayurvedic tea and homemade cookies, and they commented on the sweeping advice that they got from their teabags. They said that if nothing else worked out then they could get work coming up with words of wisdom for teabags.

'Live and let live,' said Vera

'Dare more than you dare,' suggested Cissi.

Cissi studied Vera in the light coming in through the window and got up suddenly.

'You have to be "fall", with that skin and your warm, green eyes! You can have this; it's way too dark for me. Classic shopping mistake.' Cissi had fetched the hair-coloring kit from her bathroom and put it in front of Vera.

'Fall?' Vera thought she had heard incorrectly, but Cissi explained that she was sure that people were right for certain colors, and that colors – and thus even the people suited to them – were divided into groups named after the seasons. Cissi started talking about the debate in color-analysis circles about whether you could be a blend of color groups, and if so how the colors were blended.

Vera smiled at her friend's complicated theories and let Cissi convince her. She already had brown hair. According to Cissi, the toning would just 'make your hair shinier and give it little chestnut highlights,' and it warmed Vera that Cissi was so generous and positive. Sleep, eat, work and study was all she had done for the past few months, and now she felt like it would be good for her work on the welfare project if she fixed herself up a bit. She used to do it, after all. Maybe it was time for the old Vera to make a comeback?

'Everything in life has pluses and minuses,' said Cissi philosophically.

Yes, maybe so... Vera thought about Saturday.

'Can I take out your braid?'

Vera nodded. Her host loosened the hair-tie carefully and freed Vera's hair. She began to lift and pick at it as she continued:

'And the trick is to do something about, or downplay, the negative and emphasize the positive.'

But if you can't do anything about the negative? Saturday's failure: it hadn't been so easy then. It hadn't been a matter of 'downplaying' things.

Now Cissi let go of her hair and looked worriedly at Vera.

'Hey – what is it?'

Vera shrugged her shoulders and smothered a sob.

'Was it something I said?'

Vera writhed as if in physical pain. 'No... it isn't your fault, it's just that... If it doesn't *work*, what then?'

'If what doesn't work?' Cissi sat down on a stool in front of Vera. 'I would say that you have a lot we can build on, so when we're done you'll be...' She stopped herself. 'Ah... look even better, I mean.'

Vera shook her head again.

'It's my... husband.' She had to make an effort to get the word out. 'Adam. I was supposed to be with him in Stockholm this weekend, but I couldn't stay. I just couldn't. It felt completely wrong.'

Cissi looked at her sympathetically. 'You couldn't bring yourself to stay?'

'No. First there was a song on the bus that made me... I got off and threw up in a dog-waste bin. And then, in the apartment. I was going to stay, but it was like my body refused. I felt really bad.' Vera took a shaky breath.

Cissi looked at her. 'Okay.'

They sat quietly for a while before she continued.

'But you made the best of the situation, didn't you? Because, you know, it's like Gunde says, "you can't fool your body".'

Vera smiled palely, remembering the iconic cross-country skiing world champion. She dried her face a little embarrassedly and nodded, 'Yes, it's like Gunde says.'

She laboriously twisted off her engagement and wedding rings and put them on the little label that was attached to the teabag. The label's message encouraged her to be proud of who she was.

Cissi thought they might as well go ahead and do everything at once, so when Vera was sitting in Cissi's tiny bathroom with her hair, now a worrisome orange, in a sticky heap under a plastic bag, Cissi lit a powerful lamp on the mirror. Vera had washed her face carefully and even put in her contact lenses in honor of the day. But Cissi wasn't impressed. She pointed to places where Vera's skin was dry and chapped and where Vera's thick, dark eyebrows stuck out.

'Oh, sorry. We've only just got to know each other and here I am saying things like that. Flat-out rude. It would be like you coming up to me and blurting out, "well, here's a muffin-top!"' Cissi grabbed the fat around her waist.

'No, it's okay,' said Vera, smiling palely. 'It's like when my mother-in-law came to the apartment. She cleared off the whole kitchen counter and pointed out all the stains. I actually told her that a lot of daughters-in-law would be offended, but not me. In the first place, it was mostly Adam who did the dishes. But even if I had lived there alone...' Vera shrugged her shoulders, 'I'm not interested in competing for "cleanest kitchen counter". It would be another thing if we were going to operate on it.'

'Okay. But now you're taking... a break from Adam?'

Vera nodded and looked at the light indentation that the rings had left in her finger after years of wearing them. 'Yeah, I guess so.'

Cissi went out to the little table where they had sat drinking tea. She came back with Vera's rings and placed them carefully in her lap.

'Don't forget them. You know, you can't dump him on me,' she tried to joke, but went on quickly: 'Uh, so the mother-in-law cleared the counter. What did she do after that?'

'She got cracking with the steel wool. And I guess that's what you feel like doing too?' Vera asked, dutifully forcing her rings back on.

Vera was surprised at the amount of work Cissi put into the renovation project. She wondered if this was what it was like to have a big sister. They took a break for lunch and then Vera scrubbed the bathtub to get rid of all traces of orange hair dye. Otherwise, it was just simple, goal-focused work, and after four hours in Cissi's little apartment – after Cissi had curled Vera's now chestnut-colored hair and made up her face – it was time to go into town and get kitted out for the banquet.

'Formal attire means long dresses for women.'

'So what does "formal attire, *at a minimum"* mean, then?' wondered Vera.

'A *gorgeous* long dress!' Cissi took a draped, gold-colored creation out of her full closet. 'This is what I'm wearing.'

Vera glanced at herself in the mirror on the way out. She saw her usual jeans and her favorite sweater, but what was above the beige jacket felt foreign. She struggled with a desire to go back in, wipe off half the make-up, and put her look-at-me hair in a ponytail – that's what the old Vera would do. But Cissi was already halfway down the stairs. *This isn't even my kind of thing. I hope I don't see anybody I know*, thought Vera as she shut the door behind her.

Cissi knew Lovisa, who managed Formal Clothes on Norrland Street. When Vera had tried on everything that was left in stock in size 8, there were only two dresses that were remotely possible. One of them was a violet-blue fluffy chiffon and the other was a rust-red silk dress with cap sleeves and hand-embroidered copper pearls on the bodice. Vera didn't like the violet one; it was too much like a wedding dress. When Lovisa suggested cream-colored evening gloves to go with the red dress, Cissi thought that decided it. It was true that Vera was usually as shy as a wallflower, but if, for once, she was going to a banquet, why not show off her fantastic figure in the red dress? And it was a perfect color for her as well.

Fantastic figure? Vera shook her head and showed Cissi how the dress was too big across the bust.

'No, that, that's your...' Cissi seemed to be searching for a word that was not too critical, and she lowered her voice, 'non-existent bra's fault. We should have done that first – found proper underwear...' Cissi turned to Lovisa.

'Can we borrow it for a while today and check to make sure it's right? You probably won't need to make any alterations; the length is just right and it fits perfectly at the waist! What does it cost to hire it for the weekend for the banquet if she pays now and takes it without any alterations?'

Then Cissi's cellphone rang; it was an indignant guy on the other end. Cissi waved at Vera to finish up the deal and she walked away towards the bridesmaids' dresses as she talked into the telephone: she didn't have time to come right now, but yes, she was downtown. Sure, they could meet if he wanted.

'Was that your boyfriend?' Vera wondered, as a sales assistant carefully wrapped up the red dress with the copper pearls.

'Huh? No! God, no! That was just Freddie, my little cousin. He might show up later. But he's okay for a 15-year-old.'

When they left the store with the party dress protected inside a large garment bag, Vera felt uncomfortable. She understood that the fortune she felt she had paid to rent the dress was actually a bargain price because of Cissi's friendship with Lovisa, and it was a relief that the banquet problem was now solved. But if she had felt dressed up before, now it was full masquerade.

Vera didn't have very much money left, so the miracle bra that was needed would have to be found at the big, low-price chainstore at the city mall. Cissi guessed that it would take a while, so she used the opportunity to try on clothes too. After about 20 minutes, when she still hadn't found a single bra that fitted, Vera began to feel downhearted. Cissi came back with her arms full of clothes. She hung most of them over the door of the changing room next to Vera's, but draped a few things over Vera's door as well.

'I couldn't help myself. Try these on, I think you... What's wrong?' Cissi broke off when she saw Vera's sad eyes.

'Nothing fits.' Vera let her arms fall to her sides and shyly revealed the bra she had tried on. Cissi studied Vera and the dozen alternatives that were hanging in the changing room.

'Excuse me, is it okay if I...?' Cissi fiddled with the shoulder strap and the strap across Vera's back.

'But, Vera,' she said reading the label, '34A – are you sure about this? I think it looks too big. You have it fastened on the hooks farthest in and it's still loose.'

'A is the smallest they have,' said Vera with a small voice.

'Yes, yes, but it's *here* that it's too big!' Cissi pulled the strap away from Vera's back demonstratively.

Cissi went out to the underwear display and came back with several new bras. 'I read somewhere that over half of Swedish women wear bras that are the wrong size. You should have 32B, or maybe even 30C; try these!'

'But isn't B for... well... a normal-sized bust?' Vera didn't take the garments that Cissi held out to her.

'Yes, and C is large – for you. Geez! 32 or 34 inches around the body! You are slim enough for several people! You could easily share a little with me,' said Cissi and smiled kindly.

'Yeah, so shouldn't I have 32A?'

Cissi's phone rang again. 'Nah, try these on; you'll see.'

Cissi went out and answered the phone. Vera heard her describe where they were.

Cissi was right. These fitted much better. But most of the ones she had chosen were generously padded models that Cissi said were designed to 'highlight her charms'.

What a strange expression, thought Vera. *Who is this highlighting supposed to charm?* A brief thought in Adam's direction pained her. It seemed like an impossibility. Even when she stretched herself far beyond her comfort zone.

I don't like surprises!

She broke out into a cold sweat. Suddenly she felt how much her knee ached and how tired she was. She sat down and rested a while, observing the stranger looking at her from the mirror. Vera closed her eyes and waited for the pain and nausea to subside.

'It was Linus. Stupid asshole!' a guy just outside the changing room said glumly. Vera started. *Who is he talking to?* He carried on complaining.

'The teacher went, like, nuts, and now everybody has to write a whole fucking essay about love!'

'Well, if you call somebody a whore, it's good that the teacher reacts. I think what he did was exactly right!' It was Cissi; she had come back with more clothes. Vera realized that the young guy with her must be cousin Freddie. He continued indignantly.

'But, honestly! Otherwise – no class trip! And there's no reliable stuff about love that you can pinch from the internet either! I checked – nothing!'

Vera sat and listened as Cissi tried to help Freddie, who was having a 'mega crisis', and a smile crept over her face. She and Cissi were so different, but there was still something that felt very familiar. Now Vera realized what it was. Cissi was a problem solver, just like she was. But Cissi had completely different knowledge and skills, and her repertoire of solutions seemed impressively broad. The least she could do was allow herself to be helped. Vera put on the long gloves and got up resolutely. She had guessed that the chocolate brown push-up bra would work but the question was: how would the rust red creation fit now?

The dress was surprisingly heavy with all the silk fabric and the embroidered pearls. Unexpected questions popped up in Vera's head: *Who sewed all these on? I wonder what her life is like?* Vera managed to pour the silk over her head and down onto her body, and she got her arms into the dress. After trying unsuccessfully to bend her arms backwards and pull up the zipper, she realized that she needed help. She knocked lightly on the wall of Cissi's changing room, went out through the swing doors, and turned her back to Cissi. Vera had glanced in the mirror and thought it looked promising; maybe it would work after all?

'Well, look at you! Oh, hold up your hair!' Cissi waited so that she wouldn't catch the zipper in Vera's chestnut-colored curls. Vera smiled and obeyed, and when Cissi pulled up the zipper she felt the dress settle perfectly across her hips and waist. When Cissi was finished Vera let down her hair and carefully twirled around once. Cissi smiled broadly and nodded in satisfaction, like a sculptress in front of her creation. Then Vera noticed that someone else was looking at her, and she looked in that direction.

At first he looked like an anonymous catalogue model in his relaxed dressiness: shirt hanging out, blazer, long striped scarf and a cap pulled down low over his forehead. After a second, though she realized that it was Peter Stavenius. The weirdest thing was the way he was looking at her. She had wondered about her neighbor sometimes, what he really did to conquer so many hearts. Now she was seeing it with her own eyes.

He looked at her like she was the only person in the whole world, and as if he really liked her. Well, 'liked her' was too weak. He looked like he had been waiting for her his whole life and now stood there, completely attentive, ready to do anything for her. *God, he's a good actor!*, she thought, impressed despite herself, caught in the confused locking of their eyes. *But why are you looking at* **me** *like that?*

That was when she realized. He didn't recognize her, because he had never seen – and even now wasn't seeing – *her*. It was all the fakery that he was seeing, and he clearly appreciated it. The new hair color and the shiny Hollywood curls, the fake, painted eyelashes, the lip gloss, the rented dress, and, of course, the well-padded chocolate-brown bra. She had dressed up as a 'pin-up chick' and suddenly she was on Mr Sex Machine's radar. She was suitable prey for the predator.

Then a pretty, dark-haired girl approached Peter with a corset provocatively pressed against her body, obviously flirty and intimate. Vera wasn't surprised that she had never seen the girl before. The scene illustrated perfectly why Peter's inappropriate gaze had caused her to have such unpleasant associations. Vera fled back into her changing room and let the swing doors hide her blush of indignation. Safely alone again, she sat down and tried to calm her racing pulse with deep breaths.

'*That* one!' Cissi said, sticking her head into Vera's changing room. Vera hopped nervously up off the little stool. *Shhh*, she wanted to say.

'Ooh la la!' emphasized Cissi and lifted her arched eyebrows suggestively.

Don't you recognize Peter? 'Do you think so?' asked Vera and tried to look relaxed.

'Yes! What a heartbreaker!' said Cissi with conviction.

Vera grimly took off the formal gloves, no longer able to hide what she felt in her heart.

'Right. Exactly. And that's nothing worth betting on. It's really nothing worth having.'

Cissi stared uncomprehendingly at her. 'What? A girl needs it sometimes, right? It does the trick. Of course you should buy it. No doubt about it!'

13

Jujutsu belongs to the Japanese martial arts family of budo. *Ju* is translated as soft and responsive, while *jutsu* means method or technique. The name communicates that it is the art of defeating an opponent using as little physical strength as possible.

Peter's first book about his martial art

Peter's eyes had been drawn like a magnet to the reddish brown curls, and to his joy he realized that it actually *was* the girl from the changing room who was sitting on the bus he climbed onto for the ride home. She was real and she was travelling east on the number 8 bus, just like he was, at the same time! He sat tensely, wondering why she looked so familiar. Had they met when they were out somewhere? He thought that he ought to find out her name. He didn't want to lose her again, not without knowing something about her.

But then strange things started happening.

The first was that she sat next to Cissi, the hippie lady from the department. Maybe he had seen her with Cissi? But that didn't feel right. They were talking. He sat diagonally behind them and strained to hear what they were saying. It was then he realized that the voice he had recognized from the left-hand changing room had been Cissi's. *She's a friend of Cissi!* Well then, he could just ask Cissi who she was and needn't worry about losing her. Cissi said, 'See you,' and got up. When she moved to the back of the bus to get off, Peter hurriedly looked away, out through the window, as if he didn't want her to see him. Afterwards he wondered why he had done so.

Then things got even stranger. As soon as the bus started moving again a teenage boy slunk forward and sat down next to her. Peter recognized him. It was the kid with the jeans and the big unruly hair who had been waiting outside the changing rooms. Peter considered for a brief moment, looked around in embarrassment, and moved lithely and quietly across the aisle to the boy's now empty seat, only two seats behind her. He listened tensely.

'You know, she brings up sex all the time. *That's* not what it's supposed to be about!' the boy complained.

'Well then all you need to do is explain that to her.'

She sounds kind, Peter thought affectionately and a strange certainty filled him.

'I'm sure she'll help you,' she continued.

'Yeah, but I think you can help better. You're like, married and everything!'

She's married! His heart sank like a stone – he hadn't thought of that. She might actually be happily married, faithful and forever unavailable.

She looked out of the window, but the youngster looked pleadingly at her, 'please?'

Peter realized with some discomfort that he himself might not have been fully informed about the ages of all the girls he'd picked up in the city, but none of them had been *that* young, had they?

'There's no rush. As long as it's, like, before the class trip,' the teenager continued.

'When's that, then?'

'In the spring.'

'I'm really not the right person,' she said, and Peter felt relieved.

Her curls spilled between the seats when she turned her head and studied the boy; she shook her head a little, and Peter got the sense that she was amused.

'Alright,' she said finally.

Hah, so much for being faithful. If you're going to help guys hungry for love, the least you can do is stick to ones your own age, thought Peter helplessly.

The kid looked satisfied under his giant hair: 'Awesome! I'll, like, come over some time. I'll check with Cissi about where you live and stuff.'

The kid got up and moved to a seat on the other side of the bus, the one Peter had been sitting in before. He put on his headphones and turned the music on. *I'm Mister Lovva-Lovva*, bragged Shaggy so loudly that it was audible to everyone on the bus.

Tinnitus is what you are going to get, Mister Lovva-Lovva, thought Peter sourly, again feeling like he was not at all himself. But there was something familiar in that voice – the feeling that he had heard it before grew stronger. And how could he be so strangely certain that she was kind? The truth crept up on him slowly. When she got off at his bus stop and he saw that she limped toward Stipend Street, he was certain. The woman from the changing room was the dull, grey girl on crutches – his wall-banging neighbor Vera Lund-something. *Gren? Berg? Kvist?*

A cold fall wind made him shiver, and he put up the collar of his tweed blazer. He waited a while to give her more of a head start. He couldn't bring himself to catch up and talk to her. Embarrassment paralyzed him.

Of course, he had never before seen her in anything other than ugly old jogging clothes with a fuzzy braid down her back. Yet from the moment he had seen the beauty in the red dress, he had felt like he recognized her. But how could he not have seen that *it was the same person?* And what should he do now? When Vera opened the door to the dorm with her key, Peter heard a cheerful voice ring out in the stairwell:

'Looking good today, luv!'

Peter's steps felt heavy on the stairs, like someone who was hopelessly far behind. But Matt had not seen her radiantly smiling in that dress; he had just seen her in her normal gear on her way to her room.

That's different, a completely different thing, he said in his own defense.

Vera's door was closed when he came into the hallway. He was glad that he could slip into his room unseen. Through the wall he heard music: it was loud and hard with distorted guitars.

Vera often listened to music, but this was the first time he had heard her listening to hard rock. *She must be in a strange mood.* Peter's state of mind improved. Maybe she had been as affected by the eye contact as he had? And equally self-conscious about how to take some kind of reasonable next step, given that it turned out that it was the two of them who had suddenly discovered each other, despite the fact that they had been living wall-to-wall all fall? *Although, of course, she had recognized him immediately; was that why she had looked so... surprised?* The questions spun around in his mind as he lay on the bed with his hands behind his head and listened to Vera's unusual choice of music. He lost track of time, and when he realized how late it was he had to grab a couple of sandwiches on his way to martial arts practice.

On the bus down to the clubhouse Peter realized that there were both advantages and disadvantages to the fact that it was Vera. An advantage was that although she certainly was married, her lawfully wedded husband was nowhere in sight. He realized that he had never seen any trace of a husband. *Doesn't that suggest it's not the world's best marriage?* Another advantage was that Peter had plenty of opportunities to see her; they practically lived together!

The disadvantages were, of course, harder to think about. She hadn't made any secret of the fact that she didn't like him, and he hadn't exactly given her any good reasons to do so. He got that. He realized suddenly that he had never seen her dimples before she was standing there outside the changing room, because he had never seen her happy before!

The bus stopped at the first stop just west of downtown and Peter got off, determined to do whatever it took to see more of those dimples. It happened to be one of his absolute specialties: when he wanted to, he seldom failed to make women happy.

The workout was gruelling, and not only because he had not eaten enough. After a short warm-up they went straight on to randori and Peter was paired with a new guy from southern Sweden who had to be 15 kilos heavier than he was. He was good and Peter had to concentrate fully in order to avoid a severe beating. When he managed to get Vera completely out of his head and began to learn the big newcomer's style, he managed to bring him to the floor several times.

After practice he was completely exhausted. His arms hung at his sides, aching and almost unusable, and he felt satisfied as he got into the shower. He still had it, the talent to concentrate fully and take in the present, to softly feel where his opponent was going, to follow along in his opponent's direction, but then to apply his own power in exactly the right way to steer things to where he wanted them. His thoughts returned all too easily to the memory of Vera smiling in the red dress, and it spread a lovely sweetness through his body. Peter hurriedly dried off and got dressed.

He was hungry. Hungry in so many ways. But something unfamiliar held him back. In any other case he would have asked her directly, but now he opted for Cissi instead.

The next day he found Cecilia Åström in her office at the department. He started with a little small talk about the summer course and how nice he thought it was that Vera had wound up in his dorm – he knew that it would have been a big lie only two days ago, but now it was an astonishing truth – before he got to the heart of the matter.

'By the way, I heard that Vera was going to some...' He thought about the occasion on which Vera might wear the red dress and guessed, 'ball?'

'Uh-huh, yeah...' answered Cissi, focusing on her computer screen. 'You know, the university's annual fall festival, the fall banquet.'

Peter was surprised. 'But ordinary introductory-level students never go to that, do they?'

Cissi turned toward him. 'Who said Vera is ordinary?'

'But, I mean... how did she get an invitation? Is some relative being awarded a doctorate?'

'We're all going. She's part of our...' Cissi turned back towards her computer screen, 'You know... Sturesson's... Future Wealth and Welfare project.'

'Oh, damn, I'm part of that too,' Peter heard himself say.

'Really?' Cissi tucked her red hair behind her ear as she turned back towards him with surprise. 'Are you the advanced level student? I thought it was Tomas Lern?'

Tomas Lern – top of the class. The light blond go-getter and math genius, who was aiming at a lucrative career in finance. Wooden and awkward, but the only one in class who got the right answer on the test question about derivative construction. Probably because he had already studied four semesters of applied physics. Or because he was simply devilishly smart, Peter admitted to himself.

'Tomas? Really?' Peter shrugged his shoulders. 'I'll check with Sturesson. Maybe I misunderstood something.'

He was lucky, because Sturesson was in his office, and the red light outside was not on. Peter knocked on the door and boldly entered: 'Excuse me, do you have a minute?'

The greying man stroked his goatee. 'Peter. Absolutely! Take a seat.'

'I thought I would let you know that I have checked into my… workload at Great Escape during the fall. Turns out, it is not going to be too much. Basically just board meetings, and there are only four per year.' Peter smiled brightly from the visitor's chair.

'Yes?' said Sturesson, looking at a loss.

'Yes, so I would like to accept your offer on Future Wealth and Welfare.'

Åke Sturesson's eyebrows travelled upward and he sighed deeply. 'Really? You tell me this now? It's just that… it is just too late for that.'

Peter's heart beat hard, but his voice sounded normal and relaxed.

'Oh? Pity. But I should offer congratulations. You have already got a lot of work done?'

'Well, I wouldn't say that,' admitted the Professor. 'But I have had time to talk to someone else. Lern is going to do it.'

'Oh, Tomas Lern? Yes, he and I have taken all of our economics courses together. Excellent choice,' said Peter and nodded, while in his head he thought, *what was it that Sturesson said he wanted?* 'He is a really good mathematician. And if he has said yes, and you are completely satisfied, then there is no reason to change your mind. You know that he studied applied physics to begin with? You will get really advanced derivative calculations in his cha...'

'He studied applied physics first?' interrupted Sturesson with a worried frown.

'Yes, and imagine what a good springboard it will be for him to have published his formulas in the project publications. One of the big banks will hire him immediately.'

Åke Sturesson rubbed his beard anxiously, stretched for a binder on a shelf and started looking through it. 'Yes, of course. But in the application we promised a more popular science approach. And we are going to present it at a big press conference in May. I need to ask him...'

'Yes, ask him what he does best. I think that's a good move,' said Peter, suspecting that victory was almost his. 'And be sure to tell him that he gets to take part in a press conference in the spring.'

Knowing Tomas, he would rush to turn down the position. *I'm doing you a favor, buddy.*

'Otherwise, are you willing to jump on board and write something more accessible?'

'Me? Absolutely!'

14

Reproduction refers to the worker's daily recreation of his own or others' labor power. This includes everyday tasks – such as food preparation and laundry – that maintain life and the worker's ability to show up to work. Much of this household work has historically been the responsibility of women, which is why reproduction is of particular interest to feminist economists.

From Vera's reading in the university library

Vera refused to buy the brown bra; she said something incoherent about it 'not being her.' But she thanked Cissi for her help and bought a simple white bra that fitted properly. She also returned the red dress to Formal Clothes. Cissi didn't understand. Wasn't the problem solved? she asked.

Vera tried at first to explain. 'I felt like I was in costume.'

'Life is a theatre,' Cissi shrugged her shoulders, 'Who isn't in costume?'

The objection was on the tip of Vera's tongue. *Why should I want to be dressed up like Playmate of the Week for assholes?* Vera sensed that Cissi wouldn't have anything against being looked at the way Peter had looked at her, and she could imagine that Cissi would look like a real bombshell in her low-cut, gold, draping dress at the banquet next weekend. But Vera felt all wrong in the red outfit, and she decided that she would go to the second-hand shop to look for a long dress that was more discreet.

When she got home, Vera put on 'Enter Sandman', turned the volume up high, and went into the bathroom. She washed off the make-up, removed her contact lenses, and put her hair up in a ponytail. After carefully wiping her glasses, she put them on. Vera looked at herself in the mirror, changed her mind, took out the hair tie, and arranged her chestnut-colored curls into their usual braid down her back.

She hated feeling like a cliché, and she realized that she had spent half the day doing just that. As much of a cliché as the girl in the endless parade of American films where the premise is that if the smart, boring girl in glasses would just take off her spectacles and go on a crazy shopping spree to buy provocative clothes, she would discover that she could hook up with the most popular hunk in school. It was like they were trying to drum into the ears of girls everywhere the message that happiness lies in trying to live like Paris Hilton. *Consume more*, thought Vera, and shivered uneasily. She realized that she needed to eat.

Matt and Vera had eaten dinner together and they were still sitting at the table talking when Peter came into the kitchen with a bag from the local grocery store. Peter's hair was wet and he was carrying a gym bag. He glanced toward the table as he put the milk in the refrigerator, and when he saw that Vera was there he stood up so quickly that he hit his head hard on the cabinet door that he had just opened. Peter smiled tentatively, glanced shyly at Vera and quickly disappeared out of the room with his hand over his forehead.

Although it wasn't her intention, Vera heard how critical she sounded when she asked: 'When, in fact, was it his week to take care of the kitchen?'

Matt looked at Vera in surprise: 'What are you talking about? Did something happen?'

'No, *I* don't know.' She shrugged her shoulders and bit into her flat-bread sandwich.

'So you're just negative for no reason?'

'I'm not negative!' Vera knew how unconvincing her answer sounded, and Matt looked at her critically.

'I didn't suspect that about you.'

Like you know anything, thought Vera, and immediately felt ashamed of herself. *Why am I so touchy? It's not Matt's fault!* She tried to fix things.

93

'No. Well, you know. That girl, Sandra, the one who eats here sometimes. And her, the Asian one...' Vera gestured with her hands, sweeping them from beside her face downwards in front of her body to illustrate long, loose, dark hair.

'Aye. Linda,' Matt nodded.

'And today, downtown, I saw that he...' she went silent, looked down at the table, 'made contact, like he wanted to be with a third one.'

'Aye. Lots of lasses. But maybe he can't control his, what do you call it, his charisma?'

'He is a complete "spaller"!' Vera exclaimed.

'Huh?'

'It's a north Swedish dialect word but I think it came from English. It means... something unstable. But even such a spaller could at least try to control himself!' She took another bite.

'Are you sure? That girl today – maybe she is Miss Right?'

Vera thought she heard steps from the hall, as Matt continued.

'Maybe he'll be faithful to her for the rest of his life?' Matt got up and picked up his plate. His brown eyes twinkled mischievously and he suddenly began to sing. An unexpectedly rich baritone filled the dorm: 'Where do I begiiin, to tell the story of how great a love can beee?'

Vera tried to stop him. She stood up hastily and got a piece of flat-bread stuck in her throat. She shook her head, coughed, sat down again and waved her hands helplessly. Matt stopped singing, sat down beside Vera and thumped her on the back.

'Oh! Do you want me to...?'

Then Peter came back into the kitchen. He had put on clean clothes and fixed his hair, as if he were going to see someone special. He looked at Vera, who had recovered sufficiently that she was at least getting enough oxygen. She put her plate down on the counter before she hurried out of the kitchen blushing.

'I'll wash my plate later,' she whimpered between coughs.

✖

Vera spent a lot of time at the university library. She had an idea what she wanted to write about, something that was needed to secure future welfare. She surfed online and searched the library catalogue using the words 'economic reproduction', 'care deficit', and 'basic needs'. She copied stacks of journal articles and borrowed books. It got dark early, and she hobbled slowly home, leaning against her bicycle up the hill through the rustling pine grove, her head full of things she wanted to have said. It was only when she was going downhill that she carefully rode her bike, because she could not bend her left leg enough to pedal a full circle. *Adam wouldn't like this*, she thought as the bike rolled downhill and she exposed her weakened leg to the risk of even greater injury. *But do 'we' even exist any more?* The question pained her.

On Monday she went to the department to see Cissi and discuss her chapter. Cissi was upset. There was some problem with the financing for her graduate studies.

'They won't let me finish,' said Cissi gloomily. 'Unless I agree to teach more, of course. If I teach full-time then there is money to pay me.'

'But doesn't that just delay the problem?' wondered Vera. 'How are you going to finish your dissertation if you teach full-time? Isn't it better to take out a student loan and finish your research?'

Cissi shook her head, 'Not allowed. No student loan after you've been accepted to graduate studies. Maybe I'll have to settle for making it halfway and finish with a Master's degree? She wiped a little tear from the corner of her eye and gave a forced smile. 'But now we're going to talk about your chapter!'

It still felt only half thought-through and unstructured, but thanks to Cissi's guidance, Vera sensed that she was beginning to see a pattern. *A basic problem with the economy as it exists today is that it is much more profitable to exploit a finite resource and mass-produce completely new stuff than to take care of something old and repair it when necessary*, thought Vera as she sat on the bus on the way to the second-hand shop in Ersboda. *Not to mention taking care of old people.*

The second-hand shop was located in a big warehouse

space, and to the right, beyond the shelves with knick-knacks and porcelain, were the used clothes. Vera looked through the assortment of full-length party dresses and found four that she thought might do. But it was more difficult in the changing room; three of the dresses were out of the question. There was only one dress, a green, empire-waist creation, that she could even imagine wearing to the banquet, and that was too big.

She sat down, disheartened, and wondered what she was going to do. She had to wear something, and pretty, full-length dresses didn't grow on trees. She stood up again and faced the mirror, pinching the back of the dress, with its many shades of green. It immediately fitted better. She liked the short sleeves and the square-cut neckline. The dress reminded her of the ones in Jane Austen films. Vera thought that the dress would work if she took it in at the back. Solveig at Solbacka – she had been a seamstress – *maybe she can tell me what to do and lend me her sewing machine?*

Vera decided to chance it, so she paid the modest price for the dress – a quarter of what it would have cost to hire the red one. But she knew that, in contrast to the red one, which – with the brown bra – was ready to go, this one would require her attention. *So appropriate,* thought Vera, *I have to devote time to reproduction.*

When she went to Solbacka that afternoon she filled her backpack with a little food to snack on and the green empire-waist dress. After her shift she knocked on Solveig's door. The old woman came to open it in her wheelchair and smiled radiantly when she saw Vera. After Vera had given her the fruit and bread and they had chatted a while, she summoned up her courage and asked:

'Solveig, I wonder, would you be able to help me with something?'

Vera was invited into the small apartment. She looked around with interest at the walls, where bits of fabric and ribbon competed for space with photographs of a younger Solveig sailing, sailplaning and riding elephants. In several of the

96

pictures she was with a happy man with a long, kind face.

'Is that your husband?' asked Vera, pointing to a picture in which Solveig and the man were embracing in front of a display window.

'Yes, that is my Gustav,' said Solveig warmly. 'And there is my studio, which he helped me set up.' She pointed at the picture. Studio Sun was painted on the enamelled plate that stuck out from the well-preserved wooden building.

'Yes, you used to be a seamstress,' said Vera. She picked up her backpack and pulled out the green dress. 'I have a… job you could call it, at the university. And as part of the job I have to go to a party, one where I have to wear a full-length dress.'

'Ah. Are you going to the fall banquet?' A professional interest glittered in Solveig's eyes as she felt the fabric of the dress. 'Hmm, silk voile with Belgian lace.' She looked at the price tag and smiled. 'You got a bargain, I can tell you that!' Solveig looked at the seams on the inside, 'Well made. I'm guessing the 1960s.'

'Yes, it is lovely, but, well, it doesn't fit properly. It's too big.' Vera held the dress up to her body to show her. 'But am I right that it can be taken in somehow and shortened?'

Solveig told Vera to put on the dress. She took out a pincushion and had Vera stand in front of a full-length mirror. With clever, practiced hands she pinched and pinned the dress. Vera watched her with admiration, but also with growing concern over the amount of work it was going to take to alter the dress. There was no way it could be done in 10 minutes by sewing some simple seam up the back, as Vera, in her ignorance, had thought. It was just as her father always said, *If you think something is simple, that's usually because you don't have any idea how difficult it really is.*

'You're still limping?' asked Solveig, as she calmly concentrated on the job in front of her.

'Yes, it feels like my leg is a little dislocated all the time. I think the meniscus is torn and a fragment isn't in the right place, so it chafes and the knee locks up. But I have another appointment with the doctor next week, and then they surely have to understand the problem, because it hasn't healed even though it's been six months.'

'Oh, that doesn't sound good.' Solveig looked at Vera with concern and continued working in silence. After a while she asked, 'How are things with you otherwise?'

There was something about Solveig's kind tone and the way she gently handled the dress. Copious amounts of salty tears started rolling down Vera's cheeks.

'It felt so obvious!' She said the word as if she had said *despair.*

Solveig calmly worked on.

'But now I feel completely lost. Everything is just... like a big black hole. And I chose it all myself!' Vera's voice was terribly thin, as if she had lost faith in everything.

'Yes, you young people today, it isn't so easy for you,' said Solveig softly, handing her the roll of paper towels that was stuffed in between the geraniums on the windowsill. 'You have so much freedom, and when things become difficult you blame yourselves.'

She rolled her wheelchair back a little and leaned her head to the side to study her work from a distance, then she rolled forward and started pinning again.

'So what have you chosen that is so wrong, do you think?' she continued softly.

Vera dried her face with a bit of paper, shrugged her shoulders and smiled wanly.

'No, just small things really. Like my education, my job, and my husband, for example.'

Solveig lifted her eyes from the bodice of the dress and looked searchingly into Vera's face. 'Oh my,' she said at last.

'Because I can't handle this,' said Vera, her voice shaky from the pain.

Solveig looked at her attentively: 'What is it that you can't handle?'

'I can't even keep my own promises!' When she said it, Vera realized that that was what was most unbearable. Adam had forced her into a corner in which even her own discipline didn't work.

'Well, what promises?'

She took a deep breath and her voice was a weak whisper.

'To love my husband in sickness and in health.'

Solveig paused in her work with the dress and looked up at Vera. 'Well, I don't know about that. I don't know if I think it means that you *have to* love.'

Vera bit her lip. Solveig started on the hem of the dress and puffed as she bent double down to the floor: 'One thing I think I have learned in life is that everything we do because we have to, becomes... half-hearted, or even dies.' She straightened up again, pushing the white curls from her worried, wrinkled forehead.

'Oh, this isn't going to work. Should I stand on a stool?' Vera pointed and Solveig nodded lightly. Vera fetched a wooden, blue-painted stool from the kitchen. She stood on it and soon the pinning resumed, this time with Solveig working at a much more comfortable level.

'Weren't you and Gustav married?'

'Mmm.' Solveig's lips were tightly clamped together around lots of pins.

'But what do you think that you promised him then – and what did he promise you? Didn't you promise to love each other until "death did you part"?'

Solveig sat quietly until she had used the rest of the pins she was holding in her mouth. Finally, she answered calmly: 'I love him still, even though death has parted us. But that is not because I promised once upon a time. I saw it more as if we had promised to be kind to one another, to support each other and to wish each other well, even when we faced adversity. Or perhaps particularly then.' There was a sad look in her eye and she was quiet for a minute before she continued.

'In any case, I don't think one can... what is it everyone says these days?'

The old woman thought for a minute as she adjusted some pins and checked that the right and left sides were the same length. Then she found the words.

'Achieve. I don't think one can just achieve love. It can't be forced. It just comes when it comes – and exists when it is nurtured. So! Climb down!'

She reached out with her hand so that Vera could hold it as she carefully stepped down from the stool. What had initially felt like a tent in shades of green that could fall off at any minute had now, with the help of a considerable number of well-placed pins, been formed around Vera's fine-boned frame and shortened to exactly the right length. Even at this stage, it was an impressively precise piece of work.

Vera took the stool back to its place. She realized that her and Adam's love had not been nurtured particularly well. *Maybe it was my fault?* Maybe her mother had been right and she shouldn't have gone abroad with Basic Needs after Adam changed his mind and didn't want to? The months apart had definitely not been a recipe for success.

'It feels like there is something... wrong with my internal compass. I was so sure that I had made the right decision. But then everything turned out wrong. So now I am trying to do something entirely different. The exact opposite of very wrong ought to be at least a little bit right, anyway?' pleaded Vera.

'A completely new man?' asked Solveig neutrally.

'A different project. A completely different job.' The reply came fast and Solveig looked at Vera attentively. Then she leaned back in her wheelchair looking pleased. Softly, she turned Vera towards the mirror and caught her eye in the reflection.

'Look. You look like a siren of the forest.'

Vera saw that it could definitely be called a pretty, full-length dress now. She looked lovely, but still very much herself. She was comforted. She had felt backed into a corner, faced with unacceptable choices. But now, looking at herself in the well-fitting party gown, she actually felt hopeful. *Perhaps there are choices that are both possible and not unsustainable after all?* Vera sat down on the sofa and gave Solveig a spontaneous hug.

'Thank you so much!'

'Oh! Watch the pins,' smiled Solveig.

Vera wrinkled her forehead, 'But maybe you can show me?

I don't know, how do I sew all this so that it comes out right?'

Solveig smiled kindly and stroked Vera's arm lightly. 'With my old eyes, it's too dark for me to sew right now, but I can have it done by Wednesday if you come back and try it on.'

'But that's too much to ask!'

'Not too much for you.'

15

1 PIECE OF DRYER LINT
For the lint opener: Walk up to a woman, stop, wordlessly remove lint (hidden in the palm of your hand) from her clothing, ask, 'How long has that been there?', then hand her the piece of lint.

Neil Strauss, 'The Game'

One evening, as Peter sat eating a sandwich studiously, Vera came in holding a piece of paper full of handwritten notes. She looked deep in thought. She put her notes down and opened the pantry. Peter took the piece of paper and began to read. In the middle were the words 'Redeeming reproduction' with a circle around them. Around that were lines to other words, which were also surrounded by lines to still more words and sentences.

'What is this?'

She started when she saw him. Peter took that as a good sign.

'It's my mind map,' she answered and opened a cupboard. Peter looked at the swarm of notes and found something interesting at the bottom left of the page.

'Okay. What have you discovered that can destroy all of Sweden, or wait, the whole planet?' A peculiar nervousness made him sound more teasing than he had meant.

Vera had taken out a bowl and a spoon, crisp flat-bread, milk and homemade lingonberry jelly. She crumbled the flat-bread into small pieces in the bowl. 'I don't claim to have discovered the undervaluing of reproduction.' She dropped dollops of lingonberry jelly on the pieces of flat-bread. When she had poured milk into the bowl, she looked up at Peter.

'But what do you have to say about a career as an unpaid

stay-at-home dad? And as long as you're home, you may as well take care of your old, sick father-in-law as well?'

Are you suggesting that I should stay home with our kids? He was only 24 years old and, sure, he had always thought that he wanted a couple of kids, some time in the infinitely distant future, after 30. But now Peter was taken by surprise by an unexpected feeling – he found himself strangely attracted to the idea. He felt an impulse to ask the question aloud, but realized that the possibility of having children together was not the right place to begin.

She put the milk in the refrigerator again and closed the door. She walked right towards him, and he felt his pulse quickening. For no sensible reason, he stood up, holding the piece of paper, taking advantage of the fact that he was bigger and stronger. Vera tried to reach her notes a couple of times, and he noticed that she smelled of something mild, good – some soap or other. Peter wanted to make it last longer, but Vera seemed irritated.

'But I guess you have never taken care of anybody in your whole life?'

Of course I have! Peter thought, but, strangely enough, he could not come up with a single good example. She collected herself and stepped away from him:

'This is ridiculous. I'm not going climb all over you.'

It sounded like a statement of intent. As she took her snack and left, she nodded towards her carefully written notes, 'But those are really important. Give them back when you are finished playing.'

Peter stared after her at a loss as she walked away, then at the flat-bread and lingonberry jelly that she had left behind. He took a bit of the bread, dipped it into the jelly and put it in his mouth.

The taste sensation was new and unexpectedly complex; the lingon was tartly sweet, but the crispy bread was rich and a little salty. *Remarkable.*

He still hadn't managed to communicate sensibly with Vera, and he didn't know what he should be doing differently.

She didn't seem at all interested in acknowledging what had happened last week. It was true that she had nicer clothes now, but she had gone back to wearing her glasses and putting her hair in a braid. It irritated him; in the same way that it annoyed him if he was served cold food at a restaurant – here was someone who wouldn't pull themselves together and do their job. Looking as good as you possibly could was something he considered almost a duty. And he expected it, particularly from girls. All women in his vicinity, except his mother when she was depressed, went to considerable trouble when it came to their appearance. He suspected some of the results were real triumphs of effort. Like Sandra, for example. He knew that she had hair extensions, a spray-on tan and probably a new nose. And there were other things that he experienced as *look but don't touch* – he remembered well the day that she didn't move her mouth at all, because she had just had her lips done. And she also had the best-looking silicon breasts that he had ever been up close with; they managed to be unbelievable in a sufficiently believable way. He had noticed that few men, and not many women either, failed to notice Sandra, a magnificent five feet 10 in height. It was a triumph of effort, but she looked like glamor model Victoria Silvstedt, at least at a distance.

He sat down and pondered the complicated notes. One thing was clear; Vera was damned serious about her studies. It was like a code, and he realized after a while that the smallest, most code-like notes were references to pages in books. He didn't recognize any of them from when he took the introductory course: *Green Economics, Global Women, State of the World.*

The riddle that was Vera Lundberg seemed more complicated the closer he looked.

*

It was Friday night and Peter was with Matt at the big partying place downtown. It looked like it was going to be packed, because it was teeming with people even though it wasn't yet 11 o'clock. Matt had been so highly motivated to make contact with someone of the opposite sex that he had even brought some dryer lint, so he could pull a 'lint opener' from the pick-up manual. With Peter's encouragement and not a little nervousness, he had chosen a girl he thought looked nice – a cute girl with short hair.

A little shakily, he approached the chosen one and pretended to remove the lint from her back. He showed it to her: 'Here, trash from your back... ehhh.' He peered at her shyly from under his protruding eyebrows.

She turned matter-of-factly towards Matt and took it:

'Oh, um. Thanks.'

Then she turned to the guy on her other side, held out the ball of lint accusingly and chewed him out for 'never cleaning the lint' out of their dryer.

Bollocks! There was nothing about that in the pick-up manual.

Matt returned to the bar and Peter kindly passed him a beer.

'Listen... no big deal. We all get rejected sometimes.'

'Seriously. I don't believe you.' The Brit shook his head and looked almost sorrowfully at him. 'You're the kind of guy who can get any girl he wants.'

Peter smiled at the flattery and took a swallow of beer. *That isn't entirely unlikely, in fact.* Then Peter darkened a little. There were actually drawbacks to that too. Like with Linda yesterday, after she had seen him with Sandra. She had called and bombarded him: she had cried and screamed; she had apparently not understood that Peter hadn't promised anything. She had thought that she was his girlfriend. He didn't tell Matt that Linda had 'ended it' because he'd been 'unfaithful with that plastic bimbo'.

'Hey, Peter!' Matt blurted out, already in a better mood. 'I know – let's make a bet! The next girl who comes through the door! Check it out, check it...' He made a dramatic noise like the filmmakers used in *Jaws*. 'HER!'

It was Vera who came in. Completely unexpectedly. Peter had been out at least once a week all fall, and he had never seen her out before. She was in the company of Cissi and moved carefully through the throng of people. Her hair was loose and she was wearing jeans and an ivory blouse with brown embroidery that showed off her collarbones. Peter's pulse quickened. Matt had also discovered that *Exhibit A*, the chosen guinea pig, was their dormitory mate, and he smiled.

'Oh, no, that doesn't count. That's Vera. I stand corrected. Not *all* of them prefer you, you know. You can get any girl you want, except Vera. She thinks you're a... Oh, what was it? Spaller?' He looked questioningly at Peter as he used the strange word.

Peter had to exercise enormous concentration to hear Matt, but the last part of what he said was drowned out by the increasingly loud music.

'What? What did you say?' shouted Peter.

Matt turned toward his friend and repeated himself slowly and clearly directly into Peter's ear: 'Any girl you want, except Vera!'

Matt's yelling hurt his ear, and Peter shuddered.

'Did Vera tell you what she thinks of me?'

Matt nodded.

'But what did you say she said? 'Sprawler'?'

'No. Spaller,' said Matt in his broad Sheffield accent.

'Spaller? What does that mean?'

'You tell me – you're the one who's Swedish!'

Now Matt's attention shifted to the right. An interesting blonde was approaching. Peter saw Matt summon up the courage to try again.

'Hi! Fancy meeting you here!' said Matt, using the Swedish verb *stöta på*.

The girl stared at Matt before she quickly fled to another part of the bar.

'Whoops!' an involuntary grin broke out on Peter's face. 'You need to put the accent on the little word – stöta *på* – because then it means, like, "bump into", otherwise it means... uh, "hit on".' He touched Matt on the arm in a gesture of brotherly affection, and then went off to see where Vera was.

The sorrowful Englishman remained alone at the bar, mumbling down into his glass. 'Stöta *på* not *stöta* på? God, they're picky.'

✱

For some reason it felt like Vera kept slipping away from him. She wasn't like other women, who seemed to be drawn to him.

That made the challenge even greater and something like a competitive streak had awoken inside him. But he knew a place where she would be forced to stay for hours, where they would 'meet the network in a suitably formal context', as Sturesson had expressed it when he informed him that Tomas Lern preferred not to join the project, and that it was splendid that Peter could help out on such short notice. Peter had looked for her during the graduation ceremony, had hoped to sit near her, but he had realized too late that she had skipped that part. To absolutely no purpose, Peter had suffered through four hours of *'Take the ring... Take the hat... Farewell,'* painfully struggling against drowsiness as a soporific number of strangers proudly wed themselves to Knowledge.

But then the evening came. He saw her at once in the sea of buzzing people in party clothes. Vera had hatched like a butterfly when she took off her dark coat and revealed her slim arms and a shimmering, dark green, full-length dress. Boredom and drowsiness disappeared. Perhaps it wouldn't be such a bad evening after all?

He followed her at a distance. The messy bohemian hairstyle exposed her small, protruding, slightly pointed ears. At the sides, her dark hair was pinned up with white flowers, while other curls fell untamed between her girlish shoulder blades. Vera found Cissi in the crowd, took a small flat-bread canapé and a glass of champagne spiked with cloudberry liquor. Cissi looked good this evening, Peter noted as he helped himself to food further down the buffet. She had done something unusual with her red hair, and she was wearing a gold dress befitting a film star.

Like most of the other young men in the room, Peter was in a black suit and tie. It was that or white tie and tails for the men. When Peter saw Sturesson and Sparre on the other side of the hors d'oeuvre buffet, chatting with other men, he thought of a gaggle of penguins whose only defining features were their different sizes and forms. Sparre was the tall, slightly stooped, darkly sharp-eyed one. Åke Sturesson was the greying, irascible

107

terrier. He didn't know the others. Peter's gaze fastened on the small, round, reclining man with spiky strands of hair behind his ears – there was something vaguely familiar about him.

Åke caught sight of Peter and waved him over; he was in the middle of an enthusiastic toast, '…and the making of history. Cheers to a ground-breaking research project on Future Welfare and Prosperity!' Sturesson carefully looked all the penguins, and finally Peter as well, in the eye before taking a swallow of the cloudberry champagne. This was followed by a similar round of small nods in the direction of each individual in turn.

Peter felt like a zoologist observing the strange behavior of an exotic bird, and a small smile crossed his face as he thought of Kalle. Then Sturesson spoke again, in English.

'And this, gentlemen, is young Peter Stavenius, the only son of Lennart Stavenius, the famous entrepreneur in the travel… yes, yes.' He broke off when the men nodded. The round one with the plumes of hair offered him a meaty hand.

'Morley, Anthony Morley.'

Sturesson started listing all of Morley's accomplishments. Peter nodded, but realized with embarrassment that the obviously world-renowned academic probably seemed familiar to him only because he had seen that kind of Antarctic seabird in some animated film. Sturesson continued in English for Morley's benefit.

'I'm actually an old friend of the family. Lennart and I were at Stockholm's School of Economics, class of '76!'

Peter suddenly realized that Åke Sturesson had actually visited them at home in Stockholm about 10 years ago. *When we were still a family*, popped into Peter's head.

Sturesson continued absentmindedly: 'Yes, I almost forgot, we have the girls too. Come, come.' He took his gaggle of penguins with him, over to Cissi and Vera, who had now been joined by Lilian, the department secretary. Peter's eyes were drawn like a magnet to Vera. She was not good-looking in a way he could handle, like Cissi and so many others this evening. She was beautiful in an important and disquieting way. *Different, like a mythical being.* When he moved towards her, he suddenly felt that she reminded him of someone or something that he had been attracted to since he was a teenager.

The mythical being looked serious when they formally shook hands. Her handshake was pleasurable and the memory of the cool, strong softness remained in his hand. *Perhaps she's cold?* He smothered a sudden impulse to keep hold of her and warm her up.

16

Vera sat at the banquet with a linen napkin on her lap. She was nervously expectant. Next to her sat Anthony Morley – a corpulent Brit in late middle age who was introduced to her as 'an authority in the science of economics'. *An expert in something so super interesting!* Her respectful shyness had restrained her, through the appetizer, through the reindeer fillet with chanterelle and aquavit sauce, through the wild raspberry sorbet. But now she drew a deep breath.

'So, what do you think about prosperity in the future?' she asked.

He looked at her with watery eyes. She glimpsed a flushed, red neck behind his bow-tie and wondered how many refills had made their way down his throat into that impressive belly.

The intrusive examination was transformed into an expression of delight and he whispered: 'What future do you have in mind... Are you talking about later tonight?'

The thick wedding ring shone on his chubby hand when he gestured as if to make a toast.

Just then, the banquet hall filled with the sounds of a spirited sing-along: '*O jerum, jerum, jerum! O, quae mutatio rerum*!' Everyone suddenly seemed to know exactly what they were supposed to do during this peculiarly choreographed ritual. Prim Lilian, who sat diagonally across from Vera, caught her eye and whispered instructions: 'Bang on the table!'

People were rosy-cheeked and jumped cheerfully up on their chairs when it was their faculty's turn to do so. Peter, who had unexpectedly showed up on the welfare project, had clearly done this before. Cissi had not, Vera realized when she saw how uncertainly her friend stood up with the law faculty. Morley blinked at her in confusion and, when it was their turn and Vera was about to climb carefully up on her chair, he suddenly roared. He half-stood and clumsily tried to wrap his arms around her legs.

'Oh, wait a minute…'

For a second, Vera feared for her bad knee, but he missed her and collapsed into a black-and-white heap on the floor. As the other table burst into song again, Lilian gestured to Vera to meet her under the table. Hidden under the tablecloth, she met the waiting secretary face to face. Lilian spoke quietly: 'How is he?'

Vera looked at Morley, who was still lying on the floor, happily mumbling to himself.

'Pretty well, I think. Although he's…' she said and made a little grimace.

'Discretion, Miss Lundberg. Never embarrass a professor! I'll come around and we can… prop him up.'

Lilian was on her way around the table before Vera could say another word. She looked out from under the table and saw only shoes. Now everyone was standing on their chairs singing at the top of their lungs.

'So brothers, close our circle fast, to fend for joy and glory!'

Alone under the table, Vera wondered what she had got herself into.

✳

Vera and Cissi stood along the wall, close to the stage that had been specially erected on the window side of the dance floor's dark parquet for the fall festival. As 20 or so big-band musicians in peppermint-striped pants climbed up on the stage, Vera asked: 'So, is Peter Stavenius part of the project?'

'Yes!' said Cissi enthusiastically. 'And thanks to him we got extra money for it!' Cissi swept her brocade shawl over her shoulders.

'Huh?'

'Of course, we don't *know*, but Lilian said that an anonymous donor had given the department two million kronor. And since the Stavenius family is rich, with masses of contacts among research councils and bankers, it isn't completely unlikely that there's a connection.' Cissi looked thoughtful and then continued: 'Whatever. Amongst other things, the money is going to go to my salary, so, *phew*, saved by the bell.' Cissi happily pretended to wipe sweat from her brow.

Cissi was going to be able to finish her dissertation! The thought made Vera happy, but at the same time... the whole thing felt wrong.

'So everything is fine and dandy now?' said Vera, sounding harsher than she intended. Cissi started.

'What do you mean by that?'

'Well...' Vera stopped herself. She realized that Peter's position on the project was at least more natural than hers; he was an advanced student in the subject and had even taught it.

Some discordant toots and howling came from the direction of the brass section.

Cissi studied her with a worried frown. The student band began to play a classic jazz tune. Vera mumbled 'see you later' to Cissi. She stared at the floor as she carefully made her way toward the door and did not see where they came from: Åke Sturesson, Lilian, Peter and Morley were suddenly standing in her way. Morley was reasoning with Peter.

'Like father, like son, huh?' and he thumped Peter on the back.

Vera tried to pass them, but Sturesson stopped her and yelled over the music, 'Now it's time to dance, children!'

Nobody reacted. Sturesson guided the group towards the dance floor and waved encouragingly at Vera: 'Women are in great demand this evening, so the choice is all yours!'

He nodded towards Morley and Peter. Vera looked at the ruddy professor and her dressed-up dorm-mate. Everyone waited. Finally, Lilian gripped Morley's well-filled jacket sleeve and said, 'Shall we, Mr Morley?'

Supported by Lilian, Morley staggered away towards the dance floor. With a well-practised maneuver, she deflected his hand, which had glided a little too far down her stylish, dark-blue dress. Vera and Peter remained where they were. Sturesson smiled and moved towards department head Lange.

'May I have the honor?' asked Peter, looking into Vera's eyes and bowing slightly from the waist like a stiff toy prince in some make-believe Disney saga.

'Thank you, but I'll pass,' said Vera, and left.

Vera's shoes had almost no heels at all, but her entire right side ached after an evening of favoring it to protect her left. She was forced to sit down and rest on a chair by the stairs. Over on the dark parquet dance floor she saw how Cissi took Peter by the arm and led him forward. In the midst of the billowing crowd, they began to dance – happily, almost flirting. Vera wondered how much longer she had to stay. When, according to all these unwritten rules, was it legitimate to go home? And through the dull pain, spied an irrepressible glimmer of hope – soon it would be the fifth of November.

17

That we need a radically new economic rationality is, at this stage of history, overwhelmingly self-evident. A Green economics – or ecological economics, as I prefer to call it – transforms our destructive economic logic because it subordinates economics to the process of life, rather than, as has been the rule so far, placing life at the service of economics.

Manfred Max-Neef, 'The Gaia Atlas of Green Economics'

For the first time in his 24-year life, Peter had been rejected by a girl. The unknown feeling was unexpectedly hard to take, and when Cissi appeared and invited him to dance to the big-band classic *Just A Gigolo*, his mind was still reeling from Vera's wounding words: *'Thank you, but I'll pass.'* Why wouldn't she even dance with him? What had he ever done to her? Maybe she hated *Just A Gigolo*? If so, that was something he could sympathize with.

'How is Vera, really?' Peter nodded to where Vera was sitting as he guided Cissi out to the dance floor.

'The City hotel's Jooohn Travolta,' sang Renhornen's vocalist, in a pitch-perfect voice.

'I actually don't know. She seems so bitter and strange tonight,' said Cissi. 'I wonder if it has anything to do with her...' She broke off.

'What?'

'No, I don't know. It's none of my business, but I have a feeling she and her husband are separating. I've heard that can make you really unstable.'

'Ah! No, it probably isn't easy.' It was a relief, and Peter struggled not to look pleased. Something else came to mind, making him feel a little ashamed.

'Yes, and maybe she's in pain; have you seen how she's still limping?' *That must be why she didn't want to!* How could he have failed to see that? Maybe because he had been so preoccupied by the fact that he had suddenly realized what she reminded him of: the hair with the flowers, the small, sticking-out ears and the lovely dress made her look like an Elf – the wisest, most just, beautiful and capable mythical being in Tolkien's world, which had enchanted his boyhood room. *A creature that was above human frailties, one that did not fall for simple flirtations, but instead faithfully committed herself for life.* Peter's heart pounded harder, as if he were close to answering his most important question.

'Well, just because your knee hurts it doesn't mean you have to be negative about the successes of the welfare project, does it? That's nuts!' said Cissi. She felt a vague worry: *Was I wrong to choose Vera?* She glanced at Peter and wondered what he would say if she asked the question out loud.

The singer in the peppermint-striped skirt and tailcoat could really sing: *'I ain't got nobody – nobody cares for me, nobody, nobody...'*

Cissi shook off her dour thoughts and focused on the moment, the experience of a party and the glamor of being in the arms of a good-looking man who, surprisingly, knew how to lead a woman on the dance floor, despite the fact that he wasn't from Norrland. *Things could be worse*, she thought, and saw the party lights reflecting in her gold dress.

After the rewarding dance with Cissi, Peter returned to Vera, who sat over by the stairs, distractedly watching the half-moon behind the naked birch trees outside.

He knew more now and wanted to talk about the future. 'Does your leg hurt?' he asked.

Vera started and looked at him. 'Yes, you could say that.'

'Yes, otherwise you would be expected to do your duty as Woman on the project,' he emphasized with what he thought was a charming, teasing twinkle in his eye. 'We're going to have to see how this pans out, us working together and everything...' He took a step closer.

Vera looked at him as if he were behaving threateningly. She got up smoothly using just one leg. *Light and strong*, thought Peter. *No surprise that an Elf can get up like that.*

She looked at him briefly before firmly grabbing the stair rail, turning her back to the party and hobbling down the stairs: 'Yes, I'm going to have to see how it pans out for me.'

He recognized an unfathomable determination.

And once again, she had turned her back on him and left.

*

Peter didn't understand. Every other time when he, uncharacteristically, had been the one to make the advance, he had immediately been victorious. But with Vera... His usual way of making contact didn't work, exactly when it was important that it did work, *just when he had actually met an Elf in real life.*

Of course he knew she was a real person – a nurse in her late twenties from inner Västerbotten. But there were several puzzle pieces that pointed directly at something that he longed for, something completely unique. She was beautiful in a hard-to-discover, secret way; she was petite yet strong, wildly curly-haired yet disciplined, superior yet good-hearted, stubborn yet evasive. She was completely unlike all the other women he had known and he sensed instinctively, without really knowing why, that she had something he needed.

When Peter realized that Vera had actually rejected him numerous times, he understood that he had approached things all wrong. *The definition of idiocy is doing the same thing over and over again, but expecting a different outcome*, as his Uncle Ernst used to say.

She was completely different from all the other women he had met. Obviously, he would have to use a completely different approach to get close to her. But different how? There were endless ways to be and do things. How could he get Vera to change her mind? How could he get her to see him the way young women usually did?

A wave of understanding washed over him, and he realized that he needed to get to know his opponent, something his jujutsu instructor had been nagging him about for years. Luckily, Peter, who sometimes had trouble even remembering women's first names, recalled masses of seemingly unimportant details about Vera. Thus, he had no difficulty remembering that Vera thought books like *The Gaia Atlas of Green Economics*, *Global Women*, and *State of the World* were worth reading. He went to the library and looked for them. The only one that wasn't out on loan was *Green Economics*. Peter realized that Vera probably still had the library's only copy of the other two. In a fit of uncharacteristic ambition, he borrowed other books on welfare and economic development instead.

He called his father and said he couldn't come to the board meeting next week, because he had too much work to do on the project. Lennart had sounded unexpectedly negative. When Charlie couldn't come to board meetings it was usually accepted with considerable understanding. And Peter had thought that Lennart must have been a driving force behind him even being asked to join *Future Wealth and Welfare*. Perhaps Lennart had not realized that the project would take time away from Escape, and maybe even from his usual studies? If so, that was typical of his father. *He always wants to have his cake and eat it too*, thought Peter, with an irritation that surprised him.

Peter was also surprised that he was even considering reading about welfare. As usual, he found it difficult to read the books from cover to cover. But he read the headings and summaries until he thought he understood the important parts. It was unexpectedly interesting to pit 'the richest one per cent' perspective against the argument about welfare and well-being for everyone. The books about welfare on the reference list that Åke had distributed to the members of the project were about the welfare of Sweden as a whole and the welfare of the European Union.

Vera's brief and jumbled book took a fuzzy global perspective.

It was suddenly the welfare of all of humanity, and, as if that weren't enough, even the whole planet's. In fascination, Peter realized that it was fully possible that the scrawled pencil notes in *Green Economics* were Vera's. He therefore made sure that he read everything that was circled, marked and underlined. It started with a quote from some Manfred in the preface, which claimed that we needed to change economic logic. *As if logic can be changed just like that! Either it's logical, and then we already know it, or it's illogical*, thought Peter.

Then came a depressing list of complaints. The Industrial Economy. Rape of the Earth. Exploitation of Women. Destruction of community. Disposable people. Money in trouble. Catalogue of shame. And finally, the question, 'All for what?' to which the response was, 'Above the poverty level, the relationship between income and happiness is remarkably small.' *The richest one per cent who go on Great Escapes would beg to differ*, thought Peter, remembering the classic line that people can say what they want about money and happiness, but it was better to cry in a limousine than a bus.

No wonder she's bitter, if she spends her time reading stuff like this!

He skimmed the pages restlessly and read a clearly circled passage that claimed that half of the world's population did two-thirds of the world's work, earned one tenth of all income and owned less than one per cent of all its assets. It was referring to women.

Suddenly he realized how wrong it had been when he said that Vera was expected to 'do her Duty as Woman in the project'. For him it had been a humorous way to offset the deeply private humiliation of asking someone to dance and getting a no. He realized now that there was a significant risk that, for Vera, it sounded like he was demanding that she conform to a World Order. An order which, if she agreed with the stuff in this mixed-up book, in her eyes put unreasonable demands on women for a remuneration that was entirely too small. Peter also understood that, at least for her, it was a completely different and worse type of humiliation. And, above all, it wasn't his. With the social gifts that his mother's nurturing had honed in him from boyhood, Peter knew that one could joke about one's own humiliation, but never about other people's.

Peter put down *Green Economics*. If he carried on reading stuff like this, would he become as gloomy as Vera? And even if Peter was strangely drawn to her, despite that unattractive quality, it certainly wasn't something he aspired to himself. He lay a long time with his hands behind his head and thought. This could be a really good game. He imagined how he and Vera would debate, and how he would convince her that her pessimism was exaggerated. He was satisfied. Yes, half an hour with Vera's book had done the job. He thought he understood more about why she was like she was, and how he could get her to change. He was like a spy after a successful mission. He had broken a code and entered, in order to dig out decisive information. He turned off the light with the satisfied feeling of having done his homework.

18

The night before the fifth of November, Vera woke up in a sweat, pulse racing. She had had a strange dream about a doctor who stood sorting people into different lines, injured and uninjured. In the dream, Vera's aching left knee was a pulpy mess due to a gunshot wound, and she wound up in the line with the injured. After a while a small, furious dwarf in a red cap showed up with a yardstick and declared that the line for the injured was too long, because it was longer than his yardstick! The doctor obediently changed his mind and his decision. Vera was moved to the line for the uninjured, and showing him the gunshot wound to her knee made no difference. When she awoke from the dream her cheeks were wet with tears.

With a pounding heart, Vera hobbled over to her desk and turned on her computer. She did a search on the comforting words *Healthcare guarantee*. So it was that, at 2:41 in the morning on the fifth of November, Vera realized that, because she wasn't yet in a queue for an MRI scan, all the time she had waited so far didn't count, and the healthcare guarantee period had not yet begun. She toyed with a conspiracy theory that pharmacy companies bribed doctors not to treat joint injuries too quickly, so that they would have the opportunity to sell a lot of pills, then rejected the idea.

But there must have been some reason why they wanted to keep her off the x-ray waiting list? The other horrible suspicion was not so easy to reject; it stuck to her like her now ice-cold pajama top. Because there it was on the screen: *The guarantee regulates only the period of time within which one is to be offered treatment which has been approved by qualified healthcare professionals*. It was obvious that everyone wanted the numbers to look good, so that the Swedish healthcare system wouldn't fail to meet the guarantee in 30 or 40 per cent of cases! So no decision about treatment means no visible healthcare waiting lists? Or perhaps, in practice, fewer treatment decisions, more acceptable visible healthcare waiting lists?

She didn't know how much time she had spent staring at the comforting words on the screen. In her obliviousness, they had lulled her into a false security. She realized that now.

After some time, she became aware of the fact that she was chilled to the bone. She forced herself to get out of the chair and went to take a warm shower.

She got all the way to Cat Stevens' *Morning has broken* on her playlist of songs to fall asleep to on her cellphone, before she finally drifted off for a couple of hours. Then the alarm went off, and Vera dragged herself out of bed in the November darkness.

✖

This time the orthopaedic specialist was a younger man named Modin. Once again she was asked to lie down on the paper-covered bed, and he felt, pried and pulled on her leg to examine its flexibility and functioning. He was concerned that her knee was still locking and that the muscles in her left leg had lost half of their volume, even though she was trying to practise the exercises that she was able to do. Seeing the large difference between her left and right thighs, he decided that she needed to be put on the waiting list for an MRI.

Yes! Finally! Vera had time to think, before Modin went on, somewhat embarrassed.

'But, unfortunately, there's quite a long waiting list. You shouldn't expect it to happen before late spring.'

Late spring?! Her heart sank again; her voice almost didn't hold.

'But that's impossible! I've already waited since May. Do you mean that I might have to live with a smashed meniscus in my knee for a *whole year* before I even get an MRI?'

'We mustn't draw hasty conclusions. *If* a piece of the meniscus is out of place then we will see it on the MRI. I'm sorry, but unfortunately that's how long the waiting list is.' Modin asked briskly if she was still a student and whether or not she needed a

121

sick note – and if she wanted a new prescription for Diclofenac – before he offered her a firm handshake and the appointment was over.

When Vera limped past the waiting room with a disobedient tear running down one cheek, a dark-haired nurse suddenly came up to her. She discreetly pushed a note into her jacket pocket and whispered:

'Call this number and ask for Erland. Sometimes patients don't show up, and if you can come on short notice, well...'

'Thanks! Erland?' whispered Vera back, and she felt a ray of hope returning.

Apparently there is a secret passage through the wall!

As soon as she reached home Vera locked herself in her room, called the secret number, and said the password. Her call was forwarded, but Erland was at lunch, and when she explained why she was calling, the woman's voice on the other end expressed surprised irritation.

'So you mean you're not a doctor?'

Vera wondered what that had to do with anything. 'No, I'm an anesthetic nurse.'

That fact did not mollify the woman on the other end in the least. She sounded impatient, as if she were straining to express herself properly to an irritating child.

'Yes, but *now* you're calling as a *patient*? It is your *own* presumed cruciate ligament and meniscus injury that you're talking about?'

Now Vera understood that the secret passage through the wall was for people on the Inside, and she felt like a heavy stone was rolling in front of the entrance and blocking the little ray of light that she had seen. Vera could no longer hold back her despair and she sobbed out a little 'yes' in response. There was a deathly silence on the other end of the line. Then Vera heard the rustling of paper.

'Aha...' The gatekeeper woman on the other end seemed to be engaging in an inner struggle with herself, and she finally folded. 'There is a cancellation here for the eighth of January.

So what is your name? Your healthcare number?'

The last thing the woman who guarded access to Erland – the secret shortcut through the waiting list at Norrland's University Hospital – said to her was, 'I hope you know that I'm being *nice* to you!'

When Vera hung up the phone she felt strangely guilty. But when she wrote MRI and circled Tuesday, 8 January in her calendar, it felt like she was grasping her last available lifeline. The scans would be done, and then they would see that her knee could not heal on its own. She would finally get help.

19

The first project meeting for *Future Wealth and Welfare* was held in a classroom in the rectangular, functional Social Science building, with its white-painted interior. Only Vera was absent. Peter was surprised and disappointed. He also noticed that Cissi was stressed that Vera had not come, which was not a good sign. When Sturesson asked about her, Cissi tried to smile as she said, in an affected tone, that Vera 'was at home in bed with a 100-degree fever'.

Peter drew two quick conclusions: it wasn't true and Cissi was a terrible liar. He saw how Cissi's fair-skinned face clouded over with worry as Sturesson went through the main components of the project. Their chapters were to be published in a book with a 'popular science' touch, and it was to be presented at a crowd-pleasing, public press conference. After that, Sturesson explained, more in-depth research would be conducted in stage two of the project, which would be published in international journals as it was completed. Sturesson then devoted himself to wishful name-dropping, and Peter didn't have the energy to listen to the details. But that the speaker's dream was to use the project to establish a 'pre-eminent research center' in Umeå was impossible to miss.

After the short break, Sturesson and Sparre began to assign the tasks for the project: 'everything from globalization, tax policy and Europe's aging population' could be problematized. Peter recognized the approach: impeccably systematic and with long, verbose texts. And mind-numbingly dull.

When Cissi turned on her cellphone after the meeting she had a text message. It was from Vera. She had written that she was quitting the project. A small, digital 'sorry' ended the message.

Cissi was so angry that Peter quickly suggested that they go to her office and discuss things. On the way up in the elevator, thoughts raced around in Peter's head. Cissi growled something inaudible though clenched teeth, and when they had closed the door to her office she raised her voice.

'Why the hell is she doing this? Putting me in hot water with my boss just because she's suddenly got it in her head to do something else?'

Peter's thoughts led him to an uncomfortable suspicion. There was only one explanation that fitted with everything he knew. The more he thought about it the more sure he was. But he could not bring himself to say it. Instead, he said:

'No, I don't think she suddenly lost interest. Quite the opposite. I've seen her working really hard; my guess is that she'll have a full draft of her chapter soon. I think it's called "Redeeming reproduction".'

'Yes, I know! We've spent *hours* talking about it!' exclaimed Cissi. 'But then what the hell is she up to now?'

Peter had never heard Cissi swear before. But he could quite understand. She had put a lot of money on one horse. And that horse was called Vera Lundberg.

Peter felt a strong desire to make everything right. 'I'm going to try to talk to her.'

Cissi stared at him in surprise, 'Why?' Then her face clouded over again beneath her red hair. 'What do you think you can say to her that will make her a reliable person?'

If there was anything Peter thought about Vera, it was that she was reliable.

✼

When Peter learned from Matt that Vera was at Solbacka, he looked up the address and went directly there. This game would demand an entirely new tactic. He would have to coax her, a bit like he used to do with his mother when she was upset. With sweaty palms, he practised different ways of saying it.

He asked around at the retirement home, and a woman told him that Vera had probably just finished her shift for the day, but that she sometimes stopped by to visit Solveig Marklund in Wing D. Peter looked around, unaccustomed to the institutional environment. A slowly shuffling man with Scottish plaid slippers and a wheeled walking frame helped him find Solveig's door.

He whispered a thank you and knocked.

A frail woman's voice answered from inside, 'Yes? Come in!' she called in surprise.

Peter took a nervous breath and turned the door handle. He stepped into a strange, female world filled with crocheting, yellowing black-and-white photographs and a scent of... *those old-fashioned flowers that his grandmother used to have on the veranda*! He smiled a little at the memory. Grandma's house had been full of strong plant fragrances. Out of reach of her grandchildren she had a whole cabinet filled with small, dark bottles with various herb extracts that she determinedly claimed were useful against every imaginable kind of affliction. One extract was good for treating chicken pox; another for coughs. 'In the olden days, they would have called me a witch!' she used to say, extremely pleased with herself, conscientiously caring for everyone around her who was in need.

He felt them looking at him from the small kitchen: a curly, white-haired old woman in a wheelchair and Vera were both staring in surprise. And he could understand why. In his expensive designer clothes, he was like that black Porsche that someone sometimes tried to park among the hand-painted bicycles on Stipend Street. Impossible to melt into the surroundings. But it couldn't be helped. *Force majeure*.

Warmed by the memory of his grandmother's house, Peter pointed carefully at the red clusters of flowers on the kitchen windowsill behind them – 'geraniums?'

'Yes, my Mårbacka geraniums. And who might the gentleman be, if I may ask?' The old woman rolled towards him in her wheelchair, an expression of kind curiosity on her face.

'Oh, sorry. My name is Peter, Peter Stavenius. I'm looking for Vera.'

'Yes, she is here, as you can see. By all means, come in.'

He did what he could. He took off his handmade Italian shoes and the wool Armani coat. He unbuttoned his shirt cuffs and rolled up his sleeves before pattering over to the table.

'Would you like a little tea, Peter?' Solveig looked questioningly at him from beside the kitchen counter.

'No, thank you, I'm fine.'

She rolled herself back to the table again. He felt how the white-haired woman studied him, curious but friendly. He felt Vera's gaze and met it nervously.

'I've come directly from the project meeting. We missed you.'

Vera stared down into her rose-patterned teacup and Peter continued, 'I saw the text you sent to Cissi. But you can't quit now. In the first place… Cissi recruited you because she thinks you have your own, interesting perspective, and she thinks there is a lot to it. Also, you've got pretty far with it already, isn't that right?'

Vera held her cup in both hands and looked at him tentatively, 'Mmmm,' she said finally and took a sip from the cup.

He took a deep breath and continued:

'Then there's the fact that… well, you know Cissi. She's furious.'

Vera blinked, surprised. After a second she shuddered and answered quietly, 'Oh, I didn't think of that.'

'What's happened?' asked Solveig kindly.

Stressed, Vera wiped her hand across her forehead and said: 'You know, the project I was selected for. I just felt like…' She glanced self-consciously at Peter and went quiet.

Peter looked at her and continued: 'You felt maybe that you wouldn't be allowed to do it the way you wanted to?'

Which was code for his gnawing suspicion, and Peter turned red in humiliation. Vera also turned red and nodded.

Solveig looked from one to the other. Vera broke the silence: 'Yes, and anyway, I slept really badly last night because I was in so much pain. And I felt like I just couldn't keep at it when it felt… meaningless.'

The word pierced Peter as if she had said it about him.

Vera wiped her nose with a rose-patterned napkin. She sighed and, turning toward Solveig, continued.

'So I quit. It's just that it's affected my advisor, who has really helped me a lot.'

She looked so sad that Peter forgot himself. 'It wasn't that bad. And you don't have to have much to do with me. I mean, to get your chapter accepted. Talk to her. Explain the situation. I am sure it can be resolved.'

Vera looked at him with worried eyes. She finally nodded with her lips clamped shut. She looked at the wall clock and got up, taking her cup and saucer with her.

'I'm sorry, but I have to go now. Solveig, thank you for the tea.'

Peter also got up. 'It's lovely in here!' He nodded towards the hand-embroidered lace tablecloth and the elegant porcelain. 'Perhaps I inadvertently barged in while you were celebrating something?'

'Sadly, no,' said Solveig with a little quiver in her voice. 'It is rather the opposite. Vera might have to stop coming to work here.' The old woman followed Vera into the hall in her wheelchair.

'Why is that?' *She's thinking about quitting the project and quitting here too? What is she planning on doing?*

'My body just aches so much.' Vera took her jacket off the hanger and sighed. 'I probably have to take sick leave because of the pain in my lower back.'

'Well, I can understand if you are in pain.' Peter squatted gracefully and tied his shoes.

Vera and Solveig looked at him. He stood up and rolled down his shirtsleeves. 'You've been limping for – how long now? Six months?'

Vera nodded. Peter put his hand on his hip: 'I think you have knots in your... gluteal muscles from walking crooked. That makes your back ache. I have a friend who hurt his foot in a bad kick when he and another guy were practicing jujutsu. Before he was operated on, he got a bunch of problems in other parts of his body, and that was after only a few weeks. Because, you know, he walked crookedly and his whole body was tense.'

Peter reached for his black coat and felt pleased – *maybe everything could be put right?* – and when he heard Solveig suggest that Vera get a massage, he didn't stop to think. 'Yes, massage is a good way to get rid of knots in your muscles, to get the circulation going again. I've been training jujutsu a while, so I know a little bit. I can massage you if you want.'

Vera looked terrified as she stood at the door, on her way out of the geranium lady's home: 'Thanks, that's kind of you. But honestly... I don't want you to touch me.'

Peter stayed where he was, paralyzed in Solveig's hall, when Vera left. He blushed. He had forgotten himself in the hope that he could help her. But it was clear that she would never let him. *So forget it. Go ahead and limp and hurt, if you're so picky about who touches you!*

The corners of his eyes prickled. Solveig looked kindly up at him and awkwardly reached out and touched the back of his right hand with her silky-soft old fingers.

'I want you to know that it isn't like Vera to... be like this. But she is suffering because of her knee and she is deeply disappointed about many things.'

Peter felt the question forcing its way out: 'Where is her husband, anyway?' *The one who should be massaging her.*

She looked carefully at his face and weighed her words: 'I don't know. Things can look good on the surface. But then it turns out that they are something else entirely. I don't know if she knows any good men.'

20

'Beloved child.' 'Love thy neighbor as thyself.' 'Love yourself.' 'You are the only one for me.' 'I just love that film!' Love can be understood in many ways. Write a 3-5 page essay that answers the question: 'What is true love for you?'

Freddie's school assignment

There is no up and down in space.

Vera was quite young when her father explained that it was only when you were close to a celestial body that the direction towards its center could be experienced as down. Since Vera was on earth, she could experience both up and down. And in the quiet, ice-cold darkness, she was zooming around with all other known life forms at a speed of about 30 kilometres per second. She was part of the crew of Spaceship Earth, fastened by an invisible umbilical cord in the life-giving orbit around the sun.

There was no up or down in space. Yet Vera nonetheless felt that there was. She was hanging upside down, or rather a little crookedly downward. The earth was on its way towards the northern hemisphere's winter solstice, and it was the Australians, on the other side, who were right side up and had the sun, warmth, life, and summer. Now was the time when the northerners lit candles and gathered to see through the winter. Weak beams from a low-lying sun would visit Västerbotten in the middle of the day, like a small comfort, even when the season was at its darkest. But that was all.

If I were a wild animal. Or lived in a tribe in the Stone Age, those people who carved images of moose on the flat rocks at Stornorrfors. They would have had to leave me to die, thought Vera, in despair because her body wouldn't heal, only got stiffer

130

and more painful. Then God or nature or whatever miracle it was that arranged the elements into the unimaginably complex form that was human life, would erase the specimen Vera and start over again, make a more sturdy version instead. *Survival of the fittest.*

And that wasn't the only thing that was upside down. Another strange thing was that Vera had been reprimanded by Peter Stavenius. A reprimand that she couldn't help but think was justified.

He had appeared like an alien in Solveig's kitchen. Vera could never have imagined that her dormitory neighbor might remind her of her father. But Stavenius sat there in his expensive clothes and behaved like her father, although, she reluctantly admitted to herself, in a better way.

He expressed himself kindly, softly and carefully. Like Sven-Erik would have. But then he had told the unpleasant truth, pointed out her neglect. Which Sven-Erik would never do, even if he ought to. Peter had not been accusing or angry. He had just matter-of-factly explained how Cissi felt, something that Vera, the instant she heard it, realized was very likely true. How could she need Peter, of all people, to say something before she realized it herself? Everything was really upside down.

She found Cissi in her office. Vera knocked timidly. Cissi looked up and her expression darkened, but she gestured in a way that said, 'Come in and sit'.

Vera closed the door and sat down. There was no reason to stall; best to just get it out. For her own self-respect if for no other reason.

'I'm really sorry. It was wrong of me not to come and talk to you in advance,' said Vera, staring nakedly into Cissi's eyes.

'Yes, it was really wrong!' Cissi sounded angry. She swivelled on her chair and crossed her arms, as if trying to defend herself. *Peter was right,* Vera realized.

'I completely understand if you are angry with me. It will affect you if I quit. And that is the last thing I want to happen. You have really helped me *a lot.*' Vera realized how true this was.

Cissi looked searchingly at her from behind the barricade of her elbows, but stayed silent. Vera continued:

'There is no excuse for what I did. But I still can't use my leg and now...'

If one knows the cause of a problem there is always hope that one can do something about it. Hanging upside down in space, she took hold of the rope ladder of understanding that Stavenius had extended to her when he had turned up so absurdly.

'I've got knots in my muscles that hurt more and more every day, and in new places. My lower back is a complete mess.'

Vera thought about how terrible the past night had been. Lying awake in pain, she had examined her dilemma from all angles and realized she couldn't solve it. She just couldn't bring herself to return to Adam and pretend that nothing had happened, even if she knew it was a risky conclusion to come to. She anticipated that it would have far-reaching consequences. Consequences she was terrified of.

'I hardly slept at all. I don't have the energy for anything!' she admitted with tears in her eyes.

The tension in Cissi's jaws relaxed, but her voice was chilly. 'I vouched for you, and the least I expect is that you contact me in advance and explain what's going on. I felt it at the banquet, that you were about to bail. But you wouldn't say anything? You just send a damned text? That I get afterwards!' Cissi stared at Vera and continued. 'What exactly happened at the banquet?'

Vera looked up tentatively. 'It's hard to explain, but I felt that the money and Stavenius... I just got a strong gut feeling that it isn't going to work, that no matter how much effort I put into it, what I write is going to be... rejected. That's what it feels like.'

'For God's sake!' Cissi's anger rekindled. 'Sure – strange things happen in academia. A drunken Morley who took a nosedive under the table, professors who don't do what they should. I get it! But if you do a good job, it gets noticed! It's entirely up to you! So don't come whining to me! If you don't come to the meetings, you obviously can't be part of the project. But blaming that on someone else is just plain wrong!'

Vera sat in silence and Cissi lowered her voice worriedly:

'I realize, in fact, that I don't know you. Do you have some kind of addiction problem? Are you psychologically unstable or something?'

'Serial killer,' answered Vera gravely, but Cissi's expression didn't change a bit. 'Like I said, I'm in pain, and you know that I have some… relationship problems,' Vera continued. 'But that's all. And I'm usually not like this. I have no memory of ever doing anything like this before.'

Now Cissi smiled crookedly. '"*I have no recollection of that,*" said the American President Nixon.'

'Now I feel like I am going to do my best on the project and not worry so much about everything else.'

Cissi's arms slid down to the armrests of her chair, but she remained quiet.

Vera suddenly felt worried and her voice got weaker. 'Is that okay for you? I mean, if you still think I should be part of it?'

Cissi put a kind hand on Vera's shoulder. 'Of course I do! By the way, do you know what? I have now seen *From the Heart of the World* about the Kogi people. I think it's really interesting. I actually started to wonder why so few economists study natural resources. It's a perfect example of the limited resources that we need to conserve in the best possible way.'

'You're right there. Maybe you should write about it?'

'I already am, but maybe I ought to focus on it more,' said Cissi thoughtfully.

Vera got up from the chair, grimacing involuntarily.

'Are you taking some kind of painkiller?' wondered Cissi.

'Do you think I want to develop an addiction problem?' Vera smiled fleetingly and leaned against the wall for support. 'Have you any idea how many pill-popping anesthetic nurses I've seen?'

'At least take something at night so you can sleep. Nothing gets better if you don't sleep. And go to a masseuse and take care of those knots. I know a woman called Annika who's world-class.'

Everything really was upside down. She, with her medical training, was getting healthcare advice from Cissi. But she was grateful. There were people who cared about her.

✖

133

Vera had eaten Saturday night dinner at home with her parents on Lingon Road. When she realized where the conversation was headed, she tried to get away by leaving the table and taking her plate to the kitchen, but her mother Gunilla stubbornly followed her. Out of earshot of Sven-Erik, she anxiously launched into her questions.

'Why in the world didn't you stay at home with Adam? Why did you leave Stockholm after only a few hours?'

Vera loaded forks and knives into the dishwasher in silence as Gunilla's frustration continued to leak out of her like burning lava out of a volcano.

'When Eva and Krister told me, I was completely taken aback; I didn't know anything – I mean, what was I supposed to say?'

Vera took a deep breath and leaned against the counter for support. She directed her attention to the dirty dishes with an appeal for mercy. 'Mother, it's complicated. I just couldn't stay.'

'What do you mean, "just couldn't stay"? And he calls here looking for you; says that you don't answer your cellphone. Why won't you even talk to him on the phone?'

Vera felt her mother's chafing worry, how incomprehensible everything was for her. Gunilla fixed her eyes on her daughter and went at it with what Vera knew was the strongest argument she had.

'At least remember that you were married before God. If there is *anything* that you were raised to understand, it's that marriage and its vows are things one has to respect!'

Her father came into the kitchen with the last of the things from the table. Vera fled downstairs.

Sven-Erik found Vera sitting on the floor in the empty closet in her childhood room, crying exhaustedly. He squatted and gently stroked her back. Vera looked up at him without drying her tears. 'I don't want to have any contact with Adam right now! Why is that so unacceptable?'

'It isn't unacceptable. It is your choice to make. We just wonder why, you understand that, don't you?

Yes, she understood that. *But can you understand how bad it can get if I start talking about it?* How would Gunilla... What would she do? She leaned against her father's hand and tried to collect herself.

'I'm sorry. I'll try again; it might work out. But just not now.'

'Okay. Okay.'

He pulled her up from the closet floor. She groaned in pain as she sat down stiffly beside him on the bed. He asked: 'But is there anything I can do? Is there anything you need?'

She looked into the empty closet. 'I need my clothes and things that are still in Stockholm.'

'My office is going on a trip to Stockholm in two weeks and nothing is planned for the evenings, so we could pack a few boxes. I'm sure Olle will help.'

Vera felt a little comforted. 'That would be great. But how can I get them up here?'

'We'll figure it out. We can send them by train.' He put his large, warm hand carefully on her knee. 'You can't be trying to move and carry stuff when your knee hasn't healed. We'll fix it next week; I'll give Adam a ring.'

The thought that her father would also talk to Adam... It took a while before she could identify the repressed feeling that filled her – shame. On the other hand, wasn't the risk that Adam would confide in his father-in-law non-existent? And she realized how much he did for her, he who only wanted good things for her, who sat there waiting so patiently.

'Thank you, Daddy,' she said finally. She twisted off her engagement and wedding rings and put them on the nightstand in front of her. 'Can you take these too? I need to... give them back. Because whatever happens, we probably have to start over from the beginning.'

At that moment, Gunilla came into the room. 'Ah, this is where the two of you are hiding. What do you mean, "start over from the beginning"?'

Gunilla looked at them and then at the rings on the nightstand. Something black appeared in her eyes. Shocked, she covered her mouth with her hands and rushed out of the room and up the stairs. Sven-Erik worriedly watched his wife disappear, sighed, and picked up the rings.

The die was cast.

✖

Vera had worked late in order to be able to turn her chapter in to Sturesson, and she hobbled carefully up the stairs around 9pm. She heard the music all the way out in the stairwell. When Vera opened the door to the noise, she also heard a buzz from the kitchen and moved curiously in that direction.

Lotten smiled with a sweeping gesture at the sea of bottles on the kitchen counter.

'Welcome! Tonight's theme is drinks.'

Matt had rolled up his long sweater sleeves and was whipping cream by hand. He was talking loudly to a vaguely familiar youth. 'I don't believe that "be yourself" crap for a second.'

'No?' replied the gangly kid in confusion. It was Cissi's cousin.

'I believe more in… think of someone you can pretend to be. Maybe James Bond or something. He has tons of girls!'

Lotten looked at Vera and spoke quietly. 'He has tried that for over a year now. But he's a real cutie, reminds me a bit of Noel.' She blushed a bit and twisted her engagement ring. 'When he finally gets a girl he will spoil her rotten.'

Vera knew that Lotten missed her fiancé. 'Tough having him in Dublin?'

'Yes. But he's Irish, so I guess I made my bed… And he's working flat out at the restaurant; when I finish in the spring I'll join him there.' She smiled. 'You should come along to Dublin in the summer and see La Nueva Casa – a dream come true. Or a dream under construction in any case.'

Vera smiled. *Dublin? Maybe?*

Matt took a hot Irish coffee and went to sit on the sofa in the TV room. Vera looked in curiously. Almost everybody who lived in the dorm was there, plus some guests. Peter had Sandra with him, and Matt bowed politely at her: 'Stirred, not shaken, for the lady!' He glanced at Freddie.

Vera looked at Matt. 'Hey. What are you up to? Do you know Freddie?'

'No, darling,' Matt answered, slightly drunkenly, and put his arm round Vera's shoulders. 'This young man comes along, asking for you, claiming that you promised to teach him... about love.'

Vera had completely repressed it: *she*, of all people, was supposed to be an expert on love. And she had promised to help Freddie with that essay. Matt's arm lay horizontally over her shoulders, his face close to hers. He looked into her eyes and blinked playfully: 'So I believe that I'm the one entitled to ask questions here.'

Vera saw out of the corner of her eye how Peter was staring at them.

Lotten smiled and nodded towards the big-haired boy on the sofa. 'Yeah, Freddie here has been getting some brilliant little tips about love.'

Sandra slurped her hot drink carefully. Peter reacted as if by reflex, 'Don't slurp!'

Sandra started uncertainly, leaving a small cream mustache above her expertly lipsticked pink mouth. Vera looked at Peter and then Lotten.

'*What* did he say?'

Lotten repeated it in her confident southern accent, 'Don't sluuuurp. Brilliant.'

21

I'm just a gigolo and everywhere I go, people know the
part I'm playing.
Paid for every dance, selling each romance.
Every night some heart betraying.
There will come a day when youth will pass away – then
what will they say about me?
When the end comes I know they'll say 'Just a gigolo'
as life goes on without me.

'Just a Gigolo', Irving Caesar 1929 / Louis Prima 1956

Peter had come to Åke Sturesson's office for some guidance.
His contribution to the project was also going to be his overdue
undergraduate thesis, and he was supposed to have brought a
draft with him. But all he had managed to produce were a few
subheadings under the rather general title of 'Wealth in the 21st
century'. Peter sat wondering if the Professor also knew that
he had flunked the test on decision making. But Sturesson only
said that Peter ought to write about the importance of taking
advantage of the freedoms of globalization and concluded the
guidance session with the encouraging comment: 'Stavenius,
you obviously have considerable insights into that.'

It had been difficult for Peter to get going with the work, so
it actually would have been a relief if his supervisor had simply
made a decision for him. But Sturesson got up and opened the
door. His audience was over.

'Write a bit more and turn it in next week. I'll look it over
with the other drafts and get back to you after Christmas. Now
it's time for some mulled wine!'

✳

The refreshments at the department's advent celebration included the traditional Christmas treats. Every room was lit up with an identical triangle-shaped electric advent candlestick placed on the windowsill, and Lilian had decorated the tree with red baubles. *Pumlor*, as Peter had learned that people in northern Sweden called them. It was one of those peculiar expressions people up here thought was a regular Swedish word. They said it, and then stared in confusion when people didn't know what they meant.

Like 'spaller', or whatever the word was that Matt said Vera had used, thought Peter as he took a swallow of the warm, Christmas-spiced mulled wine. He thought he would go and ask Lilian if she knew what it meant, when he noticed that she was talking to Jeanette – the little blonde who had used his only clean towel, and whom he hadn't seen since. Lilian stood with her hand on Jeanette's stomach and a delighted expression on her face. Peter suddenly had trouble getting enough air, as if his lungs understood something his ears still hadn't heard.

'Oh! Well, congratulations! When are you due?' asked Lilian. She cocked her head, smiling.

'It's supposed to be the end of May,' said Jeanette, stroking her round stomach.

Peter had to make an effort to breathe. Vital parts of his body seemed to have stopped working. Images flashed through his mind of a stranger trying to wash off his sperm. And glimpses of a completely unthinkable life, a life together with Jeanette taking care of a child that he had sired. Or an every-other-week-with-child arrangement that would change his life almost as much, carrying him painfully far away from his dreams. *I'm only 24 and I don't even know the woman!*

He went over to Jeanette, mumbled something about needing to talk, and took her into an empty office a bit away from the advent party. When he closed the door he noticed his hand was trembling.

'Are you pregnant?'

'Yes,' answered Jeanette calmly.

'But, I know that it broke, I mean… You didn't say anything.

139

Does that mean it isn't mine?'

'No, it isn't yours.'

'Are you sure?' Peter found that it was a little easier to breathe.

'Yes, I'm sure.'

Peter felt that his pulse had begun to calm down too... *but...*

'How can you be sure?'

Jeanette looked at him with what he now saw were brown eyes.

'Because I was already pregnant when I slept with you.'

Peter sat down on the desk. 'Who's the father, then?'

'Henrik, my boyfriend, the guy I live with,' said Jeanette matter-of-factly. 'So you don't need to worry.' She averted her eyes, smoothed down the long shirt covering her stomach, opened the door and went out.

Peter remained sitting there in the dusky room, his heart pounding. He felt like he had avoided a major catastrophe by the skin of his teeth. Relief mixed with anxiety. Without a doubt, women were treacherous – *it was just like his father always said!* Peter felt sorry for the guy. How would he himself feel if the mother of his child was unfaithful? And, to top it off, while pregnant?

Unbelievably immoral. And imagine if he had managed to get stuck with a child with such a monster?

The rest of the day, relief was mixed with the nagging worry that follows from the thought that he had been saved by something as unreliable as pure luck. He went over and over his relationship with Jeanette and wondered if he had made an unusual mistake, one which, in his normally happy-go-lucky life, he usually didn't make. But the pattern was the same, no significant deviation. Late that evening Peter remembered it. He had actually been told something that could be considered a warning. What was it Kalle had said about the book on pick-up artists? *There are risks, and the point comes at the end.*

Matt looked surprised when Peter knocked on the door and asked if he could have the now well-thumbed copy of the book. Peter recognized how uncool it was, but it couldn't be helped.

He had a strong feeling that this was a book that he needed to read all the way through to the end.

✖

Christmas had come round again. Ever since his parents' divorce, the family celebrations had become an intricate patchwork of small, well-planned visits here and short stops there. What in Peter's childhood had been a glimmering, candle-lit winter paradise with Christmas tree, snow, holiday TV specials and presents was now a barely passable cracking sheet of ice that he and his sisters skilfully navigated. Today, a good Christmas meant that the Stavenius siblings had lightly and gracefully succeeded in running across the ice without falling into any freezing holes of bitterness along the way.

This year it was lunch with his mother and Christmas Eve night with his father. The only thing that was strange was that Viktoria was absent, because she was spending Christmas with her new boyfriend. Peter had thought it was a little early to be starting all that. And Vicky was only 16 years old; surely she ought not be with a guy over 20? But if his mother and father thought it was okay, he wasn't going to make a fuss. In any case, Peter needed to go home and take care of eight-year-old Sofia's patchwork Christmas.

Peter had borrowed his father's second most expensive car to drive himself and Sofia out to the modest suburb that Birgitta had made her home for the past seven years. He glanced at his little sister, sitting there in her lovely Christmas dress and her tangled hair. He realized that Sofia couldn't remember any other way to celebrate Christmas than what they were doing right now. Her parents' separation had redrawn the map when she was busy learning to walk up stairs. Peter remembered how the tension rose in the luxurious duplex apartment before his parents went out 'for a walk'. While Sofia, gripping her long-suffering brother's hand tightly, methodically learned how to tramp up and down the stairs, 20 times in a row, he knew that they went off to argue. Seven years later, behind the wheel of a German luxury car, Peter felt a wave of affection for his little sister's innocent Christmas joy. He realized with surprise that it was perhaps Sofia who gave him the stability to survive Christmas, rather than the other way around.

His father had never been any good at fixing girls' hair. And just as Peter had suspected, the first thing Birgitta did after giving them welcome hugs was to carefully begin brushing Sofia's hair, a worried frown on her face. 'How are you, honey? Didn't your daddy brush your hair?' she asked.

'No problem. We just forgot. I can do it myself,' said Sofia, confidently taking the hairbrush.

'Do you want pigtails or a braid? Or maybe a ponytail?' asked Birgitta.

Peter saw his mother's enormous love for the baby of the family, and he knew how difficult it was for her to live without Sofia every other week. Since Birgitta missed half of the time, it was as if she did not realize that even Sofia was growing up. In mom-time the girl might be six years old, but in reality she was in the second grade and would soon be nine.

'But, oh! I want it loose, Mom!' She put down the hairbrush firmly and ran into the townhouse's little living room, tossing her long, light blond hair.

'Moozaart!' called Sofia.

Lunch passed without any major mishaps, and Peter even managed to engage in a little polite small talk with Göran – the humble piano teacher for whom Birgitta had destroyed their home. It had been a complete mystery to Peter all these years. He loved his mother as much as a son could, but that made it all the more difficult to understand how she could go and fall in love with such a measly, withdrawn character when she was married to the stylish and handsome Lennart. In what possible universe could 'beige' Göran be preferable to Lennart?

His father had said it was just as he had always thought: basically, women were completely untrustworthy. You can give them the whole world, but then they just decide they want something else. The best strategy was 'don't try so damned hard,' he used to say, double whiskey in hand on Saturday nights.

They navigated their way through lunch, skilfully balancing on the ice patch. But before coffee was served Birgitta became so angry that she began to cry. Göran had gone to the kitchen with the dishes and Sofia was playing upstairs with the household's dishevelled little Cairn Terrier, Mozart. Peter had begun to relax and had accidentally blurted out that it was 'remarkable how life could change just because Vicky wanted to learn the piano'.

'Is that what you think happened?' asked Birgitta, looking at him indignantly. He realized too late that he had slipped up due to his own carelessness. Now he would just have to put up with the ice-cold bitterness that was coming.

'Yes, I can imagine that's what Lennart said, anyway.' She spoke quietly but spat out the words. 'The happy housewife who has everything, but still leaves her poor, innocent husband for someone else.'

Peter didn't know what to say. She turned and looked right at him, saying something complicated and incoherent. Deep within the confusing barrage of words Peter made out two questions: Did he not agree that one is an adult at age 24? And now that he was an adult shouldn't he understand – or did she mean was he grown up enough to hear? – what had really happened? Peter looked quietly at his mother and weighed her coded questions. *She wants me to say yes. She needs me to.*

When he nodded, everything poured out of Birgitta like a spring flood.

'We had you when I was young, before I had had time to discover my own ambitions. I was content to stay at home and take care of you, and my mother was alive and could help me. You were with grandma a lot.'

Yes, I was, Peter remembered. He thought about the happy, secure feeling he had experienced at Solveig's, just from the scent of geraniums.

'Then we started Rooms when you were three, and Lennart and I shared an intense professional life. I realized that there was so much I wanted to do, and I loved the creative aspect of it! That's why I have my little company today; I am fascinated by how you can use space to form your life and surroundings. That is my way of expressing myself and my talents.'

Peter nodded again. He knew that it was true. He looked around the room. Even in a mediocre townhouse in Bagarmossen, she had created a cozier and more functional home than the large, impersonal luxury apartment that was Lennart's place of residence. The kids preferred to live with her, even though their father bought them more things and clothes and took them to restaurants all the time. It was hard to say exactly why, but his mother and the spaces she created exuded a life force.

'I love kids, and when we had Viktoria I was thrilled. But that was also the beginning of a journey into darkness for me. Lennart wanted to sell Rooms because I couldn't work with the creative side of the business when I was home with Vicky, and he didn't listen to what I wanted. He sold our furniture store, which was going to be... which felt like my life's work... and used the money to start his consultancy business. And I tried to go back to being a housewife, to direct my creativity inward, towards the home.'

Peter well remembered the years she was describing. The early 1990s were filled with attention and creativity focused on their home. For him it was a bright memory. How could she describe it as a descent into darkness?

'I thought those years were great,' said Peter softly, but Birgitta flinched as if he had slapped her.

'Perhaps they were good years for a child. And really good for Lennart. He started in the travel business and began to bring clients home for dinner. Three-course meals, expensive and complicated – that was what was expected. I enjoyed setting the table and organizing things, but the food was always a source of anxiety for me. And Lennart didn't help one fucking bit!' The ice-cold bitterness was now accompanied by a hot vein of anger, and she pushed her chair back vehemently. 'He assumed that I was a machine, an events machine, one that also took care of the kids and kept the home functioning. And when I once hired a caterer to help, that wasn't good enough either!'

Peter thought back to the strained parties and how tense Birgitta usually was, wound tighter than a drum, on those Friday nights.

'But why didn't you just tell Father?'

'I tried! 'He just said that it was "natural that I was tired", and that it was "okay that I had my little outbreaks; they were nothing compared to Inger's".'

Peter smiled despite himself. Yes, his father's mother had a rage that surpassed everybody's. It was no surprise that his father wasn't frightened of Birgitta's comparatively mild temperament. She looked at him and her indignation increased.

'There's nothing funny about it!' she said. 'It was terrible. I felt like I didn't count. The only thing that was important was Lennart and his big projects, which were going to bring in so much money. For him, as it turned out.' Tears filled her eyes. Peter looked down at the jagged scar on his left thumb and remembered with a shiver the horrible summer night 16 years ago.

'I know,' he said, 'to have Vicky a month early, to give birth completely alone. That must have been really rough.' He pushed his chair backwards to get closer to her, put his arm around her shoulders, and leaned his head against hers.

In a low voice, she said: 'Yes, but it wasn't just that. It wasn't just something that happened once. I shrank afterwards. I became smaller and smaller and Lennart became bigger and bigger. Too much depended on me. Lennart didn't need to take any responsibility at home; I had always done it. Everything revolved around him and what he wanted. Then when Sofia was born... the world's finest, most lovable little girl!'

Birgitta looked up at him with her tear-streaked face, as if she were forced to defend herself, to prove that she also loved her third child, before she continued.

'Then I tipped over the edge, down into the darkness.'

'What darkness?' Peter handed her a napkin and gestured awkwardly that she should wipe her face. He remembered that Birgitta had stayed in bed for months, crying, and no-one had understood why. That was when grandmother Inger had come to live with them and take care of the children. Father had said that it was a 'female thing' and that it would heal on its own.

'They called it "postnatal depression".' Birgitta sobbed, dried her eyes and saw from the napkin that her mascara had run. 'But in my case it was just the logical final step on a journey away from my self-confidence. I felt like I was imprisoned in a cage, and the walls crept closer and closer until the bars cut into my skin.'

Peter both remembered and didn't want to remember, and perhaps he appeared quizzical, because his mother tried to explain.

'You know what I mean – my self-imposed responsibilities and principles, my responsibilities to you children, Lennart's expectations, others' expectations and how I actually felt. I got pills and such, but nobody tried to help me come back to life. Except for you kids, as much as you could. And then Göran, whom I just happened to meet, and who actually cared about me, noticed me. I was forced to escape. In fact, I think he saved me.'

Saved her? The piano man? Peter sat silently. Birgitta straightened up and took a deep breath before continuing.

'But, of course, Lennart didn't understand anything. He thought, "things have always been so good for us". He said that I had betrayed him without warning. And he made sure that I signed the papers so that I got the summer cottage and a bunch of debts, and he got the apartment and the company. Of course I agreed to it. His Great Escape was just a trap for me, and the only thing I wanted was to be free so that I might be able to survive.' The tears started again. 'I had to accept living without my kids half the time. Just because Lennart… And all the time, I've known that you think what I did was wrong!'

She sobbed against Peter's shoulder and her sorrow seeped into him. He searched for words that wouldn't be lies but wouldn't hurt her even more. Finally, in a thick voice, he said, 'No, mother, don't think that. I had just got used to all the doting and love.'

Birgitta freed herself and looked questioningly at her son. 'But do you think that a person should stay in a situation that is breaking her down? Love doesn't mean letting someone hurt you.'

They heard a gentle knocking. Mother and son looked in the direction of the noise and the dining-room door as it opened.

There stood Göran, thin-haired and wearing his ridiculous Santa tie, with a thoughtfully set serving trolley. 'Sorry, but I was thinking that we probably want coffee and dessert now...'

Peter looked up, saw the kind face beyond the bowl of homemade ice-cream, his eyes locked on Birgitta's. And he realized something important.

✖

On the way back to Lennart and Strand Road, Peter sat thinking about the enormity of what he had heard. He knew that his mother had spoken the truth; he knew her so well that he could rule out everything else. Dizzyingly new perspectives opened up. Imagine if his mother wasn't a traitor to the family who did completely unpredictable things because of her untrustworthy female nature? Perhaps she was just a person like himself, his father, or whoever, who was trying to save herself from an impossible situation? Peter felt like the continental plates had shifted under his feet. How could he, who had learned so much from his mother about social graces and responding to others, have failed to understand her deep need? He had been, what, 16 or 17? But what about all the years since? Had those years scrambling around on the patch of ice all been because he refused to see a more complicated picture of the divorce than the one his father described?

Peter questioned himself the whole way into town, and he felt like crying for the first time in years. When the car slid into the darkness of the tunnel at Söder, his left eye brimmed with tears which he immediately dried. When they came out on the other side, he shot a quick glance at his sister. She relied on him as a rock and a constant in her life; had she noticed anything?

Sofia looked thoughtfully out at the midwinter twilight. Peter forced a smile and lightly touched her fine coat.

'How are you, honey? What are you thinking about?' he asked.

'Is Mommy my real mother?' Sofia asked, looking at her big brother with her innocent gaze.

Peter stared at the road and tried to hold his voice steady.

'Of course she's our real mother. Your mother, my mother,

Vicky's mother. And she loves us a lot.'

'Then why does she live with Göran? Why doesn't she live with Daddy?'

'Because she… needed something from Daddy that she didn't get. And after a while she was just sad all the time when she lived with Daddy. But Daddy didn't understand.' *And neither did I.*

'Why did she move when I was born?' Sofia drew her eyebrows together.

'It just happened. It isn't your fault. And isn't it better that Mommy is happy and that you get to be with her every other week, than her being at Daddy's and lying in bed crying all the time?'

Sofia didn't look convinced. 'Why couldn't Daddy give her that thing she needed, so she would be happy at home with him?'

Why can't people change? thought Peter.

Peter felt the need to talk to his father about his new insights, but a suitable occasion didn't present itself. Lennart's new, even younger woman – the slim, nervously smoking Carla – took up most of his Christmas Eve. Peter wandered restlessly around in what he had thought of as his home and which was now Lennart's masculine and expensively decorated luxury apartment, with the exception of three untouched children's rooms. Well, not exactly untouched… Peter noted with irritation that his room was cluttered with shopping bags from expensive designer boutiques. He stacked the ones that would fit on the armchair in the corner and carried the rest to Lennart's spacious bedroom. There were a half dozen pairs of shoes, several handbags and tons of expensive clothes laying around. *Why couldn't Carla take care of her stuff?*

Peter went out into the living room and stood in front of the large windows. He looked out over the view: Nybroviken, Skeppsholmen and Söder, liberally arrayed with shiny Christmas lights. Sofia sat on the huge, expensive rug playing with the new TV games console she had been given as a present.

A perfectly ordinary Christmas. And yet so different. Peter

sat down on the low Italian leather sofa and continued reading *The Game*. He didn't notice when Carla came and sat down beside him. But the leather creaked when she edged closer, and Peter stiffened. It wasn't the first time that one of his father's young flames had made unpleasant advances. He usually tried to keep his distance and pretend he hadn't noticed, but he felt a stab of tired disappointment that Carla was also so deceitful. *Women who can't be trusted. What do they want? A younger body? The heir's money?*

He couldn't repress the memory of Rebecka – his father's previous fiancée. Only a month before the planned wedding she had provided an answer to the question. First she said she had got cold feet, which was literally true, as he found out when, drunk on liqueur, she climbed in under Peter's covers clad only in a tiny pair of panties. She had pressed herself against him as he lay helplessly groggy with sleep and trapped against the wall, and whispered in his ear: 'I get too little. I want more sex.'

Fortunately, the engagement between Lennart and Rebecka had been broken off the next day, so Peter had never had to breathe a word. *I hope that Father doesn't know, that he never finds out, what she did.*

'Peter?' Carla bent forward. Her breath didn't smell of liqueur, but of cigarette smoke.

Peter twisted his body so that he was farther away from her and she was more directly in front of him. *Keep the enemy in view. Arms protecting the flanks.*

'Yes?'

She nervously fingered a shiny new bracelet. *Which she certainly got from Father – diamonds worth maybe six figures? At least she's wearing them, rather than letting them lie around in a bag in my room!*

Carla played with her hair and looked at Sofia, still sitting on the floor with the TV game. Then she put her hand on his arm.

'Do you… I mean, Lennart. Do you think he's a good father?' Carla's expertly made-up grey eyes looked nakedly and almost pleadingly into his. A sense of relief spread through his chest and warmed his voice to surprised kindness.

'Yeah, hell. Sure, Dad is good.'

Peter and Carla smiled at each other for a moment, before she got up and went back to Lennart and Peter could return to his black book.

Thus far Peter had read that nerds who had learned systematic seduction techniques had started to sell courses to other insecure guys and had pulled in enough money to rent a house in Beverly Hills that was to be called Project Hollywood. The author explained that men could now learn what women had long known: how to make the best of your appearance, and what to do in order to seem interesting to the opposite sex. Using the artist name of Style, he taught new generations how to go from nerd to master seducer. Numerous gimmicks and tricks to get into girls' panties were successfully tested and documented.

'What are you reading?' Sofia looked wide-eyed at her brother, sitting on the sofa with the black book with James Bond-like silhouettes of provocative women on the cover.

Peter started as if he had been caught with pornography – and in a way that was what it was, he thought guiltily. *An autobiography about living pornography in real life?* He put the book down as if it were on fire.

'Ahh, just a book.'

Sofia looked at the silhouettes on the cover. 'A book about Barbie dolls?'

Peter smiled and hugged his little sister. 'Yes, you could say that. A book about Barbie dolls.'

She crept up beside him on the sofa and tucked her small, stockinged feet under her dress. She thumbed through the book with interest.

'What tiny print. Can you read it to me?'

Should Sofia's Christmas Eve world be invaded by 'a penetrating analysis of the secret pick-up society'? He took the book away from her and looked at the clock.

'I don't think you'd like it. Let's watch Christmas cartoons on TV instead!'

He turned on the TV and put his arm around his sister's small shoulders. They were just in time. Tage Danielsson's Christmas story had already started:

'Mother says, "One must do one's duty in life",' said Karl Bertil. "A task well done gives an inner satisfaction and that is the foundation upon which society rests."'

Perhaps it was the very idea of having a child with someone like Jeanette. Or Birgitta's confession about her last years in the duplex apartment. Or was it perhaps just the tower of shopping bags on the armchair in the corner? Whatever it was, the nightmares he had on Christmas Eve night were terrible.

Drenched in sweat, Peter woke with a strangled scream. He sat up, breathing heavily as if he had started to drown. When he turned on the light, his brain tried to understand what had caused the dreadful feeling.

But the dream was gone; there was nothing left except a fading abyss of anxiety, absurdly accompanied by the big-band version of *Just a Gigolo.*

22

Washed up on land, finally,
Ice-cold rag clinging to my removal boxes
Is it okay if I keep them in the garage
– just for a while?

Vera's dream

Vera came home to the snow-covered village late on the evening of 22 December. It was dark, but the sturdy, souterrain-style house from the 1970s glittered with Christmas decorations. She stood on the porch with what little she had brought with her and braced herself. She took a deep breath before stamping her feet to shake off the snow and opening the door.

'Hello?'

Sven-Erik and the cat met her in the hall. Daddy's friendly gaze peered out from under his bushy, greying hair. Under his open terrycloth bathrobe he was wearing silk boxer shorts with Santa Clauses on them and a faded t-shirt with the text *Vindel River Relay Race* stamped across the front. Vera smiled when she saw that he still maintained the tradition of wearing the Santa Claus underwear, which she had given him as a Christmas present around 15 years ago. The cat rubbed itself frantically on her leg, while Sven-Erik tied the belt around his now slightly round stomach and gave her a bear-hug.

'Why does it have to be Christmas before we get you home?'

'I thought you were going to say, "Why does it have to be Christmas?"' said Vera, still in her father's strong arms. He let her go and looked at her.

'No, it's going to be lovely. Your mother is in pretty good shape now, anyway.'

Vera hung up her outdoor clothes. 'Is she working tonight?'

'No, no. She gets off any minute. I put the kettle on...'

'I'm tired,' said Vera. 'I think I'll go to bed.'

Sven-Erik watched his daughter as she made her way down the stairs to her room.

Vera helped with the Christmas preparations, but stayed out of the house as much as she could the day before Christmas Eve. But then the day came. And the whole point was that you were supposed to spend it with the family. The others were not coming until it was time to watch the Disney Christmas special, so it was just the four of them for the herring-and-stockfish Christmas lunch: Vera, Sven-Erik, Gunilla, and Grandpa Ivar, who was combed and outfitted in his dress shirt. Gunilla had been calm at the start of the meal, but became increasingly upset the more she thought that Vera was avoiding her questions. When the subject of Adam came up – he had called his mother-in-law regularly during Advent in an effort to talk about Vera – it became too much for Gunilla.

'You said that you would talk to Adam!'

'No, Mother, I said that...'

'You didn't call Solbacka about a full-time position either, did you?' Gunilla interrupted.

Vera looked away. *So much for Mother being in good form.* There was the same old risk of a volcanic eruption brought on by Christmas stress, laced this year with her daughter's unbearable failures: risky international aid work, separation from a fine doctor husband and, to top it all, a refusal to work. Vera knew roughly what was coming, but the words burned anyway.

'I really don't understand you! You will be 30 soon; you have no proper job, no husband, no real home – and all your belongings are in boxes in our garage!'

Sven-Erik tried to put a calming hand on his wife, but she rushed out towards the laundry room and garage, yelling as she went, 'And you don't even *try!*'

Vera tried to bear the onslaught. Ivar sighed and looked at his watch. Sven-Erik picked up his plate and looked encouragingly at Vera.

'Come, Vera. Let's take a second helping. I think the ham turned out really well this year.'

It was actually nothing new. Her mother had always been like this – worryingly searching for flaws in her only child. Like when Vera had suddenly shot up in height when Gunilla had just completed a course on eating disorders. Of course she thought Vera had anorexia, because she was too thin. Or when her father had been at the Nolia trade show and bought a new tar contraption to light the fireplace. Her conscientious mother, who had been reading in a parent-teacher newsletter about being alert to 'sweetish odours', marched right in on a board game of Spin the Bottle, turned on the light and demanded, threateningly, 'Who's smoking marijuana?'

Naturally she meant well – in her way. And Vera usually managed to keep things under control. With the help of self-discipline and a talent for being adaptable, she avoided provoking Gunilla's fears. But Vera could not talk honestly about the worst year in her life, not even to her father, because she feared that he would thoughtlessly tell her mother, and then the volcano would most likely erupt as never before. Or would it be more like an incident in a nuclear power plant? Only Sven-Erik's absorbing acceptance could then, like control rods submerged in a reactor, prevent a chain reaction that would otherwise risk crushing everything.

The only person she had opened up to a little was Grandpa Ivar, in the spring, just after she had come home. But she had not got very far before stopping herself, because she was ashamed. As soon as she got close to what had happened, in an effort to be matter-of-fact, she was filled with an ice clump of sorrow surrounded by an isolating shame. Vera was bearing secrets that she hadn't told anyone, and it was not doing her any good. It was a malevolent loneliness.

Vera fled from the Christmas lunch down to her old childhood room. She looked at the bookcase, where books about orphan Kulla-Gulla were squeezed in beside Kitty books, old schoolbooks beside arts and crafts projects and sports awards. There was more than 10 years' worth of dust on her graduation cap. On that shelf, she could go through her life, year by year, like the rings on a tree. One of the least dusty things caught her eye. Although she knew how bad it would make her feel, her hand took down a photograph in a white paper frame with gold rings. Suddenly completely drained of energy, she sank down on the patchwork quilt. The nose of her worn teddy bear pressed into her back. She stared at the picture and held her breath. When she relaxed the world grew blurred through her tears. She didn't know how long she had been sitting there, aching, when her mother's voice cut through the air from the floor above.

'Vera,' she called, 'do you hear me? Adam is on the phone!'

She dried her face quickly, wetting her left hand. *Where does all this come from?* Vera had had no idea how many tears had been waiting to come out. She forced out a shaky breath, and tried to sound natural, but her voice came out strangely weak.

'Oh, okay.'

'Aren't you going to talk to him?' The reproachful undertone had no problem travelling the distance down to the basement. After a silence her mother continued.

'Vera! What *is it* with you?'

Vera fled to the family room.

Gunilla gave up and hung up the phone. The last thing she called down was like a command. 'I told him you would call later.'

Vera twisted the wedding photo into a hard cone and went over to the fireplace. When she heard footsteps on the stairs she dried her cheeks again, which were stiff with salt. It was her father. Vera relaxed and sat down ceremoniously on the stone hearth in front of the fireplace. Feebly, she leaned on her left hand, which hid the tear-stained, ripped-up memory. With her right hand, she stacked the logs so as to create a good fire. She worked curls of birch bark between the logs. Sven-Erik fetched a large, old leather pouffe and pushed it over. He helped her up on the pouffe and then sat down carefully beside her, although

155

he barely fitted. Vera leaned slightly against him and shakily drew a breath.

'I know. "Don't make mother sad." Sorry.'

He gently handed her a last stick of wood and lifted up the cat, who was worriedly rubbing Vera's leg.

'And I *will* take care of those boxes!'

Sven-Erik nodded and put his arm round his daughter's stooped shoulders.

'Yes, yes. That's no problem.'

The cat's insistent purring mixed with the Christmas music from upstairs.

'But full-time at Solbacka? Is she trying to kill me?' She looked at him indignantly. He softly stroked the cat's back.

'There, there. Things'll work out.

He isn't just saying that, thought Vera. *He really believes it.* Vera lit the white paper in her left hand and used it as a torch to light the fire. The birch bark quickly guided the fire to the dry wood and the warmth was just starting to radiate when Gunilla's voice once again travelled down the stairs.

'Vera, Sven-Erik! They're here!'

She heard the hall filling with Uncle Mats and his family – aunt, cousins with their partners and children. They were in a festive mood. Vera winced and got up heavily, using the hearth to help her off the low pouffe. She put the fireguard in place before she left but didn't notice that the wet, tightly twisted photograph had landed on the hearth outside it.

Vera had always thought that *Lady and the Tramp* was a calm and relaxing part of the Disney programme that they, like millions of other Swedes, still watched every Christmas Eve afternoon. But this year was not like others.

This year, Woody Woodpecker was like balm for her soul in comparison. And she was not prepared for it at all. The romance of it was unbearable, and it didn't matter that it was about cartoon dogs. When the languorous *'Oh this is the night, it's a beautiful night and we call it bella notte'* started up, Vera excused herself and, eyes filled with tears, carefully climbed past her cousins' children, all dressed in their Christmas finery,

156

who were playing on the carpet. She fled to the bathroom with a lie about the stockfish not agreeing with her.

✱

The old Volvo was so full of removal boxes that the windows fogged over. Vera wiped the passenger window so that Sven-Erik could see where to turn to access the student accommodation. The inner courtyard hadn't been cleared and the car left patterned tire tracks in the soft, untouched blanket of snow.

He asked about Adam. 'He hasn't been violent towards you, has he?' His voice trembled. 'Because, if so, I forbid you to listen to your mother. In that case, you *may not* go back to him. You know that crap about "I only hit you because I love you"...'

Vera looked at him and shook her head. 'No, I know.' Her father was the epitome of flexibility and seldom categorical, but she was well aware of his immovable opinion on this question. 'I know. "Those who hit, you leave." But it isn't that... Park here. It's closest.'

Sven-Erik and Vera struggled to get the armchair up the stairs. It took a long time thanks to her halting, toddler-like steps, and he had to take most of the weight. Finally they reached the hallway where Sven-Erik had already left a couple of removal boxes. Vera took out her keys. It was quiet and empty on this Thursday, 3 January, just as she had said it would be. Not a soul on all of Stipend Street – except for her and Sven-Erik, and they were finally going to resolve the problem of all those boxes in the garage.

As they were squeezing the armchair into her room, they heard a rhythmic pounding from next door.

'Someone is here, anyway,' declared Sven-Erik.

'Oh, oh, oh, oooohh,' moaned a man's voice from the other side of the wall.

Aha, Stavenius, thought Vera and noted matter-of-factly that it was the first time she had heard his voice in the middle of the act. *It must be something really special this time.*

Sven-Erik, puffing, straightened his back. He looked amused.

'You have a neighbor at home? It doesn't sound like he's alone, either.'

There was a thunderous noise from the next room and a door banged open. Sven-Erik looked out into the hall. He stiffened and stared mutely. Vera followed him to see what had shaken her father's usual equanimity.

It was Peter Stavenius, his blond hair dishevelled, dressed only in underwear, a pair of jeans round his ankles.

Sven-Erik smiled tranquilly. 'Things seem to have got a bit wild in there.'

'Yeah, I mean... You could say there's been a little accident,' said Peter as he quickly pulled up his jeans. He gave a start and slapped himself on the abdomen as if he had suddenly developed tics.

'A little accident?!' echoed Vera. She saw her father's surprise at the acid tone she couldn't hide.

Peter blushed and fiddled with his hair in embarrassment before crossing his arms over his naked stomach.

'Yeah, I don't get it... why would I have done that?'

She felt like... Well, she didn't really know what, but *can't he hear what he sounds like?* She went silently back into her room and heard the rest of the conversation from in there.

'Peter. Hi. Dorm neighbour of Vera's. I'm here studying for a resit test.'

'Are you now? Sven-Erik, Vera's father. You aren't overexerting yourself, I hope? That could wear you out, you know.'

23

'I'm the world's greatest pickup artist,' he grumbled in my direction. 'How come I don't have a girlfriend?'
'Well, maybe because you're the world's greatest pickup artist.'

Neil Strauss, 'The Game'

Catastrophe was perhaps too strong a word, but it didn't go well when Peter tentatively suggested to Lennart that women in general, and Birgitta in particular, might not be completely unpredictable. Lennart immediately went on the defensive and started interrogating Peter about what Birgitta had said to him. Then, when he was all worked up, Lennart started in on Peter for missing the last board meeting of the year. Charlie had managed to find time to come from London, even though he had been busy getting promoted and earning yet another million pounds. It would have been one thing, Lennart had said irritably, if Peter had got around to finishing his degree. Instead, all he had heard was that his son had failed the decision-making test *and* neglected to hand in some chapter or other to Sturesson on time. 'Good-for-nothing,' was his father's uncensored judgment, and it didn't help much that Peter promised to go back and swot up before the resit.

It was not unusual for Lennart to be critical of his son, but this time, for some reason, Peter couldn't let it go. The phrase 'good-for-nothing' haunted him for several days. It echoed in his head, as if it confirmed something he had heard somewhere else. *Good-for-nothing? Incompetent. Useless. Worthless. Incapable. Bad.*

Peter had a strangely fateful feeling about New Year's Eve. Charlie was home for the holidays and called to invite him to some spectacular celebration or other, but Peter turned him down. Charlie sounded surprised – Peter had always said yes before to tagging along when his successful cousin was on a mission to spend his bonus in Stockholm's most exclusive nightclubs. He had been the proud wingman. He had felt how their power of attraction multiplied when the two of them – rich, good-looking cousins – appeared together in Stureplan, Stockholm's playground for the upper class. Once, they went into a bar and the effect, measured in the number of interested glances, was so noticeable that Charlie had whispered that they had 'top-notch head-turn quotient'.

But on this unusual New Year's Eve, Peter did not dress up to greet 2008 in style. Instead he lay on the couch reading *The Game*. Earlier, the character called Style's description of the good that could actually come from a well-developed ability to attract new acquaintances had felt consoling. But now the book seemed to be a feeble consolation, because, when he took up where he had left off, the pick-up society's foundations began to creak alarmingly. Project Hollywood degenerated into a reality freak show. It was sex, betrayal and drugs, mixed with trying conflicts about girls, housework, money and power over the pick-up classes.

Another character called Mystery, master seducer number one, suffered a bad case of jealousy and fell apart. Several other elite pick-up artists felt like they had become sex-addicts and turned to religion and asceticism to cure themselves. One went to an ashram in India and another to a strict Jewish school in Israel. Just when Peter was wondering why they were taking such drastic steps as celibacy and solitude, his cellphone rang.

Who calls at four o'clock on New Year's Eve? Peter was pleasantly surprised to discover that it was Kalle. 'You're coming into town? Great! What do you have in mind? "Wherever?" Yeah, there are some good places… Vanity? Sure, I can arrange that.'

It turned out that Kalle was at his parents' house in Knivsta and felt like celebrating New Year in town. Peter met him at the train station and, as they walked over to the rock club, they updated each other on the fall semester – Kalle's experience teaching high school in Kalmar, Peter's fifth semester of economics, the project and a few other things. Kalle asked curiously about 'lame Florence', and Peter thought he managed to sound neutral in his answer about Vera. Kalle said that he missed the dorm and spoke longingly about Umeå University's annual spring rounders tournament.

When they reached Vanity, Peter easily got them past the long queue. The atmosphere was festive and a few of the rock club girls, decked out for New Year's Eve, tried to make eye contact with him. Peter felt strangely uninterested. He brooded over what he had read, trying to understand what had actually happened over there in Project Hollywood, the luxury villa that had slipped into filth and decay. Since they were early, the bar was still quite empty when Kalle and Peter picked a place and sat down.

'I've almost finished reading that book, *The Game.*'

'Yeah? Good.' Kalle took a swallow of Guinness and looked pleased.

'But I don't get it. It's so damned all or nothing! Now some of them are moving to monasteries and don't want to have anything to do with women.'

'Mmm.' Kalle reached for the bowl of peanuts.

'But why?'

Kalle looked at him tentatively, shrugging his shoulders. 'Maybe because, having seduced a bunch of wives and girlfriends, they've realized: "Shit! It worked!"'

'Yeah, right, here today, gone tomorrow.' Peter attempted a cool grin, but a wave of insecurity and betrayal, deeply rooted in his teenage years, surged up from his gut and made his eyes burn. *They have discovered for themselves that you can't trust women.* And yet. Mom clearly hadn't left them just because she was struck by an irresistible attraction to Göran the hunk. That was obvious, and he believed her when she said that she had done it in order to survive.

'But the girls in the book don't seem to be suffering. They just seem to be behaving like pigs,' said Peter.

'Huh?'

'You know, hanging out in bars looking for one-night stands.'

Kalle looked at him neutrally. 'Kind of like the guys in the book? Or like... you?'

Peter stared down at the ice bucket behind the bar and started as if it had been poured all over him.

'But...' *I don't? And anyway...* 'But there's a difference, isn't there? Guys are, well...' *What is it Dad says?* 'More, by nature... you know, the birds and the bees. Bees fly around, flowers stay put.' *Sow their wild oats*, that was what Lennart used to say.

Kalle looked skeptical. 'What do you mean?'

Peter didn't answer, and indignantly took a gulp of beer.

'If you mean that girls are flowers and guys are bees, then you're...' Kalle's hand gesture clearly communicated 'nuts.'

'Because, you do realize, of course, that bees have sex with bees and flowers with flowers? I mean, otherwise, what kind of offspring would we get? Flying roses?' Peter didn't look very amused but Kalle grinned at the image before continuing.

'Flowers offer the bees food so that they can fertilize each other despite the fact that they can't move. And if you're thinking about the sex lives of bees, I assume you would want to be a female? Do you know how many drones service a queen bee? And I haven't even mentioned what happens when...'

'Fine! What about mammals, then?' interrupted Peter. 'We're mammals, and males sow their wild oats, at least until they are married and have to control themselves.'

'Wow! You sound like someone from the 19th century; that's how people first studied primates!' Kalle pushed his glass away and started pointing animatedly at the bar as if it were a blackboard.

'All observations that didn't fit with Victorian norms were ignored. Only the "right" kind of animal sex was recorded, no homosexuality, no promiscuous females. But the truth is that animal sex is more or less "anything goes", and the evolutionary pressure for promiscuity is equally strong for females and males.'

'Huh?'

'Married women also have to control themselves sometimes,' grinned Kalle.

'What do you mean, "evolutionary pressure?"'

'Don't forget the whole point of sex.'

'What is the point of sex?' This was something Peter really wanted to know.

'Well, in terms of pure evolution, it's about two things: to bring information together and to build ties of co-operation so that offspring can survive.'

Peter hadn't expected this. 'Bring information together?'

'Okay, let me start at the beginning.' Kalle looked at him patiently. 'Life on earth has existed for more than three billion years. For about two billion of them, there was life without sex. But after that, developments really took off. You could say that sex was invented by single-cell organisms that wanted the information stored in other cells' DNA. Both individuals benefit from it, because you get *the best of both* rather than just a replication of the same old thing. New mixes, new variations, fantastic development – you know, millions of species. And when we get to mammals – like you say – then it starts to be a lot of work to ensure that offspring survive, so the ones with several care-providers have a better chance. That's why pregnant chimpanzees... well, their milk glands swell, their uterus gets stronger and they have as much sex as possible with as many males as possible.' Kalle took a handful of peanuts and began to put them into his mouth.

Peter went ice cold. 'What the hell? What are you saying?' *Pregnant? Jeanette?* He shuddered.

'Yes, now we get to reason number two. Offspring whose mothers behaved like that probably got more food and help, so they were more likely to survive. Because every male that the female chimpanzee had sex with knows that it *might* be his offspring. Of course, we might argue that that is also reason number one.' Kalle's thick hair fell across his forehead as he thoughtfully picked between two molars.

'Huh? What do you mean, reason number one?'

'Information. The best DNA. It takes a lot of effort for a body to create a child. Obviously she wants the best possible hereditary material to start with. "May the best man win," you know. Oh, and did you know that you can tell by their balls how faithful primates are? Bloody fascinating!'

As the noise level in the bar increased and the place became more and more crowded, Peter sat wanly, listening to Kalle explain that, by measuring the testicles of apes, you could determine how monogamous the species had tended to be during its evolution. Apparently, the big male gorillas didn't need to invest in more than small nuts because their sperm didn't need to force their way through the sperm of other males. By contrast, chimpanzees had gigantic ones in order to equip themselves for the fight to reach the egg. The dry conclusion of the researchers was that, theoretically, based on gland size, human sexual fidelity was somewhere between that of the gorilla and the chimpanzee.

Peter felt dispirited, and the abandoned child inside him felt like crying.

Peter left the club early. He wasn't in the mood to meet new people anyway, even in the unlikely event that someone was interested in meeting a person who was standing at the bar talking about ape testicles... When Kalle wandered off happily in the direction of the stage and the live band, Peter went home to his father's empty apartment on Strand Street and anxiously continued reading *The Game*.

Having lost Katja, whom he had so longed for, thanks to his general unpleasantness, Mystery sunk into a serious psychosis. Style bravely fought against his mentor's schizophrenia, but all that remained of the pick-up guru was an unstable human wreck. Bitter and patched-up with anti-psychotic drugs, Mystery disappeared inside himself, oscillating between suicidal thoughts and a desire to murder his father. Another master pick-up artist described how he felt like a bucket full of holes – he kept trying to fill himself up, but everything just leaked out.

Peter decided that Mystery's big problem was that he always thought the grass was greener on the other side of the fence – he was incapable of appreciating what he had.

Incapable. Good-for-nothing. Worthless.

Peter decided there and then to invite Sandra to dinner and to make sure that he valued what he actually had.

At midnight, Peter turned on the TV and went over to the big windows to watch the fireworks from the outdoor arena at Skansen, the city zoo. Surreally, they appeared just before they were shown on TV, and from a different angle.

'*Ring out, wild bells, to the wild sky*' said the authoritative voice from the TV.

'*Ring out the old, ring in the new; Ring, happy bells, across the snow; The year is going, let him go; Ring out the false, ring in the true.*'

✳

Peter travelled up to the midwinter darkness of Umeå on 2 January. It turned out that Sandra was also back in town. Surprised, she accepted his dinner invitation. He had dressed up a bit and booked a table at the little tapas restaurant. Sandra was attractive, fashionably dressed and well groomed, as usual.

Peter sat and tested the idea that he might perhaps be able to fall in love with Sandra. Undeniably, she had many advantages, and the soft light from the candle on the table didn't reveal the hardness he often noticed in her face. Approvingly, he reminded himself that she had more brains than people assumed; sometimes she seemed to be playing the dumb blonde. And he liked her being so social and goal-oriented. *But...* He caught himself remembering how it had felt to hold the whole of Jeanette's smaller breasts in his hands, how sensitive they had seemed to be, and the sexual closeness he had felt between them. He felt a stab of lust at the thought of how she had responded to him in the shower, and it turned his stomach. He put down his knife and fork in agitation, and thought about what Kalle had said. Getting aroused by knocked-up-swollen breasts and a pregnancy-induced sex-drive caused by some other man? Definitely a perversion he didn't want.

He looked at the woman in front of him, coveted by so many men, and suddenly wondered what she had looked like before her plastic surgery. Tall and slim, with a fantastic posture and long, blond hair – maybe she had looked like Galadriel, the Lady of Light? But no. *Being an Elf was not about... it had to do with other things than appearance.* His mind wandered to comparisons, thoughts and feelings that were much more difficult to handle. *No! Pull yourself together! Stop cultivating your damned inability to appreciate what you have!*

He began to eat, reminding himself that Sandra was damned good looking and that men of all ages flocked around her in whatever bar she went into. And, damn it, the looks her cleavage usually attracted! It would be completely crap if he couldn't appreciate it.

Peter wondered if he was hooked on the idea of a dream woman put together with all the best parts of all the women he had been with – and no bad qualities. If so, it was an unfair, impossible ideal; he understood that. Was he a combination of the best of all the men – certainly no small number – that Sandra had ever dated? He clenched his teeth. No, compared with a cut-and-paste ideal, reality didn't have a chance. But ideals are just an illusion, a recipe for disaster. Sandra was robust and cheerful. He could definitely have a lot of fun with her. But he wished that she could relax, let herself go. He looked at her again in the flickering candlelight and thought: *I've noticed that she also likes the sight of them; but how does it really feel to have those hard, stretched breasts?* He had no problem with the scars, being careful and not putting his weight on her, or keeping to the very front of the right one, as she usually reminded him, but… *Fuck! Why did I let us break Rule Number One!*

Rule Number One was a souvenir from the London trip last summer, when he thought he had played his cleverest game yet. He and Charlie had been hanging out at a bar in the City, talking about sex, when one of Charlie's acquaintances had shown up. Sally (or was it Nelly?), whom he vaguely remembered as a young Halle Berry type, had cockily joined in their conversation with the coolest, perhaps most honest, pick-up line he had ever heard: 'They're all faking it anyway.' She proceeded to develop her argument with words that Charlie helped translate: 'But they all want the man to call their bluff.'

Peter had been inspired to engage in a masterful game of mirroring. He had listened and absorbed her world, and then gave it back to her in his own words – the best trick in the book to communicate that he was the man for her. Sufficiently drunk and creative, he had suddenly hatched Rule Number One of Reliably Good Sex. Predictably, too many drinks later and with the help of some additional risqué theorizing, he got his prey. Unfortunately. Because it had actually been the worst catch of his life. The next morning he had been hung over and felt like shit... Now, six months later, he understood that his depression had not just been a consequence of too much alcohol. He had a word – fuck, a whole cheesy big-band song – for the feeling.

A wave of discomfort washed over him, and he decisively turned his gaze back to Sandra. Was it because he sometimes felt that she was living up to expectations in a slightly mechanical way? Because she often wasn't relaxed and drowsy afterwards, but rather sad or irritated? It was part of the mystery of women, but he had a feeling. And he knew that it was down to him as well; he probably just needed to make a little more effort so that she could stop pretending and start experiencing it for real.

He tasted the next dish and was surprised by the fresh taste combination of coriander, lime and shrimp. He concentrated on what Sandra had to say. For once she seemed thoughtful, almost worried. She hadn't wanted to order much food, and she sat mostly poking at it.

'You know, I was really surprised when you called and said what you did,' she began tentatively. 'I thought that you weren't interested in a... a more serious relationship?' Her light-blue eyes looked questioningly at Peter. He shrugged his shoulders and took a swallow of beer to win a little time. He didn't want to lie.

'Oh, I don't know. My mother says that you're grown up when you reach 24.'

Sandra looked at him silently. He saw that she didn't think he had answered the question, so he continued, more truthfully than he had intended.

'When you're an adult, isn't it time to rise to the occasion and make some decisions, to stand for something? And then you wonder, what's the point of all that non-serious stuff?'

"All that non-serious stuff?' There was an unidentifiable

gleam in her eye, and Peter stiffened. Then Sandra smiled and looked almost relieved. 'Exactly. What is the point of the non-serious stuff? Um, I don't know how to say this. I don't want you to be sad or anything. But I think you actually seem pretty non-serious. It isn't personal. I think you're really sweet.' She leaned towards him and pushed away a strand of hair that was hanging down in his face. She impulsively squeezed his upper arm before sighing and pulling away from him again, as if denying herself a misleading temptation. 'But I want someone who is, you know... Someone who is going places.'

Peter suddenly lost his appetite. Sandra continued proudly.

'*I* am going places. I've signed three new contracts, and my blog now gets several hundred thousand hits. It's complicated with contracts, so I contacted a really good...'

A new hit song rang out from Sandra's cellphone. With lightning speed, she stuck her hand down into the latest obscenely expensive handbag someone had given her in the hope that she would blog something nice about it. She stood up and spoke briefly, a delighted, blushing smile on her face. Then she ended the conversation and sat down again.

'That was Robert. He's coming to get me in a few minutes.' She gazed eagerly out through the restaurant's large windows. 'He isn't even 40 and he already has his own law firm. Business law. And he helped me with the contracts. My dad is super-impressed.' She looked sympathetically at him and stroked his cheek with her hand, with its bright pink nails.

'Some day you'll find the right one too.'

It was like a sick sketch, Peter thought later. He sat at the table, alone with all the small plates, after a tall, well-dressed guy with a shaved head and a long, aristocratic last name had swept in and picked up his girl. Robert von Law Firm who wasn't yet 40 had even been friendly and shaken his hand.

When they were gone, a question popped up in his head, with a word that filled him with an uncomfortable feeling: *I wonder if that guy, Robert, is... well hung?* It was a phrase that literally spoke of a meat market, that reduced manhood to a cut of flesh, like any other piece of fillet or sirloin publicly evaluated at the butcher's. Peter remembered uncomfortably that it was Sandra who had made him wonder, and had in fact made him feel compelled to measure himself while erect. He had found out that he was, in that respect, normal and like most others.

On the other hand, Sandra doesn't strike me as a woman who would be satisfied with normal and average... Peter cut off the meaningless, destructive thought. *Knock it off!* And what about that 'his girl' business? Had Sandra been his girlfriend? It was actually a little unclear. He knew that, until pretty recently, she had at least wanted to be. And that was what counted. The insight burned like acid as he sat there staring into the oil lamp. It was the fuel he usually ran on, collecting admirers who constantly confirmed his market value by wanting him. That he wasn't really interested in them was another thing. Peter Stavenius usually came, saw and conquered.

I'm not going to climb all over you – he suddenly remembered Vera's voice. Peter felt horribly empty and strangely relieved at the same time. He paid and pulled on his Italian wool coat. Outside, it had begun to snow. The snow fell gently in big, fuzzy flakes that appeared out of the darkness in the light of the streetlamps. He turned up his collar and climbed into the taxi he'd ordered.

He would go home to Stipend Street and at least make sure he passed his resit.

He had studied late into the night and didn't wake up until a pale daylight lit up his dorm room. Peter guessed that it was 11 o'clock as he pulled on his jeans and went to the bathroom to prepare himself for another day of studying.

'Alone in Siberia. Yippee!' he muttered at his dishevelled image in the mirror. But, as he sat on the toilet, he began to suspect that he wasn't as alone as he had thought. First it sounded as if there was someone out in the hall, then he heard a weak scratching and snapping from above. He looked up, but there was nothing there except for his ordinary bathroom ceiling with its single light, shower curtain rod and slightly moldy vent. He flushed and got up, pulling up his underwear but leaving his jeans around his ankles. He washed his hands and splashed cold water on his face. He made a half-hearted effort to fix his messy morning hair, but stopped abruptly, turned off the water and listened. The bizarre noise from the ceiling had started again, this time louder.

Peter took the mop that was leaning against the wall and pounded its long wooden handle on the ceiling a couple of times. The crackling accelerated and Peter stared in fascination. The noise was coming from the vent above the shower. He pounded probingly and systematically at various distances from the vent. Twisted like a mountain birch with his feet still locked together by his jeans, he ignored the uncomfortable position as he pounded again, staring bewitched towards the mysterious snapping. After a while, small, strange, grey flakes started falling out of the vent. *What the hell is that?*

When he unintentionally hit the round plastic edge of the vent, the whole thing came loose. The vent fell off, and with it came a grey ball of fur and hundreds of insects. Peter looked down into the bathtub. A disfigured rat lay completely still in a small but growing pool of blood. The six-legged bugs continued to rain down from the vent. Some landed in his hair, others on his bare skin. He dropped the mop and scrambled out of his room screaming. Rodents and bugs had never been favorites of Peter's, and now he just wanted to get as far away from the horror as possible.

Out in the hallway, a total stranger stared at him. Peter froze, feeling completely naked. He had been right; there *was* someone in the hall. He seemed to have come from Vera's room. After the first alarming moment, the man looked at him kindly, as Vera appeared at his side. It was then he saw the similarity. Prominent, dark – albeit greying – eyebrows, defined cheekbones and a careful softness. *Vera's father, of course!*

Sven-Erik Lundberg seemed to be quite a decent sort. He felt like the right person to ask. Peter took the shy, reluctant man into his room. Sven-Erik looked bashfully towards the messy desk and then inspected the bathroom.

'A mouse... and silverfish,' he confirmed. 'Not a small infestation, either. You'd better call someone.'

When Peter hung up the telephone with a sigh, Sven-Erik asked, 'Are they sending Anticimex?'

Peter nodded worriedly.

'Yes, well, of course, you can't stay here. Is there somewhere else here in town you can go?'

'No.' *Why does everything have to get so fucked up?* Peter pulled on a long-sleeved t-shirt and straightened up. He tried to sound unconcerned. 'It'll have to be a hotel.'

'But... surely that's unnecessary? Vera, can't he stay in your room?' It was clear that Vera did not appreciate her father's suggestion, but it didn't matter anyway. It wasn't an alternative. Peter shook his head.

'No, they say that it's probably the whole ventilation system. Nobody can stay in the dorm tonight.'

✳

Peter sat in the back seat of the Volvo. It was a strange experience. He had stumbled right into Vera's world, and the feeling of unreality got stronger when the cloud cover began to disperse from the south, and long, faint rays of winter sunshine appeared. A dozen or so miles west of town the landscape became hillier and fresh snow blanketed the forest, lakes and mountains. When the car came out into glades or passed a large ice-covered body of water, the world glittered magically in the sparse light. *Tavelsjö.* Peter was reminded of Carla's expensive bracelet.

This was unfamiliar territory, and he had never before felt so close to Vera. He was riding in the family car as if they were old friends. The car reversed into the drive of a wooden house from the 1970s on the outskirts of the village. The twilight created a background of pink and purple streaks against the darkening blue sky. When Peter opened the door to climb out of the car he heard Vera whisper something to Sven-Erik. It sounded like she

171

said, 'you should choose… ' Peter closed the door and suddenly felt like a foreign body, an unwanted fifth wheel. *He should choose… what? Should he choose to get rid of me?'*

There were lights on inside, but Peter felt no desire to go into the house that was Vera's home. Despite the fact that he had only been appreciative and positive towards her, for some reason Vera continued to be dismissive. *What have I actually done to her?* He felt the cold through the thin soles of his shoes, and regretted that he hadn't put up a stronger resistance to Sven-Erik's natural hospitality.

The other two remained in the car for a brief moment before Sven-Erik climbed out. He seemed amused, almost giggly, and when he was close to Peter, he said, 'Well, Peter! Things aren't always what they seem! Apparently, sometimes it is just a mass of silverfish!'

There was no mistaking the warmth in the man's eyes. He looked at Peter through the dusk, and briefly rested a friendly hand on his shoulder. Peter was surprised by the good feeling his host's little gesture aroused in him. He felt almost comforted, without having known that he needed comforting. *A gesture towards a person who is good enough. A competent person,* thought Peter. *Human kindness.*

His courage returned as he walked shivering through the crunchy new snow, carrying the few belongings he had brought with him. He went into the house where Vera had grown up.

As they stood in the hallway, Sven-Erik said that their current task was to get Vera's removal boxes out of the garage and to her dorm room in town. With a mischievous grin he told his astonished wife that he had enlisted an assistant to help with the lifting. Peter and Sven-Erik chatted pleasantly while they dug out the last of the boxes, which were inconveniently buried behind the summer tires, a snowmobile and numerous pairs of skis.

There was something about Sven-Erik that made Peter feel at ease. When the older man caught sight of an old, stained scarf, it prompted him to tell a story from Vera's childhood, and it didn't feel at all strange. Peter was being treated like a friend of the family and had just begun to feel like one when Sven-Erik disappeared into the house mumbling something about how Peter should give him a minute because he had forgotten himself and, of course, 'should put the coffee on'.

Perhaps he sent his daughter to the garage with the car keys, because Peter wasn't alone very long before she came out to him and the neatly arranged boxes. Vera had put on a thick, green sweater. Strands of hair had come loose from her braid, and they curled out haphazardly along the sides.

A quiet neutrality, a no-man's land, existed between them. He had noticed in the car that she was not wearing any rings on her left ring finger, and he guessed that the removal boxes had something to do with that.

An idea came into his head. He realized that it was childish – his sudden impulse was not so different from whatever it was that made him pull pretty Sara's hair in the second grade. He certainly couldn't say that he had done it to help protect against the cold when Vera opened the garage door on the winter darkness. Nor was it an attempt to break the embarrassing silence. He had years of practice enduring his parents' massive silences – they created a force-field that could wake the dead. More than anything else, it was an effort to recreate the cozy intimacy that had filled the fluorescent-lit garage only minutes before. He knew that he was taking a risk, but as she was opening the trunk of the car, he took the old scarf that Sven-Erik had found and wrapped it around his neck. There was a *conversation piece* if there ever was one! He waited silently. In the margin between light and darkness, they silently worked together packing the final boxes in the trunk of the Volvo.

When she had closed the car and garage doors and dried the mist from her glasses, she shot him a furtive glance. *She has green eyes!* Unusual, clear, dark-green eyes with lighter streaks farthest in. She spoke.

'Take that thing off. It's filthy.'

'It's blood,' said Peter.

'I know.'

'He told me what happened.'

'Oh, really?' she said guardedly. 'So let's hear Dad's version.'

Peter slowly took off the bloodstained scarf from the late 1980s and held it up like a piece of evidence.

'When you were little, you and your friends were out playing in the snow with a puppy named... Blockhead or something?'

'It was a Labrador, brown. He was called Dopey.'

'So, he got run over by a car...'

'A road grader.'

'A what?'

'Um, a... with a sharp edge, a snowplough.'

Christ, what a know-all! Peter smiled. He put the mint green, tightly stitched acrylic scarf back up on the storage shelf next to the wood stain and continued.

'Yeah, whatever. The other kids were scared and ran off. But you took off your scarf, made a tourniquet, put Dopey on the kick-sled and took him to the vet!'

She smiled inwardly a little and nodded. For a moment everything was calm and still. Pleasantly relaxed.

Then came the sound of shuffling steps from the house. Soon, Vera's grandfather Ivar filled the doorway. He wore slippers, baggy wool pants, braces and a plaid shirt. The big black-and-white cat followed him, rubbing itself on his legs. Suddenly, Vera made a peculiar noise, as if she herself had a cat inside her. The muscular animal stopped and looked at Vera. When she made the soft purring noise again, he answered with the exact same sound, and went over to her. She lifted the cat into her arms with a gentleness that touched Peter. She stood there in her fuzzy green sweater stroking the cat. Purring, the cat stretched upward and rubbed its cheek against Vera's jaw, below her ear. *And that hair that looks like she just got out of bed...*

Peter looked down at the floor and swallowed before he met Ivar's inquiring gaze. He tried to sound unmoved. 'Can she talk to cats?'

'Vi waal hoava na kaffi,' said the tall, slipper-clad man mildly.

What the heck kind of language is that? Icelandic? Ivar put his right arm firmly around Peter, who again mustered his courage to look at Vera.

174

She nodded towards the doorway. 'Grandpa was an impatient lumberjack. When his horse was worn out, he did the hauling himself, so you'd better go with him.'

Peter let himself be guided into the house by the surprisingly strong old man. He turned toward Vera and whispered, 'But what did he say?'

He thought he glimpsed a hint of a smile behind the cat when she answered, 'coffee time.'

There was coffee, home-baked coffee cake and several kinds of cookies. Vera and her father discussed healthcare, the threat of a strike, and how nurses were dissatisfied with their salaries. Peter felt that something was being left unspoken, landmines that one might unintentionally step on if the conversation became too freewheeling. He listened and watched; he wasn't unsociably silent, but his comments were politely brief and smooth. Sven-Erik's and Vera's disagreement continued.

'But if we let private companies provide healthcare then we'll end up like the USA. Only the rich can afford healthcare when they need it,' said Sven-Erik worriedly.

'But Daddy, you can have different healthcare providers and still have tax-financed insurance that covers everybody! Then the people who work in the healthcare system could earn more money, and we could use hospitals and clinics in smarter, more efficient ways, and patients would be able to choose...'

'And then only the rich would get the healthcare they need! The way it is now, with the regional government providing healthcare, everybody gets the same,' interrupted Sven-Erik.

Peter could tell by Vera's angry astonishment that her father didn't usually interrupt her like that. And that her anger resonated deeply inside her.

'What kind of argument is that? Even if American healthcare is expensive and exclusionary, that doesn't prove that Swedish healthcare is efficient and fair! Surely we can think of more than two ways to organize healthcare on this planet!'

Sven-Erik nodded and mumbled, 'No, you're right, it doesn't prove anything.'

'And you sit here saying "same healthcare!" Do you really

think that if I were an elite athlete, that I would have had to live with my knee like this since May? I mean, you can't really believe that, can you? They fly Zlatan Ibrahimovic up here when his knee ligaments are inflamed – for the sake of football! And when Mr Star Skier Elofsson pulls a muscle in his butt, they send the ambulance helicopter to get him.'

'Lela – they call 'em soft-tissue injuries,' emphasized Ivar as he tucked a sugar cube firmly between his dentures. This time Peter thought he understood what the old man said, *but Lela*?

A hint of a smile flashed across Vera's face as she looked up at her grandfather. She spoke to him with a broader dialect than usual, as if she had been infected.

'Yeah, yeah. I've got nothin' against Zlatan. Sure, I can wish him the best for his knees. An' Elof, he even pays tax in Sweden. I'm just sayin' it's not equal for everyone.'

She went on, looking directly at Sven-Erik. 'People like me, who limp around with a leg that they can't even straighten out completely, we don't even get put on the waiting list for treatment until more than six months after the injury!'

Sven-Erik looked worried. 'What?'

'And then you feel like a criminal. I called a man called Erland and begged... well, it was a woman who answered, and I...' She hesitated and glanced at Peter, but then continued. 'I broke down crying. But at least I got an appointment for an MRI, on Tuesday, in fact. As long as they don't choose that exact moment to go on strike.'

As Vera wiped away a tear from the corner of her eye, Sven-Erik leaned towards his daughter sympathetically. He hugged her clumsily and looked worriedly at her left leg.

'Oh, honey. Can't you straighten it out? I have noticed it hasn't healed, but why didn't you say anything?'

Vera shrugged her shoulders a little and wriggled out of her father's arms with an embarrassed glance at Peter. Peter felt like he shouldn't be there. Everyone was finished with the refreshments, so he had the perfect excuse. He got up and helped Gunilla clear the table. In the kitchen, all he could hear was the running water, clattering dishes, and Gunilla, who talked about

Vera: her nursing training, how good she was with old people and her happy marriage to Adam Henningsson, the apparently fantastic husband and successful surgeon.

By the time they were finished with the dishes the dining room was deserted.

'Where do you think they went, Peter? Do you think they went back out to the garage?' Gunilla took his arm confidentially and once again he found himself being dragged through the house, only this time he was being steered by a small, determined nurse's assistant rather than manoeuvred like a two-by-four. On the way Gunilla confided that, unfortunately, it seemed as if Vera had 'had a little falling out' with her husband. 'But of course,' she went on, 'they'll patch things up again, she and Adam. Because what God has joined together let no man put asunder.'

With these words of oath in his ears he was hit by an unmistakable garage odour mixed with another, indeterminable scent. Peter rounded the doorway to the hall that served as the family's laundry room seconds before Gunilla. The only thing he saw was Vera's eyes. She needed him. She appealed to him with a look of terror as she threw something behind his leg. His body reacted with lightning speed. It was a reflex directly connected to Vera, because he moved to catch it before he had time to formulate even the first letter of a reply. Her answer seemed equally involuntary and immediate; those dark green eyes glittered as if she liked what she saw, and a warm happiness filled Peter.

Holding something damp in his hand behind his jeans, he reluctantly and with careful self-control pulled himself out of this perfect moment and back into reality. In a daze, he became aware of the scene around him: Sven-Erik stood uncertainly in front of the laundry-room shelf, a strangely guilty look on his face. Directly inside the doorway was a large laundry basket. The other smell seemed to be emanating from it, the smell that wasn't fumes from oil or gas, but not laundry detergent either. Gunilla seemed unaware, as if she wasn't even in the same room. Taking control of the situation, Peter looked directly at Vera. The sparkle of appreciation that he was sure he had seen in her eyes was gone, but she still sought his help. This time he didn't follow her in a reflex action; rather, he was fully conscious of her wordless direction. Without Gunilla noticing anything, he balled up behind his back the thing Vera had thrown to him. They had made a connection. He knew exactly what Vera wanted him to do, and he turned gently towards Gunilla as he continued his efforts to distract her.

'Adam. Yes. I just hope I haven't caused any problems for you?'

Gunilla smiled politely at the guest whom fate and hundreds of *Lepsima saccarina*, better known as silverfish, had brought into their private sphere.

'No, no, it's fine! We'll just make up a bed downstairs.'

Gunilla and Sven-Erik went into the house and Peter saw the intoxicating energy in Vera's eyes transform into something that, sadly, looked like dull, humiliated gratitude. When she quietly passed just inches from him, he took a breath and controlled a strong impulse to touch her, to try to get her to stay. Alone in the room he looked at the balled-up thing he had been hiding. It was a rag stained with red splotches. The smell he hadn't been able to identify was cheap red wine.

He threw the rag on top of the wine-stained towel that was already in the laundry basket and followed the Lundberg family into the house.

Peter didn't know exactly what it was that did it. Was it their brave disagreement, which seemed to rest on a solid foundation of respect for the other's right to a different opinion? Was it their wordless co-operation in cleaning up the wine and, later, cooking dinner? Or perhaps it was how they played music together? After dinner, Sven-Erik and Vera had got out their guitars and begun to sing and play. Neither of them had a fantastic singing voice, but it sounded good; they played together extremely well.

Maybe it was the accumulation of all these things. Whatever it was, when evening came, Peter knew that today he had witnessed one of the closest relationships he had ever come across. And remarkably enough, it was between a grown daughter and her father.

At first it was just an observation, a fact that he hadn't evaluated one way or the other. Vera and her father were very close. Period. But then the uninvited feelings came along and destroyed his status as impartial observer. The first was a kind of reverent fascination: what a thing, to be so totally accepted, so obviously good in each other's eyes. This feeling soon transformed into a darker relative, jealousy in the face of the knowledge that Vera had grown up so completely *capable* in her father's eyes. Surely that was the source of Vera's integrity; it explained the natural dignity and authority she carried on her slight frame. *Maybe that's why she is an Elf?*

Yet Vera had not actually told her father before now about the problem she was having getting treatment for her knee. *So close but so alone?* Peter felt confused, like he had missed an important piece of the puzzle. And then, finally, the memory of the two partners' joint shame about the wine on the laundry-room floor. Perhaps a lifelong project to *hide-and-smooth-over?* The minefield he had sensed beneath the surface from the moment he had stepped into the house? A new feeling filled him then; it lacked contours, but was definitely neither admiration nor jealousy.

The sofa had been made up. Peter stood dressed for bed and looked around in the weakly lit family room. Something strange lay in the ashes of the fireplace, and it piqued his curiosity. He squatted down and carefully picked up the twisted white thing with the burned edge. He carefully unfolded the handmade cone, his heart beating as if he were doing something forbidden.

It was Vera as a bride. She looked very young, almost childish, and happy. She had a bouquet of summer flowers and stared artlessly and innocently directly into the camera, directly at Peter. With a sting of something unfamiliar he shifted his gaze to Adam Henningsson, the perfect husband, at least according to Gunilla. He stood there in his dark suit, a dark man with short hair, clean, sharp features and a proud bearing. *He looks good... and intelligent,* thought Peter reluctantly. *Only 32 and already in demand as a specialist!* Gunilla's proud voice echoed in his head. It was apparently something extremely unusual.

Suddenly the floor creaked behind him. Startled, he turned around. There was Ivar in his slippers and an old, brown striped terrycloth robe. The old man shuffled around in an amazingly quiet way. He looked kindly over Peter's shoulder at the fire-damaged photograph. Then he pointed carefully with his broad index finger and spoke softly.

'Spirited gal tha' Lela.'

It turned out that it wasn't so dangerous to be caught snooping in the ashes by Ivar, but Peter didn't want to be noticed by anyone else. He whispered back.

'Lela? You mean Vera, right?'

Ivar nodded.

'Lela said that 'bout herself when she was little, y' know. Yeah, too bad that *käarn hennarsh sku va se oherrans ojaäm.*'

Lela said it herself she was little? But what was too bad? 'What did you say?'

Ivar looked worriedly at him from under his bushy eyebrows. He moved his lumberjack's finger to the groom.

'Jå, n'Adam. I tro han had vy uti å sjåa ve nagger fruntimer.'

Slowly Peter recognized the Swedish in the broad, rural dialect. 'Ah! Her husband, something with the ladies?'

Ivar nodded sadly and began to go towards the stairs that led to the upper floor. Peter risked raising his voice a little, and Ivar stopped near the stairs.

'You mean that he, did he…? Was he unfaithful?'

'What?' whispered the big, brown-striped man.

Peter padded quickly over the creaking pine floor. He held up the photograph and repeated the question right into the old man's ear.

Speaking more clearly, Ivar said, 'Nothin' I know for sure. But something she said direct she come home. Somethin' hurt her bad.' He began climbing laboriously up the stairs, but turned around and worriedly finished his thought.

'An' her knee ain't good neither. She's real unlucky for now.'

Later that night Peter lay awake in the dark. Suddenly he sat up and got out of bed. He stubbed his toe on something, and it made him whimper. He continued towards the fireplace, groping in the dark on the mantelpiece. He accidentally knocked over a box of matches, and it landed with a rattle.

'Damn it!' he whispered to himself and pawed around on the floor.

Squatting, he found the box and took out a match. He lit it and directed the flame towards the fireplace. There was the damaged photograph! He picked it up and looked at her again. *Lela... Vera – what a beautiful name!* An unusual name for an unusual person. Then he was filled with another feeling.

'Real unlucky'?

Strangely depressed, Peter let the flames devour the wedding picture. In a few seconds it was nothing but ashes.

24

'Her name's Linda. She's really, really nice – and terribly upset!'

Vera looked at her father in indignation. Peter had just got out of their old Volvo, and Vera had an uninterrupted moment in the front seat with him. She sighed. *If anyone can afford to stay at a hotel a Stavenius can!* But, of course, it was just like her father to invite him to stay overnight with them while Anticimex came and gassed or sprayed or whatever they did... Sven-Erik didn't know anything about Peter's behavior, how difficult it had been, for example, to try to comfort the beautiful Asian with the long, glossy, black hair when she came to the dorm when Peter was out, distraught because he had cheated on her.

'Really? Otherwise, he seems like a decent young man,' said Sven-Erik and took an ice-scraper from the plastic pocket on the inside of the car door. 'But that was a hell of a thing, an unbelievable number of silverfish, I mean...'

'Are they called silverfish or night creepers?' wondered Vera.

True to his Västerbotten roots, her father couldn't resist making a pun. Giggling, he said that it almost seemed homeopathic, 'evil shall be driven out with evil – an unbelievable mass of *night creepers*, yes, that's what it was!'

That was one of Sven-Erik's unusual talents. However down she was, he managed to use his sudden flashes of humor to surprise her, enabling her to laugh and forget everything for a moment. She couldn't resist it this time, either. She giggled herself and added that something had probably gone wrong with the homeopathic concentration. Not even she thought that Peter's copious numbers of women could measure up to the plague of insects of biblical proportions that had invaded his home.

Evil shall be driven out... she thought again as her father got out of the car. Something overpowering in the words crept under her skin and pulled her down into a paralyzing memory. 'It was for your sake! I thought you liked this kind of stuff!' she had wanted to scream.

The first time she caught Adam surfing online pornography, her main reaction was one of surprise. He was so darned prudish, worse than she was, in fact. He wanted it to be pitch-black during their rare physical contact under the quilt on their double bed. Was he that curious? And what he was looking at could hardly be called soft porn. When she discovered him, at two in the morning, looking at a picture of a girl not wholly unlike herself – albeit studiously posed and in completely different clothes than she usually wore – he bombarded her with what she thought were unnecessary, exaggerated excuses.

That was the night before the first Sunday in Advent 2005, and Vera had thought about it for a week. She had read in a relationship column that couples that had been married for seven years had the best sex, and she realized that that would definitely not be true of Adam and her, unless somebody did something radical. That was how it felt, too, radical, when she went into town and bought clothes like those the woman on the screen had been wearing. The night before the second Sunday in Advent she showered in a mood of strange nervousness, then put on the small, uncomfortable pieces of fabric with metal studs on the bodice, the salmon-pink corset with thin black lace and little matching panties, and the garter belt and stay-up nylon stockings. She felt like she was in costume and painfully far beyond her comfort zone, but what wouldn't one do for one's husband, in the hope of having at least a half-normal seventh year? She lay down on the bed and then sat up again, not really knowing what she should do. Finally, she gathered all her courage and called out, 'Adam. Come!'

'What is it?' came the reply from the office on the other side of the apartment.

'I have a surprise for you.'

Oh, God! She pulled herself out of the memory, dried her eyes and climbed out of the car into the quiet, winter darkness.

✖

Vera braced herself when Peter helped her pack the detritus of her life, which her dad had brought home from the apartment in Stockholm. When Ludde came, she felt like she needed to hide her face in the comforting softness of his fur. Ivar must have noticed her tear-filled eyes, because he devoted his energy to getting the guest to follow him into the house for coffee. 'Sometimes you need to be left in peace with your sadness,' as he had said when she had tried, but failed, to tell him what had happened when she came home.

She looked gratefully at her big grandfather as he dragged Peter away, and she wanted to turn off the ceiling light in order to collect herself a little, alone with the cat. It was when she fumbled for the light switch behind the storage shelf, her face buried in the cat's fur, that she accidentally knocked something over. She managed to prevent it from breaking by thrusting out her foot and catching it at the last minute. Pain radiated from her ankle, which had taken most of the weight of the falling object. She gently released the cat, which hadn't appreciated the jerky movement, and saw the foreboding sign. A large spot of red wine on the laundry room floor.

Here they come. The consequences. Vera put the corkless wine bottle back on the shelf. She saw her last few months through Gunilla's worried, darting eyes. Injured abroad under dangerous circumstances, a separation and moving house, leaving her previous practical career path in favor of something abstract and woolly. And very little in the way of explanation. Because it would have been even harder for Gunilla to accept the explanations.

The hard fluorescent light revealed everything, and nothing could have felt darker.

'Veera? What are you doing? The coffee is getting cold!' Gunilla chirped in her artificial, we-have-company voice.

Vera felt a tingling in her whole body. She would have to deal with this later. She turned off the light and closed the door behind her.

After coffee she had a chance to discreetly tell her father what had happened. Everything else had to be put on hold while they performed the familiar routine. They rose from the table in silence.

Faced with the puddle in the laundry room, her father only said: 'Let's leave it alone. It'll be okay.'

He took a dirty towel out of the laundry basket and started to wipe up the wine. The message was familiar. They would be the control rods and dive down into the nuclear reactor together. They would do the absorbing in order to prevent an uncontrollable reaction, an explosion of poisonous radioactivity. She took a rag from the shelf and helped him. It felt comfortable and familiar, but nonetheless untenable in a way that Vera didn't recognize.

'But is this really...?' She regretted it as soon as the whisper crossed her lips. She felt a strange relief when her foolhardiness was interrupted by Gunilla's voice from inside the house. 'Of course, we still hope they will patch things up, she and Adam.'

The animated Gunilla was undoubtedly on her way to the garage. Vera blushed with shame. Why was she telling Peter Stavenius about Adam? What would she do next? Now that they had a complete stranger visiting, perhaps they should take the opportunity to bring him out to the laundry room to inspect some dirty laundry? Her thoughts were suddenly interrupted by the anxious realization of the immediate problem facing them.

Sven-Erik stood up as if he had been caught doing something shameful and skilfully threw the wine-stained towel into the laundry basket by the door. Peter appeared first. Vera knew that the rag she held in her hand risked shattering Gunilla's illusion that no-one had discovered her secrets, something that would have unforeseeable consequences. She had no choice. She threw caution to the wind and sought eye contact: *Help me!*

In the space of a couple of dizzying seconds Peter had smoothly caught both the telepathic instructions and the guiltily thrown rag. Unbelievably in tune with the situation, he managed to both hide the wine-stained cloth from Gunilla and politely engage in small talk with the simmering volcano. During their secret transaction, they were alone in the universe, it was only Vera and Peter engaged in a moment's dance, perfectly synchronized as if they were one.

Afterwards she felt sick from the tension. The whole incident left her with an unwelcome debt of gratitude that she didn't know how to deal with. His surprising and beautiful perceptiveness would remain forever etched into her memory, yet it was soon overpowered by her irritation at his way of flicking his posh-boy hair and at the ugly signet ring that reminded her of how many times she had seen that hand on the bodies of different women.

They had been called to the department even though it was only 4 January, and Vera was filled with expectation. She knew that she had done a thorough job on her essay. She may not have been a car mechanic who also happened to be a student of the finer points of financial markets, but she was an aid worker with a burning interest in how the distribution of resources in the world affected people's health and welfare. She also thought that economists paid way too little attention to human rights, health and a life with dignity for everybody. It was mystifying. Surely these achievements were the whole point of economic development? Development lifts entire nations out of poverty, wasn't that what they usually said, the experts?

Cissi and Vera had to wait outside Sturesson's door, because the traffic-light sign next to his door glowed red beside the word 'busy'. Cissi asked quietly, 'So, how was Christmas?'

'Well, you know. Like it usually is.' Vera squirmed. What should she say? *The worst Christmas I've ever had. Thanks for asking.*

'What about you? How was yours?' she hurried to ask.

'Yes, nice. A bit too much good food, though,' smiled Cissi as she lightly patted her hips. 'And Christmas presents are really hard. How are you supposed to know what adults need and want but haven't yet bought for themselves?'

I actually got good Christmas presents this year. Vera had asked for a massage from Annika, the woman Cissi had recommended, and her father had given her a coupon for five treatments. Gunilla had given her a new bathing suit, because the old one was see-through from all the chlorine. It fitted really well, even if tomato red wasn't the color she would have chosen for herself. And the gift that warmed her heart even more – the tiny jar of Arctic raspberry jam from Ivar. She had a grandfather who understood more than one might guess – that much was clear.

She smiled inwardly, lost in memories of picking Arctic raspberries as a child. The warmth of high summer and secret paths. The small, ruby-red treasures, well hidden under the high grass near the riverbank. The scent of sweetness that could only develop under northern summer skies. And the walks home, her little fist in her grandfather's giant one, proudly comparing the priceless cups of berries they had managed to find. Ivar hadn't said anything when he carefully handed her the little Christmas present, but as soon as she opened it she understood what he meant: *Rubus arcticus* – so good that it heals whatever's broken.

They heard a metallic noise and the traffic-light sign switched to green. Vera nervously took a deep breath and followed Cissi into the Professor's room.

What happened next was very strange. Sturesson and Sparre were sitting in there with Peter, and they looked inscrutable. When the women entered the room, Sturesson rose hastily and gave them the drafts they had turned in before Christmas. Vera and Cissi were told that a problem had arisen with the project, and that they should go out, read the comments on their papers, and wait for further information.

Cissi left her paper on the table in the staff canteen and went to the bathroom. Left alone, Vera looked out at the panoramic view of the snow-covered campus. The sun hung low in the sky, spreading long rays of weak sunshine. Vera read the short comments on her chapter. Then she looked up and stared at a corner of the large window that was decorated with hoarfrost. Beautiful crystals that were a reminder that even life-threatening cold is not devoid of beauty. *Death's beauty*, thought Vera and shivered.

Cissi and Peter appeared.

'There are so many respected scholars involved,' he said. 'So now there isn't enough room for three student chapters. There's

187

going to be one instead. After we finish our chapters they will decide which one to include. We write, they pick.'

'So two of us are going to do all this work for nothing?' asked Vera.

He nodded, unmoved. 'Yes, that's how it's going to be.'

After a long silence, Vera turned to Cissi. 'You and I may as well give up now, in other words.'

Cissi looked uncertainly at her draft, which was still unopened on the table. 'What makes you say that?'

'But Cissi! Don't you get it?'

'Well, I do have some faith in my own education.'

Vera got up and put her right hand on Peter's shoulder. 'Call yourself a man?'

A slight shiver passed through Peter, as though he thought he was supposed to answer the question, but Vera was looking at Cissi.

'No? Pity. But perhaps you have a world-famous father and an uncle who are best friends with the research council?'

Her sense of discipline directed Vera towards the door. *That's enough.* Driven by something new and black, something that was powerful enough to overcome her well-developed self-control, she paused in the doorway and spat out, 'But two million and a peach-fuzz mustache doesn't mean that you have anything sensible to say!'

Vera left. She was cold, but in her indignation, she refused to acknowledge that warmth that her hand now missed. Her fears had been justified. It had probably never been a way forward. *But now what? What will happen with the money? Am I going to have to move?*

✖

Peter Stavenius was like a sharp stone in a shoe that was too small – he invaded her already painfully limited space. The task that had given Vera the energy to get up in the morning was being threatened, as was her livelihood, the income that allowed her to maintain her own home, one that wasn't Adam's or Gunilla's.

188

If she were the type that could be driven to a nervous breakdown, surely this was when it would happen? *If I have the volcano gene, I am going to lose my self-control and destroy everything in my path.* A horrifying thought flared up inside her. She sat down, forced herself to take a tentative breath and tried to come to her senses. *I will never be like my mother. I would rather die.*

Half an hour later, Vera stood in the dorm kitchen beating eggs and water for an omelet. She sliced a couple of potatoes and a tomato to go in it. She thought about the day's depressing decision and realized to her shame that she had overreacted in the staffroom. Cissi's work still might be chosen for the project, even if her own had no chance. Once again, she had been mean to Cissi completely without reason. She promised herself that she would try to repair the damage the next time she saw her. That's if they ever saw each other again… maybe it was all over.

Peter came into the kitchen. Without a word he bent down and took the best frying pan out of the cabinet. She sighed as she realized that she would have to use the bad one; the one with the Teflon surface shredded like terrycloth thanks to the careless use of metal cooking utensils. Peter whistled softly as he took an expensive pepper steak out of the refrigerator. He turned on the stove, and she saw out of the corner of her eye that he was looking right at her, just a couple of inches from her left side.

'What the hell was your problem today?'

'What do you mean, "what was my problem"?' She turned so that she was looking directly at him, and she resisted the impulse to take a step back.

'Why did you give up so fast? It's a competition. So what?'

Vera didn't answer, but instead put the scratched frying pan on the burner next to Peter's steak. She turned the burner up to six as he continued.

'And what did you mean when you accused me of having nothing sensible to say? Sturesson thinks I can contribute, actually, given my background.'

He sounded strangely stressed, pugnacious. As if she didn't believe that they valued his participation in the project. She

189

– the one who wasn't even a car mechanic – had to make do with question marks in the margins. *In order to secure long-term welfare development we need an upward revaluation of maintenance, care work, childcare and education*, she had written. Sturesson had responded with red question marks. The comment at the bottom of the last page was, *'Normative texts like this cannot be published.'* The only question left was who they would prioritize: the flashy, moneyed heir to a successful export firm or their own graduate student?

'What makes you think you're more suited than Cissi to write about welfare? She's been doing research for years, and you come along, still wet behind the ears...'

Peter put down the spatula in irritation and interrupted her. 'What is it with this peach-fuzz mustache crap?'

'Honestly, you really don't seem all that interested. Right? I mean, the thing you handed in before Christmas?' She put a generous dollop of butter in the pan to keep her dinner from sticking to the ruined Teflon and poured in the eggs. When she thought of it, she turned back towards him. 'It's your father who wants you to, isn't it? "Stockholm School of Economics' finest graduating class"?'

Peter stood in silence. Vera wiggled the frying pan and dropped in the leftovers from last night's dinner. She poked the edges of the omelet a little with the spatula. *If the famous Great Escape Stavenius wants his son in a fancy Swedish Research Council project, then of course they would arrange it. And young Mr Biggest-Best-Handsomest would deliver a shopping list.*

'Your whole self is a wandering peach-fuzz,' she muttered.

'What about you? You just chicken out!' Now he wasn't his usual, teasing self. He raised his voice in anger. 'If you're so fucking superior then go ahead and beat me!'

Vera suddenly wondered whether Peter was even aware of the tailwind that he had flown in his whole life. *How can he believe that everybody has an equal chance?*

'You don't know what you're talking about,' she said doggedly.

The only sound in the thick silence that followed was the

190

sizzling of the food. Vera turned away, thinking that they had finished talking. But he caught her against the refrigerator. He slapped his palms loudly against the door, one on each side of her head. He leaned forward and looked her in the eyes.

'Why are you just quitting?'

Vera struggled to remain calm.

'When you grow up you will also understand that you have to know when it is time to give up.'

Peter's turquoise-blue eyes glittered hard and implacable. 'Right. Let's all grow up and hide wine-stained towels so that mother can keep on drinking in secret!'

In that instant, Vera lost all ability to hide her emotions. She caught a glimpse of what looked like regret in Peter's expression, which until that moment had been completely stone-faced, but that just made things worse. She saw that he saw, and she felt shame at the fact that she had revealed her miserable weakness to him. She fled to her room. Blinded by tears, she ran right into Matt, who was just on his way into the kitchen. And this humiliating limping! She wanted nothing more than to pull herself free and run away from everything. But she couldn't run, no matter how hard she tried.

Tuesday, January 8. They would finally do an MRI and find out that her knee could not heal on its own. She clung to the thought that she would finally get help.

25

If Peter had imagined that Sandra might turn him down when he tried to open up and be serious for the first time in his life, then he would never have made the effort. But what was done was done, and it left Peter with a new, unpleasant feeling. Rejected. Incompetent. *Not serious. Not going places.* But how the hell was he supposed to be going places when there were no particular places to go? He tended to think he was fine where he was.

Peter's highly polished self-confidence had become a bit tarnished, so it was comfortingly flattering when Sturesson called and asked him to come to a meeting. They were going to talk about the project. Peter ironed his expensive new shirt, the one that brought out the color of his eyes, and put on his formal Boss trousers. He put a little wax on his hair and looked at himself in the mirror. He would have been at home in any meeting, anywhere, with the richest one per cent.

Look like someone who knows what they're doing, in any case. Peter had not been very old the first time his father had said this to him, adding 'because people buy it'. A bit like the guys in *The Game*: How to get a girl to think that you are soul mates in 30 minutes. It didn't matter that it wasn't true. *The show must go on.*

The department was empty on this first Monday after New Year. But they sat waiting for him in Sturesson's office, the Professor himself and Professor Sparre. The older men rose when he came in, and they shook hands.

'How's your chapter going?' asked Sturesson, as he crossed one trousered leg over the other.

'Well, I've chatted a bit with my uncle…'

'Ernst Stavenius?' Respect shone in Sparre's deep-set eyes.

'Right. And I thought it would be interesting to look a little closer at the finance industry.'

'Fantastic idea!' Sturesson sounded relieved and looked at his colleague.

'Yes, absolutely. The finance industry as the engine of growth, and with you as author. I mean, a young guy, up and coming. It will be excellent.' Sparre nodded happily in Sturesson's direction. The other man consulted his watch.

'We better let the girls in now.'

Sturesson pushed a button next to his desk and after a noise that Peter interpreted as a warning sound, the door opened. Cissi and Vera came in. Peter sat up straight. He knew that he looked good. Vera did too. She was wearing a sand-colored blouse and her long, shiny hair was pulled up into a high ponytail. She stood there, with her small elfin ears sticking out, just a foot away. Peter stood up and looked around the room for more chairs. There were none. In the meantime, Sturesson had already managed to speak with them, give them some papers and send them on their way again.

Sparre turned towards Sturesson. 'Right, where were we? Yes, I was going to say... It fits. A chapter on the supply of capital and growth fits really well. And it does the job. I mean, according to the preliminary outline we drafted. That decides it, I'd say.'

'Huh? What?' Peter was still standing. *Why... what is going on?*

'Yes, it's good that you are writing about the finance sector.' Sturesson motioned for Peter to sit down again. He sounded oddly distracted and spoke carefully, searching for words.

'But I have some... maybe... unfortunate news.'

The whole thing was strange. When Peter went to look for 'the girls', he wondered why Sturesson and Sparre hadn't told them that they had changed their mind. Instead of three chapters from their group, only one was going to be published. In other words, it had become a competition. Start, finish, judge's decision, victor.

He found them in the deserted staff canteen and dutifully gave them the message. Cissi seemed to take it pretty calmly, but Vera hit the roof. And in the middle of her outburst – before he understood that she was being ironic and strange – she put her hand on his shoulder and asked if he called himself a man. It felt like half of his brain had stopped working. He stood there in confusion, in a haze of possibilities. Nervous, but fully prepared to lifted his gaze to hers: *Yes, I am a man. I want...*

But Vera continued to talk about something completely different. She claimed that 'nothing sensible' would be said, and when the words peach-fuzz mustache contemptuously crossed her distracting lips, his humiliation knew no bounds. His enchanted hope turned to disappointment and anger. What the hell did she mean? And where was his survival instinct? His concentrated focus on the present and his opponent's movements? His state of readiness for absorbing punches and kicks?

He took comfort in the fact that Cissi didn't seem to have noticed the slaughter that had just taken place. When Vera left, Cissi just shook her head in disappointment and said, 'when did she get so cynical?'

'What? What are you talking about?' said Peter's mouth, without any help from his brain.

'Yeah, well, it is disappointing news. And maybe that's what will happen. Maybe it will be only one chapter from us, and maybe it won't be hers. But before we know more... She just quits. Gives up. Folds.'

✖

There's no fucking way it was for my father!

In the middle of the fight in the dorm kitchen his blood boiled in anger because of what he couldn't say. Vera claimed that he was part of the project because he was 'daddy's little golden boy', and she said that damned peach-fuzz mustache thing again! Just because he didn't have the world's thickest facial hair. If she thought that was the sign of true manhood, well, that was harsh.

Anger powered his revenge. He knew things about her that he didn't intend to let her get away with, so she ought to drop the 'I'm so grown-up' crap. He knew that it was match point before he even said it.

194

'Right. Let's all grow up and hide wine-stained towels so that mother can keep on drinking in secret!'

He had expected to feel triumph. But when her face fell in despair and she limped away, he felt like a major shit. *An Incompetent, Unserious, Major Shit.* And then it got even worse. When Matt made to hug Vera in the kitchen doorway, he tried to get her to look at him. Eyes full of tears, she fended him off and disappeared. Matt looked accusingly at him.

'What the fuck, Pete? What's happening here?'

Peter stood paralyzed as Matt rescued two smoky frying pans from the stove and tried to turn up the sluggish fan. The Englishman then asked if the eggs were Vera's. He took out a plate and carefully picked at the unburnt top half of the omelet to loosen it from the pan. *She really isn't any good at cooking*, thought Peter passively through the cooking fumes.

Matt poured a glass of milk and got a tomato from his shelf in the refrigerator. He put it on the plate with the destroyed omelet and grabbed a fork and knife.

'What are you doing?'

'She was going to eat, wasn't she?' He stared harshly at Peter, who was standing next to his burnt pepper steak. 'That probably means she's hungry, don't you think?'

The Englishman took the food and went off to Vera's room.

26

When you try your best, but you don't succeed
When you get what you want, but not what you need
When you feel so tired, but you can't sleep
Stuck in reverse

And the tears come streaming down your face
When you lose something that you can't replace
When you love someone, but it goes to waste
Could it be worse?

Coldplay, 'Fix You', 2006

Vera sat at the dining table with Sven-Erik and Gunilla. They had just finished dinner. On the wall next to the table hung the large, framed wedding photograph that had previously been hidden among the removal boxes in the garage. Vera nodded uncomfortably at the enlargement from that other time. 'Why did you hang that up?'

'Well, you two are so lovely, and so well suited to each other. And Eva has called and said that he is completely crushed, that he'll do whatever it takes to get you to come back.' Gunilla managed to sound reproachful, despite her sympathetic, worried expression. *The way you look when talking to someone who doesn't understand what's for her own good.*

Sven-Erik's voice interrupted the tense silence.

'So, how's it going with your project?'

Vera didn't answer. She looked down. Her parents waited attentively.

'I don't think I'll finish it,' she finally admitted.

'But why not? Isn't it really important to you?' Sven-Erik sounded worried.

'Yes. But it's over. There's no point doing any more. Just a waste.' *Meaningless.*

Gunilla turned to her husband as if she were defending her daughter against an attack.

'Exactly. There's no point in too much education. That's what I've been saying the whole time!'

Vera sensed that Gunilla thought she was consoling her daughter.

'That you aren't one of those... university people isn't anything to feel sad about. You know what you're good at!' Gunilla tried to give Vera a friendly hug, but Vera pulled free and stood up forcefully. Sven-Erik reached out to her, but it was too late. With tears in her eyes, Vera screamed at her mother, propelled by years of repressed rage.

'I am not like you, Mother! I want other things, don't you get it?'

Pale, Sven-Erik rose from the table and tried to stop his daughter. Vera turned towards him. 'I can't deal with this sick game any more! "Don't make Mother sad." Well, what about me? What about when I'm sad?'

Sven-Erik and Vera stared at each other across an abyss of sorrow.

'Do you have to hide in the garage and booze it up in order to count around here?'

It was as if a bomb had exploded on the table. Gunilla covered her mouth as if she had been the one to utter the Unmentionable. Sven-Erik looked blankly at Vera as she turned to go. Out.

Father and daughter travelled through the darkness towards town and the student accommodation block. Vera sat staring out of the window almost the whole way; the only sounds were the snow tires against the road and the windshield wipers' intermittent rhythm.

'You know that dwarf guarding the line of injured people that you dreamed about?' wondered Sven-Erik suddenly. 'What kind of hat did you say he was wearing?'

Vera dried a tear that had stolen down her cheek and looked at him in confusion. She didn't even remember having told him about the dream.

'Was it perhaps one of those, what are they called...?' With his eyes fixed on what little world was visible in the glow of the headlights, he used his right hand to trace a rhombus above his head until he recalled the word.

'Mitre! It's called a mitre.'

Her father's question slowly worked its way into Vera's tired head. When she realized what he meant, a wan smile passed over her face. But tonight he was not just playing with words as usual; she understood what he was communicating. He could change his mind. The old, die-hard Social Democrat could actually come to see that perhaps he had trusted too much in the county government's decisions. If there is only One True Authority and that Pope decides not to help you, well, then you're helpless. There is nothing you can do. *Maybe that's why Daddy thinks everyone can change, adopt new ways of thinking and test new things? Because he can?*

They arrived in Ålidhem. Lights shone warmly out into the winter evening from a few of the dorm rooms. Sven-Erik wiped a new, untamed tear from his daughter's cheek. With a soft whimper, she suddenly broke the silence she had held for all those miles.

'Damn it! She took malicious pleasure in it!'

Her father looked at her in disappointment.

'But Vera, just because things are hard for you right now...'

'"You can't handle it! I was right!"' Vera mimicked angrily.

'Why did you say it? Why did you bring up her... problem?'

Vera guessed what he was about to say and braced herself. Her father found it hard to be critical, but he sighed in exhaustion and continued.

'Just because things are difficult for you right now doesn't mean you should go after your mother like that. Surely it was unnecessary? You know there is nothing to be gained from it.'

Vera looked at her father. They had reached it: the boundary beyond which her father would never change. And this time it felt like a separation. They didn't hug before she climbed out of the car. There was no way over the abyss.

She had never felt so alone.

On Monday 7 January the nurses went on strike. On TV, the union representative said that the strike posed no threat to anybody's life, because emergency healthcare was unaffected. Nonetheless, the strike would have an impact. Vera felt a strange mix of sympathy for her colleagues' demands and dread about her own situation. There was only one thing to do: find out the facts. In her shaking left hand, Vera held the precious letter confirming her appointment for an MRI, evidence of her reprieve on Tuesday. After a long wait on the telephone, Radiology connected her to Orthopedics. They told her that the chief physician had decided that Vera's knee 'was not to be considered an emergency'. Tuesday's MRI was therefore 'postponed indefinitely'.

'Unfortunately.' That hellishly autocratic word.

It was so far past midnight that she dared not look at the clock. She connected the headphones to her mobile and listened to the music that usually relaxed her so she could sleep. But not tonight. The room was dominated by two dismal stacks of unpacked boxes that didn't fit in the hall. She had planned to take care of them, to unpack them and sort things out. But now everything was up in the air. Would she even be able to afford to stay in the dorm in the spring?

She thought about her life, how different it had been just a year ago. She had been healthy and strong, buoyed by the certainty that she was doing something meaningful abroad, filled with happiness that she could help. She had been home over Christmas, to refuel herself with a Swedish standard of living and love and support from her husband. She had thought that their time apart was only temporary. She remembered that Adam had once again talked about their trying to have a baby, and that she had said she still wasn't ready. In the past, she had thought that her desire to wait was because she wanted to do something for the wider world before a child took over and demanded most of her time for many years. It was brutally clear to her now that her hesitation had also been due to the fact that the seventh year of marriage hadn't been as she'd hoped, despite her brave efforts. On the contrary, things had got worse. When Adam had seen her in the awful salmon-pink thing with black lace, he had frozen and stared at her as if she were something evil and foreign. Humiliated, she had covered herself, her mind full of despairing questions. *I thought you liked this kind of thing? Why else do you sneak around at night looking at it?* Tears welled in her eyes as she remembered how he had tried to smooth over the disaster. 'Vera, you are always so beautiful. But you know I don't like surprises.'

Through her headphones, she heard Coldplay's lyrics about sorrow, sleeplessness and loss, and she couldn't stop her tears. She turned off the music. Her leg and back ached with stiffness and pain. She had also lost hope that massage would help. She had visited Annika, who had confirmed that there were large knots in her muscles. Yet when she pressed on them, the pain was so sharp that Vera felt like it might tear her apart. She thought that she should try to get her money back for the remaining sessions her father had bought her, because what was the point of exposing herself to even more pain?

Inside her body, at the center spot right in front of her spine, was the place where her antenna had once glowed with joy and purpose. Now that place felt more like a tightly knotted rag dripping with tears. She struggled up and opened the window next to the desk. She wrapped herself up in her quilt and rested her aching body against the table. She realized that she had been thinking a lot about fate and death recently. Imagine if she hadn't jumped out of the window in Colombia...

She remembered the trauma psychologist's words: *Misfortunes are a natural part of life and psychological stability is measured in one's ability to deal with them.* Right. Okay. But enough was enough. Now she had been reduced to a lonely fall leaf in a raging storm, helplessly blown around by forces she could not control. *Time does not heal all wounds!*

She looked down at the cycle track outside the house and thought about the God of her childhood. 'God never subjects us to more than we can bear.' It felt almost arrogant to pray, but she could no longer afford humility and she capitulated completely.

God, if you exist, hear me now. It isn't true! I can't bear what you've subjected me to! I can't do it! So... whatever! She leaned out of the window and looked up at the dark night sky. *If you want me to die, I will.* A distinct noise came from inside the room. Shivering, she pulled herself back in and looked at the clock: 3.34am.

Is someone knocking? At this time of night?

27

If you never try, You'll never know
Just what you're worth

Lights will guide you home
And ignite your bones
I will try to fix you

Coldplay, 'Fix You', 2006

He is in a foggy, dense forest. He follows a flirtatious blonde who laughingly drags him off to a solitary cabin. He experiences a familiar feeling of expectation as, somewhat tipsy, they try all her keys before finally getting in. Once inside, the woman strips off all the items of clothing that are in the way; his too. And they have sex. Sloppy, automatic sex. And they both come.

Suddenly, the mood changes; it gets darker and colder. The woman is Jeanette. Her eyes are hard and relentless as she gets dressed and leaves, locking the door behind her. With a growing sense that he has been lured into a trap, he looks through the dirty window and sees Jeanette take the cabin key from her big key ring and throw it with all her strength right out into the fog. As he watches, her silhouette takes on a new form – she is hugely pregnant and walking towards her waiting husband. The man takes her hand and they walk towards the setting sun. Soon there are three of them; far away on the horizon they are walking with a small child between them.

The cold fog forces its way into the cabin, into the room, into his body. Dusk falls and Peter tries everything; he pulls on the door, pounds on the window, yells, pleads. Nothing happens. Then he realizes what can save him: doesn't he have insurance?

He fumbles for his clothes and finds a note with a telephone number written in big, green numbers. And there is a telephone! With shaking, ice-cold hands he dials the number.

'My name is Peter Stavenius. I am calling about key insurance...'

'Yes, I know. But it doesn't apply in cases of misuse,' says an unfamiliar male voice with cold politeness.

'He's not a good man. Not a good man,' echoes Solveig's worried voice in the background before the line is broken.

Peter woke drenched in sweat, fear flooding through his body. He saw the light from the street lamp outside filtering into his room through the Venetian blind. It was only a dream. Just another hellish dream. The feeling of being doomed to waste the rest of his life locked inside an abandoned house in the fog was so strong that he had to force himself to breathe normally. He looked at the clock and paced around his little room restlessly. *It was only a dream.* But still. He couldn't shake off the feeling of being imprisoned while real life went on outside, out where he couldn't reach. And the worst part of it gripped his diaphragm like a hard, cold hand. He had gone along with it; he had done it himself, willingly.

This year, Birgitta, Göran and Sofia were spending Twelfth Night on the ferry to Finland, so the family's own distinctive traditions for taking down the Christmas tree were postponed until his mother's birthday on Tuesday. Vicky was with her boyfriend, and hanging out with his father and Carla seemed unthinkable – there was no place for a grown son in his father's life. His friends had not come back and the dorm was empty and deserted.

Peter felt alone. Not alone in the sense of being pleasantly unencumbered. This was a strangely disconnected and depressing aloneness. He had nobody. He had no place of his own, other than a few square meters he rented from the local housing authority. After a meagre breakfast, he sat down in front of the computer and played an online game for a while. He managed to waste a couple of hours, uplifted by the brief shouts of the others in cyberspace who were fighting on his team. But the emptiness forced its way in inexorably, like the cold fog in the dream, and Peter could not sit still. He got dressed and went out into the crunchy snow.

It got lighter as he passed the pond by the hospital. An inflow of warm water from somewhere had kept a small part of the pond steaming and free of ice. Some mallards that had been resting indolently, heads tucked into their shiny feathers, swam towards him hopefully, and a couple even ventured out of the water, leaving perfect web-footed tracks in the new snow. Peter caught himself wishing that he had brought along a little dry bread from the kitchen.

Fuck! I've become an old man! If he looked at his reflection in the water, would he see the decrepit face of an old person who had wasted his life? Was it only the ending that remained – game over, old boy? *Misuse.*

He walked up onto the small wooden bridge and looked anxiously into the water. A billowing, bulging surface around the mallards reflected brief glimpses of Peter. Based on them, he looked like he always did, albeit a little sad and red-nosed. But he didn't feel like he usually did. *Not a good man?*

He had gone outside without a plan. But he suddenly knew where he was going. He took a left towards Sofiehem neighborhood, and then went through the tunnel under the Blue Road and past the railroad construction site. He walked on through Öbacka Park along the river towards town. The winter sun emitted pale yellow rays from the other side of the Umeå River. On the shiny water, dull ice floes glided majestically towards the sea, as quietly and relentlessly as time. He stopped and watched the unique seconds gliding past him – fragile, beautiful and impressive. *Time flows.* He shivered and walked further along the river. He passed others along the way: a pair of lovers, a succession of dog owners, families with children, joggers, and an unhurried man with a wheeled walking frame who was emerging from the cold silence of the garden by the café boats. Peter slowed down and exchanged a meaningful look with the old man.

How have you lived your life? Are you satisfied?

The man, who looked to be about 50 years ahead of Peter,

calmly returned Peter's gaze as he gingerly began walking. The message he seemed to be communicating was, *Yes, I am satisfied.* Peter nodded his head slightly and gave a small smile. The man smiled back. Then they both continued on their way through the crunching snow in the beautiful blue light of the sadly short midwinter day.

Well-lived. Good living.

When he walked through Bridge Park, ignoring the sign that said the stairs were closed due to ice, he suddenly felt that his destination might not be such a good idea after all. What should he do? Would she even be home? After all, it was Twelfth Night. He went around the building complex until he came to the reception area.

He asked if Solveig was home. *I hope she thinks I'm a relative, maybe a grandson?*

'Which Solveig? We have three.'

Her last name? Damn! Bang goes that illusion.

'She lives down there. Building D. On this floor, I think.'

'Oh, okay, Marklund. Yes, as far as I know she is home.'

Well, at least they let me in.

He knocked with a combination of nervousness and hunger wrestling in his stomach. But Solveig recognized him and was happy to see him. After a calm conversation about the weather, the season and health, Solveig suggested they go out and eat.

'It will be difficult to maneuver the wheelchair through the snow,' said Solveig anxiously as they came out through the eastern door, the one closest to town.

'No problem.' Peter didn't mind a little physical exertion. Besides, he had seen the snowplough, so he thought that the cycle paths into town were probably cleared by now.

Even before she chose the Chinese restaurant, Peter knew that Solveig didn't fit his picture of a typical old person. Exuberantly happy, she talked about all kinds of things – types and cuts of cloth, travel and culinary experiences. After they had eaten, full and happy after spring rolls, Peking soup and chicken with cashew nuts, she held his gaze for a long time.

'I completely forgot… How are you?'

'Things are okay…' But he couldn't manage to raise his eyes from the placemat with the Chinese motif.

'Has something happened?'

'No…well, not really. But I just feel… I have started having such hellish dreams. And I feel like something is wrong.'

'Is something wrong?'

'I'm usually… I mean, someone said that I don't have any direction, that I am not going places.'

'Is that necessarily a bad thing?' wondered Solveig kindly.

'No, but, I feel like I'm just treading water. Like I'm stuck in one place.'

'You *want* to be going some place?'

'Yes!' The power in his answer surprised him. He didn't know where it had come from.

Solveig looked at him with sparkling eyes. She smiled. 'Ah! Exciting! So where do you want to go?'

The power that had suddenly filled him was just as suddenly gone. That was the problem. Where did he want to go? He had no idea. He wanted out of that fucking cabin of fear, he knew that much. But how?

Solveig lightly patted his hand with her own soft one. 'Forgive me. I'm an inquisitive old lady and it's none of my business.'

'No, it's okay. It isn't your fault that I…' He put his hands in his lap and looked down at them. 'I knew… one time there was this girl who did a really… strange thing, something that involved me. And now it feels like, like I don't understand anything! What was she thinking? I mean, why me?'

Solveig looked at him. 'She did something strange – and you were involved?'

'Yes.' He heard how pitiful he sounded. *Pathetic.*

'Is she alive, this young woman?'

'Yes, of course.'

'Well, that's good news. It's not something you can always take for granted… not back there at Solbacka at least. Here today, gone tomorrow.' She sighed and looked out at the street. They sat without speaking. Then Solveig shook off her silence.

'Well then, you can just ask her, if there is something you don't understand.'

※

Of course. Peter knew that Solveig was right. But he had tried to avoid doing so, because he could sense that it would be anything but pleasant to get to the bottom of it.

Even calling her made his armpits tingle nervously. She was unwilling, but he insisted and she finally said that she was going to the department on Monday anyway. It didn't get any better when he saw her, with her stomach almost as big as it was in the nightmare. They met shamefacedly, in secret, slinking into an empty office next to the staff canteen where they had first exchanged flirtatious glances. *Back at the scene of the crime.* Now he had to get some answers.

'I just have to say... I really don't get it. Why did you have sex with me when you were living with someone, when you were *pregnant* with his baby?' *You just don't do that sort of thing!* The question burned inside him again. How would he feel if the mother of his unborn child just... *What a traitor!*

It was as if Jeanette could hear his thoughts. Presumably she could read the contempt in his expression.

'Jesus! You're the last person who should judge other people's sex lives! What do you know about me? What do you know about what you should do when you have been trying to get pregnant for four years, and when it finally happens...' Her eyes glistened and her voice broke. 'When you finally get pregnant you find out that your partner has been unfaithful?'

Peter stared at her in silence as she continued.

'Would you have had an abortion and tried to start again with someone else? And maybe never succeed in getting pregnant again? Or maybe you would choose to be a single mother? Or maybe you would just say nicely, "I forgive you," though he would never understand what that forgiveness cost?' She stared at him confrontationally.

Peter started to realize where she was headed. There was a twisted logic in what she said. A message formed in his head:

revenge sex.

'So in this plan of yours, the idea is that your... what's his name?'

'Henrik,' said Jeanette weakly.

'Henrik knows that we... were together, in my bathroom?'

Peter felt a sticky nausea crawl its way into his stomach. He found the whole thing macabre. In his head he pictured his genitals popping in for a visit with a miraculously growing baby. A child's start in life stained, and for what? *For revenge and a moment of cheap horniness.*

Jeanette stared at the electric Advent candlestick on the windowsill; seven glittering spots of light reflected in her dark eyes. She wiped away some tears and looked absent for a moment. Then she took a deep breath and straightened up. Once again she seemed calm and unmoved.

'I didn't do anything to Henrik that he didn't do to me first. And I think that both of us now understand what we have to lose. We have put it behind us. This is a child we have both been longing for. I actually don't give a damn what you think!'

'But why me?' Peter felt violated, tricked into being the bad guy in the story. Jeanette shrugged her shoulders.

'Well, you're not exactly ugly. And I knew that you, I mean, you have a... let's just say, a bit of a reputation. I mean, you know that, right?'

She went towards the door, but then stopped and looked him candidly in the eye. 'I didn't do anything to you that you haven't already done to – hundreds? – of others.'

Peter stared at her with a raging emptiness inside as she turned and walked away.

After his meeting with Jeanette and her unborn child, Peter felt as if he had been beaten up. Something was seriously wrong. He missed the secure feeling of his first, uncomplicated analysis of what had happened. Throughout the Christmas break he had felt with every fiber of his being that Jeanette was an idiot. At first he had thought that her freckled little turned-up nose was adorable, but now he associated it with a mean, bratty kid.

Despite everything, it had felt good to be able to put the thing to rest – Jeanette was a mean, bratty kid. End of story.

But now things had opened up again. There was a new piece of the puzzle to consider. His decision. His judgment, or lack of it. Because if she was a mean idiot, why had he exposed himself to her? And he felt fear flutter in his stomach. 'A bit of a reputation?' *What did she mean by that?* 'Hundreds?' *He didn't exactly keep a tally, but, hell, it couldn't be over... 50, could it?*

Oddly enough, his parents came to mind. What if Birgitta, instead of being unpredictably fickle, was a feeling, thinking person trying to resolve a hopeless situation? What scale of other possible outcomes could have presented itself to a man capable of reacting differently from Lennart? And if there were women who could be understood, and if his mother was one of them, what did that imply about Lennart? What did it imply about him?

His thoughts turned to Vera and how much she sought to avoid him. He hadn't understood it before. Why would somebody not like him? Especially a young woman, a member of the target group with which he was usually successful? Now he understood. He was the type who had sex with anybody. Even Jeanette.

Vera was an Elf who devoted herself to helping others. He was a *Good-for-nothing without direction and with 'a bit of a reputation'*. Fuck! Obviously a person with integrity, like Vera, wouldn't want to touch him with a bargepole. How could he even have imagined that he was someone who could get her dimpled smile to light up the world like a gateway to heaven? He thought about that thing Groucho Marx used to say, that he wouldn't want to be a member of a club that was willing to have him as a member, but this time it wasn't funny. Because he didn't want a woman who was willing to settle for a man like him. He suddenly realized what was so attractive about Vera, what it was that marked her out as special. A slick seducer, used to always getting what he wants, glides in and shamelessly makes a pass at her – but she just says no thanks.

That was the type of girl he wanted!

The cruel irony cut him to the quick.

Almost feverish, he reached for his telephone and dialled Kalle. After a few polite niceties, it was as if the abandoned child in him was compelled to pose the million-dollar question: 'But what about the whole idea of family and being faithful?' *What if you don't want to have to put such things behind you in order to keep the family together?*

There was silence on the other end of the line, except for some distant laughing and high jinks. 'Sorry, what did you say?' asked Kalle, as he made his way into another room, away from his family dinner.

Peter remembered what Kalle had said on New Year's Eve, and in the mirror in the poorly lit hallway he saw that he was blushing as he wondered what 'this evolution thing' actually meant for the possibility of having a family founded on long-term faithfulness. 'I mean, something more stable?'

'Oh, yes, I see.' Now Kalle got it.

'Monogamy is actually quite risky from an evolutionary point of view. It means investing your whole reproductive potential in a single individual. You know, all your eggs in one basket. So it becomes really important to choose correctly. But some species do choose that path. Swans, I think... and wolves, foxes, otters. But then, seriously... We are humans; we have our big frontal lobes; we can decide what we want. The meaning of life doesn't need to be children. People might want to leave other legacies, like Gregor Mendel did.'

'Who?' said Peter.

'Mendel. The father of genetics. A cool guy who joined a monastery. Because, you know, both women and men can choose complete abstinence. Or people can choose to have thousands of partners. Or go for the popular serial monogamy. Or choose one person and be true to him or her.'

He made it sound like the simplest thing in the world.

Peter heard Vera come home that evening, and he was glad that he had locked himself in his room and could avoid meeting her gaze. He was sure that she would see right through him, and he was ashamed of what she would see. For the first time in his adult life, he cried himself to sleep.

✖

His heartbeat quickens. Hunted by something, he tears off his blazer and tie. He runs for his life from the fog. He trips and falls...

Once again, a nightmare woke Peter up. He spent an agonizing hour overwhelmed by cold, dark feelings. Like a lost soul, he wandered around in the dusky dorm room. Finally, he went into his newly decontaminated bathroom and took off all his clothes. He took off the gold chain around his neck, his Ulysse Nardin Marine Chronograph and the ring his father had given him for his 20th birthday. He fumbled around in the medicine chest and found his electric hair trimmer. Suddenly determined, he went out into the hall and plugged it in. He turned on the bathroom light and, when his eyes had adjusted to the harsh light, he looked at himself in the mirror: *Goodbye.*

He ran the hair trimmer straight across his head. His thick locks fell, light and dark blond strands. What was left was a pale, bald line with an invisible stubble. It looked awful! He couldn't go around like that, so there was no turning back. He ran the trimmer over his head in all directions until all his hair was gone. His head looked small and vulnerable, naked like a prisoner's – an association that felt strangely fitting. He ran his hand across it, feeling it. *At least I know it will grow back thick...* He collected his hair and threw most of it into a plastic bag that he hung on the handle of the door to the hallway. He cleaned up the rest with damp paper and threw it in the toilet. He got into the shower in an effort to get rid of the last remaining cells of his old self, but his thoughts continued spinning round and round in his head.

His fingers and toes were wrinkly as prunes when he finally put on an old, worn t-shirt and a pair of boxer shorts. He lay down on the bed and tried to go back to sleep. He was incredibly tired, but sleep still refused to come.

Peter didn't know why he had done it, or what had compelled him. In his middle-of-the-night defenselessness, he hoped that he might find some kind of relief if he just spoke with Vera. And if she saw right through him, well, isn't that what she had done the whole time anyway? He needed her clear-sightedness. Her judgment. He would not be so presumptuous as to *believe that she...* he blushed with shame. But he wanted to talk to her. She who rejected that which he should have rejected, long before he understood anything. He knew that she was there, only a few feet away – there was only the wall and a few breaths between them.

His first knock on their shared wall was tentative and careful. The second time he knocked harder and longer. Then there was an answer from Vera's room, four knocks. Encouraged by her response, Peter also knocked four times, but more softly. Then came two strong knocks in reply. It was a poor form of communication, that was true, but even so... It was like a hopeful dawn. She was there, only inches away, and she was knocking at him. With a throbbing heart, he knocked back twice. Then it fell quiet. He was alone again with his anxious heart and breathing.

Suddenly, someone tried the handle on his door. He ran over and unlocked it, saving the bag of hair from falling off when he pushed down the handle to let her in. He stood eye to eye with a dishevelled and befuddled Vera.

'Are you also having a hard time sleeping?' he whispered sympathetically as he absentmindedly handed her the bag.

'What are you doing?' Her voice echoed in the hallway.

'Ssshh – it's the middle of the night!' he whispered as he closed the door behind her.

Vera sighed. 'There's always someone who needs to pull themselves together, huh?' "Don't slurp," "don't talk so loudly in the middle of the night," and "don't..."' She looked down at the bag. 'But what?... Have you just cut off your hair? And you thought that *I* should take the trash out, right?'

Peter ran his hand over his face and quickly took back the bag. 'No, it was just hanging there. Sorry. But it's... an emergency. It just feels so real, you know? Too real to be just regular dreams?

I'm starting to think… I mean, I don't dare sleep!'

'Since you don't dare sleep, you thought that I shouldn't sleep either?'

'They aren't regular dreams. Everything just gets all mixed together, and it feels like everything is falling apart!'

Vera looked him in the eye. 'Hello, in there! There are people in the world with real problems, you know. Your biggest problem is yourself. You're so damned egotistical all the time!'

Now he saw that her eyes were swollen and red from crying behind her glasses, and her fragile posture in the light-blue striped flannel pajamas spoke of pain. From somewhere, new and unfamiliar words forced themselves into his consciousness.

'I completely forgot. How are you?'

He had apparently said the words, too, because they echoed in his ears.

She looked at him. 'What?'

'Know what? Have you noticed how being awake in the middle of the night makes you hungry? Come on, let's go out to the kitchen. I'll make some hot chocolate.'

The kitchen was weakly lit by the red Advent star that hung by the window near the table, and Peter kept an eye on the milk that was coming to the boil on the stove. Vera was apparently hungry too, because she came hobbling in with her quilt wrapped around her shoulders just as he was mixing two teaspoons of sugar and one of cocoa into mugs.

My biggest problem is myself. That I'm so damned egotistical all the time. He tested the idea as he poured a little water onto the chocolate and sugar mix so that he could stir out the lumps. He poured hot milk into the mugs until they were full of the light-brown drink.

She had turned on the floor lamp in the TV room and was sitting on the knotty, 1970s sofa with a pillow under her knee. He looked at her soberly when he reached the sofa and carefully handed her the hot chocolate.

'Yes, I guess it's true.' He sat down a respectable distance away from her, on the armchair next to the wall.

'What?' she sighed exhaustedly.

'My problem is just me. You're probably right about that. But maybe you have another problem? I mean, is something wrong?'

Vera looked at him warily. She sat quietly and sipped her hot chocolate, letting her glasses fog over from the steam. Finally, she removed them and took a shaky, deep breath.

'There is a strike. And "unfortunately", they say...' Her voice sounded weak and rueful. Suddenly she began to cry and tried to hide her sad face from him. She put down the mug, picked up her glasses and got up. She was leaving, getting away.

Peter also stood up, but this time he did not try to stop her physically. He never again wanted to feel as he had by the refrigerator the other day.

'Uh, Vera, it's okay... It's four in the morning, and I'm the only one here and... look at me.' He gestured towards his shaved head. 'This egotistical convict... would benefit from hearing about a real problem.'

A surprised twinkle lit up her tired face, and did he see a tiny hint of one of her dimples? She sat down again and he went back to the kitchen.

'Hot chocolate is good, but it doesn't exactly fill you up, does it?' He felt wide awake, more awake than he had felt for several years. He suddenly felt like he had a direction. He wanted to listen to her. And even if the feeling only lasted a few more minutes, he would be able to live on it for several weeks.

He spread butter on dark slices of bread and put several thin layers of cheese on each one. He thought it tasted better that way. He went back to the TV room and gave her a sandwich. They sat quietly, she on the sofa and he in the armchair. They drank and ate.

'Everything seems worse when you're hungry, anyway,' he tried.

He looked over at her, with her bad leg propped up on the sofa.

'Who's on strike?'

'Nurses.'

'Ah. Are you on strike?'

'No, I'm not working right now, because I'm writing... or was

214

writing… well, you know.'

She shot him a look, went silent and took another shaky breath behind the mug of hot chocolate.

Now they were dangerously close. He didn't want the new, fragile connection to be broken by their getting too close to the thing they had fought about before. He started again nervously.

'Nurses are on strike and say unfortunately…? Or who says unfortunately?'

'The chief physician at Orthopedics. Seated at the right hand of the all-powerful regional government… who has come again to judge the living and the dead.'

'Huh? Sorry, you've lost me. It's the middle of the night and I'm a bit slow…'

'I've been waiting for an MRI since I hurt myself, because my leg won't heal. I finally got an appointment, for tomorrow. But now… Unfortunately, according to the chief physician, my knee injury isn't an emergency, so I don't get to have the MRI, maybe not for ages, and this…' She gestured at her leg in defeat, 'This is… unbearable.'

Her voice disappeared again into a weak whisper. *Her real problem.* He saw the solution at once! How could he not have seen that she had needed his help for months?

'But what about Sophia Hospital?' he said.

'What?'

'If you can get to Stockholm, then I think I can fix up an MRI pretty fast.'

Vera looked at him suspiciously.

'How can you do that?'

'Well, if not this week, then pretty soon. I can call and check tomorrow. Or, later today, I mean.'

She shook her head. 'I know you're used to… but you can't buy everything. The most important things can't actually be bought.'

He looked at her seriously. 'No, I know that.'

When they left the kitchen he adjusted his stride to her slow, careful, old-person walk. She had actually got worse, and when he stopped at her door she said: 'Did you say you're having a hard time sleeping? Wait…'

She limped into her room and came back out with her cellphone. 'This is my… my music to fall asleep by. You can borrow it. And "test-try" it.'

'"Test-try" it?'

'Yes. That's what my father says. He always goes "test-fishing". Then it doesn't matter if he doesn't catch any fish. So, I mean, you can… "test-sleep".'

He took the cellphone and headphones with a warm feeling in his stomach.

Peter lay in his bed, expectantly. He felt radically different from an hour ago. When he pressed play, the music started in the middle of a song and he realized that he was starting exactly where Vera had left off. A delicate voice spoke to him, as if it were fate. And then there was a riff where the same monotonous guitar communicated different messages, depending on how the others played.

Everything depends on context. His eyes moistened with tears from the beauty and the world of possibilities that seemed to be opening up. The drums rose up and powerfully hammered home the importance of the message. If Vera had been there, she could have told him that it was when the bass went to C and the parallel minor chimed that he got goose bumps. The choir sang *Tears stream down your face and I… I promise you I will learn from my mistakes.* It felt supernatural, like a message from a higher power. Or perhaps from a better, soon to be realized, version of himself? And the deeply longed-for feeling of having a direction just went on and on, all the way to the placid end.

Lights will guide you home, and ignite your bones, and I will try to fix you.

28

Vera woke groggily, roused by a knocking sound. She sat up in bed and saw that she had slept until 8.30. She listened a little. It was completely quiet, and she thought perhaps she had heard wrong. But then the knocking started again. She pulled off the quilt, limped over to the door and opened it.

Peter was standing there with an expectant smile. 'Sorry, I didn't mean to wake you, but we have to leave at 10 if we're going to make it!' He waved some papers in the air.

Vera blinked in confusion. He continued:

'I booked the cheap tickets. Your appointment is tomorrow morning, but I thought it would be easier if we avoided the early-morning flight. And cheaper, too.' He held the papers up in front of her.

She stared at his bald head and her still half-asleep brain slowly started to recall the strange events of the previous night. She remembered him giving her his hair in a black plastic bag with elegant silver lettering, like a sick present. *What was she supposed to do with a bag of ladykiller hair?* She also remembered that her chameleon neighbor had claimed that he could arrange an MRI...

Like a starving person she took the papers he was holding out. She read that tomorrow, on Wednesday 9 January at 8.45, she was to have an MRI done on her knee at a private hospital in Stockholm. She looked at him and mixed feelings raged inside her.

'But how can...?' She heard how outraged she sounded, and tried again, releasing her other feeling, of endless gratitude. 'I mean... how did you manage to do this?'

'I didn't do much.' Peter grinned crookedly. 'Barbro at Escape is the good fairy. She heard about the situation at eight o'clock this morning. It turned out that they had a cancellation,

217

so she got back to me at 8.22 with a solution, complete with travel reservations.'

'But how was she able to...?' Inside, Vera was in an uproar. *Have I been limping around like a cripple for months, completely unnecessarily?* All she had needed to do was get in contact with this Escape-Barbro, and she would have been helped a long time ago?

He looked at her and shrugged his shoulders. 'Anyone can do it. You just need to know who to call.'

'But how much does it cost?' wondered Vera, while protests about unfairness and a feeling of great relief battled around inside her like fire and water.

'Oh, don't worry about that. It isn't expensive.'

Easy for him to say.

'You have to tell me, so I know if I can afford it!'

'You can stay for free in Stockholm. My mother insists that you stay with us – well, with her and Göran – she refuses to even hear of anything else.' He flipped through the papers to the last one and read, 'You'll need to pay for the MRI, which is 3,200 kronor, plus 400 per ticket, so around 4,000.'

Just 4,000 kronor! She sat on the plane and looked out over the Umeå River's icy delta as they took off. It felt ridiculous that she had gone around with a barely usable knee since May waiting for an examination that even a poor church mouse like her could manage to pay for. A miserable 4,000, including the trip. And the regional government didn't think it could spare even that much to help her? Not even from the taxes she herself had paid? When her eyes filled with tears, she turned away and looked out of the window. But mainly she felt angry. *Why didn't they even care enough to tell her that the option existed?*

It wasn't surprising that, in her desperation, she had agreed to go to Stockholm with Peter Stavenius. Apparently, it was his mother's 48th birthday, and Vera was invited to a 'strange thing that Göran does'. She glanced to the left where Peter sat next to the aisle. They had a seat between them for the sake of her leg, and he had helped her to prop it up using their bags, so the trip would be as painless as possible. When he had been wearing his hood to protect against the cold, his baldness hadn't been so obvious, but now, sitting beside her, his hairless vulnerability showed again. She wondered why he had done it. *What is Barbie going to say when she finds out that Ken has suddenly shaved his head?*

But that wasn't any of her business. She looked down at the sea. *Finland is over there.* She saw the wind turbines in Holmsund. They looked like the future, in a good way.

The plane started to roar and whine and she stiffened in fear. Was she going to die now, she who had been so willing to accept death just a few hours ago?

'How are you doing?' He looked at her in concern.

Is he asking me again how I am feeling? Her fear was pushed aside by the memory. The strange feeling she had got last night when he insisted that she eat something, while at the same time listening to her until she had explained her problem. For the second time his behavior reminded her of her father's, and she was just as surprised this time. The whining from the plane continued and she asked, 'What is that noise?'

'That's just the sound barrier; soon we'll be travelling faster than sound.'

Three hundred and something meters per second? She looked doubtfully at him. 'But isn't it only Concorde that flies faster than sound?'

He shrugged his shoulders carelessly. 'Maybe. But it sounds like this every time you take off, at exactly this point. It's no problem.'

Then the noise stopped and the plane again whistled along quietly through the air. He was right, although he had been wrong. And she would probably survive today, too. She would survive and she needed to fight.

✳

His mother, Birgitta, met them at Bromma airport. She looked young, with clean-cut features, thick blond hair cut in a short style that suited her, and attractive, soft clothes. *Easy to see where he gets his good genes from.* Peter gave her a hug.

'Happy Birthday...'

'I'm so pleased you could come!' said Birgitta as she hugged him back. A moment of worried surprise swept over her when they had released each other, and she asked about his hair. Peter stepped back and answered evasively that he 'needed to do something new'. Then Birgitta turned towards Vera. A genuine, warm smile revealed an even row of teeth as they greeted each other, and she immediately took Vera by the arm to help support her limping walk.

'Peter, can you take the bags? The car is just outside; I snuck in through the taxi gate.'

Vera sat in the back seat beside Peter's little sister Sofia, a girl of primary-school age who glanced at her curiously. In the front, mother and son chatted calmly and Vera fell into an exhausted sleep. They seemed to reach their destination much too quickly. Vera woke up unwillingly and felt like she was freezing. When they walked from the car to the townhouse, Peter opened the gate for her and asked, 'Oh, are you cold?'

Birgitta looked at her son as she went to unlock the door.

Vera nodded, glancing uncertainly at him as she slowly passed through the gate. As they made their way up the steps to the small front porch, he whispered. 'Uh, Vera, that thing I said about your mother and all? I didn't mean to.'

Vera looked at him guardedly. 'Okay. But...'

'I probably didn't get how sad one can be at such moments.'

'But it was true,' said Vera.

'What?'

It was painful, and the price was an overwhelming gulf between her and her father. Rejection. But it couldn't be helped.

'That was why it hurt. Because what you said was true.'

He looked at her thoughtfully. When they had taken off their outdoor clothes Peter squatted next to his shy little sister.

'Sofia, did you know that Vera can talk to cats?'

Full of admiration, Sofia took Vera's hand. A little grey cairn terrier darted around her legs, energetically wagging its tail.

'This is Mozart,' said the girl. 'But you know, I have lots of pictures of cats. Do you want to see them?'

The girl's room was wallpapered with cat pictures. Vera read the captions: Norwegian Forest cats, Persians, Abyssinians and Russian Blues. Wouldn't that be something – Ludde, a farm cat from Norrland, among these magnificent specimens. He might not be so handsome, with his random black spots that somehow managed to miss his nose, leaving it pink. But none of them looked as robust and practical as Ludde, thought Vera, and she was sure that none of them were as loyal. She felt a stab of longing for the old cat.

'And I got this from Peter.' Sofia lovingly hugged a realistic-looking stuffed cat, but at the same time she was on her guard. 'Are you his new girlfriend?'

Vera looked out through the window, down at the row of townhouses next door.

'No, we just live next to each other at university. He has quite a few of them, does he?'

'What?'

'Girlfriends.'

'Um, I think so,' said his little sister.

Vera sat down carefully on Sofia's bed.

'And, you know, no-one wants that. To be one of many. If it's going to work out, well, you want someone… someone who thinks you're special. Someone who sticks up for you, someone you can always rely on.'

Like I thought I had! She felt a lump in her throat. She had to stop thinking about Adam, otherwise she was going to start bawling right in front of this kind little thing.

Wide-eyed, the girl whispered, 'Yes, exactly, like Cinderella's prince.'

No. 'Win the beauty contest at the ball.' That wasn't what I meant. No surprise that women could turn into witches and treat each other so badly, if their fate was to be decided in a murderous competition in a humiliatingly small boxing ring. *'Who is the fairest of them all?'* If she were the second prettiest

221

at the ball, then Cinderella would be doomed to scrubbing floors on her hands and knees for all eternity. If she is prettiest and wins the competition, what happens later? Because eventually someone... *sexier* is bound to come along. The lump hurt and Vera bit her bottom lip hard. *But I refuse to be some witch in a pathetic catfight. I will step aside. I have already stepped aside.*

'I think that Peter is almost like a prince,' said his little sister brightly.

Vera took a deep breath and smiled a little sadly at Sofia.

'Yes, of course. He is... your prince brother.'

✖

Just in time for dinner the family was joined by a thoughtful Göran, who, with an expectant look, snuck in and hid a present, and Viktoria, a lanky, slender, doe-eyed teenager with braces. Vera looked around in the kitchen as she helped with the salad. She felt as though she had walked into a copy of *House Beautiful:* 'Rounded minimalism and soft, natural colors with well-chosen accents in red create a cosy feeling of warmth.' The colors were even reflected in the food, and Vera couldn't help wondering if it might have been planned. They ate a roast with potatoes au gratin, lingonberry and 'tanterelle', as Peter had apparently called them when he was little.

At dinner it became clear that Birgitta was worried about the teenage girl and her older boyfriend, and the more concern Birgitta expressed, the more sullen the girl became. The tension increased after the main course, and when Viktoria stormed upstairs Birgitta looked anxiously in the direction she had fled.

Shortly afterwards, when they were helping to clear the table, Birgitta mumbled: 'I wonder... if she has a healthy attitude to relationships.'

'What do you mean?' asked her partner.

'It's not so easy for her, you know, given what happened to her parents,' continued Birgitta, looking guilty. 'I mean, the way her father behaves, and the way...' She looked at Peter and stopped herself, with a quick glance at Vera.

'Has something happened?' Peter sounded worried.

Birgitta was quiet, but in the silence her expression said, 'That's what I am afraid of.'

Later, when Vera came out of the bathroom, she happened to hear Peter's intense but quiet voice from the living room.

'You don't have to do anything you don't want to. And if he doesn't respect you for that, then he's a worthless shit and not worthy of you, Vicky; do you hear me?'

Vera felt like she shouldn't be there and crept with embarrassment past the open door, hoping she wouldn't be seen. The only thing Vera saw out of the corner of her eye was his back, his naked head and his sister's long flowing hair falling around his shoulders as, sobbing, she bent in to hug him. Vera felt a strange mix of eavesdropper's guilt at hearing such private things about the lives of strangers, and surprise at witnessing yet another unexpected side of her neighbor. *Peter Stavenius talking about respect for young women? Or just for his own sister?*

Later that evening, when Birgitta opened her presents and the family launched into some kind of homemade ritual of taking down the Christmas tree, which also involved playing very loud Latin music, Vera was treated to yet another unexpected side of her host family. The ruddy-faced man stylishly guided his partner across the floor in an improvised tango and the pair danced, their eyes happily locked on each other. When Sofia also wanted to dance, Peter lifted her into his arms and swung her around playfully. Viktoria sat a little bit off to the side with her cellphone, rolling her eyes at her family's antics. Vera herself sat relaxed and pleasantly tired on the sofa, her right foot tucked under her left knee. She did not really know what she had expected, but it definitely wasn't this. Vera had been nervous about the trip. *But there is nothing here to be worried about, is there? Lucky them, being able to dance.* Vera had almost forgotten how she loved to dance. And tomorrow, at last, was the day of the MRI on her knee. Surely it would happen this time?

✖

The next morning Vera woke early. She looked at the clock: 5.18. She didn't want to oversleep under any circumstances, so she checked the clock radio one more time to make sure it was set properly. *A strange feeling.* She lay, in what was usually Peter's bed when he stayed at his mother's, waiting while the morning slowly arrived. She saw beautiful pieces of paper hanging on an austere bulletin board made of glass. It was Asian – maybe Japanese? – calligraphy, a precise movement captured in an inkblot. Her thoughts wandered to when Peter caught the rag next to the laundry basket. There was something in that movement that reminded her of the calligraphy.

She also thought about Peter insisting yesterday that he sleep on the sofa bed because he wasn't in any pain, but adding that he would gladly continue to borrow her cellphone to 'test-sleep'. She said that he could, but first she wanted to call her father and say where she was. He was busy getting ready for the public unveiling of the local government's new zoning plan, and sounded surprised, but happy for Vera. No trace of any accusation that she was disloyal for paying for private healthcare.

When it was finally time to leave, Peter drove Vera to her appointment in town in the family's little Ford. Peter hadn't asked if she wanted him to go with her; he simply did so. At first it seemed unnecessary, but it turned out to be a good thing, because the clinic buildings were laid out in a way that resembled a labyrinth. Between signing in and her appointment time she needed to get from entrance H to entrance K in the labyrinth. She had 10 minutes and it wasn't at all simple. Peter ran around checking different dead ends until they finally found the place.

He looked away when, undressed and with her bare legs sticking out from under a thin hospital gown, she was taken away by a very professional, male radiology nurse from Iran. Peter waited outside while she sat completely still with her knee inside the white, futuristically designed machine that hummed and whirred while, layer by layer, it formed a picture of what her knee looked like on the inside.

Then it was time to go back and wait for the appointment with the doctor. His name was Olof and he had a calm, quiet manner.

He read her medical notes, thoroughly examined her knee, looked at the MRI results that had been delivered electronically to his computer, and then asked, 'Why aren't they treating you at home in Västerbotten?'

Of all the things he could have asked, he chose the one thing she could not answer.

He promised to send her a written diagnosis within a week, one that she could forward to the Orthopedic Clinic in Umeå. They shook hands and the doctor looked at her encouragingly. 'Good luck, Vera Lundberg.'

When they flew home to Umeå that afternoon, Peter wanted to hear her music one last time. He had listened to Coldplay several times before, and he seemed to be remarkably taken by it. She was watching him curiously, when he suddenly caught her eye. He looked at her as if he wanted to devour her, the same look he had had when he saw her outside the changing room. She looked away with lightning speed, but calmed herself with the thought that it wasn't about her this time either. If anyone knew how music could make you feel, she did. *He must have a serious weak spot for Coldplay!* Reverently he took off the headphones and held the telephone out to her. He pointed at the goose bumps on his arms, tried to say something and finally just shrugged.

"'Fix you"... "Gooooose bumpppppps!" as Gunde Svan said when he saw Mogren win the World Ski Championship.

You can't fool the body, as Gunde also said.

Peter continued. 'I don't know. I mean, this song. I just want to say... Thank you.'

'And thank you, too,' came out of her mouth before she had time to think. It *was* appropriate to thank him, she realized, and, with genuine appreciation this time, she went on: 'Thank you so much for all this... for helping me to get the examination, the trip and everything.'

He looked so happy when he smiled.

Maybe she hadn't been lying when she'd said he was a prince brother? She thought about everything Peter had done in the past 24 hours, for her and for his sisters. She was taken by surprise by the sudden thought that came to her: *Imagine if he were my brother?* Amazingly enough, her first reaction was positive. She realized how fantastic it would be to have a sibling. She wouldn't have to deal with the volcanic eruptions alone, or the sick rules of the game and the abyss. A sibling would be a support in life, a joy and a comfort.

But was Peter a brother one would wish for? After she got her sandwich and strong airplane tea, she changed her mind. How would she feel being his big sister when he shaved his head in the middle of the night and tried to give the hair away? Or when the prince turned into a frog, and she was forced to comfort a stream of women whom he had betrayed, but without being able to give them any reasonable explanation?

She thought about the look of shame on their neighbor's face every time he was forced to apologize because his uncontrollable German Shepherd had come over barking, dug up their flowerbeds or chased Ludde up a tree. She looked at Peter sitting next to the aisle. He had politely declined refreshments from the flight attendant. He was slumped down reading that sick pick-up book that he had tried to educate Matt with. Kind, humane Matt who was fine just the way he was. *Unspoiled*.

In the end, the owner of the German Shepherd had admitted: 'He is incorrigible. We will keep him locked up.'

29

As mother and son were cleaning up in the kitchen, Peter started complaining. 'Did you have to bring up that thing about Vicky right now? It makes things so damned unpleasant!'

'Unpleasant?' Birgitta got angry. 'Now you sound like your father. I thought you understood that keeping quiet and sweeping everything under the carpet doesn't work. In the long run it just makes things worse!'

Peter didn't answer. She went over to a cabinet by the telephone in the kitchen and anxiously took out a notebook.

'I didn't want to say anything at dinner,' she said, 'but the school guidance counsellor called, even though it's vacation and everything. Vicky apparently has...' She looked down at the notebook and read word for word: 'low self-esteem in her relationships, which has led to an element of self-destructive and risky behavior.'

Birgitta put down the notebook, sighed, and ran her hands over her face. 'And the morning-after pill was apparently not the only reason that the school nurse decided to talk to the guidance counsellor. When I ask Vicky about it, she just says "men will be men". I mean, my God, she's only 16 years old!'

She stared anxiously at her son. 'And who are the,' she made quotation marks in the air, '"men" she knows? What male role models does she really have?'

Peter avoided thinking about what Birgitta was implying. He squirmed a little and fixed his gaze on Göran's beige sweater, which was still hanging on his chair at the kitchen table. 'Well, she has... Göran, for example.'

'She just laughs at Göran, and when I asked her to be a little nicer to him she screamed something about him being a slimeball and a home wrecker.'

Peter winced despite himself. He himself had used similar

words on occasion, and perhaps Viktoria had overheard. He realized that he had no counterevidence to refute his mother's concerns. It was true that his parents' separation had been a bitter fight, and Vicky had had a tough childhood growing up in the middle of it. That it might have made her fragile and prone to 'self-destructive and risky behavior' – he felt a tightening in his chest at the insight. Over the years he had shielded and protected Sofia, but what had he done for the elder of his sisters? Vicky, so sweet and smart behind that sullen teenage façade. *What would become of her?*

'You know, Peter, I came out of my depression with the help of a counsellor, a wise woman from Helsinki. Do you know what she told me? She said that in Finland they wash the rugs in a special contraption down at the coast, and that it is good to have the whole ocean close by, because when you do the washing, all the dirt is released and the water gets cloudy. And we have to allow it to happen, and then rinse it with clean water!'

Peter wasn't that interested in how to wash rugs, but he knew one thing. It didn't feel good to hear that Vicky might be in trouble, and his mother's bad-role-model theory about the causes was particularly unpleasant. But Birgitta had been right to bring it up, because now he would talk to Vicky.

※

When Birgitta and Göran started in with their ridiculous tradition of uninhibited dancing while taking down the Christmas tree, Peter thought – for the first time – that it felt right to join in the spectacle. Vera's opinion of him could hardly sink lower because he joked around with his sister, could it?

He lifted Sofia off the ground and looked around. He smiled at Vicky, pleased about the chat they had had, which led him to hope and believe that she would be secure enough to stick up for herself. He saw his mother happily dancing with the piano teacher. Could they perhaps be some kind of family after all – this unlikely patched-together constellation? Thinking about Birgitta's experience in the 1990s, he had recalled Vera's chaotic green book: *two-thirds of all the work, one-tenth of all the income, one-hundredth of all the capital.* He had first thought that it sounded exaggerated, or perhaps was true in some far-off hole in the Third World. But, thinking about his own parents, he realized that it had probably been something like that. If you thought of being at home with three kids, cleaning, washing, shopping and cooking as a job, then it all added up to a lot of working hours. Add to that the responsibilities of being a hostess, which she had disliked so much. For his mother, anyway, the job of housewife had been devastating. Because what could he say? *No mother, you didn't suffer, you just imagined it.*

The way his mother and Lennart had decided to resolve their problems had impacted negatively on his sisters and him. Forgiving them for that – well, he might have to work on it. And tolerance for the strange beigeness that Göran had introduced into the family? The unidentifiable Latin dance that accompanied the taking down of the Christmas tree, for example? Well, as far as that was concerned... He spun around with Sofia until she choked with laughter. It wasn't in Peter's nature to be obstinate about small things; he was rarely unwilling to try doing things in new ways.

✖

Peter longed to relisten to 'Fix You', and asked Vera if he could borrow her phone again that night. It was dark and quiet in the house when he lay down on the sofa bed. He was about to start the music when the cellphone began vibrating and ringing softly. A message – the phone was no longer set on 'music only'. Vera had entered her pin-code, so he had full access, and Peter couldn't contain his curiosity. He barely thought before he opened the new message; it was from voicemail. His thumb seemed to have developed a life of its own as it bounced across the buttons. He dialled 133 and waited tensely.

'*You have... two... new messages,*' said the female voice politely on the other end, and then the scratchy recording began. 'Darling Vera!' The man's voice sounded urgent. *Adam.* 'Seriously, what is going on? I really need to talk to you. We have to resolve this! Please call me as soon as you can.'

'*Recorded... today... 4.18am.*' commented the robotic female voice.

Quarter past four in the morning. That was when Peter had had the telephone! When the music's endless possibilities had given him a feeling of fantastic insight. At the same time, from another number... *Poor guy.* Even if he sounded calm – calling her in the middle of the night was clearly a sign of desperation. But of course, he had been Vera's husband and then ruined it. Peter shivered. He may have done a lot of stupid things in his life, but at least he had never done anything like that.

He was staring unseeingly out the window when the next message interrupted him. 'Helloooo, it's your mother. I have made a decision. I have forgiven you for that... that... attack.'

Gunilla Lundberg sounded extremely drunk and Peter blushed in embarrassment, despite being alone in the dark.

'I get it; it isn't so easy for you. Soon you'll be 30, but when you're hobbling around like a stiff old lady, it's easy to believe that you're turning 70 at least! No decent job and a falling out with Adam... and all that. But I'm going to fix it... Just take it... easy. Mom will fix it, you'll see. Bye-bye sweetie.'

'*Recorded...today...6.57pm.*'

Peter's heart pounded and unpleasant emotions struggled inside him. He had been trusted with Vera's phone to listen to music, and he had listened to her private messages. He was ashamed. And what he had discovered! Her husband absolutely wanted to talk to her. And her mother – she said she was going to 'fix' things, but it sounded like she couldn't even manage to stand up. Poor Vera, what a fucking mess! Maybe it was like this every day? No wonder she wasn't always Little Miss Sunshine.

But shouldn't he go up and tell her about the messages? *No!* protested the voice of shame inside him. *Then you will reveal that you listened to them!*

Well, replied the voice of indignant integrity, *in that case you have to give her the phone in the morning, so she can listen to the messages later.*

Peter put the phone down and thought that it was probably best; just let the robot give her the messages tomorrow. He took a deep breath and calmed his pulse. He picked up the telephone again and deleted his phone call to voicemail. Suddenly, an unpleasant feeling swept through him. He called 133 again, and the robot woman on the other end said, *'You have... two OLD... messages.'*

Damn! He hadn't thought of that. What had he done? *So fucking unnecessary!* And there was no way to get that telephone voice to call the messages anything other than old – she might just as well have said, in her polite tone, *'Peach Fuzz has... eavesdropped on your two latest, very private... messages.'*

Peter broke out in a cold sweat as he recalled the horrible locked-in-the-fog-dream: *Misuse.* He got out of bed quickly and walked around in the dark living room. He didn't recognize himself at all. Was this how his new so-called adult life was going to be? *No! This wouldn't work!* He definitely couldn't do anything sensible if he was locked in a cabin of fear.

He opened the patio door next to his mother's lush ivy plant and stepped barefoot out onto the cold terrace. He breathed in the fresh night air and looked out over the small back yard, weakly lit with discreet garden lights. *Okay. I made a mistake. So what do I do now?* The heavens were silent. Peter knew better than to ask perfection of anyone. To make small mistakes had to be okay; surely he could tell her the truth? Or... well, that the phone had signalled that there was a message, and he had forgotten that it wasn't his phone? The infinity above his head remained benevolently quiet and neutral.

His feet ached from the cold and forced him back inside. He closed the door and thought about Vera. What would be best for her? *What would happen when she heard Adam's message?* He didn't really know. Maybe she would actually be happy? A sadness welled behind his cold nose at the thought. Or would it rip open painful wounds, ones she would prefer to avoid?

And Gunilla's drunken babbling? He was more sure on that point. It would definitely do more harm than good. What in the world did Vera need to be forgiven for by her mother? When it was her mother who had the whole family tiptoeing around in a minefield? And to say such stuff to her injured daughter who couldn't get help! He sat down with the phone, called up the truth-telling woman and deleted the messages and all traces of them. If Adam was actually serious in wishing Vera well, then he could just try calling again. And Gunilla could also call later, when she was sober.

'You have no messages.'

He lay back down on the sofa and focused all his thoughts on tomorrow's appointment to examine Vera's knee. At least that was unambiguously positive – finding out what was wrong was the first step to fixing it, right?

And he listened to it over and over again: *I will try to fix you.*

They got help getting ready to go the next morning. The two women hugged and, when Vera limped down the porch steps, Birgitta stood at the door and watched her warmly.

'Thanks for everything,' said Peter softly. 'It is always nice to be here. And Vera… it's probably not a bad thing for her to get away for a while too.'

Birgitta smiled and whispered confidentially to her son. 'She doesn't know yet?'

Peter blushed and looked away towards the car, which had been pulled around to the curb at the front of the house. Göran was helping Vera with her backpack.

'Nah, I've been pretty… rotten to her. So I thought…'

Birgitta looked at him fondly, not fooled at all. He knew how well his mother understood that he usually raised and dashed women's hopes virtually non-stop, driven by the belief that happiness came from an endless stream of successes on the market. He had hoped that Vera would see him as other girls did, but it was like that psychology picture. All these years he had only seen a vase, but now he suddenly saw two profiles, and he couldn't get his eyes to see the old picture. Now he knew more about what girls thought about him, and the last thing he wanted was for Vera to think about him like that.

Birgitta was still looking at him, as if he hadn't answered the important thing: *'She doesn't know yet?'*

How could he explain to his mother that Vera had probably

known too much for months? He had thought so much about how she affected his feelings, that he hadn't even considered hers. He had not even seen her properly, only a bunch of other women, until she happened to stand before him smiling in a beautiful dress. Why would he want to remember how her smile had died when she saw him? Or how Vera had spent months trying to avoid him? How could Birgitta understand that he didn't have a chance, because how could a *Good-for-nothing without direction and with 'a bit of a reputation'* please an Elf? But there was something he could fix that would make her happier. And that was what he finally said.

'And, well, she needs an MRI, and she can get that here...'

Birgitta looked thoughtfully in Vera's direction.

'Ah, an MRI? Yes, that's good, but I think she needs more than an MRI. I think...'

She fell silent and then spoke more quietly, to herself. 'When the cage gets so small that it chafes and gives you sores, then you need to break out. But it is difficult when you need to be strong just when you are at your lowest – weak, scared, alone.'

Peter's effort to leave jolted his mother back to the present. She stroked his head quickly as she gave him a warm goodbye hug. 'Yes, I'm pleased, in any case... about the way you are now, bald or not.'

While Vera's knee was being examined, Peter sat in the waiting room and continued reading *The Game*. The pick-up chaos escalated into a tornado that crushed and destroyed everything in its path. But the author himself was saved from the worst of the maelstrom when his 'heart awoke from its slumber and did a body check in his chest'. Neil, alias Style, fell in love, but, typically, the object of his affection, Lisa – the guitarist in Courtney Love's band – didn't fall for his smooth talk the way all the other women had. Now Style knew what he wanted, but he couldn't get it. The makeover of the previous two years and his persistent practising had enormously increased his ability to make contact with women, but most of it turned out to be a huge barrier when it came to making genuine contact with the person he really wanted to reach. And it wasn't actually difficult to understand why. *What sensible girl wanted to take pity on Just A Gigolo and be with him for real?*

The all-too familiar question burned like an open flame.

On the flight home he sat listening to 'Fix You' in an attempt to keep hold of the comforting feeling of having a direction. She sat there, just one empty seat away, and when he glanced down at her now ringless finger, he thought that perhaps there was an opening after all. It felt like it was now or never. He wished for the courage to say it. Once again he shivered at the end of the song, and he saw out of the corner of his eye that she was looking at him. Gratefully he met her gaze. Maybe it wasn't necessary to say anything? Maybe she understood anyway? Hope shone like the sun inside him; his heart beat so hard he could feel it – and the sublime soundtrack continued to tell him about a happy future. But after a too-brief moment she looked away. He didn't know exactly what it was, but he thought she looked frightened.

He took off the headphones and the words that ensued were a great disappointment. Instead of the truth, he came out with some nonsense about Gunde Svan the skier and lamely thanked her for the music. Frustrated, he retreated into a nervous silence.

Just like Neil couldn't get Lisa because he had been Style, perhaps he himself would never get someone like Vera? The thought made Peter's breath shallow and uneven, and he hoped that Vera wouldn't notice anything. He bent forward to get his bag from under the seat in front of him and took out *The Game* to read the last few pages. *What was going to happen?* It turned out that when Style had mastered all the pick-up tricks in the book, he was only interested in learning how to stop using them. After trying for a long time, he became friends with his adored Lisa. He behaved like an 'Average Frustrated Chump', who honestly told her everything. The former Style poured tons of notes containing girls' telephone numbers at her feet. Finally, the tall, blond guitarist in Courtney Love's band made her decision. Lisa and Neil became a couple, and she saved him from the destructive chaos.

Touched, Peter put down the black, 400-page paperback that, according to the author, told the true story of what had happened. He looked down at his hands and saw that they were shaking. *Maybe there's a chance after all?* But just considering the question asked more of him that he had counted on. He, who always used to think, 'what you don't know can't hurt you'.

He took a deep breath, carefully touched Vera's left shoulder and looked her in the eye. 'Um, there's something I need to tell you.'

I have to start with the small stuff.

30

Before God and this congregation, do you, Vera Magdalena Lundberg, take Adam Samuel Henningsson to be your lawfully wedded husband, and to love him in sickness and in health?

Vindeln Parish Church, 26 June 1999

When the *Fasten Seatbelt* sign came on Peter turned towards Vera and said, 'Um, there's something I need to tell you.'

She didn't know why it aroused fear in her. She shook her head silently, but he continued anyway.

'Last night, it was stupid, but… I deleted two messages on your phone that you haven't listened to.'

'Huh?' Vera heard how pitiful her voice sounded.

'There were two messages, one from your… him, Adam, and one from your mother.' He blushed and smiled crookedly, stroking his head awkwardly. 'I'm really sorry. It was stupid.'

An enormous exhaustion paralyzed her. 'Why did you do that?' Her heart beat anxiously.

'I don't know… It beeped and I kind of, like, forgot that it wasn't my phone… or something. It was just a stupid thing.' He looked pleadingly at her.

Anger forced itself through the fog of exhaustion. 'A stupid thing? You just don't get it, do you? There's no room for some stupid thing!' Her voice shook. 'How was she? Was she… drunk?'

Peter nodded. Vera turned away and crossed her arms across her chest, but he didn't let her be.

'Vera, Vera…' He cautiously touched her left arm and she relented and let him straighten it out. He took his hand away, but moved his head softly until she looked him in the eye. 'No room… what do you mean?'

How would he ever be able to understand the non-existent room? He had his stable House Beautiful mother who cooked matching 'tanterelle' – what did he know about growing up in the shadow of the Volcano? *He who did nothing but take from everyone and everything all the time?* She couldn't bring herself to say anything, and caught herself trying to escape by covering her face with her hands, the way Gunilla sometimes did. *Like her mother!* The thought made her cry. Trapped helplessly on an airplane. He spoke quietly and intensely, as if trying to be discreet would help.

'Please, I really don't understand. How can it be such a big deal that you didn't hear her drunken nonsense? And you can call her back as soon as we've landed. I know that I have… Your cellphone is dead, sorry, but you can use mine.'

Aching with guilt and worry, his words didn't help. She let out a shaky sigh.

He continued: 'Your mother is an adult. You could have been out partying…' He read her face. 'Okay, you've never gone out partying. Have you never…? Never been drunk?'

She recalled an incident when she had helped her father make posters; she'd been dizzy and slightly nauseated. She shook her head. 'A bad trip caused by sniffing magic markers doesn't count, does it?'

He grinned. 'Well, okay, you could have been undergoing an operation or something. In fact, you were in Stockholm to have your knee examined. Being unreachable for half a day isn't a deadly sin, is it?'

'But… she has problems.'

'Okay, so she has problems. But you can't solve them for her, can you?'

She stared mutely at him.

'You don't have the power to solve every problem in your vicinity. And it isn't your job either…, it's not your responsibility to take care of everything.' Now he sounded frustrated, almost angry, and seemed to be struggling to keep his voice down. Vera might have been imagining it, but she thought that people in the rows in front of them were casting curious, surreptitious glances at them. She was grateful for the noise in the cabin as the plane started its descent, because Peter just continued.

'But it seems to be really difficult for you to get that. Aren't you being a bit of a megalomaniac? "Ah, do you have a problem? Well, then, of course Vera Lundberg should solve it for you."'

He stopped and calmed down, looked at her. Even harder to take, however, was the fact that he looked like he felt sorry for her.

'Do you know what I think?' he said. 'I think that you are way too hard on yourself. Your biggest problem is that you try to be perfect. And, of course, that can be nice for the rest of us. At least at the point when you're trying to help all the time. But it doesn't work. Nobody is perfect. What happens when you try to do something that doesn't work?'

The question echoed inside her, but she couldn't bring herself to answer. Finally, he continued. 'If you persist in trying to achieve something that you can't, I think that's when you get depressed and end up unhappy all the time. I think...' He averted his eyes and pondered, frustrated, for a moment, before he started over.

'I'd like to know, what do *you* want?' He spoke the words slowly and clearly.

She tried to think, though her mind was tired. What kind of question was that? The answer felt far away. He started to talk again, and, once again, it was as if he had read her mind.

'And I don't want to hear "solve the world's problems, save the world's children, help my mother or make Adam happy"... What do *you* want, for *you*?' He looked at her inquisitively.

She looked out through the window. The situation was unnerving. Frightening and liberating at the same time. She looked at her aching, powerless left leg and then back at Peter's questioning gaze. She was surprised at the answer that came bubbling out of her core, from the place where her antenna used to glow: 'I want to dance.'

He studied her with a hint of a smile, as if he were the genie in the bottle thinking, 'Interesting wish, hmmm... and not a bad one, at that.'

Peter held his hand out in front of her as the plane's landing gear hit the ground with a soft bounce. 'Okay. It will take a while, but let's make a deal. Come spring, you will be dancing.'

He sat there waiting. Somewhat confused, Vera put her hand out too, and they shook like they were sealing a business deal. *Really weird.* She felt he wished her well, and it surprised her. As they had been coming in to land, it had been as if real life had been suspended, a descent through cloud cover aided by advice from the opposing team. *Or advice from an alien from outer space. Something not of this world.* And the mood felt different. Calm and fresh, like after a powerful thunderstorm.

As soon as she was allowed to turn it on, she borrowed Peter's cellphone and called Lingon Street. No answer. With rising alarm, she even called her parents' cellphones. No-one answered them, either. Peter tried to calm her, saying that they were probably just busy at work, and that she would be able to reach them in the evening. Vera didn't know if Gunilla was working the day shift; her hours were always irregular, but it was possible.

When they got back to the dorm, Vera was surprised to find Cissi in the kitchen having tea with Matt in the warm light from the large, red Advent star and two votive candles. The table next to them was covered with skilfully drawn sketches. Vera turned to Cissi and said warmly:

'Hi! What are you doing here?'

'I've been trying to reach you, so I decided to just drop by… and I was offered a little Afternoon Tea. Super nice!' Cissi smiled briefly at Matt before continuing.

'Vera, do you know what industrial designers actually do?'

'Apparently they draw beautifully,' said Vera, carefully picking up Matt's oversized sheets.

'Yes, that too. But they watch people trying to do things, and then they come up with ideas, build and test prototypes. The goal is to find solutions that enable people to do what they want, only in a better way!'

'Cool!' said Vera, with a strange feeling of recognition. *Do what you want in a better way?*

Then Cissi noticed that Peter was standing behind Vera.

'Peter! What in the world happened to your hair?'

He touched his head and shrugged his shoulders.

Cissi looked alarmed. 'An accident that required a fire extinguisher and decontamination?'

'No, I just got tired of it. I needed something new in my life...'

Cissi turned inquisitively toward Vera. 'Where have you been?'

'In Stockholm. For an MRI and to take down the Christmas tree,' answered Peter.

'Really?'

Vera nodded and exhaustedly sat down next to Cissi.

'Did you get my message?'

'Yes.'

'Yes, I'm sorry if I expressed myself stupidly last week. I know your contribution will probably be published now that... Well, now that the situation is what it is.' Vera sighed and shrugged her shoulders.

Cissi cut a scone carefully and chose apricot from among the small jam jars on the table. Vera continued anxiously. 'I just wonder what is going to happen – do I get to keep the money from last term? Because I have spent more than half of it, and I just spent 4,000...'

'I don't think the money is going to be a problem. Not for the fall anyway. And if your chapter isn't published, then it's like we are guilty of breach of contract, not you. Check with Lilian about what you signed in the fall. Worst-case scenario, you don't get money for the spring. Sorry.'

Vera sat quietly as Cissi went on. 'I've checked up on it now, and, unfortunately it's true... They want to choose one of our chapters, and I'm not at all sure that it's mine that they want.'

She showed Vera what she had in front of her on the table. Vera leaned closer and saw that Cissi's manuscript was called *Wealth, Welfare and the Boundaries of Nature*. Cissi flipped through it and showed her: her draft also had numerous red question marks.

Vera pointed to a word and said, '"Anomaly?" What does he mean by that?'

Cissi shrugged her shoulders. 'He doesn't think it fits with the rest.'

'In religion, an anomaly is a miracle,' grinned Matt.

Cissi smiled slightly and waved dismissively with her red-splotched chapter. 'Yeah, yeah, at least this fits in with my dissertation, so I'll still be able to use it regardless...'

'That's good,' said Vera.

'And I think that you should consider the possibility of reworking your chapter a little. Who knows, maybe you'll be the one who gets published?'

Vera smiled wanly and shook her head. She looked at Matt as she leaned slightly towards Cissi and put her arm around her shoulders. 'But what a friend she is!'

Matt nodded. His deep-set eyes sparkled approvingly behind the steam rising from the cup of Darjeeling, and then he looked up. Only the Englishman noticed that Peter was standing behind his project colleagues looking thoughtful.

The atmosphere around the table was cozy, and others who lived in the dorm joined the group, but Vera felt completely exhausted. Peter took her backpack and helped her into her room.

'Uh, Peter, by the way... What did Adam's voicemail say?'

Peter looked down at the floor. 'It was short... "Please call me, we have to solve this," or something like that.'

'Ah, oh. Okay.'

Peter looked at her as if he wanted to say something else, but then he just shrugged his shoulders and left.

She had forgotten the condition she had left her room in two days ago. There were removal boxes and bags everywhere, and she couldn't find the one thing she desperately wanted – her phone charger. She didn't want to close the door and cut off the sound of the cozy murmuring coming from Matt's Afternoon Tea. She didn't want to be alone with her chaos and depressing removal boxes. But where was the charger?

While she laboriously searched the room, she remembered Cissi's words. *Breach of contract.* She thought about the promise she had made in church that beautiful summer day in a different life. To love Adam, in sickness and in health. At that moment it had felt natural and totally uncomplicated. Adam, the kind, handsome guy who had been the star of the local soccer team, popular in school, considerate and unbelievably clever. *How could one not love him?* she remembered wanting to ask the priest. She recalled how special and secure she had felt. *I'm on dry land now.* She looked forward to 'in health,' but wasn't at all worried about 'in sickness'. She knew she would be able to cope. When there was trouble in the family, you were there for each other; you supported each other. It had seemed so obvious.

But now, loving Adam was associated with enormous pain. And with shame. The bottom had fallen out of the relationship; there was nothing left to stand on. The old harmony, the friendly discussions, the fun and mutual trust felt like smoke and mirrors hiding the truth.

She had gone abroad with Basic Needs. She had left him. She knew her mother blamed her for that. She thought that Vera had destroyed the marriage by leaving. But deep inside, Vera felt that it could just as easily have happened while she was riding home on the subway from some health clinic in the suburbs. The fracture had nothing to do with physical distance. It had been there all along, molded into the marriage, mixed in among the good stuff. She had not realized it until it was too late, not before she had been lulled into a false sense of security. And all her brave efforts had not been enough to fix the fracture. Now, after the fact, Vera saw the marriage as a huge, personal failure.

She sat down on the bed, put her glasses on the nightstand and covered her eyes with her hands. She sobbed in the darkness. Suddenly, a little glimpse of light, new and unfamiliar questions appearing from above the clouds. *Is this a problem that I can solve?*

She thought about it. No, it is beyond my power... the insight came to her slowly. She forced herself to think harder about the root of the pain, its essence, and it became clear. *It is impossible for me to solve it. So it isn't my responsibility.* It was still a terrible loss, but it didn't need to be her responsibility and her shame. Tears started to fall, but they were mainly ones of relief, and she sniffled loudly.

'Vera?' The voice was soft and compassionate. 'Sweetie, what is it?'

It was Cissi.

Vera dried her face awkwardly and tried to stop crying.

'It's nothing. I'm just so, so … tired. And I can't find my phone charger. I really need to charge my phone!'

Cissi hung up her coat in the hall and stood with her hands on her hips. She looked like a resolute schoolteacher worried about an unruly class.

'You can't live like this! Talk about bad chi!'

'Huh?'

'Why do you have a mass of removal boxes stuffed in here? You don't have any room for yourself! This is a perfect example… You are both exhausted and stressed out at the same time. Right?'

Vera nodded.

'So you don't have the energy to take care of all your stuff. You just let it take over your space, which makes you exhausted and stressed, which means you don't have any energy. And so forth. Get it?'

She went over and opened the top box. 'Clothes.'

Vera shook her head. 'It isn't in there. It must be lying around somewhere. I didn't have it in… Stockholm.' Her voice weakened to the point of nearly vanishing.

'Are these boxes from… ' Cissi went quiet as if to censure herself. 'From your home with him, Adam?'

Vera nodded.

'Well, that makes it even worse! Don't you realize that every time you see these boxes it reminds you of him and whatever it is that happened? It isn't good for you. You need peace and quiet, rest from all this damned crap!'

Cissi dumped a whole box out on Vera's bed, and in the face of such determination Vera submissively pushed herself into a standing position with the help of her tired right leg. She had done so a thousand times before, and it had become increasingly painful, but this time the pain cut so sharply that she fell back onto the bed.

'Arrgh!'

'What? What is it?'

Vera groaned and grabbed her lower back. *I should have taken my crutches to Stockholm.* Using them made her shoulders ache, but it was nothing compared to this!

Cissi cast her a worried look. 'Are you taking an anti-inflammatory? Did you get a massage?'

Vera twisted awkwardly in an effort to get up off the pile of clothes on the bed. 'I am a devoted consumer of Diclofenac, but it's starting to give me stomach pain, and it doesn't help that much. The massage was a nightmare; I thought I would break in two! If you're interested, I have four treatments with Annika that you can have.'

'Did she use her elbow to put pressure on your muscle knots?' Cissi looked compassionately at Vera, offered her hand and pulled her carefully up off the bed.

'Mmmm, something about giant knots in my piriformis...'

'I know. It really hurts. My sister had pelvic pain when she was pregnant and completely stiffened up after her second child. She said that getting rid of the damned knots was like experiencing delivery pain all over again. But she went a few times and did stretching exercises, and that did the trick. Sometimes you just have to push through the pain to get out on the other side. That's what my sister said.'

I don't know if I have the strength, thought Vera. *Anyway, what's the point when I'm not getting help for my knee, which is the cause of the whole thing?*

Cissi had started sorting the clothes.

'Really nice! Wrong color, but otherwise fine. It can go to the Salvation Army. Or, what do you think? Tell me if... Worn out – toss it. Like new, but...' She looked at the bra's tag and said ruthlessly, 'Wrong size!'

Cissi went to the kitchen to get some paper bags. She held some garments up in front of Vera, and had Vera try on a couple of shirts before she decided, but within half an hour she had emptied two boxes and sorted things into different bags – *throw away, give away*, and a neatly folded pile on the bed that was *keep*.

Throw away, thought Vera. She could seldom bring herself to do that, except the salmon-pink, black-lace disaster. Feeling like the world's biggest failure, she had immediately buried it in the bottom of the bin.

While Cissi dismantled the removal boxes, Vera stored the clothes that had survived the sorting in the empty closets in the hall. The feeling of liberation was remarkably strong. She glanced at the bras in the 'give away' bag and memorized – *34A, wrong size.*

'What's in these?' Cissi asked, pointing to the bags she had found behind the boxes. They were full of outdoor clothes and exercise stuff. Suddenly more energetic, Vera took command and also put the outdoor clothes into the closets, everything except for a big quilted jacket, light turquoise with gold fur trim. She had never worn it, but Vera noticed Cissi looking at it with interest. Then it hit her...

'I've never worn that. I think... yes, see the price tag? It was 50 per cent off the sale price and it's so pretty that I bought it. But it doesn't fit at all. But maybe you... maybe you want try it on? I think it will look really good on you!'

Cissi went to the mirror in the hall and put it on. It fit perfectly over her curves, not too puffy and not too heavy. The soft turquoise and gold suited Cissi's red hair and light skin.

A feeling of happiness warmed Vera from the inside. 'Wow, it looks great! Really! It really... what was it you said? It really suits you?'

Cissi turned this way and that in front of the mirror and tested putting up the hood. She smiled and nodded. That clinched it for Vera. 'Then you should have it. And thanks so much for helping with everything!'

The phone charger had fallen off the desk behind the bags with the outdoor clothes, and it was easily spotted once they had been cleared away. Cissi was late and rushed away happily wearing the new jacket and carrying her old one in one of the empty bags. Before she left, she made Vera promise that she would use the rest of the massage sessions and continue to clean out the rest of the boxes, or at least move them to storage.

As soon as the cellphone came back to life it signalled, *'You have two, new messages'.* The first was from Adam, again.

'Darling Vera…,' he pleaded, 'please call me as soon as you can; I have to talk to you! I don't want… I can't be without my Vera. Please, honey, call me!'

'Recorded… yesterday… 11.57pm.'

Her pulse quickened. Vera swallowed and couldn't help wondering if this was the kind of message that Peter had listened to and deleted. Questions fluttered randomly around in her head. How was Adam? *It isn't your responsibility to make Adam happy… What do **you** want?* Why had Peter really listened to her messages? And why had he deleted them?

Her scattered thoughts were abruptly interrupted by a tense male voice speaking. There was an unfamiliar mumbling in the background.

'Hi Vera. It's Mats. It's… Can you call me as soon as you get this message?'

'Recorded… today… 10.28am.

Vera's heart pounded hard in her chest. She was filled with foreboding and her fingers felt clumsy and hard to control as she pushed the buttons to return her uncle's call.

It rang numerous times on the other end. She was about to give up when he finally answered. Vera sank feebly onto the bed as Mats anxiously recounted what had happened.

He had run into Eva Henningsson when he was buying coffee cake for the office that morning. Eva had asked how things had turned out for Gunilla yesterday, and Mats hadn't understood what she was talking about. Eva told him that Gunilla had driven over to their house last night, when she was 'not in good shape' – but thank goodness nothing had happened. She had been… 'unlike herself, not well at all.'

Vera understood immediately. *Disorderly. Blind drunk. Public danger. Drunk driving, punishable by law.*

The Henningssons had called Sven-Erik, and he had come at once, straight from his meeting about the new zoning plan.

He had taken her home, though it sounded like it had been a disorderly affair. Eva had said that it was fine that the Toyota was still at their house; she just wanted to make sure that everybody was okay.

Mats didn't know anything about how his sister and her husband were doing, but he went right over to Lingon Street to check on them. He found the door open, the Volvo and Sven-Erik gone without a trace, and Gunilla unresponsive in her bed.

He had called 911 and accompanied his sister in the ambulance to the hospital. She came around during the trip, but at the hospital they pumped her stomach just in case. The doctor who had just looked in on Gunilla said that she was no longer in any immediate danger, but the combination of alcohol and sedatives was life threatening. They wanted to keep her in overnight for observation.

Vera tried to say something, but all that came out was a suffocated sob.

'Don't worry about Gunilla. I'm with her. You don't need to worry now,' continued Mats, trying to comfort her. But then he continued more doubtfully. 'Um... I haven't spent much time looking or anything, but I really have no idea where your father is.'

Vera felt a cold lump in her chest. Mats continued. 'Of course, Sven-Erik can take care of himself. I'm sure he's fine.' Vera thanked her uncle. Mustering all her strength, she asked him in a weak voice to call as soon as he knew more.

For once in his life, her father had worked late. *A few hours yesterday,* she thought, and feelings of guilt blossomed inside her. It was an old, well-worn pattern. The control rods hadn't been in place. Neither she nor Sven-Erik had submerged into the storm of emotions to absorb all the negative energy. Instead, Gunilla got drunk, drove over to the Henningssons' and said and did... *God knows what?*

And worst of all, why was her father missing? He always reproached Vera for every decision she made that took her away from her mother – so where was he? Vera felt like she was missing important pieces of the puzzle, and she was very worried. A car accident? She had heard that there was a snowstorm inland. Or maybe he'd had a heart attack? The thought was horrifying. The family couldn't function without him. He was the stable, persistently positive one. He couldn't be gone. She would be alone with all of it... She would break in two right down the middle.

She was sitting paralyzed with anxiety when someone knocked on the door.

Someone came in and shut the door. After a couple of slow steps, he reached the door between the hall and the rest of the dorm room. It was Sven-Erik! She stood up laboriously with the help of the wall and walked right into her father's arms. He hugged her back and snuffled into the messy strands of hair that had come loose from her braid.

She stepped back and looked at his face searchingly. 'What happened?'

His nose was swollen; he had a long, bruised bump over his left cheek, and a huge fat lip that made his mouth look crooked. *Had he been in a car accident in the bad weather after all?*

Vera fetched her well-stocked first-aid kit from the bathroom. Sven-Erik pulled the desk chair past the removal boxes that were still standing in the middle of the room, and sat down tiredly, like an old man. She saw that he had been crying. She asked with her eyes if she could take care of his injuries. He nodded.

'Vera.' He sighed shakily, but bravely held his face still so she could work on it. 'Last night... was not a good night.'

She put on sterile, throwaway gloves and began carefully to wash and bandage his injuries, while, slowly and full of anguish, he told her what had happened. Krister Henningsson had called him when he had turned his phone back on after the unveiling of the zoning plan. He had immediately driven over and witnessed Gunilla, half-dressed and enraged, screaming at Eva and Krister because they apparently didn't think that Vera was good enough for their fine son. Maybe because the Lundbergs were ordinary workers and not from the distinguished social class that included doctors?

248

Then, in a sudden mood swing, Gunilla had sat on Krister's knee to try to explain herself, not noticing that her dress was riding up her thighs and... He gestured, humiliated. In any case, Sven-Erik had finally maneuvered her out of the house, and he tried to talk sense to her on the way home. She knew that she wasn't allowed to drive the car when she had been drinking! When they finally got home and were standing in the hall, he told Gunilla that he didn't think the Henningssons had looked down on them *before*, but thanks to her behavior tonight... That was when she... did it.

'Did what?'

Sven-Erik lifted his gaze from the floor as if it were infinitely heavy. 'It was with the coat-hanger. I didn't react quickly enough, so...' He touched his bandaged cheek and directed his gaze back at the floor again. He hung his head heavily. He lifted his arm, revealing the red-brown stains on the jacket sleeve.

'It missed my eye, but the hook caught my nose, so it bled a bit.'

Vera couldn't comprehend what he was telling her. Gunilla was capable of all kinds of things, yes. She had actually done all manner of things over the years... but she had never been violent towards anyone. Vera saw the ring on the hand that he was carefully holding over his injured cheek, and it dawned on her that her father had also promised *in sickness and in health.*

But how much sickness did you have to take before the best course of action was to end it?

She saw her father's despair and realized the scope of what had happened. That was her father's line in the sand. *Those who hit, you leave.* The last time she had seen her father, they had parted in disagreement because she had felt it impossible to keep giving in to Gunilla. Sooner or later the volcano would demand concessions that exceeded what was reasonable. There would be no room left, and everything around it would be destroyed. Now it had happened, they were past the reasonable, and she felt only sadness and fear. The fact that she had been right was terrible. It was awful that her family was gone, smashed to bits by a hellish drunkenness and a coat-hanger. The family was larger than the sum of its parts, the whole more valuable than just its individual

249

members. What would happen now? What might she have done differently?

As if he shared her thoughts, Sven-Erik said: 'I don't understand. It came completely without warning this time.'

She knew she had to confess. 'No, it probably wasn't without warning.'

'Huh?'

'I found out today that she called me yesterday; she left a message.'

'Well, what did she say?'

'I… don't know.' *Maybe the catastrophe could have been avoided?*

31

Fundamental principles of Jujutsu Kai:
1 One's own good balance
2 The opponent's imbalance
3 One's own strongest point
4 The opponent's weakest point

Vera had asked about the message from her husband. As Peter left her room he was overwhelmed by a strong feeling of loss. Perhaps he had deleted Adam's message in the vain hope that doing so would delete her husband from the playing field? But, of course, it wasn't that simple. And everything hung on what he had asked her while the plane was landing: what did Vera want? And if she even wanted a husband, what kind of husband did she want?

He understood that the person she was already married to ought to have a big advantage. She had chosen him a long time ago and she knew him well. She was like an Elf, so she would never let some infatuated peach-fuzz destroy her marriage.

The thought depressed him. He also remembered that she had actually told him to his face that his big problem was himself, that he was *so damned egotistical all the time.* That was definitely not a compliment. He looked gloomily at his reflection in the mirror. But, at the same time – if his biggest problem was himself, then he could actually do something about it! He wasn't helpless, dependent on someone else. And he truly thought that he had already started to solve the problem. He straightened up as he gazed at himself. He still wasn't used to seeing his bald head. Peter thought about the fact that Sandra had seen a man 'going places' in Robert von Law Firm.

Perhaps Peter could begin by giving himself some direction?

A professional path that didn't have anything to do with Vera? Suddenly resolute, he felt that he had an important task to do. He would write an essay about growth in finance markets.

He sat down at his desk and started to read the article on the top of the pile of articles that he had found when he searched 'financial growth' at the university library. It was about financial derivatives on Wall Street, which had experienced enormous value growth. The market for something called Credit Default Swaps had grown 100-fold since it was created 10 years ago. *One hundred fold!*

He marked the text with a yellow highlighter. He needed to dig into this further; it would definitely impress Sturesson and the others. If you wanted growth, then you should definitely focus on financial markets; they were absolutely right about that. Those guys at JP Morgan Chase who had invented the securities ought to have piles of money by now. It was guys like that who had the buying power to take a helicopter to Alaska and shoot grizzlies over the weekend.

But what were these Credit Default Swaps?

On the other hand… a new thought came to him and he lost his focus on complicated formulas. Vera had actually taken off her rings and Cissi said that she was in the process of separating from her husband. If so, then things were not exactly as they should be in her marriage. Peter suddenly remembered what Solveig at the retirement home had said.

I don't know if she knows any good men.

Derivatives would have to wait. He got up from his desk and went directly out to the kitchen. Only Matt was still there. He was cleaning up after his tea party.

'Hey, Matt. Can I ask you something? What do you think of when I say "a good man"?'

'What?' Matt looked cagey. 'Is this some… what's it called?'

'No, it's not a test or anything. I'm just wondering; what is a good man?'

'Alright.' Matt thought for a minute while his hands carefully washed the teapot in the sink. 'Jesus, I guess.'

Uh oh. *A holy man who died a martyr's death.*

'No... well, okay. Him of course. But I mean a regular person. A good man who, like... makes the people around him happy?' *A man who Mom would not have had to divorce,* he thought, and continued, 'a man you stay with because he makes you feel good?'

Matt thought for a minute and then shrugged his shoulders. 'I am reading *The Art of Happiness* by Tibet's... you know, Dalai Lama. He says that one can learn the art of being happy.'

Learn to be happy? That wasn't an answer to the question. What Peter wanted to know was how to make *someone else happy*, someone you were close to. But perhaps they weren't entirely separate things?

'One becomes happy if one practises *discipline and compassion*, that's what he says,' continued Matt.

That sounded like a pretty boring kind of happiness, thought Peter. It sounded almost like Vera, and look where it had got her. *Less* discipline and compassion felt more like what she needed!

Suddenly, Vera appeared in the doorway, tense and serious. 'There you are. Good. We need you... can you come to my room?'

When Peter got to Vera's room, which was untidy with bags and removal boxes everywhere, he saw that her father was there. His face was injured, giving it a swollen and crooked appearance, but he was skilfully bandaged around the mouth. *Nasty blow, that*, thought Peter.

'What did my mother say in the message you deleted last night?' asked Vera.

'Wait, wait a minute...' said a stern-looking Sven-Erik. He spoke slowly. 'Did you delete a message from Vera's phone last night?'

Peter nodded tensely: 'Yes, I did.'

'But... why?' Sven-Erik sighed angrily as if he were trying not to swear. 'Why would you do that?' Last week's friendly tone had vanished and a uneasy combativeness filled Peter. This was serious. He shook his head.

'I was a complete idiot to listen to it. You're absolutely right.

I should never have done it. But then when I had...' Peter felt strongly that what he said next was the truth, even if he shouldn't have done it: 'I deleted it to spare Vera.'

'Spare Vera?'

'Yes. I think she spends too much of her life trying to... anticipate and work around Gunilla. When she called yesterday, she was... drunk and said things that would have made Vera sad. I thought it was unnecessary for her to hear it.'

'Unnecessary? I'll tell you what's unnecessary!' hissed Sven-Erik through his swollen lip as he rose out of his chair. Vera looked at her father as if he had suddenly transformed into Mr Hyde, and turned back to Peter.

'Please,' she pleaded, 'try to remember. What did she say?'

Peter's heart beat uncomfortably and he felt like his body was ready to flee, but he looked steadily at Vera: 'She said, if I remember correctly...' *Do you really want to hear this?*

He tried to avoid the worst of it. 'That you are 30 years old, your life is a mess, and you're having problems with your husband. But she was going to fix things for you.'

'Aha!' Sven-Erik sighed and pressed his hands over his eyes so hard that it looked like he was going to push them into his head. 'She was going to fix things with Adam. If we had known that yesterday evening, we could have stopped...'

'Stopped what?' Peter shifted his gaze to Sven-Erik. 'What happened?'

Sven-Erik didn't answer. Vera looked at him. 'She has been admitted to the hospital for observation,' she said grimly.

'What?' Sven-Erik looked up, color draining from his face.

'Yeah, Mats called. He's with her. He wondered where you were. We need to call and tell him...' Vera reached for her cellphone, which was still charging, and spoke briefly, saying something about Sven-Erik being okay, but that he didn't want to talk to Gunilla; things had happened and they could talk more later.

Sven-Erik lashed out at Peter. 'If we had known, then none of this would have happened!'

Peter felt like he was on trial, and Vera continued presenting the prosecution's case. 'She drove drunk. She went over to my in-laws' house and... raised hell. Then she hit Dad in the face with a coat-hanger. So now the family is in pieces. It would have been really... useful if we could have prevented it!'

Vera looked at him in despair as she pushed him towards the door. 'It's best if you leave.'

It was a relief to get out of there. They were going to sit there dwelling on it, blaming themselves and him.

A guilt club for the imperfect.

Yet when she closed the door behind him he felt painfully excluded. And it didn't help that half an hour later he saw Matt helping Vera and Sven-Erik carry bags and boxes out of her room. Peter had wanted to protect and help her, but maybe Matt's way was better? *It's a more popular one, at least.* The thought stung him as he saw Sven-Erik, with his lacerated face, smile gratefully at Matt. Peter stood in the kitchen doorway and watched as Vera hugged her father goodbye.

As she limped back to her room with an air of defeat, Peter lost control. Suddenly, he was outside her room, with his foot blocking the door like a pushy salesman, and he said in a low voice: 'What you told me is terrible, and I'm really sorry. But there's something I really don't understand. It feels like you're blaming me, or yourselves or something, for what happened.'

Vera's expression confirmed what he said, but she let him follow her in anyway. He closed the door behind him and continued: 'I know what it's like when a family falls apart, how a divorce can tear you apart. I know the price everybody pays, especially the kids. I have... huge respect for your efforts to protect your family. But you were in Stockholm to have your knee examined yesterday. Even if you *had* heard the message, what could you have done?'

'What time did she leave the voicemail?' asked Vera tensely.

'About 7pm, and your Dad was working then!' said Peter.

'But I could have called Mats, my uncle!'

'Well, okay, but who's to say he could have dropped everything and rushed over then and there?' Peter heard his pulse pounding in his ears. 'Don't you get it? If Gunilla wants... if she wants to kill herself then she'll find a way! If she doesn't want to be saved, then nobody can save her. All your attempts to adapt, your efforts... maybe you think you're doing her a favor. But I'm not sure that you are, because...'

Birgitta's words came to him from across the space that, until that moment, had just been a silent observer. In the heat of the moment, he finally understood: 'Love doesn't mean letting someone hurt you.'

Wide-eyed, Vera looked at him. She quickly wiped away a little tear with her left hand. Glancing restlessly around the room, she whispered: 'She wouldn't have hurt Dad if we had known... what was about to happen and had prevented it.'

Peter tried again, hoping he could get her to understand. 'My father has never touched so much as a hair on my mother's head, but he still hurt her for years.' He lifted his hand and showed her the large crooked scar on his left thumb.

'We spent the summer that my mother was pregnant with Vicky at our summer cottage out in Stockholm's archipelago. I was seven and in the middle of my Emil-of-Lönneberga period, so I wanted to carve wood figures all the time. But I cut myself, and I must have got some crap in the sore, because after a day or so I got sick. The sore got full of pus, and I got red streaks...' He stroked his fingers up his arm to show what he meant.

'Blood poisoning?' she wondered.

'Yes, as it turned out. That night I got a high fever and was delirious, but the cellphone didn't work. We had one of those big clunky things with an antenna, like people had back then. Mother didn't want to risk it. She had no choice but to try to get me back to the mainland to the hospital. There was a nasty wind out, although thankfully not a gale. I think she was scared to death, and the waves slammed so hard against the boat that her waters broke. I was so ill that she was forced to do everything herself. She gave birth to Vicky four weeks early and alone. Because do you know where Dad was?'

Vera looked quietly at Peter as the difficult, long-forgotten feelings raged inside him. He was surprised at the bitterness in his voice. 'He was in Tibet working on his big vision.'

'What big vision?'

'To "open Shangri-La for luxury tourism". He planned to come home a couple of weeks before Mom's due-date. And, sure, he came home as fast as he could. Everything went well, we survived. But he cut everything too fine, there was no margin for the unexpected. Mom was forced to cover for him all the time. It was always Mother who had to have margins. I mean, Dad has never hit anyone, but he hurt her by not giving her any space, any oxygen – by only doing things that fitted in with his own plans and failing to notice anything else. My mother was so flexible... she let herself disappear...'

Peter choked up and turned to go. But then he suddenly thought about the main character in the drama: the small, ash-blond nurse's assistant. She had actually seemed pretty tough to him. He stopped in his tracks. 'How do you really know what Gunilla can and can't take? Has she ever had to try before? Have you ever let her take responsibility for herself?'

×

In the days that followed, Vera was as reserved as she had been before. Each of them kept to themselves, and Peter sat alone in his room. He sighed and stared at the pile of books and papers. It had become so complicated that he was forced to start over from the beginning. He reread the purpose of derivatives and recognized the description: to spread risk. He sensed that spreading risk meant loaning out more money, *but how did that make the entire system more secure?* Peter enjoyed the luxury of grasping things faster than most people, but this was like a dense forest. He was constantly forced to retrace his steps in search of something that looked like a path.

Peter sat for a long time trying to think, tapping his bald head in frustration. He finally gave up and went out to the kitchen. Vera was sitting there having tea with Cissi's cousin, the big-haired teenager. They were looking at a notebook in the lamplight. Whatever it was, it had to be more interesting than the impenetrable derivatives jungle. Peter boiled water, took out the instant coffee, and glanced over Freddie's hair towards his notes. The teenager underlined the heading for what looked like the tenth time. Other than a short paragraph underneath it, the paper was covered with erasure marks.

'I think you have to include trustworthy,' said Vera.

'I think so too,' gambled Peter. He felt strangely certain that that word and Vera were a combination he believed in. Regardless of the context.

Vera looked up warily. But Freddie was unreceptive and only sighed in frustration. 'But what does it mean? Being reliable or something?'

'Yes, what are we talking about?' Peter brought his cup over to the table, sat down across from them, and started reading upside down. The teenager had written *Real Love* in pencil at the top of the page.

Peter glanced at Vera. 'Real Love. Okay. Well, to begin with, attraction.'

Vera snorted. 'Attraction? Some people seem to experience that several times a week with different people. That has nothing to do with love.'

'No, I mean something special. Chemistry that just… instantly bowls you over. Haven't you ever heard of love at first sight?'

Fuck! That sounded like a bad pick-up line right out of The Game. Was he trying to defend himself against having reacted only to appearance, like all other men according to Style? He knew better than to argue that with Vera. *Although, was that actually what had happened?*

'What do you know about someone you've only seen for a second? Then it's nothing more than your own fantasy you fall in love with! For like, a week…' Vera's cheeks turned red. Freddie struggled to write, preoccupied with the difficult task.

Peter thought. He had started all wrong. He had tried to defend his weakness instead of emphasizing his strength. He had first noticed her when she looked different from her usual self; he understood the conclusion she had drawn. But why couldn't she imagine a more generous interpretation? How could he have known deep in his heart that the woman on the bus was kind? Wasn't the spark that drove everything else out of his mind actually his realization of that kindness? Sure, he had been slow to realize it, maybe he had the slowest power of insight in northern Europe. But that didn't make the feeling any less genuine. *How could he express that?*

Freddie looked up in frustration, and scratched around in his mass of hair with his pencil. 'That... trust-thing, Vera. Do you mean reliable?'

'Trustworthy. Yes, exactly, reliable. But also... to be able to trust.'

Peter looked directly at her. 'Yes. You can be as reliable as hell, but if the other person isn't able to trust you then...'

Vera coldly interrupted him. 'If people deserve it, then others rely on them.'

'Yes, that's probably true. Unless the one who is supposed to do the relying has been burned before.'

'Or if the one who thinks he is reliable... ' Her voice quivered: 'demonstrably isn't?'

His heart beat loudly as he looked at her. It beat so hard that he wondered if she could hear it. Demonstrably *wasn't*. That was then. *This is now.* 'But if he changes?'

She looked at him skeptically, shaking her head. 'You can't change another person.'

'No, that's true. But you can change yourself.'

There! A warm feeling spread through his chest. He knew that he was capable of changing. Surprise flashed in her eyes and she gazed searchingly at him. Freddie dropped the pencil so that it bounced against the paper and slumped back in his chair.

'God, what a fucking crap assignment! It's, like, not worth the bother!'

✖

The following Friday, Vera came out to the kitchen for breakfast with messy hair and a piece of paper in her hand. She looked worried. She sat down and put the paper on the table in front of her. Peter abandoned his morning paper, got up off the sofa and came over to look at it. It was the results from the MRI!

'So, it came. What does it say?' Peter asked.

259

Vera looked up. 'It says just what I thought.' She raised her stiff left leg. 'I talked to the doctor there. He recommends two operations. First for the meniscus, then months of training, and then the cruciate ligament.'

'So, one step closer to the Dance.' Peter smiled at her.

But Vera didn't look happy. 'The examination may only have cost 4,000, but the price of an operation is another matter. I'd guess at least 20 times as much. Minimum.'

'Yes, but, like he said, they'll probably do something about it here in Umeå, right?'

Vera looked doubtful. 'My knee is not considered an emergency, and the nurses are on strike. I had to make a major fuss just to get a doctor's appointment. I'll go in today and show them my knee and the diagnosis, but they're hardly going to change their minds.'

She sighed anxiously and skilfully braided her hair down her back in the usual way. He observed the small, precise movements of her hands, and clenched his fist at the memory: he had held her hand twice.

Peter brought his half-eaten sandwich and teacup over to the table. They ate in silence. The last time they shook hands, Peter had promised to help her. *But how*? To pay for an operation in Stockholm seemed out of the question; there was no way she would accept such an expensive gift, even if he offered it. That left only the Västerbotten county government.

'Have I ever told you that I do jujutsu?'

'Yes, you said something about it once.' She looked perplexed.

'It's, well, a way of thinking that you can use in other contexts… I mean, maybe you could use it now.'

She looked at him questioningly.

'I think you are fully aware of your weaknesses here,' continued Peter. 'You are just an ordinary person going up against the powerful county government and their… what did you call them? Almighty doctors?'

Vera nodded.

'Okay. So what are your strengths?'

Vera pursed her mouth in doubt and shook her head.

'Well, you have to have some strengths,' Peter insisted. 'Even in this battle. For example, you're a trained nurse. The Almighties have some weaknesses. They made the wrong decision, after all. It's complete crap that you've had to go around like this for months, right? Isn't that what the doctor at Sophia Hospital said?'

'Well, he didn't use those words exactly, but...' Vera nodded.

'Use your strengths and focus on their weaknesses. If you were working for the county government and made a mistake like that, what could a patient do?'

'The Medical Board.'

'What?'

'Report me to the Medical Board,' explained Vera.

'Okay, then. That's it.'

32

M69/MRI Knee Osteoarthritis Clinic
2008-01-09 (22096)

Total rupture of anterior cruciate ligament. Cartilage
of lateral patellar facet has altered signal intensity
and reduced thickness, no focal defects but signs of a
horizontally oriented injury. Distal quadriceps tendon
and patellar tendons are normal. Cornus posterius
region of medial meniscus has somewhat irregular,
oblique rupture penetrating the underside of the
meniscus. Medial and lateral collateral ligaments are
normal. Middle region of femoral condyle has slight
edema near the meniscal tear.

Olof Eklund,
Sofia Osteoarthritis Clinic

It was extraordinary, as if an emptiness had been filled.

And it had happened exactly as Peter had said during that
remarkable landing. Vera was usually the one who helped
people solve their problems, but this time, it was the other way
around. Surprised, happy and still holding the telephone, she
thought about what had just happened.

Have you ever let her take responsibility for herself? His
words had etched themselves onto Vera's brain, but she had had
mixed feelings. On the one hand, it was like a breath of fresh
air, like opening a window in a musty old room and letting in
the summer breeze. But it was also frightening. *If she wants to
kill herself then she'll find a way.* Obviously he was quite right;
nobody could be watched every minute of every day.

Peter had been right about other things too. What he'd said
had actually helped her at her next doctor's appointment at

Norrland University Hospital. She was still amazed when she thought about everything that had happened on Friday.

She had dressed in crisply pressed clothes and put up her hair. Having sensed that Orthopedics was experiencing some kind of IT meltdown – they couldn't find any of her previous emails – she took a hard copy of the diagnosis from Stockholm with her, and gave it to the doctor before carefully sitting down on the examination bed, which was covered with a paper sheet.

'Ah, yes. Vera Lundberg. Knee injury...' Vera waited patiently while the specialist read through the document. He frowned and looked up at her.

'Yes, of course this needs to be treated. As you know, however, the nurses are on strike, so for the time being we can only do emergency procedures. The strike also means that the waiting list is growing... so I can't promise anything.' He stretched out his hand to give her back the document containing the diagnosis.

'What?' Vera sat on her hands, refusing to take the papers.

'You emailed this to us, didn't you?' His white coat fluttered open as he span around in his chair. He shifted his feet, in their brown leather sandals, from the chair leg to the floor, put the papers down on his overflowing desk, and clicked his mouse impatiently, searching in vain for her email. Finally he gave up. 'Maybe you can try sending it again? We'll get back to you when the strike is over; then we'll know how long the waiting list is.' His tone was light, and he offered his hand to signal that the appointment was over.

Vera ignored it and looked at him coldly. 'So your decision is to continue doing nothing about my knee? Can I have that in writing?'

'Why do you want it in writing?'

'I am going to report the case to the Medical Board, and I need to include your decision as a supporting document.'

The doctor paled. Vera didn't move a muscle. After a moment he turned back to the screen and began typing. Vera read the words *Due to the strike...* over his shoulder. He wrote a couple of lines and sent the document off with a click.

'You can pick up the printout at the reception desk, but don't think you can use threats to improve your chances.' He looked at her sternly.

'Fine. I'll use it to improve other people's chances of getting the help they're entitled to, instead, since I assume that I haven't been treated worse than anybody else. Which must mean that there are other people in the same situation.'

Vera felt her racing pulse and sweaty palms. The atmosphere in the room was hostile. Despite her own powerful sense of indignation, the doctor's distress forced its way into her consciousness like an uninvited guest. As he opened the door for her, she noticed that the veins in his temples were bulging. *Leave now!*

'Report it if you want, but you can't claim it's my fault that Sweden's nurses are on strike!'

Uncharacteristically, Vera was up for a fight; having been coached by a space alien she was prepared for this turn of events. She remained seated on the examination bed.

'You may not be able to operate on my knee now due to the strike, but why didn't you mend the meniscal tear right after the injury occurred last spring? Why didn't you even put me on the list for an MRI until the late fall? Why was I forced to pay for an MRI in Stockholm in order to get your attention? I know something about how the Medical Board works, and I think those are the questions they're going to be interested in. Something must be seriously wrong when a patient has to live with a condition like this for eight months, or even – what did you have in mind – over a year?'

She stared at him implacably before finally getting up and limping towards the door. 'I'm going to get the printout from reception, but I'll be right back, because I want your signature on it.'

Now it was Monday morning, and she had just received a phone call from the receptionist at Orthopedics. With a cheerful voice the woman had said hello and asked, 'Am I speaking to Vera Lundberg? Yes? Well... we've just had our morning meeting and our chief physician says that it's time to help you with your knee. What do you say? Does an operation next week suit you, on Monday, 28 January?'

Amazed, Vera said yes, sure. And yes, of course, she could drop in and have some pre-op tests done. Yes, yes, thank you, goodbye.

So, *now* they suddenly had time to help her? She was going to get her operation – in the middle of the nurses' strike? She felt a strange mix of happiness – as if she had won the most important victory of her life – and guilt. Who had she jumped in front of in the queue thanks to her inside knowledge about how to report doctors to the Medical Board? *But my name isn't Ibrahimovic, and I'm not Sweden's star footballer – so it was my only option!*

Most of all she felt grateful. What had happened was extraordinary. And it was all thanks to Peter Stavenius.

The week passed. Vera went in for the tests and met the anesthesiologist. She wondered why he wanted to examine her throat and see how far back she could bend her neck. She knew it was standard procedure when a patient was going to be given a general anaesthetic, because the doctor needed to know that they could be intubated if something went wrong. But weren't meniscus operations done with laparoscopic surgery and spinal anesthesia? The anesthesiologist looked at her in confusion and showed her a piece of paper describing the operation. Hadn't she received a copy?

It was a picture of a knee reinforced with a gigantic titanium screw. They were going to drill it in and fasten it to her femur. Tendons from the back of her thigh would be threaded over the titanium and stapled to the fibula to create a new anterior cruciate ligament. Vera was confused. Were they going to remove the meniscus splinter and rebuild the cruciate ligament at the same time, even though her leg was so weak? The light-haired anesthesiologist looked at her medical notes and said yes.

Vera hesitated for a second. *That's not what the doctor in Stockholm said.*

'Don't you want the operation?' The anesthesiologist looked at her neutrally.

Orthopedics in Umeå may well have been suffering an IT meltdown to rival the Congo's, and they may well have been using dubious methods to keep the waiting lists from getting too long, but Vera believed that the surgeons, at least, knew what they were doing. She looked at her medical notes and saw that it was the chief orthopedic surgeon himself who was going to perform her operation. He was the one who had decided to do everything at once. *I really can't go on walking like this for ever, so...* She decided to trust the man who, until as recently as Friday, she had considered a cruel opponent.

'Yes, of course I want the operation,' she replied.

'Well, okay, then... Your test results look fine and you have a good, open throat. So let's do it! See you Monday morning at eight.'

Adam called just as she got home from the anesthesiologist. Fortified by some new kind of strength, she finally felt capable of talking to him. She didn't know what the new strength actually consisted of until the polite, introductory chitchat ended and he got to the point.

'To err is human, to forgive divine.' Adam sounded reproachful.

'What's that supposed to mean?'

'I want you to forgive me.'

'Let's assume that it was the first time you did it. And that you haven't done it again since. Even though we both know that that sounds pretty implausible. So what does "forgive" mean here? What are you asking me to do? How am I supposed to know that it won't happen again?'

'If you just come back...'

'If I just come back,' interrupted Vera, '... then I've changed my mind. But I'm not the problem. You're the problem! No matter how much I forgive you, it's still up to you. I can't come back until you...'

'What do you want me to do?' asked Adam in despair.

'You have to want to change. And that doesn't have anything to do with me. Nobody else can change you – it's something you

266

have to do yourself.'

It struck her like a bolt out of the blue: *that's what Peter had said!* She and Freddie had been sitting there with that never-ending homework assignment about love. Peter had come along and started harping on about love at first sight. When she had reminded him of all the amorous glances he seemed happy to cast around – not to mention all the bodily fluids – he had turned beet-red and shut up for a while. But then, just as she was thinking about her doomed marriage, he had suddenly come out with: 'But what if he changes?'

She had pondered the unexpected question, whether it was possible to get Adam to change, and her response had been pessimistic. 'You can't change another person.'

But Peter had refused to give up. He had just looked her in the eye and said: 'But you can change yourself.'

It was Adam's responsibility. And that was exactly what she needed to say. Had the space alien given her yet another new form of strength, a piece of advice that might save her marriage?

After she ended the conversation with Adam, she thought uncertainly about her neighbor, and was surprised to discover a new feeling – one of respect. It was so strong that it gave her goose bumps.

On Saturday 26 January Sven-Erik drove into town and picked up Vera. He wanted to invite her out to celebrate her 30th birthday. When they arrived downtown, Vera limped slowly and carefully up the worn, uneven stairs to the inappropriately named New Café, one of Umeå's oldest. They ordered coffee, hot chocolate and cinnamon rolls, and chose a table by the window. They looked down at the busy activity on the pedestrian street below, speaking little and grieving over the breakdown of the family. She asked how it had been, living alone at the summer cottage. 'Oh, yes, fine. It was okay. It was lovely by the river.' She thanked him for storing in his shed the boxes that she didn't have room for in her student accommodation. 'No problem, it was nothing...' he wondered why he hadn't thought of it before.

She told him about the operation on Monday, and this elicited a rare smile.

'Oh, that's fantastic. What a great birthday present!'

Yes. She couldn't think of a better present. She stared unseeingly and silently at the small package her father held out to her. Then she took it and opened it carefully. It was a lightweight watch made of titanium. So appropriate...

They sat in silence as he drove her to Lingon Street and dinner with Gunilla.

'There was something you caught Adam doing when you came home in the spring?' asked Sven-Erik. He looked at his daughter as if he finally dared pose the question because there was nothing left to lose.

Vera was thrown into a storm of feelings: fear and shame, but also something lighter and more comforting – perhaps relief? She sat silent and stiff, her mind racing with incomplete sentences and censored answers. But her father had stopped the car in front of the house, and he didn't need to hear her words. He had long suspected the truth, and now he could read it in her face.

'Cheating?'

She couldn't control her physical response. She nodded unsteadily and her eyes filled with tears. But she couldn't speak. She couldn't tell him how she had come home late that Friday night, in a wheelchair, in the company of an assistant from Basic Needs. She couldn't bring herself to describe how she had yearned for Adam, but had been unable to reach him by phone, to tell him that she was suddenly coming home from Colombia. She hadn't thought it would be a problem since she could let herself in with her own key.

The noise had hit them as soon as she had opened the door. Her favorite antique cup, purchased at a flea market when she and Adam were on that great vacation in the archipelago, left out on the kitchen counter and stained with dark-red lipstick. The tube of lubricating gel thrown on the floor. And then, what she had seen in the living room, the core of the unmentionable: *Adam with an unknown woman*, her man, so beautiful even as he broke her heart.

The details stung her. The woman was so different from herself: big, platinum-blond hair; over-the-knee, stiletto patent-leather boots; large, naked breasts pointing straight up at the ceiling as she lay fanned out on the coffee table. *Maximum height, full projection?* Adam hadn't noticed her until he opened his eyes when she turned off the deafening music, the silence abruptly interrupting the ecstasy. So completely caught in the act.

A peculiar little yowl had come out of her own throat. The poor assistant had failed in his attempts to be tactful as he quickly helped her flee the apartment in the wheelchair. He had stuttered something about 'God, what a mess,' and 'don't worry, I'm sworn to secrecy.'

Vera felt as though she had been robbed. She was ashamed that she hadn't put two and two together when she had found the huge folder labelled 'Renovations' hidden on his hard drive. She had been looking for the picture of the tiles she had sent him, but the folder had held neatly categorized porn in dated sub-folders. Over time, increasingly abnormal bodies engaging in increasingly extreme behavior. *God, just imagine the workplace injuries! Does he really want to look at this stuff? Does it turn him on?* It was so hard to deal with that she repressed it, almost managed to forget it. But since the spring it had been impossible to forget. Because now it was undeniably a fact, and a violation of the silent agreement she thought they had. Given the reality of their married life, the conclusion they seemed to share was that desire was overrated and something you could happily live without. Apparently that wasn't true at all. It was just what he wanted her to believe in order to keep her out of it! She felt completely duped – naïve, gullible, hoodwinked. And it left her with a painful emptiness, a horrible sadness that rendered her mute. Had she thought it would be less real if she didn't voice it?

Sven-Erik bent across the gear stick and hugged her. His voice was thick, his message awkwardly disjointed.

'I'm so sorry, my dear. You don't need to tell me anything if you don't want to. We'll talk later. When you're ready. Oh, Lela. It's not easy being human.'

They held the hug for a moment; then she pulled away from her father and glanced at the house.

He looked at her sadly, his hand holding hers tightly. 'Will you be okay?'

She nodded, drying a tear from her cheek.

'Shall I pick you up at 6.30? Or do you want to call? I can come earlier if you want. I'll just be at Olle's.'

Still tearful, she nodded again, leaning against him as if to absorb reason and comfort before going in. When she got out of the car she saw that Gunilla had drawn open the kitchen curtain and was watching them through the window. Everything was so strange. Vera and her huge emptiness. And Sven-Erik, who wouldn't come in with her, driving away from his own home.

Gunilla was up and about and had prepared a lovely meal. Superb whitefish from northern Norway with vendace roe from Kalix, asparagus and mashed potatoes. But the food was spiced with accusatory bitterness, and Vera found that she had no appetite. After a painfully long hour, Gunilla baldly asked, 'Why did you both leave me?'

'Mother, I'm 30 years old. I didn't leave you. I live where I usually live, in the dorm.'

'Well, what about your father? Why won't he even talk to me?'

'Hasn't he said anything at all?'

'No. He just moved out to the cottage.' Gunilla took an uneven breath and dried the corner of her eye. Vera felt her mother's pain and tried to explain.

'He isn't doing it on purpose. He just doesn't have the energy to talk right now.'

'Doesn't have the energy to talk? What kind of egotistical nonsense is that?'

'Egotistical nonsense is the last thing you should accuse him of, Mother.'

'Nobody thinks about me! First I have to stay at the hospital and now I'm sitting alone and abandoned in this house!'

Vera raised her voice in response to her mother's loud complaints.

'Why do *you* think he left you?' she asked.

'I don't know!'

'So you don't remember anything? Do you remember driving the Toyota to the Henningssons', despite the fact that you were drunk?'

Gunilla defiantly avoided looking at Vera. She got up hastily and picked up her plate. 'The least you can do is eat the tiny portion you took!'

'You don't remember yelling at them about Adam? Or sitting in Krister's lap with your dress practically up around your waist?'

Deathly pale, Gunilla suddenly leaned against the kitchen counter for support. As usual, Vera could sense how bad her mother felt. It was a grotesquely well-honed talent she'd acquired in childhood. But being merciful now would only be destructive. A continuation of the dangerous, cushioning lie that they had let her live all these years. Vera knew that she had no choice but to continue telling her the truth.

'Perhaps you remember hitting Daddy across the face with a coat-hanger? The hook missed his eye by about half an inch, so he only needed two or three stitches; but he didn't come to me until the next day, so I did what I could with...'

Gunilla had covered her ears with her hands, and now she screamed: 'Stop! Stop it! I don't want to hear any more lies!'

Vera got up and looked at her new watch. It was only 5.50, so she would have to call. She couldn't stay another minute in this house, where lies became the truth and the truth lies.

On the way out she looked at the wall in the hallway. A cascade of dark-red spots stained the light wallpaper, spots she had never seen before.

She raised her voice so it could be heard in the kitchen. 'Mother! Thank you for the dinner. It was delicious. But...'

Pale and agitated, Gunilla appeared in the doorway. Vera looked at her unflinchingly as she said: 'I'm not lying. If you don't believe me, just look here at Daddy's blood.'

Gunilla stared at the wall, and a shadow fell across her face as her daughter left.

✳

Vera was wheeled into the operating room by a kind, experienced colleague, a stylish, greying nurse she had never met before. She had fasted since the night before; she was clean and her leg had been disinfected. Vera had not taken the small plastic cup with the tranquillizer that she had been offered. She knew that she was more likely to avoid feeling nauseous after the operation if she skipped it. The operating room was bigger than she expected, but the gigantic lights, smell of alcohol, green-clad staff and shiny metal were all familiar. It might have been routine for her, if not for the fact that she was the one on the operating table. She recalled something that she had thought about countless times before: it might be run of the mill for the staff, but it was never just an ordinary day for the person about to go under the knife. They spoke quietly and calmly as they put a needle in her arm and a pulse oximeter on her finger. The man who put the mask over her nose and mouth maintained eye contact with her until she slipped into unconsciousness.

Vera woke reluctantly with a burning pain in her left leg. She looked around. Of course, she was in recovery. The nurse who had prepped her for surgery was quickly at her side. 'The operation went really well. Now your knee is stable, and if you do your physio diligently you'll regain full range of motion! For now, how much pain do you have on a...' She fiddled with the IV and lost her train of thought.

'On a scale of one to ten?' asked Vera faintly.

The grey-haired woman smiled and nodded.

Vera focused on her body and then said, 'I'd have to say... seven... or eight?'

'Okay. Let's get you some pain medicine.'

Vera watched the nurse add morphine to her IV. After just a few seconds, the pain began to subside and she slid into a languidly pleasant mood. Morpheus took her hand and pulled her weightlessly into another world.

Looking up, she sees a beautiful vaulted ceiling. It is breathtakingly high, warmly illuminated and exquisitely

272

painted with sun, moon and glittering stars. The large, round room feels magical, harmonious and perfect. But suddenly there is a powerful jolt from below ground, the foundations begin to shake and the ceiling cracks. An ominous rumbling can be heard, and the ceiling splits apart. A gap opens between the moon and the sun. Everything becomes darker, harder. There is a frightening uncertainty about the future. She gazes worriedly at the gap far above her head.

But in her peripheral vision she sees something else. She looks to the right, and through the gloom sees a youngster on a tightrope... intrepid, brave, agile and lithe, a long, blue rope around his waist.

Her heart thumps. Was it his climbing that made the ceiling split apart? No, it must have been an earthquake, surely? Worried, she looks down, but the pale stone floor appears undamaged.

'Vera! Come on! I need you!'

Who was that? She looks around, and catches sight of Adam, standing behind her and holding on to some scaffolding. Did he call for help? Vera climbs carefully and nervously up the scaffolding. Suddenly, the blue rope is in front of her and she follows it with her eyes, all the way up to the man who has climbed up to the ceiling. He has started sewing the ceiling back together! The rope is attached to the two halves in a zigzag pattern, and he hangs in the middle, using his weight to pull the sides of the ceiling towards one other. He must be the one who called her! With a terrified look down at Adam, she forces herself to try to climb higher. She takes hold of the heavy rope and feeds it up towards the solitary repairer. He continues sewing and she feels inadequate. She has climbed to the top of the scaffolding that Adam is holding on to. She dares go no higher, though she knows that nothing is more important than repairing this world.

She continues to feed the rope up to the man sewing up the ceiling, and, finally, he has almost sewn the pieces together.

'Fine suturing,' calls Adam from down below. 'Come down now, Vera!'

When she looks away from the work on the ceiling, she hears a panicked cry. The lithe acrobat is falling, just before his final stitch, which would have completed the repairs.

Vera rushes down from the scaffolding and over to the fallen man, lying lifeless on his stomach on the hard stone floor. His head is turned away from her; all his blond hair has fallen off, and his back has split open. A strong, young heart has fallen out! He was practically a boy! So unspeakably tragic.

She drops to her knees and picks up the heart. Carefully, she puts it back into his chest cavity through the split in his back. She has a small bag with silver writing on it in her hand, and she collects the blond locks in it. The bag containing the hair feels oddly familiar. She carefully turns over the unexpectedly heavy, limp body, and looks at the face on the bald head. It's Peter! Dizzying astonishment mixes with her sense of guilt. He had tried to be a hero, but she hadn't dared climb all the way up. Had he tried to help, but fallen to his death because she couldn't… ?

He suddenly opens his eyes and looks at her gravely. 'But you can change yourself.' It sounds like a challenge, a question.

Instantly, the answer flashes through her mind: 'I want to change!'

She knows what it means. Fearfully, she looks up towards the dim, frightening height where the rope is dangling desolately and the weight of the vaulted ceiling's powerful halves has pulled apart the unfinished seam.

She is going to have to climb up and sew the last stitches herself.

33

Peter sat in the white cement bunker one floor below the university library. Under the watchful eye of the invigilator, he and a hundred other students were taking their exams, cut off from the world in their bubble of concentration amid the scratching of pen on paper. He stretched his aching back and looked through his resit paper in Executive Decision Making. He knew he was going to pass, and was surprised that he had found the topic so interesting – how we actually make decisions that impact on our own and others' futures. In some cases we make rational decisions based on available information and evaluation of risk. Sometimes we're guided by a gut feeling based on information that comes from who knows where, or information we didn't even know that we had. The latter had been easy to remember. All he'd had to do was think about Vera in the red dress in front of the changing room.

The dark stranger, so strangely familiar.

But we could never escape uncertainty about the future consequences of our decisions. On that point, Peter had directly quoted the book: 'Post-decision surprise, sometimes pleasant, sometimes unpleasant, is characteristic of decision making.' And he was sure that he had answered the last question correctly: decisions are often governed by routine – the power of habit and established models.

✼

Dinner with Ernst and Kerstin unfolded roughly as usual. Fillet of beef and large glasses of red wine, which he had been allowed to partake of for several years. The biggest difference was that it wasn't just Ernst and Lennart who talked. Peter had saved up a number of questions that he wanted answered.

'Listen, you're an experienced professional, a banker of the old school. What exactly *is* the financial market?'

His ruddy-faced uncle seemed flattered and loosened his tie a bit. 'The financial market is like a brilliant machine that collects capital and decides who gets to use it and for what. The surplus that humanity has today is loaned to those who can increase it – people with good ideas about the future. Financing is what makes the rest of the economy work, what creates future returns; it creates welfare; yes, in the long run it is what keeps us alive!'

'Wow. Important job you have.'

'Yes. I think so,' said Ernst, as he refilled the wine glasses.

'What do you think about the huge financial growth in, say, the US and Great Britain?'

Ernst's face clouded over a bit. 'Well, competition has definitely increased, and there is no doubt that Sweden has fallen behind. But we do the best we can. Obviously we would like to earn the same level of profits, but we have legal frameworks that make it difficult!'

'What frameworks?'

'Capital requirements, the Financial Supervisory Authority's instructions about security, things like that.'

'Okay. But isn't that good? I mean, doesn't that protect us against speculative bubbles? I mean, before we had them… the crash of 1929 practically killed off large parts of the world economy, didn't it?' Peter glanced at his father, but then turned back to Ernst, who answered.

'Of course. But we're living in the 21st century now. Knowledge about how the economy develops – just look at Greenspan, he has managed to avert a crisis with the help of an expansive monetary policy. We have an entirely different level of stability today. That stability is used by hedge funds and investment bankers who operate from tax havens. They offer profits that we can't compete with, and it is increasingly visible in our income statements and balance sheets. The financial market is global, full of cross-ownership and unbelievably complex, and competition is constantly increasing. I won't deny that we're worried; we've lost billions to competitors! Money leaks out of the country from every direction, even from public bodies like the Local Governments' Investment Fund and investment funds owned by public pension authorities!'

'Yes,' teased Lennart, 'why can't you offer the same interest on savings as the Icelandic banks do? I have actually moved all my liquid assets to Reykjavik. You need to shape up, brother!'

Ernst threw up his hands in a gesture that signalled defeat. 'Yes, of course we understand how it looks from the customer's point of view. Obviously we all want 5-per-cent interest on our bank accounts, 12-per-cent return on stocks and bonds, or even higher returns like some of the hedge funds offer!'

There was that word again – hedge fund. Peter had a question about that too. 'Hedge funds, globally, how big are they? I mean, how much capital do they manage?'

Ernst leaned back and put his hands behind his head. With his expensive shirt stretched tight across his elbows, he looked up at the stucco ceiling and the crystal chandelier. He seemed to be calculating his way through a mass of data files. He finally sighed and said: 'Excellent question, my dear nephew. But I must admit that I am at a loss. I really don't think anybody can answer that question.'

'What?' Peter was surprised, and out of the corner of his eye he noticed that Lennart was too.

'I have a pretty good sense of the information that the Financial Supervisory Authority has,' continued Ernst, 'and I really don't think they know. Hedge funds and investment banks are private institutions, and in addition to their own capital they finance a lot of their affairs with borrowed money. I doubt that anyone has an overview of the whole thing. At any rate, I've never seen any such data.'

'Aren't those institutions the ones people mean when they talk about new finance? Do they deal in derivatives and the stuff that Charlie does?'

Ernst smiled proudly. 'Yes, it seems that he has a lot to teach his old man.' Peter looked at Lennart and felt how it stung. *Yeah, I know. Compared to Charlie...* Peter interrupted that line of thinking and asked: 'But derivatives – "securities whose value is derived from the performance of an underlying entity" – what are they, *really*?'

'I see a derivative as a form of insurance. Insurance against the possibility that the price of something one plans to purchase in the future rises, or that something one owns decreases in price. The derivative originated in commodity markets. But it's only in recent years, thanks to the development of new products, that derivatives have really taken off.'

'But the special derivative that Charlie sells, CDS, what is that?' Peter glanced at Lennart. Did he almost look a little hopeful?

'The insurance company he works for specializes in protecting against credit losses; it is more focused on that than any of the other firms,' said Ernst. 'They sell contracts that promise to compensate the other party – their customer – if an insured security loses its value, for example stock in a company that goes bankrupt. Their customers pay a premium for the contracts.'

'A success story that outshines almost everything else,' added Lennart in admiration.

'Yes, it is the world's largest insurance company, and the London office is hugely profitable.' Ernst was nearly bursting with pride.

'The biggest in the world. That's something!' said Lennart with a note of respect in his voice.

But the increase in turnover! 100-fold in 10 years? Didn't an increase like that imply that CDS contracts couldn't really be insurance? The thought went through Peter's head, but he figured that there was no point trying to challenge Charlie's fan club.

'Ernst, speaking of the competition, I would have expected you to say something about… I mean, don't high returns usually imply high risk?' asked Lennart suddenly.

'Today there are advanced mathematical models to estimate risk and put a price on it. The free market has suffered from periodic crashes – no denying that. But history shows that, in the long run, it is a superior welfare-creator. Just look at the past 200 years. What fantastic development!'

'Ah, yes… that's the easy answer about general growth across the board! But I want to know if you think I'm stupidly risking my money in Iceland, the way investors in the Dutch tulip market did in the 1600s?' said Lennart, looking directly at his brother.

'I'm not well versed in the details, but I assume that the Icelandic state guarantees deposits like everyone else. Perhaps you should think about the fact that Iceland is about as large as… Norrbotten County. Presumably, Iceland's hydro-energy is just as good as ours, but they lack the ore, manufacturing and forestry of northern Sweden. 300,000 people who basically live on fishing exports isn't the strongest tax base in the world, should the national deposit guarantees have to kick in. There's uncertainty in the markets at the moment… the American housing market is wobbling and global indexes are falling, as are dividends. To be honest, our responsibility in the banking sector, to protect people's savings while also delivering a good return on investment, is becoming more and more difficult.'

When dinner was over, Ernst and Kerstin followed them to the door. As she kissed his cheek, Peter's elegant aunt asked him, 'Of course, you're coming to Charlie's 30th birthday celebration, aren't you?'

'No, I don't think so,' said Peter, glancing at his father over by the coat rack, knowing full well why his attitude towards his cousin had changed. Being in Charlie's company no longer put him in a pleasant or admiring mood. It had become a source of pressure, of impending disapproval. 'I have a lot going on in Umeå, full-time studies and some other… projects. But give him my best and thanks so much for the invitation.'

✖

It was Monday again. Peter's cellphone rang, and the display showed that the call was coming from an unknown inland number. Peter fully expected to hear 'sorry, I must have dialled the wrong number', and was surprised when he realized that it was Vera's father.

'I know it's a lot to ask, but I'm out at the cottage; the old Volvo is stone-dead and I can't get hold of anyone else. Vera had her operation on her knee this morning, and they want to send her home. Could you go and get her? I mean, bring her home to the dorm?'

'Yes! Of course I can!' said Peter unthinkingly, heart pounding.

'Are you sure it's okay?'

'Yes, it's fine.'

After a few practical details, and what Peter understood was an unusually strong expression of thanks from Mr Lundberg, he stood staring out through the window.

How am I going to do this? The fact that he didn't have a car was the least of his worries. Maybe he could borrow Toby's? Otherwise he could always call a taxi. But... *the hospital.* He suddenly found it hard to breathe.

Peter followed the color-coded stripes that went this way and that across the floor of Norrland University Hospital until he reached a pair of metal double doors. The colorful tape was a smart trick to help visitors find their way in the huge hospital. He read the sign on the doors. He had reached his destination; she was behind these doors. He shakily pushed one open, and the physical discomfort became almost unbearable. When a nurse directed him to the right bed, he saw Vera lying there, pale and with an IV in her arm. A nauseous feeling spread in his stomach. His field of vision shrank dramatically, and he broke out in a cold sweat. He collapsed into a chair that the nurse quickly pulled over for him.

'Oh! You're white as a sheet!' He heard the nurse's kind voice from far away, as if she were in another room. She helped him take off his jacket as she talked to a colleague behind him.

'Fall in blood pressure, faint risk. Can you get... yes, thanks.' She bent down so her head was close to his and said: 'Put your head between your knees. Do you feel like you're going to vomit?' She gave him a white plastic bag that was attached to a plastic hoop. Caught in a state of repugnant powerlessness, he heard Vera's weak voice from above.

'Peter? Are you okay?'

God, how embarrassing this was! 'I'm fine. I'm not going to be sick.' With relief, Peter felt his body struggling to return to its normal condition. He saw no alternative to admitting the truth. 'It's just that... uh... when I was seven I had to spend a night alone in the hospital, in an infection ward.'

'When you had blood poisoning and your mother was giving birth to your sister?' asked Vera softly.

Peter nodded gratefully, sitting up slightly and lifting his head from his knees. 'They thought I needed to be given medication straight into my bloodstream.'

'Intravenous penicillin,' she said from the horrible, prison-like hospital bed.

'Yes, maybe, but all I remember is... all the unfamiliar adults... all the needles, how many times they jabbed me looking for a "good vein".' His voice broke at the memory of the desperate fear, the solitary anxiety. He also remembered the feeling of being saved by the arrival of his maternal grandmother, after what seemed like an unbearable eternity. In the early dawn light, she had crawled into the hospital bed with her grandson, and he had finally cried himself to sleep in her arms. *Never again... Never, ever again!*

'I understand,' said Vera soberly, just as the nausea had subsided and he was able to sit up and look at her again.

'And you've been here, all alone... and they've stuck you with needles and cut into you!' He stared in fear at her arm, with the intravenous needle and tube taped to it.

'Don't look at that, look here instead!' She smiled weakly, seemed almost drunk as she raised her free arm and touched him lightly on the cheek. He complied by turning his head so that he was looking at her face. 'I'm fine. Don't worry about me. And I'm happy, because I have a whole, new knee.'

'Yes, everything went well.' The grey-haired nurse was back and seemed to want to give him instructions. 'She has been given a lot of morphine for the pain, and here are enough pills to last a week.'

Ah! She's on morphine. That's why she touched me!

'No hair... but your heart is in the right place, I hope.' Vera put her hand on his chest and smiled at him.

The nurse smiled approvingly and turned towards him. 'Your girlfriend won't be herself for a while. First she'll be – how should I put it – more upbeat, more positive. Then, after a week, it'll be the opposite, because then she'll come off the morphine. You'll have to support her then, okay?'

Peter breathed in sharply when the word girlfriend filled the room, and now he held his breath, waiting for Vera to correct the nurse and prick the illusion. But she just blinked slowly, completely relaxed, as if there were very little of importance in the world. Peter began to breathe again, nodding seriously as he accepted the task. *Yes. I will support her!*

He looked Vera in the eye as they removed the IV. He felt an unpleasant shooting pain and grabbed his own exposed arm, but she just talked about something else. Once she got started, she continued going on about it all the way from the hospital bed, through the hospital corridors in the wheelchair, and out to Toby's car.

'I have a feeling that you're going to be the one representing the future in the welfare project. You are the younger generation. Because like you say, it's only if you have power that you can have responsibility. As for me, maybe it's just as well, now that I think about it… What I wrote feels too weak, too insubstantial; it's just a little piece in the puzzle of how to fix the problem. Seriously, something is wrong, something much bigger than my little undervalued reproduction, I can feel it. Make sure you deal with it. It's to do with livelihood, how we support ourselves. It's about life or death in the future.'

Vera stayed in the car while he signed for a special stool that she was apparently supposed to use in the shower. They managed to make their way to the stairs on Stipend Street without incident. Suddenly, there was a *ding!* from Vera's backpack. He helped her dig out her cellphone, and waited while she listened to a message, balancing her weight on her good leg.

'It was just my unfaithful husband,' she said drily as she put the phone back in the outer pocket of the backpack.

'Unfaithful? Then you should leave him!' said Peter. He ran

agilely up the curved staircase with the shower stool and put it down outside the door to their dormitory. *So lumberjack Ivar had been right!*

'That's rich, coming from you!' snorted Vera.

When he came back down, he saw that she was trying to navigate the first step with her crutches. Her movements were alarmingly unsteady.

'It's still true.' He experienced a strange mix of emotions.

'Well, I'll take it with a veeeeery...' She staggered and he was forced to take hold of her, '... large pinch of salt.'

'You mustn't fall on your new knee! I think we need to solve this some other way. I think it's best if you let me carry you up the stairs.'

After a moment of resistance as she continued trying to navigate the stairs herself, Vera broke down and gave up, exhausted. 'Okay. Okay. I'll let you!' He helped her sit down on the bottom step to rest, noticing that she grimaced in pain, even though every movement was in slow motion.

'I know it hurts like hell, but I'm going to be really careful. Our goal is the least possible pain, okay? Wait here.' He went back up, taking the stairs two at a time, this time with her crutches. When he came down, he helped her get into a standing position using her healthy leg. The process proceeded at a snail's pace, but when they had succeeded he patted his shoulders encouragingly. She put her arms around his neck and he lifted her carefully, keeping his eyes locked on hers. He felt nervous about proceeding. 'I can see that it hurts... but, yes, that's right, keep your healthy leg tucked under the other one.'

He looked at the stairs as he slowly started up with his cargo. The weight in his arms was exactly as he had imagined – light, but not that light. Distracted by her scent, which wrapped itself around his heart like soft cotton, he tried to focus on moving gently so as to avoid causing her unnecessary pain.

'I don't want my wife to be unfaithful and I definitely don't plan to be,' he suddenly found himself saying as he reached the seventh step.

What on earth am I saying? He wobbled a bit, feeling almost drunk, and was forced to lean against the railing and wait. *Try not to sound so desperate!*

'And what about all your carrying-on this fall?' She looked at him.

Meaningless, he thought anxiously, but swallowed the word. *Just more desperation!*

'Once I'm married, I'll just have to make do with memories of *la dolce vita*,' he said instead, trying to sound cool.

'Ah, I see! Best you don't mention it to your wife, then!'

Fuck!

'Or perhaps you should update your online dating profile once you're done with *la dolce vita*?' she giggled in his arms. 'Chubby 45-year-old with thinning hair longs to have children and a family. Seeks wife to listen to reminiscences of *la dolce vita* years…'

Fuck. Fuck. Fuck.

She was laughing so hard her whole body shook, making her harder to carry.

Why the hell did I say that? I'm not the one who's drugged up!

He started to sweat. Her laughter subsided into small attacks of the giggles and he moved on again in silence, one heavy step at a time.

My biggest problem is myself. No shit, Sherlock. Was there any way to save this situation?

On the next-to-last step, Vera turned her face away from him as if she were humiliated. 'Oh, you carrying me… it's such a cliché. I really hate being a cliché!'

He put her down carefully on the white shower stool, took a step back, stretched, and took a breath that did not smell of Vera.

'I know, you've always wanted to take care of yourself. But what is so clichéd about accepting help when you need it? And I'm not going to carry you over the threshold like some caged housewife, if that's what you think. Because that doesn't work anyway – it just leads to divorce.'

He unlocked the door and held it open. 'After you, free and independent woman!' He held out her crutches and said, 'Next time, you can carry me.'

'How old are you, anyway?' She stared inscrutably at him.

'Twenty-five...' ...*in the fall.*

She smiled crookedly. 'So 20 years until the profile update, then?'

'Listen,' said Peter after he had put the stool in her shower, 'knock on the wall if you need help.'

✖

Peter continued to work. He felt restless for several days. What could he say that was actually true about financial growth? If his kids found the article in 25 years' time, would he be able to defend it? He googled the phrase 'Hedge fund, record profit'. The list of hits included pages called 'Long Term Capital Management' and 'Black-Sholes Calculator'.

Just a little piece of the puzzle. That's what Vera had said. He felt exactly the same way! It was a huge, complicated puzzle, and the way Sturesson expected him to put the pieces together... Peter wasn't convinced. He felt increasingly sure that something important was hidden from sight, and he was filled with a strangely uncomfortable feeling. *Something doesn't add up!*

Feeling dazed and confused, he suddenly realized how hungry he was. He looked at the clock. It was almost two in the afternoon and he had forgotten to eat lunch! When he came out into the kitchen it was empty, but the radio was on. And there, like an old friend from the distant past, was the song that had kept him going that difficult spring when his parents' divorce had become a reality, much like the mere thought of elves. He felt as if he had received a new and important message from a higher power, one that echoed pure respect and admiration.

34

Wake up kids, we've got the dreamer's disease.

'You Get What You Give', The New Radicals

A week after the operation, just when Vera had taken her last morphine pill, Sven-Erik came to visit. Vera noticed immediately that her father was both back to his old self and different. He was propping her up with extra pillows behind her back when the thing she had been wondering about for hours finally came up.

'Vera, I really want to apologize. I've had so much to apologize for... all these years. I'm sorry that I... I definitely didn't teach you how, but you knew anyway, and when you wanted to... I wouldn't let you... put your foot down.' He sat sorrowfully at the foot of her bed and put a warm hand on her left foot, cold from the poor circulation below the swollen knee.

'Daddy, it's okay. I know you did the best you could.'

'Yes, but still. And I've been thinking about... when you thought Gunilla was pleased that you found it difficult to navigate the academic world.' Lost, he looked her in the eye honestly. 'I actually have no idea, it's like I wonder now... whether I have ever really known her.' Tears came to his eyes.

'Of course you know her! We all know her, but she has to help herself. We can't do it for her!'

He squeezed her foot with his hand. 'In any case, I think you should show her that she's wrong. You can do whatever you put your mind to!'

Vera smiled at her father. Someone knocked on the door and Vera called, 'Come in! It's open!' She wondered why her voice sounded so weak.

It was Peter. He recoiled in surprise when he saw Sven-Erik

on the bed.

'Oh, hi. Sorry to interrupt. I just wanted to ask if I could borrow your cellphone...' He looked at Sven-Erik. '...I won't delete anything, I promise!'

Sven-Erik got up and looked at his watch. 'I need to get going anyway. Bye, sweetheart.' He bent over and gave her a hug.

He stopped in front of Peter. 'About the deleting thing, I just want to say... it wasn't you who was wrong, who did wrong. What you said... it was a hard thing for an old, misguided man like me to hear, but you were right. You deserve my thanks. And I'm also very grateful that you picked Vera up from the hospital.'

He patted Peter's shoulder awkwardly as he passed him, then stopped in the doorway and looked at his daughter. 'Take care of this one. Not everybody is lucky enough to have a neighbor like him.'

Peter stared at the floor.

Vera loaned Peter her cellphone. As he left with it, he told her that he had a surprise for her. It was quiet and empty without her father. She still wasn't used to sitting around waiting to get better. She got up and hobbled over to the computer with the help of her crutches. She had entertained herself yesterday with various online IQ tests, and was in the mood to waste a couple of more hours now. She found a new test and started in. The aim was to complete a set of tasks as quickly as possible. Usually it meant figuring out which geometrical shape was missing in a pattern; some questions involved series of numbers, and a few had to do with words. Looking for patterns was an enjoyable challenge.

She had just finished the test when Peter returned with her phone. She looked up from the screen.

'You know, my father was right. Thank you.' She fell silent, thinking about all he had done for her. 'You've turned out to be a rock.'

Peter looked pleased, but his voice sounded a bit hurt, too. 'Don't sound so surprised!' he said. He pulled the armchair out of the corner and sat down.

Vera suddenly felt ashamed. 'I'm pleased Daddy said what he did. It was all true. And I also want to apologize for some stupid things I've said… it was harsh… I know that it… I mean, what I said about peach fuzz…' *made you sad, I saw it!* she thought in remorse and continued. 'It was completely unnecessary. It isn't your fault that you are who you are.'

'It isn't my fault what I look like? Is that what you mean?' retorted Peter quickly.

She turned to look at him, and his defiantly hurt expression filled her with regret.

'No, it doesn't have anything to do with what you look like!' *If it was only about that…* The strange feeling flickered through her for an instant before she stamped it out. 'I only meant that I felt like you just showed up on the project out of nowhere, not exactly hardworking, pretty young but from a circle with money and influence. But forgive me. You can't help where you come from, or how they act.'

Peter seemed to relax. 'You're right. Sturesson choosing an inexperienced undergraduate over Cissi is strange. I have… also recently started to suspect that it isn't a coincidence. What if he wants me because he wants the chapter to be about the record-breaking growth of the financial sector?'

He looked serious, and the unexpected words silenced her. Peter touched her worn cellphone carefully as he continued. 'I added a song to the end of your playlist, but you can move it if you want. It isn't exactly something you fall asleep to… Your music… it's been important to me. Especially "Fix You"…' He grinned and looked down at his hands, which held the old phone as if it were of great value. 'I've been sleeping a lot better, so…'

He reached out, put the phone on the desk and spoke solemnly, although his eyes wandered around the room avoiding Vera's gaze: 'So, anyway, here's a song in return, one that reminds me of you.'

'Okay. Thanks. I'll listen to it later.'

Peter twisted himself around in the chair and looked curiously at the screen. 'What are you doing?'

'I'm forced to sit still, so it's just a bit of fun…' She knew it wasn't the whole truth. It was also a comfort after having been tossed out of academia's influential circles, and now that she was on sick leave rather than pulling her own weight. The result on the screen said, 'Intelligence quotient 139, very superior intelligence, 0.5 per cent of the population.' *One point up from yesterday.*

'Oh,' said Peter quietly.

She clicked away the page in embarrassment, only to reveal a message inviting her to complete a membership test for Mensa. The goal of the organization was 'to identify and to foster human intelligence for the benefit of humanity'.

She could see that Peter had come up with something he thought was a good idea. 'Wait a minute, young lady, Miss IQ 139...'

And so she waited. She gazed out of the window at the winter twilight. The painkiller had started to wear off and her leg hurt a lot more. *Here comes the bitter reality...* He was back in 30 seconds with an untidy stack of paper.

'Houston!'

'We have a problem?' wondered Vera.

'Yes. I can't make any sense of this. It's hellishly difficult, like a complicated mystery. So I thought maybe you could listen and see if you get it?'

'Okay...' Vera straightened the folding chair she had under her aching leg and leaned back.

'Long Term Capital Management was a hedge fund started by...'

'Sorry, but what is a hedge fund?' interrupted Vera, feeling how far she was from being able to live up to the hopefulness she saw in his eyes.

'Oh, sorry. I forgot...'

...that I don't understand a thing about the world of finance, thought Vera.

Peter went on: 'Roughly speaking, hedge funds are to do with "enclosure", and the original idea of the funds was that you put rich people's money in them to protect the capital against fluctuations by taking... counter-positions, you might say. I think the point was security, just like the name "hedge" suggests. In practice, however, it has more and more become the opposite, and you actually play the market trying to earn money on fluctuations, not just protect against them. Hedge funds are basically elite banks playing a high-stakes game, but without the legal restrictions that ordinary banks have. LTCM was the star among hedge funds in the 1990s. They used computers and advanced math, and people working for them earned money like you can't even imagine. They yielded 40 per cent some years.'

'Forty-per-cent interest?' Vera was skeptical. 'So, let's see: assume I have a million…'

Peter raised his eyebrows dramatically. 'Just a million? You mean 10 million, I think. And what currency?'

'Um…' She looked at him for an answer. 'Ten million… US dollars?'

Peter grinned. 'Good. They don't deal with people who have a measly million Swedish kronor.'

'Okay. So I have 10 million dollars… when?'

'1996.'

'And in 1996 I place my money with LT… what was their name?'

'LTCM – Long Term Capital Management.'

'Long Term Capital Management… So in 1997 I have 14 million dollars in my account?'

'Yes. Fourteen million, one hundred thousand dollars to be exact,' said Peter.

'But… how in the hell is that even possible?'

'It was possible because they had "leverage". That means a lever, which is a fancy word for using borrowed money to get a higher return on money. They simply borrowed 30 times more money than they had in deposits and played it all. They speculated that all the small differences in stocks and bonds would counterbalance each other, and when they actually did…'

'You mean… they played it right?' wondered Vera.

'Yes, and because they were playing with gigantic sums of money, the returns on the deposits were huge, quite apart from the fact that the funds themselves earned a ton of money. Two guys named Sholes and Merton were members of the board, and they got the Nobel Prize in Economics in 1997 for the formula the fund used.'

'Aha. Award-winning master players?'

'Exactly! It's just that... only a few months after the King handed over the prize... do you know what happened?'

Vera shook her head. 'No idea.'

'They played it all wrong, and the lever fell just as hard, but this time in the direction of loss. It got worse and worse. The golden boys' Long Term Capital Management lost 4.6 billion dollars in 1998. And now it starts to get really weird, because guess what happened then?'

Vera flipped through Peter's pile of papers, and her tired brain tried to understand the money managers' complicated maneuvering. 'The investors lost their money? The fund people were forced to repay their fat bonuses and apologize profusely?'

Peter smiled. 'Exactly! That would have been the logical outcome. The rules of the game say that big gains in a free-market economy are morally justified because the investors take big risks, but by the same logic they have to take the losses when things fall the other way... And yet, three months after the prize was awarded, when the Nobel-prize-winner fund lost four-and-a-half billion, the Federal Reserve called a secret meeting.'

Peter looked through the stack of papers and showed Vera a copy of a newspaper article. The headline read, *Secret sessions that saved LTCM*. 'This time they didn't play by the rules that they otherwise speak so highly of. Instead, 14 bankers at the Federal Reserve negotiated a bailout. A bailout in the sense of rescue mission.'

Vera skimmed suspiciously through the article. 'But doesn't the International Monetary Fund say no to such deals? According to the US, at least according to what you hear about the US in developing countries, isn't it forbidden to... um... engage in anti-market activities... support companies that ought to go bankrupt?'

'That's exactly what I mean. It was obviously a case of double standards. But why?'

Vera shrugged her shoulders. Peter held up a piece of paper

with a formula written on it. 'What do you see?'

Vera looked at it in confusion. 'It looks like natural science.' Through the increasingly insistent pain in her leg, she searched through old, hazy memories from high-school science. *Could it be a formula for how gas spreads?* 'I don't know, but I'm pretty sure it's physics.'

'Physics. That sounds comforting,' said Peter.

'What is it then?'

'This is the exact Nobel prize-winning formula that they used, and that is still used to price derivatives. They claim that it creates an instrument to make the market better at managing risk. It's just that the frequency of crises has increased alarmingly of late. Just three years after LTCM was saved, the IT bubble crashed, and now Ernst, my banker uncle, says that the global indexes are starting to fall again.'

The collapse of the stock market at the turn of the millennium, thought Vera exhaustedly; even she remembered that.

Peter was still looking at her hopefully.

'Okay. So here's my idea. Sturesson and the others have decided that there will only be one chapter from us, but they can't decide how we do it. So I thought… why not do it together?' He pointed at the screen. 'You are one in 200, according to this… plus your experience, your view of the world and how you ask the big questions… Now we're talking microscopic parts of one per cent. They're gifts you have, so use them! We don't need to write about financial growth if you don't want to, but… help me understand this… incomprehensible mess!'

Vera felt sick. 'No.'

'What do you mean, no?' She saw that he hadn't expected that response from her.

'I don't want to. I don't have the energy. Anyway, it will be a waste of time.' Vera's voice was weak.

Peter stood up indignantly. 'Right! Naturally it's easiest just to give up! Otherwise you risk – the horror! – being less than perfect! Better to sit here and join some IQ club and take meaningless tests? Say what you want, but that's definitely not doing something for the benefit of humanity!'

'Sturesson doesn't want it. And he has made it perfectly clear that if he doesn't want something to be in the welfare project, then it isn't going to be in it.' She twisted, as if to try to lessen the pain in her leg.

Peter wandered restlessly around her little room.

'Okay, let's say you're right. We assume that he doesn't want... then we just have to find a way around it. Life is full of opposition; it's a challenge; you just have to see whether... which way has the best chance of working. Go under, over, around – or maybe it's just a question of timing, go before or after the toughest resistance!' His irritation became increasingly aggressive. 'But you seem to think that when you encounter barriers and opposition... then you just give up? And you tell *me* to take responsibility for future livelihoods, for life and death? I really don't get it, and I haven't even managed to put together a *single* piece of the puzzle!'

He stormed off, out into the hallway, and his parting shot was, 'I'm going to ask Cissi. It is fucking irresponsible to sense that something is really wrong and not even try to do something, to warn people!'

The door slammed behind him and a deathly silence fell in the room.

The powerful pain hollowed her out; all her morphine-induced light-heartedness was gone. In addition to the burning fire in her leg, she now felt feeble, frozen, alone and anxious. She needed to lie down. Whimpering from the pain in her left leg every time she moved, she slowly got to the bed, lay down on her back with a pillow under her knee and put her headphones in her ears. She filled the silence with the music that made Peter think about her.

The first feeling she had was one of surprise. What she heard was in sharp contrast to how she felt, because the song was happy, cocky and full of energy. When it was over she listened again, trying to hear the lyrics, and then she understood. It was what he had asked of her – *You feel your tree is breaking? Just bend.*

What if he were right? Maybe it wasn't just feeble, but actually immoral, to stop trying, to give up following that strong intuition, the driving force that had once led her to change direction? *You've got the music in you, don't let go.* She shivered and tried to pull the bedspread loose from one side of the bed and cover herself with it. She managed to cover about half her body, and started weakly tugging at the other edge of the bedspread. Maybe external opposition wasn't the biggest problem? Didn't she feel a bittersweet relief? In all honesty, wasn't it pretty comfortable not having to stick her neck out? Not having to provoke anyone, avoiding criticism?

The music filled her consciousness and, shivering from the sudden cold, the truth dawned on her. It wasn't flattering to realize that she had cast herself in the role of submissive martyr. To face the fact that she had passively accepted the convenient excuse that it was other people's fault, that she had tried but there was nothing more she could do.

What had she actually expected would come of Kogi Mama's mission? That challenging the world order would be simple and painless? That professors, world leaders and huge companies would stand up and applaud the questioning of almost everything they did? The insight was sobering. It was true. She gave up too easily! What Peter was suggesting was frightening, but perhaps that was exactly what was demanded of her to fulfil her personal mission in life.

She was full of questions and the song delivered the answer straight into her ears. *Don't give up, you've got a reason to live. Can't forget, you only get what you give.*

35

Moral hazard: occurs when an actor is not required to bear the full negative consequences of his actions. This gives the decision maker an incentive and a tendency to be less careful than he would otherwise be.

Definition Vera found online

Why is this a good idea?

Peter thought about Vera's question. From the very first time he had met her, she had forced him to think bigger. And now, when that was precisely what he was trying to do – *please join me and ask your questions* – she didn't want to! He left his papers in a messy pile on his desk and, disappointed, went out to the kitchen for a drink. As he reached the kitchen it suddenly occurred to him how she had looked: increasingly pale and shivering. *Which is what the nurse had told him would happen!*

A week had passed, and now, just when he needed to keep his promise, what had he done? She had called him a rock. Right. Nice rock that went and attacked her, just when she was feeling at her worst. Wasn't he also the genius who had told her a few days ago that her problem was that she took too much responsibility? And now he had yelled at her for taking too little! He hadn't thought about how she must be feeling.

He went back to his room and opened the cabinet above the closet. He pulled out his grandmother's warm blanket and knocked on Vera's door. He heard a weak 'what?' from inside, and went in. He found her lying on the bed. She had not been particularly successful in making a cocoon with the thin bedspread.

'Listen… sorry I sounded like that.' He put the fluffy, woollen blanket over her, and the gratitude in her eyes warmed him. 'I noticed you were freezing. Does it hurt a lot?'

'Mmmm.'

'I understand. I'm sorry. What can I do?' He looked at her night table. 'Panadol? Is this all you have now?' She nodded. 'Should I try to get something else?'

'You need a prescription for anything stronger. I just have to try to put up with it. But this blanket...' She looked surprised. 'It smells like an oil I got from a medicine-man in Colombia.'

'Did you go to a medicine-man? May I ask why?'

She smiled wanly. 'No, I helped his daughter after a difficult birth, and I think he wanted to give me something valuable.'

'Really! Do you still have it?'

She nodded. 'It's in the bottom drawer of the dresser.'

'Can I look at it?'

'Mmmm. It's a little calabash with a carved cork, decorated with a spiral that looks like it was done with black finger-paint. Counter-clockwise means ascending.'

He closed the drawer and looked in fascination at the small, handmade wooden bottle.

'South American Indians?'

'Yes – indigenous people. They're called Kogi; it's rare to meet them; very few of them speak Spanish. They live in the Sierra Nevada, the world's highest coastal mountain range. They see themselves as elder siblings, morally responsible for all of humanity. Their Kogi Mama, a kind of medicine-man and chief, pointed at the valley... where it had been clear-felled; all the trees were gone, and there was erosion. And he looked directly at me and asked: "Little brothers and sisters, what are you doing?"' Her eyes were bright with fever and she looked pitiful under the blanket, yet she was glowing, and Peter understood why. It was fascination, wonder. She went on, 'It was mystical; I know that sounds flaky.'

He shook his head and sat carefully down on the edge of her bed. 'No, I don't think it sounds flaky.'

When she pulled the blanket down a little, he could see her whole face and her serious expression. 'It felt like a mission, my life's mission. Then, when the guerrillas attacked, and I hurt myself, that's what I focused on.'

'The mission?'

'Yes. What are we doing? *Koyaanisqatsi* – a crazy, unsustainable way of living.'

Peter carefully removed the cork from the calabash and lifted it to his nose. '*Koyaanisqatsi*? It smells distinctly of lavender, like the blanket, and perhaps rosemary... tea-tree?'

Her dark eyebrows shot up. 'Aha, so you're an expert on plant oils?'

He carefully replaced the cork and shrugged his shoulders. 'My grandmother was a...' *I shouldn't say witch...* 'herbal medicine fan.'

'Well, if you can figure out those scents, you should apply for a job making perfumes or something,' she smiled weakly. 'Kogi Mama said it is made with seven different plants and that it helps against fever and infection.'

'Not against morphine abstinence and pain after a knee operation?'

'No, unfortunately not.' She smiled crookedly and shifted with a grimace. 'Listen, I think I need to elevate my leg more.'

Peter took a pillow from the armchair and together they rearranged the pillows under her leg. He left the calabash on the night table beside her.

'Are you comfortable? Is there anything else you need?'

'I think I've lost some blood, I'm craving liver pâté. I guess I need iron.' Her pale cheeks colored. 'I mean... I get it every month, if you know what I mean.'

'Okay, I get it. Liver pâté. I'll see what I can do.'

'By the way, thanks for the song. I think I recognize it. Late 1990s?'

'Mmm. New Radicals. *Maybe you've been brainwashed too.*' He carefully finished adjusting the pillows around her leg. 'Is this okay?' He started to get up, but didn't want to leave without... 'Like I said, I'm sorry... Obviously you need rest. I'll try to solve my mysteries myself.'

She looked at him as she fiddled with her headphones.

'I was thinking about that. I think it might have a lot to do with *Koyaanisqatsi*. And that makes it my mystery too. So I'm in. But I think we need all three of us to be involved, so can you ask Cissi too?'

Warmth spread through his body and he broke out in a broad smile. 'Absolutely! But perhaps we should wait a few days until you've recovered a bit more?'

She nodded. When he made to leave, she put on the music and his pulse increased when he heard the line: *You're in harm's way. I'm right behind. Now say you're mine.*

✖

A week later the three of them met at the university for lunch. He had chosen a time when they would have the cafeteria more or less to themselves. Peter turned to Cissi.

'This thing that doesn't add up – maybe financial growth is only part of the story? In any case, I think it's better that we take control and make sure the best of all three of our parts is included; otherwise they'll have the power. They'll be able to pick just one of them, and readers will miss out on the rest.'

Cissi's eyes sparkled with adventure.

'Yes! What an exciting idea! Why not do something unexpected?' Cissi sat back heavily in her chair, and they heard a cracking sound as she fell diagonally backwards onto the floor, an astonished expression on her face.

Vera looked at her in concern. 'Are you okay?'

In a second, Peter had helped her up and pulled over another wooden chair to replace the one whose leg had broken off.

Cissi blushed in embarrassment. 'Thanks, I'm fine, it's okay.'

Vera stared at the broken chair. 'What a spaller it was!'

Spaller again – so that's what it means. He understood the sense of vulnerability. He was familiar with what it feels like when something you believe in 100 per cent suddenly collapses.

✖

Peter had just finished eating when Matt kindly showed the guest into the kitchen. Despite the fact that a trim black beard now covered half his face, Peter immediately recognized the man from the burned-up wedding picture. Instantly, he felt his entire dinner revolt against him. Adam looked even better in person, and the only likeness he had to Peter was his height.

'Peter, this is Adam, Vera's husband,' said Matt.

'Oh, really? I thought she had separated,' Peter said without thinking. He noticed that Adam was still wearing his wedding ring.

'Why would you think that?' said Adam, studying him with his dark, clear blue eyes.

Because you've been unfaithful, you stupid fucker! Peter kept his mouth shut, took his dish to the sink and rinsed it with the warm water running full blast.

'Where *is* Vera, by the way? I've been trying really hard to get hold of her...' He laughed nervously. 'Or is there something you're not telling me, guys? Does she sleep here... or has she gone and found somebody new?'

'No, Vera lives here. She hasn't met anyone else as far as I know; or have you noticed anything, Peter?' Matt looked at him, and Peter worried that his racing pulse might make him turn red.

'She's working on a welfare study. She has a lot to do on it at the moment.'

Adam looked frustrated. 'I just don't get it. Why would she decide to study economics and stuff like that all of a sudden? She's an incredibly good anesthesiology nurse.' He stared glassy-eyed out of the window. 'She is really... outstanding. At her best when it really matters.'

Peter's cheeks started burning. He put the last of the dishes into the drainer and dried his hands on the least dirty dishtowel he could find. He tried not to sound defiant. 'Did you know that even on morphine Vera has an IQ of 139? So I'm sure she's a brilliant anesthesiology nurse. But she's good at other things, too.'

He caught a glimpse of Adam's watchful expression before the outer door suddenly slammed and the sound of crutches could be heard from the hallway. Adam turned quickly and went to meet her. Peter couldn't help looking towards the doorway, and he saw that Vera's expression communicated a desire to escape as Adam embraced her.

Peter kept himself within earshot of the married couple. He spread a thick layer of liver pâté on a piece of rye bread as he listened to Adam explaining that he had finished the kitchen and had managed to find that FSC-certified walnut wood that she wanted.

'So now... all you have to do is come home, and I'll make you lasagne!' was the last thing he heard Adam say before Vera's door closed.

Peter hesitated a few seconds before he went ahead and knocked.

'Come in!' yelled Vera. She was sitting at the desk, so he put the pâté sandwich and glass of juice down in front of her.

'Here you go. Iron.'

'Thanks, that's kind of you,' said Vera. 'Adam, this is my closest... neighbor, Peter.'

A short, tense silence followed.

'Yes, we just met out there.' Adam nodded towards the kitchen and offered Peter his hand. Peter reached out and took it. He registered Adam's slightly too-firm handshake as he met the man's penetrating blue eyes. He suddenly felt as if he were being scrutinized by an opponent before a match, and he didn't flinch. Instead, he saw Adam questioningly shifting his eyes back to Vera as he left.

Peter shut himself in his room and sat on the bed. He tensed uncomfortably in order to press his ear against the wall. He had difficulty discerning what they were saying, until Adam suddenly raised his voice in a burst of emotion.

'Please come home! I miss you so much!'

Vera's response was too quiet for him to hear. His throat constricting, Peter collapsed in a heap on the bed.

Fucking Don Juan!

The impossible had happened, and it had started with a tempting spark in the fall, which had secretly taken root and developed. His mother had seen it straight away. Now that he knew Vera better, it was even more obvious and it frightened him. The slightest hint of a smile on her face was the highlight of his day. He also caught himself reliving precious moments, like the one in the laundry room when she had silently spoken to him, and his body had followed her instinctively, with a strong feeling that it was born to do so. Everything was right with the world – harmonious, fascinating, beautiful and good – when he was connecting with her. But there was a downside, and it was horribly obvious now. When they weren't connecting, everything died; the world became cold and empty. Abstinence tore at him, and he longed for those precious flashes of contact.

His rational instinct for self-preservation protested: such dependence on another person – especially one who had mainly dismissed him – was anything but healthy. He was badly affected by this fixation, and even if he now knew better than to follow *The Game*'s recommendations about what to do in such cases, he missed his old independence. There was a lot that was wrong and unhealthy about his old life, but freedom from the whims of another individual was a fantastic thing. Given that she was now behind a closed door on the other side of the wall, doing God knew what with her legally wedded husband, it was a freedom he yearned to have back.

Lying helplessly on his bed, he set a goal for himself. He would free himself from his dependence on Vera, but without numbing himself with meaningless, transitory relationships. He would exercise discipline and become a new man worthy of an Elf. But, he told himself – and this was the key – he would be worthy of *any* Elf. He would just use Vera's superb judgment to measure how he was getting on. If she wanted to be his friend, a genuine friend, then he would know he had succeeded. He was only 24 years old. Even if he had learned the hard way that Elves don't exactly grow on trees, he comforted himself with the thought that he had plenty of time to meet one later, once he had changed.

But it was such a shame. He felt in his bones that they could have been great together. *I have done all I can; she still doesn't seem capable of even considering me*, he thought sorrowfully. *Would she really rather go back to her unfaithful husband?*

36

Vera hadn't expected Adam to show up at the dorm. He was charming and eager when he showed her the pictures of the new kitchen they had chosen together and which he had now installed. She looked at their airy, two-bedroom attic apartment on the little screen, so spacious compared to the cramped little dorm room she lived in now. Happy memories of their joint renovation project caught her off guard. What a team they had been! Everything had gone smoothly, each knowing what the other was going to do, what practical support the other was about to need.

'It looks nice,' she admitted and smiled sadly, her head full of memories. She recognized how much she missed the closeness she thought they'd once had. After listening to Adam's appeals for a while, she heard the sorrow in her own voice when she posed the important question.

'What really happened to us?'

He sat on her bed, looking down at his hands, and the air in the room suddenly turned oppressive. She avoided talking about the most painful aspect of what had happened to them. 'Why didn't you want to do voluntary work abroad, like we had talked about for so many years?'

Adam looked relieved. 'Regardless of the backwater you find yourself in, you deliver the best care possible… But I would go crazy. Volunteering in a developing country was something *other people* wanted me to do. I'm best at precision, at exactitude – preferably with a little…' he smiled crookedly, '… sprinkling of spatial artistry. I come into my own when I work with plastic.'

'Yes, that's true enough.' She remembered a firefighter whose face Adam had managed to reconstruct after a gas explosion. And then there was the 35-year-old woman who had lost one of her breasts to cancer. Adam's reconstructive surgery was so good that it was difficult to see any difference. *His precision really helps people.*

'And the remuneration reflects it,' Adam continued. 'Only Torsten earns more than I do. We're really growing; we're one of the biggest in the world now. And I'm the only one in the Nordic region who doesn't have *a single* dissatisfied patient! No long-term pain, no crookedness, no capsular contraction, and no significant loss of feeling reported.' He looked at her with a pleased expression.

'What about the woman who called us at home, crying?' protested Vera.

'But she got herself pregnant, didn't she, which caused her breast implants to swell. It's not surprising that complications arise in such situations; there's not much I can do about that.'

Yes, God forbid, her body reacted naturally! thought Vera angrily. An unpleasant tangle of memories from Adam's workplace forced its way into her consciousness: his overbearing boss bragging that their department had *'produced a million happy women, not to mention their husbands.' 'Thanks Hollywood.' 'Yes! Our business is all about profit and success!'*

'Anyway, I switched to facial plastic surgery in the spring, and I'm also doing some intimate plastic surgery for men. It's even more difficult; the margin for error is even smaller.'

'What?'

'Longer, thicker. Testicular enlargement is also becoming more popular in other countries.'

Was the department trying to produce 'a million happy men' these days? 'Not to mention their wives?' Vera understood that the clinic must be making a lot of people happy, but she still found the whole thing absurd. 'Do you think it's an appropriate thing to do?'

'It's a free world; you can do what you want with your own money, right? The fact that the people who come to us aren't always the most gifted or blessed with the strongest self-esteem...' He shrugged his shoulders, and the fracture in the relationship, the fracture in Adam, was suddenly visible. She reacted with contempt.

'So whatever the customer is willing to pay for – you just do it?'

'Beauty is in the eye of the beholder. I don't make moral judgments about it.'

Yes, you most certainly do! And you do so in completely contradictory ways! The strength of her outrage frightened Vera into silence – she dared not speak her mind.

Adam got up and went over to the window, looking out on the winter darkness.

'It was really nasty, that thing with the guerrillas.' He turned anxiously towards her. 'You'll stop doing that volunteer job, now, won't you?'

Vera sat quietly at the desk as he continued.

'Did you know that I'm part of an operating team we have at the clinic that works overtime to treat facial deformities?'

'Yeah… I remember those cleft palates you fixed here in Umeå,' said Vera.

'Yes. The kids… I heard that their speech development and everything was really good. And we're getting better and better at it. Can't that also count as volunteer work?'

Vera didn't answer. After a moment, Adam tried again.

'I know you don't want to come and work at the clinic, otherwise… I promise, you would be the best, and would make good money, too. But I have something…' He went out in the hall and came back with a page he had ripped out of the newspaper. He unfolded it and put it down in front of her. 'There's a vacancy for an anesthetic nurse in the thoracics department at Söder Hospital. Right up your street – and the hours are good, too. Apply for it!'

She stared vacantly at the job advertisement in front of her as Adam squatted down beside her. Teary-eyed, he looked at her, took her left hand and pleaded, 'Please come home! I miss you so much!'

Her eyes welled with tears. 'It's really hard for me, too, you know. I've never been an adult without you. I feel all alone.'

'Yes! That's exactly how I feel too! So I'm going to fight for you! You said I have to change because the problem is mine.'

He groped around in his pocket and looked pleadingly at her. 'I know I screwed up; it's true. But I'm changing, I'm hoping…' He held out the rings she had asked Sven-Erik to return.

Vera pulled her hand away. 'I assume it reappeared? That… "Renovations" folder?'

The color drained from his face, and he backed away and sat down heavily on the bed.

'Yes, Adam. I found it. When I was going to choose the tiles for the kitchen! And then…' *after a week of doubt and tears…* 'when I decided to bring it up, to ask you about it, I just wanted to see how bad it was… I mean, I wasn't planning to completely overreact or anything!' *At least there wasn't anything illegal in it, or violent, was there?* She remembered her gnawing anxiety. *Just a load of women who definitely weren't me.* 'But it was gone.' *So I let it go, as if it had been just a nightmare.* 'But it reappeared? Have you always had a folder like that?'

Adam hung his head and sat quietly, with his fingers buried in his hair.

'When I was in Colombia, a wise person told me that I am good at trusting people,' Vera whispered, with tears running down her cheeks.

Adam looked at her, eyes red from crying. 'Yes, you are, and I love you for it.'

Rage swelled in Vera. *You just don't get it!* She stood up, because she had to get away from him. 'It was true then. Because I *had* trust. I don't any more.'

Adam stood up and came over to her, tried to take her in his arms. But his gesture just intensified her painful feelings. She leaned back, held up her hand as if to keep him away and raged at him: 'It takes a long time to build trust, but only an instant to destroy it!'

And I forbid you to touch me again!

She got a lump in her throat at the thought of what her eyes had communicated. Adam looked at her in shock and retreated to the bed. She sat down in the armchair and cried quietly, her face buried in her hands. After a few minutes, she managed to calm down enough to lift her head and look at him again.

305

He still looked lost, but whispered, 'But with more time, you can rebuild trust. Right, honey? That's why I've started... I am going to solve it; I'm in therapy; he said I need to "come to terms with women's roles".'

And therapy's going to teach you how...! A burning pain behind her eyelids and in her throat kept her silent.

'And I promise; I'll wait for you. The others just make me feel bad; it doesn't mean anything. Because no-one can ever take your place.'

When he had gone, she sat alone, struggling with the anxiety-demons, knowing that she had to make a decision and feeling torn in two. *It doesn't mean anything?* To her it meant everything, and she felt that she had to make a choice. No, it was more that she had a responsibility to make a decision. *No-one can ever take your place.* But why would she want that place?

She turned on her computer, and with unsteady fingers typed the word 'divorce'. The computer responded immediately with hundreds of hits. It turned out to be remarkably easy to separate. Under Swedish law, all it required was that one of the spouses wanted to separate, and that he or she filled out a form and sent it to the district court. In the past, she read, a divorce was always based on 'irreconcilable differences', but now you didn't need any specific reason. Okay. So she wouldn't have to describe the sinkhole that had opened up under her when she came home from Colombia in a wheelchair. *I wonder if Daddy is going to do it?* And it was strange, because just as the question had formed in her head, Gunilla called.

Vera was surprised to discover that they could speak calmly with one another for 10 minutes, and that she was able to tell her mother that she didn't have the energy to see her if she was just going to scream and deny the truth. Gunilla said that she was going to 'start on a program', and after a lot of beating about the bush Vera realized that she was talking about going into rehab. Perhaps most surprising of all, Gunilla ended the conversation with a peace offering.

'I'm glad you're trying to do the project again, I think it will be... good.'

Vera noticed that her mother's words had cheered her up. Mainly because it meant that Daddy was obviously talking to her again. That was progress, whatever he decided to do about his marriage.

※

They took a break in the cafeteria. The light hanging over the table gave the secret little rebel group a round, well-lit space in which to gather, and the place was almost empty. Most students hadn't yet returned from the Christmas break, and there was plenty of space on the sofa for Vera to prop up her leg with her winter jacket.

Cissi held her warm mug. 'Sturesson and Sparre emphasize the importance of competitive growth, a rising GDP. They're always talking about how we and the rest of Europe need to figure out how to support an aging population. It requires increased productivity, an influx of foreign labor and stuff like that.'

'Right,' said Peter. He turned to Vera and seemed to be gathering his courage. 'I have read your draft, and it's good. But I have to admit that I have some... objections.'

'Okay?' said Vera, looking at him with curiosity.

'I mean, reproduction is obviously completely necessary, since there's no humanity without it, but I still feel like we finance welfare with the help of production, that is, the creation of tangible value.'

'Ah, the old "givers and takers" argument?' She looked at him inscrutably.

'Yeah, something like that.' Peter met her gaze without flinching.

Cissi looked at them. 'It's true that the private sector is taxed so that we can pay for public welfare, but the things provided by the public sector create an environment that enables the private sector to create value – infrastructure, education, child and elderly care...'

'Also, a lot of the burden of reproduction takes place outside the paid economy, in the home, before we even have anybody who can go out and work,' said Vera.

'But what is it that creates prosperity?' insisted Peter.

'Obviously we need both. If it sounds like I mean something else then I need to reformulate the argument,' admitted Vera. 'But it's still interesting that those who talk about givers and takers seem to mean that everything women do in the public sector is taking, while everything that men do in the private sector counts as "giving" to society and to the takers. I would argue that it is more a question of long-term versus more immediate value creation. But look at what you're writing about, financial growth.' Vera looked at Peter across the table. 'The argument is that we have a free market because when people act in their own interest, it supposedly creates the best possible entirety for everybody. And that outcome is guaranteed by everybody having access to all the information and acting rationally, right?'

'Yeah, that's the fundamental principle,' said Peter, and Cissi nodded as well.

'In that case, stocks and bonds should never be incorrectly priced, which means that you should never be able to profit by making "smarter" investments than other people – but isn't that exactly what the typical finance job is all about?'

Cissi looked amused. 'Yes, you're right.'

'So that means that according to the market economy's own values, stockbrokers must be takers.' Vera noticed that Peter was trying to wrap his head around that idea. She went on. 'I saw a list of the highest-paid positions in Sweden, and guess which one topped the list? Stockbrokers!'

Cissi looked slyly at Peter. 'Yeah, why should they be earning money on other people's money? What value do they create? They don't produce anything, and the service they provide... it isn't like they're teaching kids to read or something.'

Vera took a sip of her tea as Peter turned to Cissi.

'My cousin is a superstar of modern finance, and I guess he would say that he creates growth. But I talked to a... key figure in Swedish banking. He says that regular banks feel like they're being driven out of business by financial actors that operate outside of established legal frameworks. There isn't any transparency in their operations; nobody has an overall picture of the capital movements they're responsible for; the money can come from anywhere, can go anywhere… you know, the City of London, Wall Street, all the secret island tax havens.'

'Huh? What are you talking about?' Cissi looked confused. 'Is it illegal?'

'Well, it's unregulated, and that probably makes it *easier* to engage in illegal activities – money laundering from drugs, trafficking, mafia stuff,' said Peter. 'But the shadow banking system isn't illegal. Governments actually encourage its growth.'

'Everybody wants a piece of the pie?' asked Vera.

'Yes, of the strongly growing pie called financial turnover and profit,' confirmed Peter, and Vera suddenly had a flashback of him in the laundry room.

Cissi was still skeptical. 'But you said that they operate outside of established legal frameworks?'

'Yes, they avoid taxes and jurisdictional limitations, and there's a lot that isn't public, that's confidential.'

'But it's completely legal?'

'The shadow banking system is legal,' answered Peter.

Vera continued eagerly, 'If it's so much of a secret… How do you find out how they think?'

Vera saw something bottomless in Peter's eyes, but he didn't answer.

Cissi took her chapter out of her bag, put it on the table and folded her hands over it. 'Regardless. Do you know what welfare is really about?'

Peter looked at Vera as if she were the answer to the question. Vera held his gaze, took a breath.

'Energy,' said Cissi.

Yes, it's you, his unbelievably turquoise eyes seemed to be saying. Vera felt her cheeks get warm – *what are you saying?* – and she quickly shifted her gaze to Cissi's harmless stack of papers and concentrated on what Cissi was saying.

'Throughout human history, it's always been about energy, often in the form of food. Food is equivalent to labor power, which is the basis for all other value creating activity. People who started farming accumulated a surplus, which made it possible for them to do something other than spend all their time looking for food. They had time to build big houses and roads, to educate themselves, to create art and to build cities. Food surplus is the foundation of civilization. But then, about 200 years ago, the West also discovered extreme energy reserves. First coal and then oil. The entire industrial revolution is founded on our ability to exploit energy stored underground.'

'Yes, that's true, ancient, stored solar energy,' said Vera, safe in the tame, unemotional part of her brain that handled natural science. 'Isn't the era before the dinosaurs even called Carboniferous?'

'Don't ask me. I have no idea,' said Peter, and Vera avoided looking at him.

Cissi pulled two books out of her bag, and Vera read *Peak Everything* from the cover of the top one. *So everything is great?*

'Heinberg,' said Cissi. 'He claims that the 1900s was the last century in which we could keep on growing as we had got used to. We entered it with 1.6 billion people and 100 years later we're closing in on 7 billion. And the curves for our consumption are even steeper. He claims that his generation alone, those born in the 1940s, have used half of the planet's non-renewable resources.'

'Uh-oh. That sounds ominous,' said Vera. *So it's all downhill from here?*

'Yes, doesn't it?' Cissi's large, grey-blue eyes were serious. 'And then...' She showed them book number two, with the even grimmer title of *Collapse*.

'Diamond explains how past civilizations either survived or died out based on their ability to adapt to the limitations of the natural environment.'

Peter skimmed through the thick book's table of contents.

'If you want a quick understanding of what he means, I suggest reading Chapter 2 about Easter Island,' said Cissi.

'In the Pacific Ocean?' wondered Peter.

'Yes, the puzzling little island that a Dutch ship happened to find on Easter Sunday in 1722. To their great surprise, they found a few starving savages and almost 400 gigantic stone statues, artistically placed in the middle of nowhere.'

'Huh?' said Vera.

'Yes, it's a mystery,' said Cissi. 'Read it, you'll see.'

Peter grinned. 'I have a soft spot for mysteries, so maybe I will.' His expression darkened as he flipped through the book. 'Otherwise it seems like it's mostly about war and famine and misery.'

'Read Chapter 9, too. It's about two civilizations that managed their resources sustainably.' Cissi nodded in the direction of the book. 'They had completely different strategies, but they did the right things in the right way. So there's always hope.'

'Yes, that's true,' said Vera. 'If changes were always for the worse, then we might as well all give up. But a lot of changes have been for the better. Child mortality rates are declining throughout the world. And just think about how much information we now have access to thanks to the internet, and I mean...' She shifted her gaze to Peter, because it was mainly meant for him: 'Injuries heal, people help each other, things resolve themselves. People can change.'

She saw how much he had to say in response. Her pulse rose alarmingly and she forced herself to tear her eyes away. *Say something! Anything!*

Cissi watched them in silence.

As if he had heard Vera's silent appeal, Peter returned to thumbing through *Collapse*. 'This book still feels a little bit like... you can have the plague or cholera, the choice is yours!'

'Well, in that case, I definitely pick cholera!' said Vera. *This is something I know about!* 'Cholera is definitely no fun, but you can fix it. You know...' she looked eagerly at Cissi. 'People would come to us crying, carrying a relative they thought had died on the way. But often, they only looked lifeless. You just needed to be quick, find the vein, often in the groin, where you could put in an IV.' She saw how Peter shuddered, and remembered how he had almost fainted at the hospital. But this was a story with a happy ending. 'After a while, after we had given them a couple of pints of fluid, they usually perked up, and then we could take care of them until they made a complete recovery. I can't really describe it. It just makes you feel so good! It's an unbelievable feeling!' The memory made her eyes fill with tears of happiness. 'To see the person recover, and the family!'

'Helping made you happy?' smiled Cissi.

'Exactly. That's just how it was,' said Vera thoughtfully.

'It's called a helper's high,' said Cissi.

37

I can't. I'm involved now. You let go, and I'm gonna have to jump in there after you.

Jack Dawson, from the movie Titanic, *by James Cameron, 1997.*

Peter realized that he was like a well-oiled weathervane. He had just decided that he had to stop hoping that Vera would fall for him when, still lying helplessly on his bed, he heard her raise her voice in pain. 'It takes a long time to build trust, but only an instant to destroy it!' He sat up at once. The disobedient hope filled him again, the world had brightened and color had returned to it. *Yes, you have good judgment… Trust takes a long time – well, you can have all the time you need!*

After that, their collaboration on the question of future welfare began. When he had the courage to say what he thought – and Vera was equally frank in return – he was filled with a sense of recognition, as if this was just what he had been longing for. Late one evening he realized that their conversation had been like the fascinating space he had seen Vera and her father occupy, when they had disagreed with one another, but not quarrelled. The space where respect and curiosity supported an infinitely open atmosphere, alive with the possibility that one – *or perhaps both* – of them would change their mind.

One evening in the dorm, Matt waved something squarish in the air and said, 'She says Jack Dawson!'

Peter stopped. 'Huh?'

'You asked me about a good man; she says that this is what 9 out of 10 women would say.' Matt held out the object he had in his hand. It was a rental film, the old tearjerker *Titanic*.

'What? Who told you that?'

'My sister Lauren… and she consulted lots of her friends, too!'

Peter vaguely remembered the old film, but his curiosity was piqued, and he was sure he would watch it now with new eyes. They loaded up with snacks and beer, put the film on and settled themselves on the sofa.

Toby sauntered in, looked at them in astonishment and asked, 'Are you going to watch *Titanic*?'

'What are you doing here? Aren't you looking after your daughter this week?' countered Peter, suddenly embarrassed.

'We switched, so she's with my ex. I didn't have the energy to commute. It takes one and a half hours to Skellefteå, and we have a couple of long days this week,' sighed Toby.

'Do you want to see what women, according to a reliable source, really want?' wondered Matt carelessly.

'According to what reliable source?' wondered Toby.

'My sister, and the world. It is actually the world's most popular…' Matt looked questioningly at Peter.

'The world's most-watched film,' said Peter helpfully.

'Yeah, the world's most-watched film. That must count for something!' said Matt.

So they sat there – Peter, Matt and Toby – while the March twilight outside the window cast bluish shadows on the snow. Peter watched Dawson with undivided attention. Leonardo di Caprio played a poor but carefree young man who saved a rich man's fiancée from a spectacular suicide, keeping her from throwing herself off the stern of the gigantic Atlantic steamship in desperation, right into the ship's deadly cold, black wake. And then there was the young artist's motto: *Making each day count*. Peter thought it sounded reasonable.

'Not exactly rocket science, is it?' he said to Matt.

'What?' Fully absorbed by Kate Winslet's portrayal of the red-haired, High Society beauty, Matt stared as she climbed up on the bow rail with Jack behind her. 'I think she's gorgeous!'

'Uh, hello! We're supposed to be studying *him*, not her,

right?' smiled Peter.

'*God*, this is romantic!' sighed Matt quietly when they kissed in the sunset. After a while Peter turned to Toby instead.

'There isn't anything particularly unusual about this, is there? The point is that women basically want what we want. Don't you want to have fun, be yourself and marry the one...?'

Peter fell silent, because she had come into the room and was standing behind them. She moved so quietly without her crutches. It seemed like she hardly limped any more. She looked like something from the cover of a health magazine. She was wearing an orange, short-sleeved shirt and drying her loose, freshly washed hair with a small towel. She stood so close that he could see from the light of the film that she had a sprinkling of freckles from being out in the sun as winter slowly receded to make way for a new Norrland spring.

'What are you talking about?' asked Vera.

'Sssh...' admonished Matt. 'We're studying a good man!'

'Goodman?'

'No, a Good Man – a man you stay with because he makes you feel good.'

Peter blushed in the darkness when Vera sat down. There was about four inches between them. A space filled with electricity. The idea that he would be able to accept just being her friend was laughable! Peter wanted so much more. To rest his leg against hers, to let his arm rest against hers, or at least to brush against her foot. She dried her hair slowly and listlessly on the towel. Her movements, her scent and her warmth – she felt magnetic, and it took all his energy to force himself to sit still. The biggest moveable object that humanity had thus far succeeded in building hit the iceberg, and the catastrophe unfolded, but Peter could think only of her. How could he reach her? How could he get her to come to him? He thought about their shared curiosity, their shared mystery – the impenetrable logic of finance. *How can we find out how they think?* Suddenly, the answer was obvious.

He leaned towards her a bit, brushing her arm for a second, and whispered, 'Uh, Vera... I've been thinking about this new

315

finance thing. I think I can find out how they think.'

She turned and looked at him happily. She whispered back, 'Yeah? Okay.'

The pulse of energy left him breathless. He saw affirmation – she was confident that he could do it! Attending Charlie's victory party and exposing himself to Lennart's unflattering comparison of him and his cousin would be a bitter pill to swallow, but it was worth it.

Rose was hoisted down from the Titanic in a lifeboat, gazing at Jack in a long, painful goodbye. Matt sniffled loudly, and everything was suddenly way too sentimental. Peter felt an uncomfortable embarrassment.

'Not very manly, Matt!'

He looked up, vulnerable, open and confused. 'Huh?'

Vera bent forward and lightly tousled Matt's hair. '*Very* manly, I think,' she said in a soft and intimate voice that Peter found worrying.

She got up to leave and he looked down at her fingertips.

Brilliant performance. Stroke of genius. Seriously. He realized that being with Vera was demanding. She had standards, and he wasn't sure he could live up to them. He thought about Sven-Erik and Ivar and sensed that Vera was used to a different kind of masculinity than the one he had managed to cultivate. And then here was this guy who... *just gets it right*? He looked at Matt, who was once again completely lost in the film, and felt strangely ill at ease.

Peter grabbed a pillow and turned his attention back to the film, trying to focus on the reason they were watching it. *Jack and Rose.* Love that lasted only a few hours. Reciprocated love – fantastic, sure, *but what then*? That was the big question. How do you live a happy life together? Peter thought about other realistic endings – like his parents', two people who didn't seem to live on the same planet any more. And how many people live their whole lives haunted by memories of short, breathtaking sparks of love that are never allowed to catch fire?

The tragedy unfolded. The boat sank, and people turned into violent savages in the struggle to survive. Because the piece of wreckage he found couldn't hold them both, and because Jack was such a gentleman, he gave his place to his beloved Rose, and froze to death in the icy cold Atlantic waters, his lifeless body sinking to the bottom of the ocean. Peter realized in astonishment that he hadn't thought of that, the self-sacrificing death. *Maybe a good man must be a Jesus after all?* He looked around and saw that Matt had completely dissolved into tears, while Toby snorted and got up.

'It's easy to be Mr Perfect if you drown on Day Two. Give them day after ordinary day of changing diapers, spike that with 90 nights of colic, and then see what happens.'

✖

Peter looked at himself in the mirror. As recently as last June, he had been a wide-eyed, admiring finance-wannabe. As he held out a pink shirt against his chest, he thought that the job in hand wasn't particularly difficult. All he needed to do was play himself, except as he had been six months ago rather than now. *God, I look like a right brat!* he thought, tossing away the shirt and reaching over the ironing board for another one. Charlie hadn't seen him since then, so obviously he thought that Peter was as he'd always been. So if it was at all possible to find out what was going on inside Charlie's head, then he had a good chance of succeeding. He decided to wear his light-blue striped shirt with the white collar. He realized that he needed to do something about his hair. It had grown out about half an inch, and it stuck out all over his head. He looked like a fuzzy duckling – not a good look if he was going to blend in at Charlie's 30th birthday party. He needed a haircut.

When he came home from the barber's, he met Vera hurrying out of his room with a stack of papers.

'Sorry, I didn't know,' she mumbled, eyes wandering as if she were trying not to look at him. She looked strange – upset, maybe.

'What?'

She disappeared into her room and Peter went into his, hung

up his jacket and continued into the little bedroom. He started when he saw something shiny and black on his pillow, like a long, outstretched cat. It was Linda's hair.

She was lying under the covers.

'*Jeesus*, do you guys always just barge into each other's rooms without knocking?'

'We're working on something, a sort of group project...' sighed Peter, stroking his freshly cut hair. Only at the front was it still long enough to tug.

'Close the door, for God's sake!' hissed Linda, still under the covers. 'And what the hell have you done to your hair?'

'What are you doing here?' All he could think about was what Vera must have thought.

Linda lifted the covers and scooted backwards a little. All she had on was the black underwear she had bought that life-changing Thursday last fall. She patted the bed. 'Come here, handsome! I heard that you and Sandra broke up, and that you seemed... a bit lonely, so I thought maybe you missed me.'

Peter's heart beat in agitation. *No, no, for fuck's sake, no!*

Linda twisted a little, desire in her eyes. 'I know what I said before, but I can't stop thinking about you. I thought, maybe he can change. Maybe I should give him another chance.'

Peter stood next to the window with his back towards her. He struggled to sound calmer than he was. 'I know that I haven't been... very nice to you. I understand now what you thought, and that you were disappointed. I'm sorry. And I want to change. Or rather, I *have* changed... because now I know what it means to be in love. In love for real.'

He stood with his arms folded and glanced at her warily. He saw her take in what he was saying and stiffen. She climbed out of the bed and angrily collected her clothes.

'And it isn't me you're in love with? *Fuck*, Peter! You change for someone else? Do you know what that feels like? We are talking *years!*' She disappeared into the bathroom with her clothes. She came back out after a few minutes, irately pulled on her coat, and shoved her handbag under her arm as if she wanted to smother it.

318

Peter extended his hand, palm upward.

'The hell I'm shaking hands with you!' she spat.

'Fine. But can I have my key back?'

She snatched her key ring out of her bag, but she was shaking so much she couldn't get the key off. Frustrated, she dropped the whole thing in his hand and let him do it.

'"*In love for real.*" Right. And you believe that, do you?' she mumbled as she took back her keys. Before she left she pointed a sharp finger in his chest and said slowly, 'Things are going to go fucking badly for you. Do you have the slightest idea how much crap karma you've attracted?'

✖

The halogen lights created a sense of being underground. Peter stood on the thick, burgundy carpet and glanced at his reflection in the mirrored wall of faceted glass. Taking a deep breath, he straightened his silk tie and fiddled nervously with the expensive tiepin.

Okay, bring it on… you can do this!

What he saw in the mirror reassured him that he had been right – he looked like his old self. As for his behavior, he would just have to rely on his background and social skills. He ran his fingers lightly though his waxed hair before opening the door and joining the loud throng in the fashionable nightclub where Charlie's festivities had already begun. With luck, barely anyone would notice that he was late. Peter smiled and greeted people as he made his way through the crowd towards the birthday boy.

As usual, Charlie was stylish, gregarious and smartly dressed in an obscenely expensive black suit, his chestnut-brown curls falling just over the collar of his blindingly white shirt. He was talking to two men – Stureplan finance types, by the look of them. Although they were smiling at each other and holding up their champagne glasses in a toast, their body language communicated competition, almost aggression.

Peter accepted the obligatory glass as he approached Charlie and went into action.

'So, here's the cocky bastard who scorns his old colleagues!'

319

said the shorter of the strangers to Charlie.

The other one, blond with slicked-backed hair, narrowed his eyes. 'Yes, and apparently his own first million!'

Ah! Stockbrokers from Charlie's first job, then?

'Nooo, not at all,' said Charlie. 'I just said that it's not hard to make money if you are something of a salesman and get good kickbacks. But that doesn't mean you create any value.' The stockbrokers looked at him questioningly. Charlie turned towards Peter.

'Well look here, cousin dear! So you managed to drag yourself away from the hinterland?' he said as he gave him a backslapping hug.

'Yes... you don't turn 30 every day,' mumbled Peter. He shook hands with the stockbrokers, who introduced themselves as Erik and Stefan.

'They were just asking me what I do now, how it's different from what they do,' explained Charlie and turned back towards slicked-back Stefan. 'At Financial Products we actually create money! We're the biggest insurance company in the world; we're leaders in financial engineering, and we help the market get closer to the ideal condition – put simply, we make it more complete and effective!'

'Yes,' said Erik, reluctantly impressed. 'We've heard about your phenomenal growth... But you're gambling pretty hard, so how come you still get to keep your triple A credit rating? I don't want to belittle you or anything, but, I mean, aren't you creating a fastest-to-the-door situation? Think about Russia in '97. They also had great ratings, but, fuck, it just... *poof*... disappeared!' He laughed and downed his champagne in one gulp.

Charlie turned to Peter. 'Erik traded Russian government securities when Moscow defaulted on its domestic debts and declared a moratorium on foreign creditor payments, and...' Charlie pursed his lips, and began talking as if to a small child, 'the poor baby has never recovered!'

'I had money on the screen when I went home that evening,' continued Erik, 'but the next morning, when I turned on the computer to check my holdings, the screen was completely blank. Everything was gone! Fuck! The whole market was pissed off...'

'You shouldn't listen to this.' Charlie turned to the stockbrokers, 'You're just jealous because you didn't earn five million pounds last year!'

Stefan smiled wryly and thumped Charlie hard on the back. 'You psychopath!' he said admiringly and followed Erik, who was on his way to refill his glass.

'Psychopath?' wondered Peter.

'Oh, there was a study that showed that a high percentage of successful traders are... emotionally cold. It was something about being able to handle large sums of money without being nervous, daring to take risks. So, in financial circles, calling someone a psychopath is the highest compliment you can give,' grinned Charlie.

'But you're not a psychopath, are you?' *You have your flaws... but you're hardly an ice-cold madman,* thought Peter.

'No,' admitted Charlie. 'Of course you get nervous sometimes, but I'm damned good at playing the part!'

'"You look like you know what you're doing, Stavenius",' quoted Peter, and his cousin nodded. They had both heard that ad nauseam.

'But what did you mean by kickbacks?' asked Peter.

'Oh, that was when I worked at the bank as a financial advisor, right after I graduated from business school.'

Peter nodded. If nothing else, his father would never let him forget it.

'The way it works, investment funds sweeten their arrangements with traders so that the trader earns money if he advises the customer to pick their funds. So that's what you do! It's an easy way to make money.' Charlie shrugged his shoulders. 'And that's what Stefan and Erik still do; basically everybody in Swedish finance does it.' Charlie looked around condescendingly, as if the people he was talking about might be listening. 'You know, they liquidate positions, try to float along adjusting to shifts in risk...'

'But kickbacks,' wondered Peter, trying to sound relaxed.

'Isn't that just another word for bribes?'

Charlie didn't seem to notice his cousin's intense interest in every ounce of information he revealed. He shrugged his shoulders, 'Sure, you could say that. But the funds increase in value, so everybody wins – the customers too.'

'But you got into stocks after the IT crash, in 2002. Didn't all the stocks go up?

You earned a million, and your customers were pleased, despite the fact that the increase had nothing to do with you. When stocks go up, you take the credit, but when they go down, you throw up your arms and blame everything on 'the Market'…

Charlie looked inscrutably at him, then sipped his champagne and held it up. 'Do you know what makes champagne *Tête de Cuvée*?'

'Huh?'

'How you produce one of the world's best champagnes year after year?'

'No idea…'

'No. And the world's best vineyards don't know either. It's weather and wind, which differ from one year to the next.'

Peter took a breath: 'Vineyards always deliver wine, otherwise they don't get paid. Stockbrokers, on the other hand, sell their services year after year – both when markets go up and when they fall – based on their supposed knowledge about stocks.' Peter watched his cousin's reaction. 'But in a perfect market, there should be no incorrect pricing of securities, so there shouldn't be anything to gain from making "smarter" investments than others.'

Charlie lowered his glass very slowly and stared at him as if he had just uttered a secret password. He took a step closer and whispered triumphantly, 'Cousin! I *knew* you had it in you!' He tapped Peter lightly on the forehead with his finger. 'Everyone who can count knows that, in the long run, the advice of stockbrokers is worse than leaving things to chance!'

Adrenaline coursed through Peter. He tried to sound blasé, as if what Charlie had said was nothing more than trivial gossip. 'So if I put my money in "actively managed funds"…?'

'Yes, you're paying the stockbrokers' profits and salaries, so you're earning less, and statistically speaking you get nothing out of it!' Charlie looked around the room, as if to assure himself that nobody had heard him.

An insight suddenly flashed in Peter's mind: *Vera was right!* The first million before 25 – the Holy Grail, the rite of manhood, he had been… *A taker!* The so-called hero is standing here and admitting it! Peter's heartbeat wouldn't settle, and a mass of disconcerting emotions threatened to distract him. But his brain remembered its mission, and he pushed on, seeking information that he could never get by reading.

'But what about the impressive growth at your current job?'

Thank God I don't sound like I feel! thought Peter, almost surprised at how relaxed his voice was.

Charlie straightened up proudly. 'We're product developers. We're the ones who create the growth. We make what the market wants – products that attract international capital.'

'What's the annual turnover? I heard Ernst say that he didn't know.'

Charlie shrugged his shoulders. 'If Dad doesn't know then nobody does. But it doesn't really matter. The more the better,' he grinned. 'If I remember right, I heard something about a BIS estimate of 600 trillion.'

The number was too big for Peter to grasp, but he asked, 'BIS?'

'Bank of International Settlements, closest thing to the UN that finance has.'

'Oh…' Peter was trying to remember everything. He couldn't exactly pull out the little notebook he had in his inner pocket in front of his unwitting informer. He needed time, and as he and Charlie followed the crowd out in the direction of the fine old hotel where dinner would be served, he tried to ask less factual questions.

'But listen, why your group? I mean, why is your company in London the one that is creating this fantastic growth?'

Charlie looked flattered. 'We have some of the world's sharpest minds. And we work a lot, sometimes 80 hours a week. But we also get a fair share of what we create!' He put a brotherly arm around Peter's shoulders. 'When you've graduated next year – and make sure you take a lot of math courses, okay? – then I can introduce you around the company if you want. You're welcome to join us and help create big profits!'

'But big profits imply big risks, so what happens if things go the other way?' wondered Peter.

'Are you too scared?' grinned Charlie, but continued frankly. 'If you work alone and do idiotic things then you will wind up out in the cold, of course. On the other hand, just like with Erik and Stefan – you also wind up out in the cold if you don't take sufficient risks when others do, because you don't give your customer the increase in value others are getting.'

The wind blew small, icy snowflakes into Peter's face and he froze. They didn't have to walk far, but he suddenly felt almost ill. *I should have worn warmer clothes.*

Charlie lowered his voice and leaned in closer. 'And if the firm has good contacts, then even serious mistakes can be resolved.'

'You mean like with LTCM 10 years ago?' guessed Peter, holding his breath.

'Exactly!' Once again Charlie's eyes glittered with what looked like respect. 'Because if you owe a million then it's your problem, but if you owe billions, then obviously it's the bank's problem!'

'What did you say?' shivered Peter as he pulled his thin coat more tightly around his neck.

'Nobody had a clue, everything was a secret. But then they met, all the bank directors at McDonough's – and that's when they realized it wasn't just their bank; *everybody* had loaned money to the fund! I've heard that Long Term's leverage at the end was 125!'

'What? They owed... 125 times their own capital?' Charlie nodded. 'Yes. Of course, it's hard to say exactly how much it was, because they were so heavily in derivatives, but that was the figure they said, and all of it risked disappearing. It threatened the whole financial system!'

Peter squinted into the driving snow and let the dizzying message sink in. He looked down at his Italian shoes, which were way too thin for the cold weather and left black marks in the white slush. He hoped his expression didn't reveal anything as he said, 'So, too big to fail?'

'Exactly. And then the banks that contributed to the bailout got shares in the fund and could just wait it out. The whole crisis ended up cancelling itself out, I think. So the financial branch learned a lesson – "stick close to the Washington Consensus",' said Charlie.

'What does that mean?'

'The US national bank... the Federal Reserve, the ones who arranged the meeting, they're more like an association of banks than a government body. And, anyway, the US is pushing more and more for financial regulation to be open Counterparty, that is, that in large private banks...'

'Huh? Now you've lost me.'

In a frustrated whisper, Charlie continued through clenched teeth. 'There was some talk about her... that Brooksley Born woman claimed that "swaps are futures", and argued for regulating everything. But we had powerful forces on our side – so it didn't happen! We still have the right to sign private contracts without bureaucratic interference. Thanks to that, the American market has continued to grow at a good rate. That's why we are particularly focused on developing products for them. The products I have sell like hotcakes – bankers, pension funds, everybody wants them. They yield 12-per-cent interest and with our swaps the risk is non-existent!' said Charlie proudly as they turned the corner and headed towards the entrance of the splendid old hotel. Soon they would be out of the cold.

Twelve-per-cent interest with non-existent risk – that doesn't sound like a functioning market economy, thought Peter and asked, 'There must be some amazingly strong product supporting the whole thing. Or is it the lousy competition? What is it that increases so much and is risk free?'

Charlie stopped and looked him directly in the eye. 'Peter, I'm saying this because you're like a brother to me. If you are going to work in finance, forget production! Only unprofitable old bankers worry about such things. The goal is simple: we attract more customers with more money. Working in the financial sector is about anticipating what others are going to do, acting at the right moment, attacking from above. Taking advantage of the freedoms!'

The law of the jungle. Peter recognized the feeling he had now from his fruitless efforts to read his way to an understanding of the impenetrable logic.

'You mean "it's only a rumor, but it's a good rumor"?' guessed Peter as he passed through the luxury hotel's gold rotating door.

'Exactly! Those of us who are the best, we aren't just number crunchers. We understand psychology. Do you know what Soros did so brilliantly in the fall of '92?'

In the lobby, on the stairs with the thick, blue carpet, Charlie was suddenly pounced on by two young women with fake tans. Kissing his cheeks, they bombarded him with chirping phrases like 'it's been *soooo* long' and 'how *are* you these days?' Peter took the welcome opportunity to sneak away and ask the hotel receptionist if he could get some painkillers for his headache. He fished around for his notebook, feeling like some kind of foreign spy as he locked himself in the bathroom and quickly scribbled down what he had heard.

Tables were set for a three-course meal for 140 people in the hotel's beautiful Winter Garden. 'With extremely high incomes,' Charlie had said, 'come extremely high expectations.'

Peter was lucky to be placed at the same table as Charlie, so despite his dull headache – and after exchanging pleasantries during the appetizer with his aunt Kerstin, who was seated next to him – he returned to their conversation: 'Charlie, tell me, what did Soros do so brilliantly in 1992?'

All eight of them at the round table with the cream-colored tablecloth turned their faces politely towards the birthday boy, who was wiping his mouth after the smoked shrimp in wood sorrel sauce. Peter knew that Charlie had no problem being the center of attention; the question was what he was willing to reveal to a larger audience.

'What he did so brilliantly...' Charlie paused dramatically and looked around at his well-dressed guests, 'was simply the old foolproof trick – short sell and tell.'

The woman next to Charlie, who wore her hair in a short, flattering style and had big, lively brown eyes, reminded Peter uncomfortably of *'Halle Berry' from London*. She might be close to 40, but her tight dress emphasized a body in top form. Did all of Charlie's women friends look like that? This woman was lighter skinned and spoke Swedish, but she still gave Peter unpleasant associations that made his headache worse, despite the medicine. *Another piece of my disintegrating dignity. I need to take it easy with the alcohol*, thought Peter.

'You mean...' wondered the Swedish Berry as her elegant nails fiddled with a pearl in her ear, 'that he bet money that the pound would fall, and then spread a rumor that actually forced a devaluation?'

'You make it sound like you can get away with betting on a horse and then stoning the others in the middle of the race,' objected an unusually large man on the other side of the table.

'Nah,' said Charlie, 'I call what Soros did being convincing in his pronouncements about the pound... and the lira, and the Swedish krona! And he earned money. A billion dollars on the devaluation of the pound alone, if memory serves. Do you remember when we had 500-per-cent interest in the fall of '92?

The giant nodded his head. 'Nobody in Swedish finance can forget that!'

'No, not even me, and I was just a kid,' said Charlie. 'It was expensive and useless trying to defend the krona. But now, that's enough, good people! Cheers!'

When the table thinned out in the pause between the main course and dessert, Charlie leaned towards Peter and said, 'I see Eleonore gets to you. Is it because she looks like...?' He raised his eyebrows meaningfully.

Is it that obvious? Peter looked down at the table in humiliation. He felt that the strain of the evening was causing cracks in his façade.

'I heard from Sally that it didn't go very well. After the damned bragging you did, I thought it was... pretty funny. Talk about overselling and under-delivering!' grinned Charlie.

'She talked to you?' He looked at his cousin with dread.

'Yeah, I happened to ask about it.' The corner of Charlie's mouth turned up teasingly as he said: 'Misery, I think that was the word she used. Misery.'

Peter rested his head on his arms and groaned. The worsening headache was starting to make him feel like his head might explode. It wasn't news that the whole encounter had been a flop. All his vague memories from that evening suggested it. He knew that the drunker he had become, the cockier he had sounded, while his actual ability to perform had declined at the same speed as his bragging had increased. His clearest memory of the... *what should he call the lamentable affair? Attempt?*... was that she had put her hand on her breast, and he had seen the characteristic marks on her left ring-finger. He had become anxious. *Adultery.* He had asked about the kids in the family. 'We have no children,' she had said. But even if it were true, it didn't matter; his desire evaporated. He really didn't want to. But since he was a man, that wasn't okay. If a man says A, then he's always expected to say B next. If he doesn't, it's okay to label him defective. That's what reigning social norms dictate. But Peter was not a man who could combine an erection with strong feelings of maudlin self-contempt, and he refused to feel ashamed that he wasn't a machine. Still, the situation gave him plenty of other things to be ashamed of.

'You don't think it would have been smarter to lay off the bragging a bit? Give yourself a chance to, say... be a pleasant surprise?' suggested Charlie, the teasing grin still on his face.

A shameless, outspoken flirtation. It should have stopped there. *Why is it that only women have the right to say A as confidently and convincingly as they damned well want, without automatically committing themselves to B?* He should have allowed himself to say A, period. Because that part of the evening had been fun. Peter realized that he had been most interested in her thoughts; it had been her disarming honesty that fascinated him and piqued his curiosity. She had said, 'They're all faking it anyway.' *What does that mean? Explain!*

328

But then he thought again about her missing rings – *so much for honesty*. He felt almost bitter.

Charlie bent forward towards his gloomy cousin. 'Don't worry about it. So what; you were humbled in the act of love. It happens to everyone. And one time doesn't count.'

Peter had heard that before, but he never understood it. *How can it not count? One is one – not zero!* But worried wasn't the right word to describe how he felt. Humbled? Was that the right word? Humiliated? Mortified? Now he was getting close. That was a part of the feeling. But 'act of love'… how could it have been that? He didn't even know her!

The truth was that the gigolo in him had neither abstained from the depressing adultery nor delivered what she, after all his bragging, had expected. Adultery in the form of a failed drunken quickie. *The most meaningless of the meaningless.*

Peter felt like the lowest form of life. His head was pounding and his whole body felt like shit. He was close to tears as he sat there in the beautifully decorated, buzzing party room. He felt his cousin grab his shoulder awkwardly.

'What the hell, Peter! Let's just forget about it.'

Peter took a deep breath and nodded a bit too anxiously. He tried to pull himself together and forced himself to remain sitting despite his desire to flee.

'Anyway, what I want you to know when you choose a career…' Charlie looked around and lowered his voice to speak confidentially to Peter. 'Listen to what I am saying – finance is where the money is. Being an entrepreneur today is an unnecessarily difficult way to make money! Perhaps with the exception of owning a giant chain of discount stores – think Walmart. Do you want to own a bunch of stores with cheap junk…? Or do you want to follow the best? Because we see it clearly in the City of London. These days, all the talent flocks to finance.'

No it doesn't! thought Peter, like a drowning man who suddenly sees something that can save him. A wave of warmth washed over him as he recalled Vera's face so close to his in the darkened room when they were watching the movie. She would never give the lowest form of life a look like that! *One she believes in.* In that moment, he had been that. And that's what he wanted to be! He was filled with a strong desire to tell Charlie about his neighbor with an IQ of 139.

Charlie must have seen objection in his expression, because his voice suddenly hardened to the point of ridicule. 'The only question is whether you can hack it, whether you have the talent and the nerve,' he challenged, leaning back in his chair.

If I'm enough of a psychopath, you mean?

'Otherwise, if you're going to have any chance of earning multi-millions per year then your best bet is to sell cheap junk, pay slave-labor wages, no benefits...' grinned Charlie.

Peter felt an unexpected urge to complete the evening's mission. 'But what about the stuff Ernst is always talking about? What about providing for ourselves in the future?'

'Yes, thanks. Customers, creditors and stockbrokers make a good living, we have no problem accumulating money,' said Charlie, sipping on the expensive cognac that had been served.

'As Erik said, money is numbers, lines on a computer screen. What real value do you actually create? If a lot of people want their money at the same time, and it turns out that the value... doesn't exist, does it all collapse?'

'A big customer on Wall Street has a whole room full of math geniuses from India.' Charlie twisted his brandy snifter thoughtfully, and the caramel-colored liquid swirled around in the warm light from the candelabra on the table.

'A turbaned guy seemed a bit unstable last week,' continued Charlie as both of them stared as if hypnotized by the cognac's golden dance. 'He babbled something about "fat tails", that the derivatives insure against small losses, but not the big ones, that risks are widely dispersed...' He giggled, 'Like mines hidden throughout the whole system – and that there's going to be one hell of an explosion. He got all agitated and screamed that "we pretend to be investors, but in reality we're..."'

Charlie put down his glass – he rounded his tongue and put it against the roof of his mouth in an effort to mimic a Hindi accent, and with sweeping gestures he said, 'Deadly fucking chicken racers!' Charlie let his raised eyebrows sink back to their ordinary position and laughed. But Peter was not amused. *Little brothers and sisters, what are you doing?* echoed in his head.

'Yes, exactly. Why not object?' The question came out of Peter's mouth unbidden.

'I think they took Cuckoo Bird to the nuthouse,' came the unconcerned reply from within the brandy snifter.

Peter was filled with an unpleasant feeling that he associated with high blood pressure.

'Yeah, well, you don't seem to know where the money will come from either. Do you really know what you're selling?'

'I sell CDSs on CDOs – and it's a damned good deal for all concerned!' snapped Charlie, staring him in the face.

Now they had reached the final battle. *Now is when I have to pull myself together and persevere,* the last lactate-burning minutes of the match. Peter felt sick, and feverish now too, but Charlie didn't seem sober, so were they even?

'A CDS is insurance against bankruptcy,' said Peter in a conciliatory manner as he bent forward. 'But what are CDOs?'

'Collateralized Debt Obligations. Damned good product.' He threw up his hands. 'They are tailor-made packages of mortgages... different levels of claims. That's what the quants – the quantitative analysts – sit and calculate.'

'Mortgages... house loans, right?'

'Yes, US house loans. But it's not just that; I don't actually know how Goldman created them – a well-placed partner, by the way.' Charlie blinked meaningfully. *Washington Consensus?* wondered Peter quietly as his handsome cousin continued. 'CDOs have to be packaged particularly smartly.' Charlie shrugged his shoulders.

'But the 12-per-cent idiot-proof interest you mentioned? US growth isn't anywhere near that, is it?'

Charlie rubbed the lip of his brandy snifter glass with two fingers.

'No, but you know... house prices just keep increasing there, so if somebody can't pay their loan then the bank takes the house and sells it at a profit. The income is high enough to pay the lender, to cover our financial service fees, *and*, last but not least, to provide a good return on invested capital! And our sales have increased enormously. Just look at the figures since 2000. We rule! I've actually surpassed the best at Goldman's now, and now I sell them naked!'

Peter turned icy cold. 'But what happens if US house prices fall? Or, rather, *when* they fall? There'll be tons of people who can't pay, all at the same time. You've sold insurance... but insurance is built on the assumption that only a few will need to collect! How the hell can you afford to keep your promises otherwise?'

Charlie leaned over to get closer to his cousin, looking at him with bloodshot eyes. 'You wonder why I work *with* the system, succeed brilliantly and earn 70 million kronor per year? When instead I could pull the emergency brake, make enemies of all my customers and colleagues, hell, the whole financial sector, and wind up on the outside... only to see my place filled by some eager intern from Oxford?'

Peter looked at the man he used to want to be like. 'But, I mean, what about your... conscience? Or, aren't you at least afraid of being unmasked?' asked Peter finally.

'What do you mean, unmasked? Almost everyone I know in finance is doing the same thing, or trying to, anyway. Stop acting like you're Mr Righteous Investigative Reporter out to dig up the truth!' A shadow came over Charlie's face and he suddenly spoke as if talking to himself. 'In any case, it isn't that easy to find out.'

'But you're telling me...' asked Peter with his heart in his mouth.

'Well, I don't know about telling. I'm just giving you a tip, because, damn it, you're like my little brother. If you want to make big money, come and join us.'

'You don't really think I'm secretly digging for dirt, do you?' asked Peter. He was exhausted and needed to bring the conversation to an end.

'That would be something,' grinned Charlie, and he smiled at Eleonore's silhouette as it smoothly slid back into the chair next to him. 'Heir to Escape yapping at its customers. Nobody is that stupid, surely?' The dark woman raised a perfectly pencilled eyebrow at him quizzically, and Charlie turned back to Peter.

'You know it's a race – you run or get out of the way. The most skilful win. There will always be downturns, but the market regulates itself, it's a natural law. And the alternative...' Charlie turned and was talking to Eleonore again, 'More regulation would just dampen the financial world's inventiveness, and innovation is the source of wealth. Right?'

To Peter, the last part sounded like a defensive, pre-rehearsed speech.

The guests enjoyed an elaborate display of fireworks from the hotel balcony overlooking the Baltic Sea bay that graced the eastern shore of Stockholm's oldest neighborhoods. Peter remained inside, resting on one of the plush sofas, but when the guests streamed in again, it was as if the warmth around him suddenly increased his nausea, and he rose and moved against the tide, out into the cool air. He stood with his elbows against the thick, stone balustrade. *What is he actually saying?* The question spun around in his head feverishly, and he experienced a strong sense of falling head-first onto the cobblestones below.

He suddenly realized that he wasn't alone. Carla was there, lighting a cigarette about three feet away from him. *Fuck! I'll look like Rose at the stern of the Titanic if I don't stop hanging over the edge!* He straightened up as casually as his spinning head allowed, and exchanged a little chitchat with Carla. Peter looked at her, the latest in his father's line of young girlfriends. She stood there thoughtfully; slim as always, one arm across her waist like a belt, a support for the other arm, which she was using to smoke. She held the cigarette between her elegant fingers, and took a deep breath. He hesitated, but felt compelled to ask her something important.

'I know it's rude to ask, but that question at Christmas... are you two thinking... I mean, are you pregnant?'

Carla looked at him as she picked a flake of tobacco off her tongue with her free fingers. She flicked it off, shook her head and took another deep puff. Peter felt relieved.

'Okay, in that case I actually wanted to... I've thought about what you asked, and I want to explain my answer a bit. Lennart is probably not... I mean, sure, he has been a good father sometimes, but I think you need to ask more of him. The mother has the right to.' He fell silent and looked at the scar on his thumb. It always reminded him of terror and vulnerability. '*The child* must be allowed to ask more of the father, too. And if he hasn't managed to deliver by the time he's in his forties, then I have difficulty seeing how he is going to do it now. He isn't interested in changing.'

Carla stood completely still, unreadable.

Peter continued. 'I'm sorry to be saying this now, but you did ask... and I don't want to mislead you. It's a pretty important decision.'

Carla sighed a bit shakily, blinked with her mascaraed eyelashes in agitation and nodded curtly.

'Yes, it's an important decision.'

She crushed the cigarette butt with the point of her elegant high-heeled shoe and went back into the warm, well-lit hotel.

Alone on the balcony, Peter started to feel cold again; his head was spinning as he went back inside. He felt abandoned – as if he had believed in God, or at least in adults who had things under control, who took responsibility and could be trusted. Peter felt that he would never be able to look at the world in that way again. What he now knew had worrying consequences. Though exactly what they were was unclear.

He wanted to go home to the anything-but-glamorous dormitory, because at least there he had some sort of stable ground under his feet. He felt no such thing here. He ran into his uncle Ernst on his way out to the taxi. 'I have to get going. I think I'm coming down with something. But give my best to everybody and tell them I said thanks. What a great party!'

Ernst nodded in a fatherly way and helped Peter on with his coat. Peter suddenly had an idea. 'Mr Chairman of the Board?' He watched his uncle respond with the dutiful expression he usually assumed when matters of responsibility arose. 'We're due to revise the risk analysis at our June meeting, right?'

'Yes, that's correct,' nodded Ernst.

'I want to put something forward on that point. Can you add it to the agenda?'

Ernst studied him. 'You have something you want to put forward about the risk analysis? Okay, duly noted.'

The fever and headache got worse, and the shivering started on the flight back up north. The journey seemed to take forever, but he finally arrived. He dragged himself from the taxi up to the dorm.

And there she was!

The words tumbled out of his hazy brain. 'Hi... you weren't here when I had to leave, and I didn't want to call... because it felt like one of those stupid things, a giant misunderstanding, I mean, when you don't see the other person, you know?' He leaned against the wall, suddenly exhausted, so exhausted, and tried to finish explaining. 'But I just wanted to say that what you saw yesterday in my room... I mean, Linda...' The words came out as smoothly as if he were trying to push a car with the handbrake on, and Vera looked embarrassed.

'No, you don't need to explain. Besides, I like her. And anyway, it's none of my business who's in your room.'

He whimpered weakly and turned towards the wall. He felt faint and as if his head were going to explode. *But I want you to think it's your business!*

'How are you?' She sounded worried. 'I think you...' She put her hand on his forehead. 'Yes, you have a pretty high fever.'

'Yeah, I'm going to go and lie down.'

He staggered into his room, dropped his bag in the entrance, and fell onto the bed. Although he had left the door wide open, she knocked carefully before she came in with a large glass of water with lemon juice.

'You need to drink lots. It's important.'

He sat up with a groan, obediently took the glass and drank.

'By the way, how did it go? Did you find out how new finance thinks?'

'I don't know.' Dizzy with exhaustion, he didn't know if he was lying. He tumbled backwards onto the bed.

'Okay,' she smiled softly, 'but, at least you tried!'

She hesitated at the door, turned and looked at him lying on the bed.

'Peter, knock if you feel like you can't manage, if you need help.'

She turned off the light and closed the door.

He drank the rest of the lemon water and managed to undress and shower. He put on his old sweatpants and a t-shirt and, shivering, climbed back into bed. The next morning, Vera knocked and came in to see how he was doing. He felt even worse. He was dizzy, had a dry cough, and his whole body ached. She was holding something white. She was just explaining that it was an ear thermometer, when her phone rang.

'Good morning. Yes, but our hero...' She blinked at Peter and silently formed the word 'Cissi.' 'Apparently it was a giant party for his cousin from the world of finance... We'll have to wait to hear about it, because he's not well at all. But I'll be there. See you at nine!'

Concerned, she sat down next to him on the bed and took his temperature with the help of the white instrument, which bleeped in his ear.

'Oh!' she said when she read the display. '103 degrees! You really are sick! I wonder if we should call the clinic?'

'No, I just have a cold. Go on... keep working.' He smiled feebly.

The days passed and Vera worked out a routine. She checked on him, took his temperature – which she wrote down on a piece of paper on his desk – and made sure he ate something and drank a lot. Despite the fact that he felt faint as soon as he got up, he was very motivated to keep himself clean. Now that she was coming by at least twice a day, it was not the time to give up his habit of showering every day. It felt good, but it took the effort of a mountain climber just to get into the bathtub... Except for the blood-poisoning episode, Peter couldn't remember ever feeling so powerless. Each stroke with the toothbrush was strangely slow. He felt as though his fever kept climbing and climbing. After five days of monitoring his temperature, Vera looked really worried. But when she suggested that he probably ought to go to the hospital... He refused and forced her to promise.

Never, ever again!

×

Oh, what a magnificent city Charlie shows him! Fascinated, his eyes roam up to the extravagant architecture of the façades – magnificent imperial buildings and huge, polished-glass complexes. The forces that build such things, the power! And everything welcomes him; in the company of his urbane, sophisticated cousin, he is admitted into a world of style and refinement. Smiling, expensively dressed people take his hand and lead him upwards in a murmuring flow through golden doors. He is welcome; he is one of the few chosen to enter the majestic party halls, with mirrors, crystal and tables overflowing with food and drink.

Curious, he leaves Charlie's side for a moment, just to see what is on the other side of the mirror... He loses his footing and falls one floor down into a room like the one he was just in above, except this one is dark. Strange. The same people are sitting here, wryly grinning with their clothes dirty and torn, like a poor theatre company of days past. They play poker. He senses cheating and trickery, but the cigar smoke's thick fog stings his eyes; he has difficulty seeing. There is a mirror in the corner on this floor too. It's black. Caught by a power he can't resist, he looks behind this one as well, and he... falls! He falls helplessly further, deeper – until he finally lands heavily in a stinking underground place.

Here there are sewers and tubes; trash; filth; yellowish, poisonous foam and mud. He hears whimpering people, sees emaciated children. Pulsing tubes stretch from the dirty people in bondage. Peter struggles, follows the tubes, echoing in agony, upwards again. To the sound of his own anxious heartbeat, he crawls through tight passages, follows the tubes, worms his way through narrow locks and shafts. He comes to a new floor, the basement over the sewers, where all the tubes converge. In the middle of the room, coldly illuminated as if from fluorescent lights... Oh, what a horror! A body so disfigured that he can hardly bear to look at it. All the flexible tubes force their way into the hanging torso – where the legs should be, there is a bunch of tubes that resemble the wriggling tentacles of an octopus. Bewitched, he wanders around the ghastly center of the room and a scream of terror fills his whole being. Because the face... the horror's face is his own!

Suddenly he is hanging there in the middle of the room, unclean, caught, violated, tricked. All the screaming sounds that vibrate from the tubes flood through him. He is stuck helplessly, every effort to escape will tear him to pieces. Anguish. And then the jerky metallic female voice issues the verdict: 'Do you have the slightest idea how much crap karma you've attracted?' His heart pounds in terror as the repulsive sound around him slowly dies out. Mute terror fills him; he wants to scream, but can't. 'Help! Help me!' He is only seven years old, a boy helplessly hanging as if on a meat hook.

And finally... a safe scent. She has come. He feels indescribable relief when his grandmother comes and lifts him down. Her soft hands free him from the parasitic tubes and stroke his skin, healing him. He cries in her arms and it is a sweet relief to hear her.

'There, there, it's okay. Everything will be fine. You'll be fine.'

38

And thou all-seeing circle of the sun, behold what I,
a God, from Gods endure.

Aeschylus, 'Prometheus Bound', circa 430 BCE

Peter wasn't as panicked as Amoke had been. The teenager had
survived the militia's cruelty, but first just wanted to die, and
then refused to leave Basic Needs when her physical wounds
had healed. *Amoke, whose name meant 'she who should only
be caressed'.* And yet there was something in Peter's eyes that
reminded Vera of that first rape victim she had cried with in the
Congo, something there that made her wonder what had really
happened that night at the hospital 17 years ago when he had
blood poisoning. Had he been overpowered against his will?
Had they pinned him down in an effort to immobilize him so
they could get a needle in his arm? Or to sedate him?

Vera didn't question the need for an intravenous antibiotic.
But had some authority lost patience and allowed medical
rationality to override human compassion? Had a little seven-
year-old, alone in the night, separated from his parents, been
coerced? Had no-one taken the time to hold and comfort him,
apply an anesthetic cream and hold his hand, explain that he had
nasty bacteria in his blood from the sore on his thumb? Had no-
one said that when the cream started to work, if he was really
brave and didn't move and sang the *Star Wars* song when the
doctor sent Luke Skywalker to fight the mean Darth Vader in
his blood, then all he would feel was a tiny prick?

Whatever had happened, it was obvious that it had left him
with some kind of hospital phobia. *That was a high price for
an adventurous little boy to pay for his father's success.* And

because Vera knew that the patient's sense of security strongly influenced recovering and healing, she promised Peter that he wouldn't have to go to the hospital. But that was before she knew how sick he would become. It was now Day Seven and the situation was becoming critical. She had practically created a mobile clinic in Peter's room, complete with equipment and medication.

Now his fever was up to 104. What worried her even more was that he was unresponsive and whimpering deliriously. 'You never said it was like this! Let me go! Let me go!' He tossed and turned anxiously, as if terrified of the sheets, and his shirt was drenched in sweat.

What else can I do? Suddenly it occurred to her. She got clean sheets from her room, a towel and, from the bottom drawer of her dresser, the calabash with Kogi Mama's fever medicine. Back in his room, she opened the window, removed his sweaty shirt. She went to the bathroom and dampened half of the towel with warm water. She washed him with the damp part, and used the other to dry him off. She saw that he was shivering in the cool air, but let him lie there with his arms over his head. She felt emotional about Peter in a way she had never felt about another patient, but she worked efficiently to clean him. *I understand that you're cold, but I can't let you get any hotter!* She carefully rolled him to one side, and with practised hands she changed the sheet from that half of the bed. Then she rolled him the other way and did the same on the other half.

Vera sat on the edge of the bed with her little wooden bottle… and… *goodness, the cork was tight*! She looked at him and was suddenly overwhelmed by a powerful memory from a school field trip in the ninth grade. The most beautiful thing she had seen among all the thousands of art treasures at the Louvre. At a distance, among all the beefy bearded men with everything from powerful toes to locks of curly hair perfectly carved out of white stone, she had seen a statue of a lithe young man, proudly bearing a torch to humanity. The teacher had told them the ancient Greek myth about Prometheus, the young Titan who defied Zeus. Through the Parisian throng, so unnatural for someone raised in the Norrland forest, she had got only a glimpse. There were so many people who wanted to see him! But it was like Prometheus was lying here now, fully alive, strong and lithe, his chest smooth and bare. Her pulse increased anxiously. *He looks like an anatomy lesson,* she reluctantly admitted; *anglus mantibulae* popped into her head as she looked at the straight lines of the jaw, nose and eyebrows and the round form of the lips. Naturally blond women with dark eyelashes were not unusual because they often used mascara and... She looked at his short hair. It had started to grow out, and it was actually quite dark blond – but those dark eyelashes were still one of many unlikely details. It was no surprise that he was appreciated by the hordes of girls who hunted him so successfully! Such public beauty was in a league unthinkable for *someone who couldn't even keep Adam when he had promised before God to be faithful,* she painfully reminded herself. With discipline, she pulled her eyes away and finally managed to get the cork off the bottle.

She knew that his beauty wasn't hers to enjoy; it belonged to all the others who flocked around him. She would treat him as she should, as a *patient like any other*! She let a generous portion of Kogi Mama's oil flow down into the soft hollow where his lower rib connected to his breastbone. She replaced the cork, and took a deep breath. Trying to ignore the strange shyness that warmed her cheeks, she forced herself to look down at her lap and began rubbing the strong camphor-scented plant extract into his chest.

She moved her hands carefully upward and then out towards his shoulders and back in over his collarbone. She continued downward to get more oil and then repeated the procedure, trying to use her sense of touch to rub the oil into parts of his skin she hadn't yet reached. Her eyes obeyed her and remained locked on her lap, but her hands registered an unexpected feeling. They made her aware of his heart beating, and she realized that she had great affection for the person who lived in there. There was a huge crowd of admirers between them, but... There was also a very odd 'but'.

He had helped her in a way that she didn't think he helped anyone else. Regardless of how much she looked away, her hands were aware of the beauty that lived inside his skin, and she wondered how many had been allowed to see it. The exquisite movement when, with impossibly fast reflexes, he had caught the flying wine-stained rag. The honest and curious expression when he had asked what *she* wanted, for herself. His courage to look for the truth even though it would turn things upside down. His unexpected abilities, his way of supporting her so whole-heartedly, but also challenging her, refusing to let her give up. *Microscopic parts of a per cent* popped into her head.

She was filled with the breathtaking notion that she – the girl who had left the statue-filled room without the slightest impulse to force her way to the front of the crowd – was, oddly enough, the person who got to see the greatest beauty in him. Vera couldn't stop herself from letting her eyes wander... *how small my hands look on him.* She found herself thinking that it was actually a bit of a shame that his thick hair was growing and would soon completely cover the bumps on his head. She didn't understand why, and it worried her a little, because she was used to understanding her feelings. She tore her eyes away from him, too taken by his naked proximity to fully understand the source of her feelings of near-melancholy about his hair. But she unconsciously sensed that his bald head was the one feature she appreciated that hadn't attracted lots of others before her.

She was also concerned that she had started to act like a cliché. She had told herself that it was because she had more money now, but deep inside she knew that the real reason she had started wearing contact lenses again – and wearing her hair loose more often – was because she wanted him to notice her. Not as he had done outside the dressing room, when she had felt like she was in costume. Now he knew what he was looking at because he knew her well enough, and she felt like herself. It was an important difference, and anyway, wasn't it harmless and human to want to be noticed? But still, it was worrying... and she couldn't fully repress the question she dared not pose directly: *Why do I want* him *to notice me?*

Vera followed the instructions that Kogi Mama had communicated to her with sign language. She rubbed oil over the entire front of his torso, but blushingly avoided the line of hair extending downward from his navel and over his flat stomach. She saw that he was still shivering, and it moved her to see the light hair on his arms stand on end. She shyly observed her work, noticing the harmonious pattern of muscles, ligaments and bones under his glistening skin. Her heart raced a little when she remembered how easily he had lifted her and carried her up the stairs.

He is not a little boy. He's a man.

As if from the cellular memory of a stone-age person, a raw feeling she couldn't fully identify rushed through her. It was as if she had lain injured on the flat rocks at the river near Stornorrfors 6,000 years ago – easy prey for a predator prowling in the night – but he had found her and carried her to safety, given her a chance to heal and survive. She was almost finished when, distracted by the feeling of having travelled thousands of years back in time, she let her left hand glide further down than she had meant to. A small, hard nipple carved a line of fire across her palm, and he moaned. She was jerked back to the present and looked at his feverish face.

Trembling, she pulled herself away from him. She felt like something was flooding through her, and she looked at her hand as if expecting to see a trace of him there. Her sense of discipline reacted with panic: *Stop! He belongs to Linda – and I'm still married! And that's all to the good – even if I am going to start over, I must know better than to even think about him.* How much fun would it be to be girl number 63, anyway, while he secretly, even in the best-case scenario, limited himself to *dreaming* about the good old days of *la dolce vita*? To go from Adam to Peter Stavenius would really be jumping out of the frying pan into the fire.

Shivering, Vera closed the window. She unfolded her other clean sheet and laid it over him, pulling it up to his chin as if that could erase what had just happened. Then she sat back down on the edge of the bed. She sat stiffly, a storm of emotions raging inside her, and an undisciplined tear suddenly fell onto the sheet. She watched the light-blue wet spot spread on the cotton fabric. She had pinioned the dangerously riotous desire that had overcome her, but she couldn't prevent herself from grieving. Why did it have to be the unthinkable Peter Stavenius who had given her so much that was beautiful?

It was all such a pity that things were as they were.

She suddenly realized how hot he had felt under her hands, how high his pulse was, and how short and strained his breathing. A fear grew in her: *he will get better, won't he?*

The rational nurse laboriously dried her tears, pushed aside all the confusing feelings, and made a decision. She had never heard of a young, otherwise healthy man becoming life-threateningly ill from a respiratory infection, not since the Spanish flu epidemic. But *he can say whatever he wants – nobody is going to die of the flu on my shift.* She dialled the health hotline number. The pre-recorded woman's voice answered: 'If you are calling about a life-threatening situation, hang up and call the emergency services.'

He twisted anxiously and whimpered; tears leaked from his eyes. She waited with the phone pressed against her ear, sat up straighter on the bed and carefully wiped the tears from his cheeks, first with the back of her fingers on one side, and then with her palm on the other. His soft hair felt like cat fur against her fingers, fingers that didn't want to stop touching him, fingers that felt as at home as if they had been stroking Ludde. She realized that her way of touching him could only be called caressing. Overwhelmed by a feeling of great tenderness, she whispered, 'There, there, it's okay. Everything will be fine. You'll be fine!'

She swallowed, shyly removed her hand and tried to repress the intimate, ardent desire to comfort him that his tears had awakened in her. She scooted awkwardly further down the bed. The mechanical voice told her that it would soon be her turn, and she realized that she already knew one thing they would say. His fever must not rise any further. A body temperature over 105 could lead to brain damage. She checked his temperature again with the ear thermometer... heard the bleep... the fever had gone down to 103.5. She was filled with relief. The crisis seemed to be over.

Peter opened his eyes, smiled tiredly through his tears, and weakly reached out and held her hand. 'Grandma?'

'No, it's just me.' Vera hung up the phone.

'Vera? I'm glad it's you...' He blinked tiredly and squeezed her hand feebly, 'because Grandma is dead.'

She stroked his scarred thumb with her own thumb. 'Did your father find Shangri-La?'

His voice was weak. 'Shangri-La is a myth. It's a dream about heaven on earth.'

39

I thought her unsinkable and based my opinion on the best expert advice available.

*Philip Franklin, shipping company vice managing director, on the sinking of the Titanic (*New York Times, *16 April 1912)*

Peter hadn't known how right he had been when he had told Vera in the stairway that she could carry him next time. She had called him a rock for the little he had done – *so what did that make her?* She had turned out to be a real friend, and he wasn't a bit surprised. He felt happy, secure and accepted, and he couldn't stop thinking about her.

He ate breakfast with a healthy appetite on his first fever-free morning. Vera came into the kitchen carrying her bowl of crushed, crisp flat-bread and lingonberry jelly. Her hair was tied up in an enchantingly messy knot at her neck that showed her elfin ears. She was wearing a tank top with small shoulder straps and a strip across the chest with some kind of Celtic pattern.

'Good morning! How are you feeling today?' She sat across from him, and a dark strand of hair came loose and directed his attention to her collarbone. *What is there to say? I'm eternally grateful; for thou hath saved me, my beauty?*

'Thanks. I feel fine. And thanks for all the… help. Do you think it was the oil from the jungle that healed me?'

A strange expression passed over her face, and she took a quick mouthful of her Norrland-style breakfast cereal and shrugged her shoulders – a gentle gesture that made her collarbone move in a way that made him lose his train of thought. He noticed the way the thin strap of her top followed the curve of her shoulder, and it occurred to him that she didn't have anything on under it; beneath the cotton was only her. He knew it was inappropriate, but he let his eyes roam downward. He realized with surprise that no décolletage in the world had ever been as enticing to him as this non-existent one. The faint outline of her contours beneath the Celtic pattern made his pulse race. He tore his eyes from her, and was forced to stare down at his breakfast for a moment before he could remember what he had been talking about.

'Yeah, I saw the wooden bottle under the bed, and since I smelled like my grandmother's medicine cabinet, I realized that you...' He stopped when he saw how she was looking at him. She suddenly averted her gaze. The look in her eyes: it was almost as if... she had been caught. She blushed quickly, from her cheeks all the way to the tips of her ears, and he suddenly realized how she must have touched him. He looked at her hands and imagined how they had taken possession of him. A feeling of intoxication spread like lightning through his body, and he felt strangely out of control, like a teenager. He scooted his chair in. *Damn it! Why couldn't I have been awake? Although if I hadn't been sick, then she wouldn't have done it.*

At the same time, something in her involuntary reaction communicated something more. If Vera didn't feel anything for him other than a grandmother's tender concern, then she would hardly have reacted like that when he asked. He realized that he would probably feel uncomfortable if it had been someone else, like Jeanette, who had secretly tended to his unconscious body. But with Vera it was sweetly promising, almost as if he hoped that her blushing meant that she hadn't been completely professional. These fascinating insights gave rise to a wonderful but puzzling fantasy, and later, in moments of solitude, he took pleasure in pondering their meaning.

✖

Something had happened to him. Was it because he had fasted for a week and lost almost five pounds (all of them from the muscles in his upper body, or so it felt)? Was it from falling in and out of fever-induced dreams? Or had it happened because of Vera's hands? He had no idea. He only knew that he now observed everything as if from a great height. He no longer felt mixed up in it, weighed down, ashamed or afraid to see. He just wanted to dig deeper, and he spent his time in the university library, following up the brief notes he had taken in Stockholm. Vera and Cissi also scoured the shelves in the large reading room. The singular library atmosphere of subdued, concentrated activity remained with him when they walked to lunch at the restaurant in Berghem, across the street from the university.

'Just look at how quickly you've healed after the operation! Your knee seems pretty good now,' said Cissi kindly as she looked at Vera.

'Yes, but I had an appointment with the orthopedic specialist on Monday, and he said it's still too stiff. If I can't bend it more than 90 degrees within a month, they'll need to go in again.'

'Another operation?' asked Peter, and Vera nodded.

'But the stiffness thing…' said Cissi. 'Have you tried warm water?'

'Yes, I do rehab in the therapy pool on Wednesdays.'

'So you do stretching? I mean, in warm water?'

'No, not much when I'm in the water. But I do stretching exercises… It's just that it's stuck; it feels impossible to bend it any further.'

'I have an idea!' said Cissi. 'I'm going to take you to the spa; the water in the hot tub is 100 degrees. We're going to get that leg to bend so you don't need another operation!'

Vera smiled, 'Oh, yes please!'

They went into the restaurant and placed their orders. As they sat down Cissi asked: 'How are you, Peter? You were in really bad shape, weren't you?'

Vera looked at him. 'Yes, I was really worried when we couldn't get the fever down for so many days, and you became delirious.'

'I was delirious? Did I say anything?'

'Yeah.'

'What?' asked Peter, his pulse quickening.

'I don't really remember. It wasn't anything I actually… thought about.' Vera avoided his eyes, bent down and fiddled with her bag before continuing. 'I was afraid that you had got some really nasty respiratory infection… When I took Epidemiology, our teacher said that we think we've defeated infectious diseases once and for all. But we waste antibiotics, use tons of them on animals and mild colds, so bacteria adapt and become resistant to them. We take penicillin for granted, but the risk is that it won't work against new strains.'

'So we're being shortsighted about it?' Peter forced himself to concentrate on what she was saying.

'Yes, shortsighted, exactly,' confirmed Vera.

Cissi's number was called, and she went to get her food. Vera looked straight at him, and what she said sounded like a confession: 'You should know that I was about to break my promise; I was calling an ambulance, but the fever broke while I was on hold.'

'I'm grateful for what you did, and I understand. Sometimes you have to break a promise.' He locked eyes with her, his face serious. The moment was interrupted by a voice calling their numbers, and he offered to get their food.

Vera smiled a little as she gave him the ticket with her number on. 'I still think you need to do something about your hospital phobia, try to get over it when you're fully recovered. I can go with you if you want.'

'Well, if you promise…' He smiled and went to get the food.

The restaurant filled up, but the noise was low-key and relaxed.

'So, Peter,' said Cissi when they all had their food, 'tell us about your visit to the wealth factory!' She looked at him expectantly as she sank her teeth into her second chicken skewer.

'Wealth factory?'

'Yes,' said Cissi as she wiped her mouth on a napkin. 'As Sturesson says, "the finance sector – the West's new, impressive growth motor".'

'Well, what can I say?' began Peter. 'When I was at the party I heard a lot of things that seemed hard to believe. That's why I've been checking it out this week.'

'Okay. So what have you got to say about the growth of the

financial sector?' wondered Vera.

'Well, there *is* growth, definitely. The financial sector is gigantic. Turnover is probably at least 12 times bigger than the world's combined production.'

Vera and Cissi looked at him in silence.

Then Vera asked: 'But what *is* it then? I mean, what does the finance sector's turnover actually produce?'

'Exactly! That's the key question!' Peter looked at her eagerly. 'Some of the financial flows do fantastic things. For example, there's this system of micro credits that have lifted millions out of poverty. That shows the financial sector's role in promoting welfare. You give a loan so the borrower can buy materials and make something with them. Then she can sell the product for a profit that covers both the loan with interest plus a reasonable salary for the work. That's the classic idea of a bank, to finance the production of things that there's a demand for, or to finance increased productivity, which also guarantees that the borrower can repay the loan.'

'Okay... but how can the financing of productivity be 12 times bigger than the production itself?' asked Cissi. Peter drew a deep breath, but he was no longer afraid to see, or to explain.

'Because most financial activity is not small-scale and close to production. Most people in finance, and all of the best-paid people, engage in activities that have nothing to do with providing for people. It's just money. It's like a giant casino. Take my cousin Charlie: he earned five million pounds last year...'

'Almost 70 million kronor in a year?' asked Cissi skeptically.

'Yes. He's apparently better than anyone else at selling some kind of insurance on what you might call a grab-bag bundle of American mortgages. I think it's completely unsustainable!'

'What does that mean? Unsustainable insurance? I don't get it,' replied Vera.

'His company is the largest insurance company in the world, and it has a triple-A rating, which is the highest credit rating you can get. But his department in London has started developing "financial products" that use the triple-A as an assurance of quality for these grab-bag bundles. Which means that they've attracted investors who never should have bought them, like pension funds, local governments...'

'What are you talking about – grab-bag bundles? It sounds like "selling a pig in a poke" to me!' Cissi frowned. 'What do the regulatory agencies say?'

'The agency or agencies that should be reacting just turn a blind eye to the fact that the whole thing is a house of cards built on the ridiculous assumption that American housing prices will never fall,' said Peter. 'And we're talking about a country that imports a lot more than it exports, that borrows to finance consumption.'

'That doesn't sound good,' sighed Cissi, putting down her knife and fork.

'No, it's seriously not good. And it gets worse. Near the end of our conversation, Charlie said something strange. "I sell them naked". First I thought he meant "I sell the pants off them" – you know, that he's the world's best financial securities salesman. And maybe he is. But then I discovered that there actually is something called "naked CDS". That means that he's sold more CDSs than there are CDOs.'

'What?' said Cissi.

'There are more bets that the grab-bag bundles are worthless than there are grab-bag bundles.'

What Peter had found out about his cousin gave him a bad feeling, and he went on: 'Charlie sat there bragging that he created growth by selling insurance that promises his firm will repay the value that disappears when American housing prices fall. So it isn't enough that he has led people to believe that it's risk-free to gamble on the US housing market at a rate of return of 12 per cent. He's even selling insurance to players who don't own any mortgages!'

'But why would they want it?' wondered Cissi.

The answer suddenly popped into Vera's head: 'They're going to earn money when the collapse comes.'

'Exactly!' said Peter, his heart beating wildly. 'They're speculating that the market is going to fall. Not exactly a long-shot.'

'But can you get an insurance pay-out on something that you don't even own?' asked Cissi, looking alarmed.

'In the world of derivatives you can. You can make any bet you want in a private contract. No limits. The derivatives market isn't regulated. A woman at the Commodity Futures Trading Commission in Washington pushed for better oversight in the 1990s, but they stopped it.'

'Too many powerful interests earning too much money on the status quo?' asked Vera.

'Exactly. And, of course, Charlie argues that he's "just responding to demand" and selling as fast as he can!' Peter heard the outrage in his voice and drew a deep breath before continuing. He looked at Vera: 'I mean, this kind of shortsightedness is fantastic for the contracting parties. It's a win-win for Charlie, who gets a commission for selling; for his firm, which increases sales; and for the customer, who buys a little insurance now and can cash in big when the housing market crashes. But it isn't Charlie's firm that will have to pay. They won't be able to. No way! So it will probably be the taxpayers who will end up bailing out these companies – and that means less education, healthcare, infrastructure. Maybe higher taxes too, because it is going to require giant sums of money!'

They sat in silence, overwhelmed by the gravity of it all. And Peter didn't have anything encouraging to report from the rest of his conversation with Charlie, either. He looked at Vera again.

'Do you know what Charlie said about the LTCM bailout? He said that, in secret, the hedge fund hadn't loaned out 30 times more than its capital, but 125 times more.'

Vera looked at him in dismay, thought for a moment, and then said, 'So Wall Street saved Long Term because they felt like they had to. They broke all the rules and saved the fund, because they had too much to lose themselves?'

Being so fully understood gave Peter a warm feeling; he nodded.

Cissi looked confused. 'Wait a minute... broke what rules?'

'Rule number one of the market economy. If you take risks, then you can either win or lose,' said Vera. 'But the banks were taken hostage by their own greedy loans.'

'Exactly,' said Peter, looking at Cissi seriously. 'Long Term Capital Management rigged the game so that, if they guessed correctly, they could rake in giant profits, but if they guessed wrong then others would have to step in and take the loss. So, of course, they were more than happy to take any level of risk.'

'And that's the key to getting away with it, right? Risk gigantic sums of money?' Vera asked Peter. 'Which is what your cousin is doing now?'

'Yes, that's right. There is even a term for it – "Too big to fail". The goal is to be too big to fail. The rules of the market economy have been set aside by smart types who have rigged the system, and they're the ones who attract the big sums of capital.'

'Moral hazard!' said Cissi. Her light skin was paler than usual and she slowly leaned back in her chair.

'Yeah,' said Peter, feeling almost sympathetic. 'On a scale beyond… it's almost impossible to grasp. We should all be in a panic. Because there is more and more money in the form of abstract numbers on computer screens, but they're really only expectations that loans will be repaid with interest. And my gut feeling is that the expectations are increasingly groundless, because money growth isn't linked to increases in productivity. But Sturesson believes – well… everybody believes – that it creates wealth, because the turnover provided by borrowed money is included in countries' GDPs. But it isn't future wealth. It is more realistic to call it the opposite of future wealth.'

Cissi stared contemplatively out of the window, as if trying to make sense of the spring sunshine. 'My cousin Fredrik has started to talk about Gandhi, about means and ends.'

'Freddie?' Vera made a gesture indicating wild hair and Cissi smiled a bit and nodded.

'Yes,' Cissi said. 'I just thought of it. Money is a means, while the end, the purpose, is to live well, which requires a good environment and quality goods and services.'

Vera felt a surge of energy and turned to Peter. 'Right. That's it. What you're saying is that financial markets are messing around with means that are completely unconnected to goals! Because money is not the same as purchasing power, is it?'

Peter felt so understood that he couldn't keep from smiling, despite the gloominess of the conversation. 'More money without higher productivity leads to bubbles that burst, or inflation – with prices rising in step with increases in the money supply.'

Cissi groped for her notebook in her bag. 'And besides... How much of current production is sustainable? If oil production peaks about now, and wealth is built on work... Do you know that a gallon of oil is equal to...' Cissi read from her notes, '... 520 hours of manual labor?'

'Yes, but it isn't as if we're suddenly going to run out of oil, is it?' wondered Vera.

'No, but it's a declining curve. According to the oil industry's own calculations we'll have the same oil production in 2050 as we had in 1980. But there'll be twice as many people on the planet and a lot more countries will be industrialized.'

'Oil production,' mumbled Vera, 'I've said it before: how can we even call it "production"...?'

Peter looked at her, '... when it's millions of years of stored energy from the sun that we are consuming?'

Vera smiled in agreement. Cissi worriedly studied her notes.

'You know...' Vera stood up. 'We really need to think. And the forest is a good place for that. I want to go up to Stadsliden, anyway.' Vera nodded in the direction of the wooded ridge a short distance away.

They walked through the residential neighborhood to get to the dark green wooded area that Vera was drawn to and then passed in among the tall conifers. Vera pulled a piece of paper out of her jeans pocket and unfolded it. 'I worked for Basic Needs all of last year, and now I've been thinking about satisfying needs – I mean, satisfying the needs of the world. That guy, the so-called barefoot economist you showed me...' She turned to Cissi.

'You mean Max-Neef?' asked Cissi.

'Yes. He says we should measure development, not GDP

growth. He means development as in society's ability to meet humanity's basic needs. Because poverty is not having your needs met.' Eagerly she stepped between Peter and Cissi and showed them the piece of paper: 'Here are the needs he listed.' She began reading aloud.

'Subsistence – physical and mental health; food, shelter, clean water, air we can breathe.

'Protection – security, care, healthcare.

'Affection – respect, friendship, love.

'Understanding – critical capacity, curiosity, education.

'Identity – sense of belonging, self-esteem...'

Peter watched her rounded lips continue to read the words on the list, but he didn't hear them, because his feelings overwhelmed him. This was what he wanted more than anything else. His stomach fluttered as if filled with newly hatched butterflies.

'A total of nine needs,' he heard her say, 'that all people share. So, if you have all nine then you're rich. If you don't, then you're poor. Money can definitely help – if you're close to starving, then a dollar a day can be the difference between life and death. But you can also be a dollar millionaire and be unhappy.' She folded up the piece of paper and continued along the path, going deeper into the forest.

'Michael Jackson,' said Cissi thoughtfully. 'He has everything that lots of people strive for: global mega-success, King of Pop, world's best-selling album of all time, tons of money, fame. He built his own amusement park, just because he felt like it. But would you want to be him?' She directed the question to Peter.

'No.'

'Why not?'

Peter shrugged his shoulders: 'I don't think he's happy.' He looked up at the blue spring sky between the trees.

'I don't think so either,' said Cissi.

'Right! The basic human needs we all share can be seen as a fixed point,' Vera said, sounding enthusiastic. 'Max-Neef says that everything we do can be evaluated against that fixed point as either a pseudo satisfier, singular satisfier or synergistic satisfier!'

'What? You've lost me!' admitted Peter

Vera looked at him eagerly. 'Pseudo satisfiers; for example, landmines. They're supposed to fulfil the need for security, but they remain in the ground and harm and kill for years after a war.'

'Pseudo?' wondered Peter. *As in pseudonym? As in not wanting to reveal your true identity?* 'Do you mean… uh… like pretending?'

'Yes, pseudo is Greek,' said Cissi. 'It means false. And I've also read that… breastfeeding is synergistic, because it fulfils several needs at once – nutrition, strengthening the immune system, attachment, contact.'

Peter was still thinking about falseness. 'Okay, so pseudo – that's when you think you're doing something that fulfils a need, but it really doesn't. Is that it?'

Vera looked straight at him. 'Right. It actually prevents it; it's a barrier to meeting the need.'

Peter suddenly felt like he had been punched in the stomach. How much of his former life had been *pseudo*? Like *The Game*? Sure, a momentary ego-boost. He had mastered the skill of attracting sexual partners without raising a sweat, and he had been good – over 50 women in just a few years. Yet it had brought him neither security, nor self-esteem nor love. The insight was too shameful to admit. Instead, he looked at them and offered his next thought.

'I get it. I realize now that we can't provide for ourselves over the long term by relying on…' *Charlie's 'product development'* he thought, but continued, '…increased financial turnover. So my point is precisely that it is only pseudo-growth.'

'Pseudo-growth,' said Cissi thoughtfully. 'As opposed to real.'

Peter's next insight was also too personal for him to want to say it out loud. *Offering 18,000-dollar trips to pseudo-heroes to shoot grizzlies increases GDP, but it's only a pseudo-success. A short-term kick for Wall Street predators, at the expense of the planet and the bear population.*

'Think about the investments for the future that could have been made with those resources!' he said out loud.

Vera stopped next to a pine tree that had snapped in two. Like a slain warrior, the powerful trunk lay on the ground in the snow beside the dangerously jagged stump. She ran her hand thoughtfully along the trunk, from where the wood just under the bark was healthy, to the place where it was reddish brown and full of holes. The center of the tree was rotten and dead, and the thin layer of living wood that was left had been insufficient to withstand the wind.

'Look at it – it was a spaller. It was rotten inside and that eventually brought it down. As my grandfather Ivar says, "It's not before the big storm that you see which tree has deadwood, but after…"' Vera turned to Peter. 'Let's stop at the DVD store on the way home. I want to see *Titanic* again!'

They were back on the sofa in Stipend Street. Vera handed the *Titanic* DVD to Cissi, who said: 'I love this film. I think I've seen it 12 times.'

'You know what? I came home one night and the guys were sitting here studying a "good man".' Vera smiled at Cissi and pointed at di Caprio's character on the DVD cover.

'A good man?'

'Yep. A man you stay with because he makes you feel good. They wanted to know what kind of man that is. It was Matt's question, wasn't it?' Vera asked, looking at Peter. His heart pounded in protest, but he nodded in silence.

Cissi smiled. 'They're good guys in this dorm.'

'Yeah, Matt is good,' said Vera simply. 'Anyone with that ambition is honorable.'

Peter bit his lip, because now it was even more impossible to speak up. Why couldn't he own up to his most important aspiration? *Fucking pseudonym*

Vera put the film in the DVD player and said, 'Do you realize that there's a similarity between what you said, Peter, and the Titanic?'

'What do you mean?' wondered Cissi. 'The insane hubris?'

'Yes, exactly! When they built the Titanic, the world's biggest ship, they thought that size was the same as stability. They even called her unsinkable! How ironic is that? And why did it sink?

It wasn't bad luck; it was just what you said, Cissi; they put arrogance and ambition above responsibility.'

Vera hopped around the menu and then fast-forwarded through the scenes. Suddenly they were at the bow of the ship in the sunset and Jack was holding Rose so she felt supported, yet free as a bird. He would caress her wingtips, and she would soon turn and kiss him. Peter sensed that he was blushing. *Is this what you wanted us to see?* He heard Matt's voice inside his head: *'God, this is romantic!'* But Vera had made a mistake.

'No, perhaps it's the next scene...?'

It was a scene in the present. The treasure hunters were telling the now elderly Rose that the Titanic's size had been a significant part of the problem. The ship couldn't turn the way the experienced, skilled captain was used to. With the other, smaller ships he had been navigating for years, an iceberg big enough to sink them would have been visible in plenty of time to turn out of the path of danger. But...

'Everything he knows is wrong,' explained the man on the TV.

Peter flew up off the sofa. He pushed the pause button and felt a strange energy pulse through him, because he suddenly remembered the most common way of making a decision, based on the power of habit and routine.

We've had extreme growth in real standards of living driven by a limited reserve of cheap fossil fuels! He remembered Uncle Ernst's definition of idiocy. Another form of idiocy ought to be repeating the same behavior on an ever-increasing scale – and expecting the same outcome despite changed conditions. *Fundamentally changed.*

Peter said, 'We're using an old decision-making procedure, because it's always worked before!'

'What are you talking about?' asked Cissi.

'What is money, really?' He turned eagerly to Cissi.

'It's a promise of an exchange of value,' she said. 'Money rests entirely on trust.'

Peter looked at Vera. 'Yes, and trust always takes time to build up, but it can be destroyed in an instant.' He felt shivers down his spine when he saw something nakedly questioning in her face, before she blushed and looked down.

Peter went on. 'And growth... in the financial sector is based on a belief that we can borrow today, and repay later with interest. It is based on a belief that we will be able to produce even more goods and services in the future; that the real, material economy will grow, which it has done relentlessly for 200 years. But...' Peter pointed at the frozen picture on the TV screen. 'Everything we know is wrong. Because when the energy supply declines and the environment is under pressure, then it will stop growing.'

'So the quest for money now risks undermining our ability to really provide for ourselves?' wondered Vera.

'And nature's ability to maintain real prosperity,' added Cissi.

'Yes!' said Peter. He continued, fumbling for his words. 'Remind me, what was it Sturesson said about Economics' most important responsibility being – to prevent... miss...?'

'Misallocation? Failing to properly prioritize resource use?' wondered Cissi.

'Yes, exactly! Now our priorities are definitely wrong. Just think about all the wise investments that aren't being made because people are making short-term profits on things which are unsustainable. Talk about opportunity costs!'

Vera looked at him. 'If we continue like this, humanity will wind up with numbers on computer screens instead of what we need – food, clean water, warmth, protection from the elements, transportation...'

'Transportation?' wondered Peter, thinking about Great Escape.

'Yes. For example, say you're having a baby and complications arise. Believe it or not,' teased Vera, 'being able to get to a hospital is a matter of life or death!'

'Or if you had wanted to flee from Easter Island with your family some time in the 1600s,' said Cissi, looking at him meaningfully.

His curiosity was piqued. He *would* borrow that book from Cissi.

'If so, our trust in money will be undermined because we'll get increasingly less for it,' said Cissi, 'and that *in itself* risks creating poverty. Trust is an important social capital that enables economies to function. Why should I give the fruits of my labor to you, if I don't think I will be compensated with something that has a stable value?'

'But whose money will become worthless?' wondered Vera.

'I heard from a trader that sometimes… *blip*, just like that, rows of numbers on a computer screen can disappear. That's what happened with Russian government securities in 1997,' said Peter.

'But the value of everybody's money is undermined too. There can be hyperinflation, where you have piles of money, but no purchasing power,' Cissi seemed to shiver, 'like Germany in the 1930s, fertile soil for the rise of Hitler and the Second World War.'

Cissi searched in her bag and pulled out a white book with a small, black swan on the cover. 'Taleb is a philosopher who worked as a trader on Wall Street. In this book he writes about how financial formulas can't handle the unusual and unexpected, like the occasional black swan.'

'But that's not what we're talking about now,' objected Vera. 'Because if money grows and there isn't enough growth in real wealth, there will be a crash that should be *expected*. The crash isn't an occasional black swan, it's built into the growing gap between people's increasing expectations and the planet's decreasing ability to meet them. Let me show you what I think he means.'

Expectation tingled like champagne bubbles in Peter's body.

Vera put a piece of paper on the coffee table in front of them and drew an upward curve. She looked at Peter. 'Financial assets. Money, in other words. Okay?'

Peter felt her concentrated energy flowing through him like water in an underground spring.

'And here…' she turned towards Cissi, 'a downward curve, because there is less and less left – finite resources. After peak everything the speed of exploitation declines because there is less and less left, in more and more unreachable places. Look at the gap!' Vera pointed to where the curves started to move apart.

'So time passes…' Vera moved her hand to the right, let her

thumb and fingers separate to illustrate the growing gap between the curves. Then she suddenly stood up. 'I think we've figured out how it's all connected! And look here...' Eager and flushed, Vera reached towards the old DVD player's fast-forward button.

'Wait,' said Cissi. 'Shouldn't the curves be like this in the beginning?' To the left of Vera's lines, she illustrated how, at first, natural resources were high and the amount of money low, and she let the lines cross and continue in to Vera's. Cissi pointed to where the curves started. 'Because even if *Collapse* shows that humanity has repeatedly overused resources and driven ecosystems to collapse, it used to be at a local level. On a global level resources have been quite abundant and money scarce.'

Vera looked appreciatively at Cissi. 'Yes! Good, Cissi! Peter, did you mean something like this?' She looked at him as she pushed a strand of hair behind one of her little pointed ears. Peter nodded mutely.

'And look here.' Vera fast-forwarded the film and then pushed play again. 'That's Andrews, the architect of the Titanic – the guy who knew exactly how the ship was constructed.'

Andrews pointed at the drawings in front of the distrustful decision makers on the captain's bridge. He showed how a tear in the hull like the one the iceberg had made would permit water to flood in and fill five watertight bulkheads. That would cause the ship to lean, and the water would continue to flow over the bulkheads, thus pulling the ship down into the depths bow first. He said that the Titanic was built to withstand water in four bulkheads, but not five.

'But this ship can't sink!' snorted an agitated man with a mustache.

'That's Bruce Ismay, the ship company's managing director,' said Vera. He's the one who convinced the captain to operate at maximum speed so that they would arrive ahead of schedule and get impressive headlines in New York's morning papers.'

'She is made of iron, sir. I assure you, she can. And she will, with mathematical certainty,' replied the architect.

The white-bearded captain stared at him, his skin glistening with sweat. 'How much time?'

'An hour, two at the most.'

The captain turned to a subordinate: 'How many aboard, Mr Murdoch?'

'2,200 souls aboard, sir.'

White-beard turned back to his mustached boss. 'I believe you may get your headlines, Mr Ismay.'

Vera turned it off and looked at Peter. He felt drunk on the flood of energy, and he was sure that she must feel it too. He caught a glimpse of a smile before he turned to Cissi. 'With mathematical certainty. That's what we're saying. Not unlikely coincidence.'

The silence suddenly became oppressive, and it was Peter who finally broke it.

'How should we... convey this?'

Cissi and Vera looked at each other for a moment, before Vera finally spoke. 'The problem with the Titanic was that they built something huge based on assumptions that proved to be false. We've built a giant global economy, and the key question is: are the basic assumptions of that economy in agreement with our physical reality?'

Peter realized exactly what she was asking. 'I feel like those freezing guys up on the mast, the ones who first saw the iceberg.'

✖

Peter felt like his thoughts had been dancing with Vera's. What a *kick*! Like a good match. No, that wasn't strong enough. The flow of contact was better than sex. Months of gnawing frustration over a puzzle that he couldn't solve were over. Because now... they had completed it a different way. Complications unravelled, mystery solved. He thought about what Vera had said when they were in the forest. He didn't remember all of Ivar's words, but he remembered the message. Things might look good on the surface, but it's not until they are subjected to pressure that you find out how stable they really are. Fortunately, most of the trees had survived the storm, but not the one that was rotten on the inside, because it was weak. *Not the one that was a spaller.*

Elated, he continued thinking and another important idea occurred to him. He went to Vera's room. She was there, sitting at her desk.

'Thanks for today... We have a lot to work with when we think together,' he said with daring frankness.

'Yes, I feel like that too,' said Vera, meeting his eyes.

Distracted by how his heart was beating, he almost forgot what he had come over for.

After a brief silence, he pointed towards his room and said: 'I just thought of something. This stuff is hard to deal with; we're coming to some pretty unpleasant conclusions. And it isn't just small stuff. It's vital. What can we do to slow down in time, before we run into the iceberg at full speed?'

'What can we do to make sure we have smaller, less luxurious lifeboats in time?' asked Vera with a smile. 'Do you mean that we should focus our strengths on our opponent's weaknesses?'

Peter thought about the awful fragments he remembered from the last fever-induced nightmare. 'This time the opponent is ourselves, our own way of life...'

'*Koyaanisqatsi.*'

'Yes, exactly, it's a whole way of life that has to change. I mean, we know the facts. The question is: how do we present them?'

She sat in silence, and he continued. 'Think about driving a car. When you first learn to drive, it's really stressful when a truck thunders down the other side of the road towards you. But then you realize that the trick is never to stare at the 18-wheeler that you're passing, but rather at the open road ahead, where you're *going.*'

Vera nodded in recognition. Peter wandered restlessly around the room. 'It's not good news, so the risk is that everybody will just stick their heads back in the sand. And then things will explode. We're going to talk about the problems, but I think the chapter should focus on solutions. What can we do instead?'

'We need to propose completely new rules of the game,' said Vera.

'Yes, we actually need a new economic world order,' said Peter. 'Let's rewrite the end of the chapter. And Sturesson wants a meeting next week; we should go together. We have to check with Cissi, but I wanted to ask you first. I thought about what you said in the forest, what Ivar said about... deadwood...'

'Mmm.' A hint of dimple flashed across her face.

He moved closer to her and said, 'I think the chapter should be called "Structural Integrity".'

He saw her think about the words for a split second. Then she spontaneously stood up, smiled so that her green eyes narrowed into happy slits, and said: 'Peter! You understand exactly! I'm so glad!' She threw her arms around him and Peter returned her hug carefully for about two seconds, until she shyly stepped back.

The situation was much more serious than he had ever imagined, but he felt strongly that he was in the right place, at the right time, and that he was doing exactly the right thing. He continued to feel euphoric for almost an hour. After that, whenever he felt like it, all he had to do was return to the memory of their singular communication, and he was filled with a sense of well-being so exquisite that it was like nothing he had ever experienced before.

40

It was early afternoon, and the spa was peaceful. It was quiet except for the lapping of the water against the sides of the pool and the soft music. A couple of visitors in bathrobes lay dozing on lounge chairs. The serene atmosphere was suddenly disrupted by three young men. They entered the pool area from the brick-colored main building, and jumped into the turquoise water, laughing and speaking in lively Italian.

After Vera had done the whole set of physio exercises for her knee – she knew them by heart by this point – Cissi directed her towards the far corner of the room. 'This is why we're here – this hot tub, 100 degrees,' said Cissi as they slowly immersed themselves in the steaming water. It was so hot that Vera shivered, but she quickly got used to it and sank all the way down until only her head was sticking above the water.

'Do this,' said Cissi. She stood with one leg forward, knee bent, the other stretched out behind her. 'Stretch your hip flexors – that relaxes the muscle knots in your backside.'

Vera stood up, already feeling that the warm water made it easier to stretch her stiff muscles. 'If I shift my weight like this, I can also bend my knee further.' She leaned forward, stretching her right hip muscles and forcing her knee to bend as much as possible. *Ouch!* She still couldn't push her knee into a 90-degree angle, let alone go beyond it.

'Work through the pain and come out on the other side,' said Cissi, sinking down into the comfortable seat carved into the hot tub wall. She shifted her gaze from the grounds and the spring snow visible through the panoramic glass wall to the Italians in the pool.

'Vera,' she whispered after a few moments, 'the small, long-haired one is watching you.' She smiled mischievously and studied Vera. 'Yes, the bronze colors of this mosaic

365

tiling definitely flatter you, and that red bathing suit is a little *Baywatch*.'

Vera snorted. 'Yeah, right, the bathing suit, perhaps!' She took a deep breath and shifted her weight a bit, forcing her left leg to bend a little more. The pressure in her knee was almost unbearable; it felt like her kneecap was a stone crushing down on something tender and ulcerous. Vera felt a flutter of fear in her stomach. *Am I ever going to be able to bend this leg again?*

'But wasn't there at least *one* of those *Baywatch* girls who hadn't had a boob job?' said Cissi.

'Hmm, on the subject of operations, I really don't know what to do. I mean, I didn't get my knee fixed until I threatened to report the specialist to the Medical Board. He said that threats weren't going to get me an operation – even though that's what happened – but I told him I was going to report it anyway. I mean, I can hardly be the only person who had to wait an unreasonably long time… So if not for myself, I should report it to help other people.'

Cissi looked towards the big, turquoise pool again, and Vera followed her gaze. The Italians were climbing out. The two older ones continued up the stairs, but the one with dark, shoulder-length curls came over and climbed into the hot tub. He settled down in the empty corner as Cissi threw Vera a meaningful look.

Vera needed a break from the torturous stretching of her left leg, so she carefully switched legs and started working on the other hip flexor.

'But now it's fixed, and the specialist did a really good job… Should I report him anyway? It feels wrong… but also wrong not to.'

Vera felt the pain in her left leg slowly recede now that she had straightened it out.

'Ugh, the moral dilemmas that arise in the draughtier corners of the welfare state,' sighed Cissi. She noticed how the bushes outside were starting to re-emerge as the snow melted and left small craters around their trunks. 'When I was in Switzerland taking a graduate course, I met a student from Russia. He said that in Russia they say "feel like a Swede" when they mean that things are going well.'

'You mean that "Life is a bowl of cherries" is "feeling like a Swede"?' asked Vera.

'Exactly. That Russian was a right cynic; he had no respect for economists.'

'But wasn't he an economist?'

'Yes, he had a scholarship and travelled between the US and England; but it seemed like he only did it for the money, like a mercenary. The only Russians he respected were writers. He said that communism and the capitalism Russia has today are more similar than different – the same ruthless exploitation and luxury imports for a filthy rich elite. The elite *this time* are the people who managed to get their hands on Russia's natural resources.'

'The oligarchs?'

'Exactly. The country has been "liberated from communism", but the media is still tightly controlled, and there is no real free market. The economy is still controlled by a few giant companies.'

'So if they make a mistake, it has large-scale consequences?'

'Yes. That guy, I told you about, Black Swan Taleb, he said in his lecture that the West has the same problem with its big companies and banks. The ones that are shaky should be allowed to fall apart when they're small, before a collapse can cause too much damage. Taleb started out as a trader, and I think he was talking about the financial market in particular.'

'Right. Like the Titanic. We convince ourselves that it's unsinkable. But everything human is fragile,' said Vera as she massaged her aching knee. She changed sides again – could she bend her knee *a tiny bit more this time*? She straightened her back, shifted her weight to her left leg and braced herself – *how much pain could she take?* From the corner of her eye she saw Mr Dark Curls looking at her... arms?

What I'm doing must look really strange. She smothered an impulse to tell him about her knee injury.

Vera turned back to Cissi. 'By the way, has Peter told you what he thinks we should call our chapter?'

'No, what?'

'Structural Integrity.'

'Oh, that's great!' exclaimed Cissi.

'I know. And then I googled it and found a definition. Structural integrity is the margin between safety and catastrophe. There's a connection to Economics – getting good return on investment. If you build a bridge then it has to be completely safe – supporting capacity, elasticity, all the stuff that bridges need – but also not prohibitively expensive.'

'Structural integrity… He's gifted, that guy,' smiled Cissi.

'Yeah.' *I know.* Vera's heart started beating faster. *A beautiful mind, too.* She looked out past the slender stems of the bushes to the sculptures that decorated the grounds.

A determined splashing indicated that the Italian had suddenly got up. Cissi looked at him, slid towards Vera and whispered through clenched teeth, jerking her head almost imperceptibly towards him, 'Aye aye, someone's standing to attention!'

Vera glanced with embarrassment in the direction of the Italian and caught a glimpse of his problem, which he was unsuccessfully trying to hide by wrapping a towel around his wide, black bathing trunks.

Cissi watched him walk away and then turned to Vera, curiosity in her voice. 'How are things between you and Adam?'

No, she didn't want to think about that. The last time he had called was after some kind of soul-searching therapy session, and the therapist had told him to practise being completely open and honest with his wife. He had told her that what she had seen, well, it wasn't the first time. She hadn't known how to react; she had felt numb, mute. But she had also realized that it wasn't a surprise. 'It's like an addiction,' he had said, with despair in his voice. 'But it also proves,' he had pleaded, 'that it doesn't have anything to do with real feelings; it's only sex.'

When is sex ever 'only' anything?

She looked at Cissi shyly. 'He's in "integrating therapy". He's "coming to terms with women's roles".' *God, how shaky her voice was!*

'Ah, he's using the classic Madonna-Whore excuse!' snorted

Cissi. 'Let me guess – you're the Madonna?'

'Mmm.'

'And somebody else is playing the whore in this drama?'

The conversation was more painful than the aching in her knee. Vera nodded and looked down at the water.

'Sorry... guessing again – passion nowhere to be seen?'

Vera blushed hotly, involuntarily answering Cissi's question.

Cissi looked at her sympathetically. 'Don't settle just because you want to feel safe. You'll only wind up creating a prison for yourself.'

Vera remained silent and Cissi studied her knowingly. 'The Russian taking the course in Zurich, he didn't just talk about Economics. In the evening he... brought up other things.' She arched an eyebrow and the corners of her mouth turned slightly upwards.

'Sorry?'

Cissi rolled her eyes roguishly and, speaking with a Russian accent, she said: '"You wonderful redhead, you look like my ideal woman. You know the many health benefits of orgasms?"' Cissi dropped the accent. 'And then he started listing them...' She laughed at the memory.

'Wow. That was direct!'

'Yes. File it under "Bizarre pick-up lines".'

'Did it work?'

'Yeah, well, good sex is healthy, everybody knows that, right? At least, everybody who had had the enthusiastic Sivan for biology. You know, she was really ambitious... we were in the ninth grade and she went through the Hite report, the Myth of Vaginal Orgasm and stuff. I don't think the boys ever paid more attention to a biology teacher!' said Cissi, grinning.

Myth? thought Vera as Cissi continued breezily.

'So anyway, I added one to his list, so it would be more complete – that the female orgasm is the best training you can have to prepare for giving birth. You, of all people, know that. It's important to be strong, so that the baby can get out, so you don't get a terrible situation like the one you described, with a little coffin or a baby buried with its mother...' Cissi made a distressed face.

The uterus is composed of smooth muscle that cannot be consciously controlled, remembered Vera.

'But I think that young Mr Popov interpreted it to mean… that I was up for it. He got really pushy, so I was finally forced to say, "No, listen, I'm going home to strengthen my immune system with my Jocke".' Cissi looked down at the mosaic floor of the hot tub – speckled brown, bronze and off-white – and seemed to lose herself in a memory, a hint of a smile playing on her lips.

'Joakim? I haven't met him, have I?' asked Vera. Cissi's expression became serious and sad.

'What is it?' asked Vera.

'It didn't last.'

'I can tell that it must have been something special.'

'Yeah, it was really promising, and I was pretty sure that…' Cissi's voice broke.

'What happened?' wondered Vera.

Cissi's eyes filled with tears. Vera looked at her sadly, recognizing her friend's misfortune all too well. Cissi looked out towards the grounds, tears running down her cheeks.

'Oh, Cissi, I understand,' whispered Vera.

Cissi shook her head violently and dried her face with the back of her hand, but the tears just continued. Vera got the message: *You don't understand!* Vera looked at her, her own sorrow an aching undertone.

'I understand that something happened, that something you couldn't accept destroyed what was special and good.' Cissi looked at her in surprise and nodded. A copy of *Cosmopolitan* was lying in front of Cissi on the edge of the hot tub, left behind by a previous bather. She pointed at one of the headlines on the glossy cover. *Love your body!* 'It took just two sentences each,' she said in a whisper.

'What?' Vera wasn't sure she had heard properly.

'Jocke used to really… value these,' said Cissi looking down at her breasts, just visible at water level. 'But once, when we were having sex, when we had been together for 13 happy

370

months – and I had started to think that he was The One – he suddenly said, "Pity…"' Her voice broke and she was forced to start again. '"Pity they bulge out at the sides when you're lying down." And then he put his hand on my stomach and said, "time to lay off the sweets, perhaps."'

'Ouch!' said Vera grimacing.

'Yeah, I tried to be cool about it, but I lost… everything.' Despite the fact that tears were still running down her face, Cissi bravely tried to smile. 'It still makes me cry. It was almost two years ago, but I can still feel like I'm all wrong when I see somebody as thin as you. Anyway, we were lying there and I was thinking that he had ruined everything, but I was trying to pretend nothing was wrong. So I forced myself to relax and said, "Are you in yet? Well, move it, then!"' Cissi collected herself with a shaky breath, dried her face and said, 'Let me give you some good advice. Whatever you do, never say that, and I mean *never*, especially if you really like the guy. And, you know, it wasn't even true. We fitted together like pieces of a puzzle; I was just really upset.'

The rippling water and a breeze of bossa nova rhythms filled the silence. Vera didn't know what to say, but after a moment she thought about a scene from James Cameron's film. 'What was it that Rose said to the ship-company boss who was completely fixated on the idea that the Titanic should be so big?'

'"Dr Freud has some interesting things to say about the male preoccupation with size,"' said Cissi, smiling crookedly. 'No, guys don't seem to realize that we have muscles down there, which we are happy to use to help ourselves, so to speak.'

Okay… Vera's prudish upbringing involuntarily asserted itself, as if trying to protect her tender ears. *Too much information!*

'Of course, people are obviously different in that department, too,' continued Cissi matter-of-factly. 'But the one time I *did* have a problem with size, it was because it was too big for me.'

Vera was now red as a beetroot, but couldn't refrain from asking: 'That's when it, mostly… stings, right?' *And can hurt for days afterwards?*

Cissi looked at her in concern, as if she wanted to ask

371

something, or say something important. She hesitated and seemed to change her mind. 'No, more like it... you know... hits the cervix too hard.'

Cervix. The word stuck in Vera's head, just like Cissi's recent reference to fatally difficult births, as if they were part of an entirely different discussion. She suddenly realized the irony. She had spent almost a year at a maternity unit, which ought to make her something of an expert about women's reproductive systems as the site where life begins. Yet she was remarkably ignorant about that site in her own body... as a place for things that... occurred before life began.

'But if that had been a problem with Jocke, we would have been able to figure out a solution,' said Cissi thoughtfully, almost to herself.

'So what happened after that?'

'We tried for a while, but it was dead. We had been like Superman; we had been able to fly, but after that it was like there was kryptonite everywhere.'

You lose all your strength and just want to throw up in the first trashcan you can find? wondered Vera.

'He became jealous, and I became jealous. We gave each other complexes and that killed the attraction. Everything human is breakable – you can say that again!' Cissi smiled sadly and looked up at the ceiling. The sound of a song by Sting was drifting softly through the room.

'He never understood that the problem was what he had said? Didn't you tell him what really happened?' Vera felt strangely upset.

'*How fragile we are,*' quoted Cissi sadly, as if to herself. She snorted and seemed to be trying to protect herself by adopting an air of distance: 'That's what can happen if you're fat and furious!'

'No, seriously, Cissi, you might have got furious but you mustn't say you're...'

'Okay,' Cissi interrupted, 'wrong word. Overweight, chubby, chair-breaker.'

'But anyone could have broken that chair! It was poorly built.

Poor quality. You just happened to sit in the wrong chair!'

Cissi looked sadly down at the water and shook her head. Vera glanced at her friend's figure in the blue bathing suit, and thought that she looked like the ideal 1950s woman, like Marilyn Monroe or Sophia Loren – minus the ridiculously cinched-in, I'll-breathe-later corset.

'There is absolutely nothing wrong with you. You have attractive curves. And you know, every day, tons of people spend lots of money, take risks and accept pain in an effort to look like you. There aren't very many people who have your shape naturally. Think about that Russian – you're his ideal woman. So it's just like the message on the teabag label says, you know...'

'What? "We're spiritual beings having a human experience?"' said Cissi, smiling.

'I was thinking of the one I got: "Be proud of who you are."'

Cissi took a deep breath, as if to clear her head, and looked at Vera. 'Have you considered that what happened with Adam might be a good thing in disguise? Maybe you're supposed to find someone more compatible and finally get to have the sex you deserve?'

Vera blushed – *What?* She didn't know what it was that was different – the calm atmosphere, the hot water, Cissi's own openheartedness? But she said something she had scarcely dared to admit before. 'It wasn't just Adam's fault. I felt a shame... it stopped me... I mean, my childhood God...'

'Ah! "Wretched, wicked human am I!" What crap! Just look at the Catholic Church. They say that birth control and ordinary, honorable sex is a sin, that priests are so holy they have to practise celibacy. Yeah, right. They become repulsive, pedophile monsters instead!' Cissi's blue-grey eyes flashed angrily as she quoted, using an authoritative male tone, "Sex is evil and leads straight to hell. I'll violate small choirboys instead, because raping children surely doesn't count."'

'Ugh! It sounds completely sick!'

'It *is* completely sick. Old men with power and wealth claiming that God is on their side, no matter what horrible stuff they do. And you can bet it isn't just Catholicism. You can find priests, imams, gurus all over the place who preach shame and guilt to others, particularly women, while they secretly engage in the truly shameful. Seriously, Vera – I know you had a Christian upbringing and all that, but do you really think God is an old man sitting on a cloud, sternly looking down at your crotch? If there actually is a God, shouldn't he have better things to do with his time? Or *her* time – because I think that *if* God exists, it's more sensible to believe she's a mother who is more interested in making it snow in the Sierra Nevada!'

Vera recognized herself in Cissi's outburst. 'When I didn't get to ask what I wanted to in Sunday school, I wondered why God gave me a brain that I wasn't supposed to use,' she replied with a smile.

'Exactly,' said Cissi, 'and the same goes for all your equipment. Woody Allen supposedly said something like, "I'm such a great lover because I practise a lot when I'm alone."' Cissi turned over on her stomach, rested her chin on her hands and looked out of the window. 'But I would say to Mr Allen that, when it comes to men, it's basically a matter of *how*. Because some of them seem to have limited themselves to practising speed. Sure, everybody can appreciate a quickie now and then, but it shouldn't be the only thing in their repertoire. So, if all Mr Allen has is speed, then I would tell him that he may as well stick to doing it alone!'

Cissi grinned as if Vera must know what she was talking about, but Vera sat blushing and wondering. She was mute in the face of the obvious and huge difference between them.

'But when it comes to women,' Cissi continued blithely, 'I'm sure that Woody is on to something. Because I promise you, 9 times out of 10, if it works for the girl then it works.'

Vera realized that she must look really puzzled, because Cissi said: 'Well, seriously, men are so damned uncomplicated! I mean, as long as you don't...' Cissi looked self-consciously down at the water.

'As long as you avoid a certain two sentences?' guessed Vera.

'Right, because not even Viagra will help after that.'

I wouldn't call Adam uncomplicated, but maybe he is, compared to me. Vera realized that she didn't know much about men.

'Also,' continued Cissi, 'first, make sure you understand yourself. And then... the world is full of attractive men to have fun with; it doesn't have to be serious all the time. Just make sure you get what you want, and above all – don't fake it! Because then the whole thing is just *about* him and *for* him, a performance.' Cissi clenched her teeth and shook her head, looking down at her hand, which seemed to be trying to wipe something off the surface of the water.

Vera recognized herself in Cissi's words, but she had never faked it. She didn't even know how – *by mimicking Meg Ryan, perhaps?* Anyway, she wasn't sure Adam would have appreciated it.

'Is that what Max-Neef would call pseudo-satisfaction?' said Vera.

Cissi smiled. 'Exactly. And they never learn! How many men go around thinking they're the world's best lover, when in fact their partners are seriously frustrated, imprisoned by their own fake-orgasm trap? Stuck with choosing between a rock and a hard place.'

'What? Who's stuck choosing what?'

'Your choice is either staying where you are, accepting an unsatisfying sex life, or saying: "Sorry, this isn't working for me; I've been dishonest about something that people should be completely honest about".'

A troubled expression crossed Cissi's face and she looked away before continuing. 'I suppose I grew up, realized that things couldn't continue as they were. So I made a decision. I tried to change things a little bit, but he didn't understand why; he thought everything was fine. So I chickened out and did the easy thing. I ended it, took the death and reincarnation route. The next guy I slept with... it was a whole new thing, completely new rules. And from that moment on, it was *a lot* better. And, like I said, it doesn't always have to be really serious.'

Cissi's eyes sparkled slyly. She signalled with her head that Vera should look up towards the stairs. 'They went to the solarium. Go and ask how long they're in town and, you know, maybe get his phone number? He's cute, right? A little *Latin*

Adventure might be just what you need!'

Vera shook her head in alarm: 'I don't think so – and how old do you think he was? 22 tops!'

'So? What difference does that make? Do you want me to do it for you? I'll get the number; you can do whatever you want with it. *Fai attenzione!*'

Cissi stood up and climbed out of the steaming water.

✖

Vera wondered what her life would have been like if she had been in Cissi's ninth-grade biology class. She would certainly have appreciated Sivan's frankness. Suddenly resolute, Vera decided that since she hadn't been lucky enough to have Sivan, she would just have to do it herself.

She went to the city library and managed to ask without blushing for pedagogical descriptions of sex for junior high-school students. The helpful librarian referred her to an issue of a magazine for kids and a lively illustrated book that described the feeling of an orgasm as scratching yourself and then sneezing. Vera read in the magazine that the clitoris has a higher concentration of nerve cells than any other part of the body – 8,000 of them forming a little 'bud of desire' tucked up between the legs. *Who knew!?* thought Vera with a smile.

Hadn't some TV comedian argued that in the 21st century girls needed a word for their bits that was as undramatic as 'willy' was for boys, so that they didn't have to spend the next hundred years talking about 'front bottoms'?

Vera rode home on the bus, smiling at the thought. Even if that comedian never accomplished anything else, he had certainly made a contribution to the lives of generations of Swedish girls.

When she got home, Vera locked herself in her room and got to know her soft folds and nerve centers. *Is it true? Are there more of them than just the obvious one? Doubtful*, she thought, *but maybe it's a matter of practice.* She discovered to her surprise that she could control the muscles that Cissi had mentioned. She began a journey to conquer herself… and almost made it.

41

Chick Crack – noun: any spiritual or psychological subject that appeals to most women but does not interest most men, such as astrology, tarot cards, and personality tests.

Tyler Durden speaking in Neil Strauss's The Game

Sturesson, clad in a grey blazer, looked at them from behind his desk. 'A joint chapter? My dear students, you misunderstand the situation. Please don't take it personally. We have simply realized that three is too many. Publishing costs and so on.'

'No, we do understand,' said Cissi placidly. 'I mean, what other reason could there be? That Vera and I, in different ways, both question the concept of growth?'

Sturesson's lips puckered as if he had tasted something tart. 'Growth is an absolute necessity – how could there be prosperity without it? Wealth and Welfare in the 21st Century is about growth. End of story.'

'But isn't Economics supposed to be about how we use finite resources wisely?' asked Vera.

'Absolutely.'

'So what Cissi is talking about is really important, that we are coming to the end of cheap oil...' continued Vera.

'What?'

'Global oil production. And Peak Everything,' explained Peter.

'Yes, yes, peak oil theory, that's nothing new.' Sturesson seemed to lose interest, and he looked out of the window at the inner courtyard.

'But don't you think that facts about energy supplies and other natural resources ought to be a more central question for

Economics?' wondered Cissi.

'There are specialists who study it.' The Professor sounded uninterested, as if he personally found it boring. 'And in any case, the market regulates it, exactly like it does everything else. If oil becomes more expensive, it stimulates new innovations, new energy sources, shale gas!'

'Talking about innovation,' said Peter. 'You were part of the group that gave the Nobel Prize for Black-Sholes, right?'

'Yes, I was on the committee then,' answered Sturesson proudly.

'Do you agree that the formula looks like physics?'

A broad smile broke out on Sturesson's face. 'Good, Peter! The foundation is actually a physics equation describing heat transfer!'

Peter felt the adrenaline; the Professor wouldn't be quite as pleased when he heard the next question. 'But how do you feel about the Prize now? I mean, their fund crashed only a few months later.'

Sturesson rested his hands on the back of his head, fingers clasped together and elbows pointing outward. He swivelled his chair so that he was once again looking out of the window, one elbow resting on a crammed bookshelf. 'Yes, there you have it... Even the best sometimes get it wrong,' he said, sounding completely unconcerned. He looked distracted for a minute, as if his thoughts were far away, before turning back to Peter.

'We only have room for one chapter. That's final. And I thought we agreed that a chapter on financial growth would fit in well with the other chapters?'

That's the thing, thought Peter. *I think it would fit a little too well.*

'Well, it's Cissi who is the most knowledgeable, so if there are too many of us, she should be the one who writes the chapter. Problem solved!' said Peter. He was aware of Vera watching him with sparkling eyes.

'Ah, that's a shame.' The Professor slowly shifted his gaze to Cissi. 'Is that what the three of you have decided? That you'll be the one who writes it? Well, then... You understand that we can't publish just anything.' His voice hardened. 'I'm warning you as a favor. If you don't fit in, you're out, as they say. And that would be a shame, wouldn't it?'

Cissi looked away. The room fell silent.

'Anyway. About the wording in the application... You'll all attend the conference, presumably?' asked Sturesson after a while.

'Yes. It wouldn't look good otherwise,' mumbled Cissi. Peter noted that Sturesson didn't seem to notice the strange glassy expression in her eyes.

'Exactly. So it's decided!' Sturesson sounded unworried and turned his attention to his computer screen.

They left the room. Peter watched Vera, who followed Cissi as she stormed through the glass doors in the corridor. *I'll take care of it,* said the expression on her face.

'I'll be right there. I'm just going to...' He nodded his head towards the bathroom door. As he retraced his steps, he passed Sturesson's open door and heard Sparre's voice. Peter slowed down and then stopped, pretending to be interested in the brochures on a small table just outside Sturesson's office. His heart beat anxiously, but his curiosity was stronger than the strange feeling of risk.

Peter heard Sparre's voice. 'I've read all the other chapters, and the last revisions are due this week. After that I can finish the introduction. But given the way things are with Monika, I don't have time to do anything else. And now this fucking amateurish...'

'I understand. Of course you have to be with Monika now! Don't worry about the student chapter; I've just taken care of it. We aren't going to get Stavenius, and it's not really going to be about finance. But Ågren is going to write something, and she won't embarrass herself. There might be some environmental nonsense, but she isn't going to risk her future!' Sturesson sounded certain. 'I have a lot to do, but I can write the summary. And we have Lilian; she'll take care of all the practical stuff. But

379

I really hope you can be at the press conference.'

The sound of a chair scraping against the floor prompted Peter to take his leave quickly. He found Vera looking for Cissi in the stairwell. She held up a steaming paper cup. 'She wanted tea, but now she's disappeared. Maybe she went outside?'

Peter looked at her grimly. 'I just heard Sturreson and Sparre talking. Sturesson said that he's sure that Cissi won't embarrass herself, because she doesn't want to risk her future.'

'But they couldn't damage her future, could they?' said Vera, looking worried.

Peter shrugged his shoulders, and they continued searching for Cissi.

They finally found her outside, sitting dejectedly on a bench. She sat hunched over with her arms crossed in front of her chest, as if to protect herself from the still-chilly spring breeze.

'Don't say, "I told you so!"' she said through clenched teeth as Vera approached her.

Vera gave her the cup of tea.

'What do you want to do?' asked Peter, and Cissi turned to look at them. He saw that she had been crying.

'Should we just forget about this?' asked Vera, glancing quickly at Peter.

'Yes, this could affect your dissertation, Cissi. It could be problematic for you – maybe you shouldn't risk it.'

Cissi warmed her hands on the cup, as if seeking strength and resolve. 'I shouldn't risk it? The whole point of academic work is being able to freely ask any question you want, to have the courage to realize that the big, the strong, the established can be wrong. At least that's what academic work is to me. If I can't do it, then I shouldn't be here anyway. And to break under pressure is not structural integrity. So, if you ask me, we *will* do this, and we'll do it well!'

'You know,' said Peter, 'there are others risking more. I heard about a mathematics genius on Wall Street who started to suspect that financial growth was dangerous. He said that derivative traders were "deadly fucking chicken racers."'

'Really? What happened to him?' asked Cissi as she got up.

'They got him committed to a mental hospital.'

'Ouch! Okay, guys, what we need now is some team-building!' said Cissi.

✳

Peter had known that Cecilia Åström was a bit alternative, so he wasn't particularly surprised when she insisted on knowing exactly when and where he was born. Nor that they were required to go to an apartment in Öbacka one week later, to visit a woman named Agnes, who, according to Cissi, was 'the city's best astrologist'.

The woman was around retirement age and tied her hair in an old-fashioned knot, but she wore fitted clothes and moved with a supple youthfulness. She looked at them over the frames of her glasses as she let them into her apartment.

'So are you the ones who are going to change the world?'

Does she mean that or is she being facetious? Peter looked at their hostess with interest, but nothing he saw allowed him to decide.

Agnes started by giving them a short lecture about how astrology had been an important part of Western culture and Christianity for hundreds of years.

That doesn't mean there's any truth in it, thought Peter. *You could say the same thing about wars of conquest and slavery.*

Agnes then asked if they wanted private consultations or preferred to sit together in a group and let everybody listen to everything. Cissi said that the whole point was that they needed to get to know each other better. Agnes smiled and nodded.

'Knowing yourself is the foundation of all forms of strength, and that goes for teams too.'

She started with Peter and expressed herself very carefully, eyes locked on his, as if she sensed that he was skeptical about the whole thing.

Peter took great pains not to reveal anything. He didn't want to give her any simple clues she could pick up on. If the

381

astrologist was going to tell him about himself based on the positions of the planets when he was born, then so be it. He didn't intend to let her off the hook by revealing information with his body language!

To his surprise, Peter discovered that she had a lot to say about him that he thought was true, particularly that he was very curious and had the ability to change and innovate. She claimed that he had a naiveté that could be detrimental to him, but he could grow out of it if he wanted to. When she said that he was attracted to intelligence and strong opinions, and that he would be happy to have a partner who was his superior in that regard, he couldn't keep himself from glancing at Vera.

With the drawings of Vera's planets in front of her, Agnes talked about a person who was uninterested in banalities and prestige. She mentioned generosity, humanity, empathy, a longing after a higher purpose. But perhaps she was too self-critical and dutiful? Then she talked quite a while about Saturn and said that Vera had probably been through a very difficult period over the past year. 'Saturn stands for cramp and stiffness,' she said, and she advised Vera to, 'relax and accept, forgive and go with the flow', and to conquer her fear of change.

'Not all pain is bad. It can be telling us something, to help us change things, find the right path and make progress.' Agnes' kind voice was interrupted by the telephone.

When their hostess went to answer, Vera turned to Cissi and said, 'Do you know what Matt said that he read in something by the Dalai Lama?'

Matt, thought Peter. *It's obvious that you like him.*

'That you should be happy that you can feel pain, because otherwise you can hurt yourself without noticing it, rot away without advance warning,' continued Vera. 'That's what leprosy is, a disease where the nerves die and the ability to feel pain disappears; the body decays.'

'True,' said Cissi. 'But isn't it nice to hear Agnes say that the worst might soon be over, that soon you won't have Saturn hanging over you any more?'

When Agnes returned, she didn't say anything about Cissi

that Peter didn't already know. He could have told the astrologist that Cissi was a generous, temperamental, creative person who needed freedom and intellectual challenges.

'And now to the issue of you as a group. It's interesting. Mercury's placement says that each of you has a good head on her – and his – shoulders,' Agnes said with a nod at Peter. 'And you have exciting and related lunar nodes with strong Uranus aspects. So there is something about the purpose of your lives and the role you can play for the world around you. It's fate and free will, what one takes in and what one radiates,' she said cryptically. 'And Uranus indicates awakening, the unconventional, liberation from old shackles. Surprisingly fast changes are possible.'

Agnes' grey-brown hair glittered in the sun that streamed in through the high windows facing the river. She looked at them curiously and asked, 'Are you casting light on new things? Making sure the world doesn't miss important signs before it is too late?'

They sat in silence. The sun sparkled on the water that was visible beyond the grassy fields. Agnes studied them and said seriously: 'The task seems to be enormous... are you able to describe and portray what's needed?'

Peter looked at the others expectantly. A suppressed giggle suddenly bubbled up from inside Cissi, 'There are rotten trees.'

'And a gigantic ship going full steam ahead, with a rudder that's too small, and conceited decision-makers we all trust, although perhaps we shouldn't.' Vera glanced at Peter.

'And there's lots of talk and little action.' He thought about the curves that Vera had drawn and the insight stabbed him. *Overselling... It won't be much fun when humanity discovers its expectations lack any connection to reality.*

'But these pictures,' said Cissi, 'are more about what happened when we started to understand, when we realized how everything fits together. They aren't part of our chapter. I mean, you can't come along dragging the Titanic into the world of research.'

'If so, that's a pity. In my experience, the bigger the communication challenge, the more important it is to have pictures,' said Agnes, looking worried. 'My advice is to look for metaphors that illustrate the most important things, and don't just keep them to yourselves; you must tell people!'

Just before they left, while they were waiting for Cissi, Agnes turned secretively towards Peter and Vera. 'I haven't devoted much time to your two horoscopes combined, but I see many harmonic aspects, and a couple of interesting tension-filled ones too. It is unusual to see it so strongly. Very unusual.' She fell silent and looked searchingly from one to the other over her glasses. 'I think you two are good together, in part because you need to become more alike.'

Peter felt his heart thumping, and was glad that the hallway was poorly lit. The words touched him deeply. But now he was unsure of his self-control. Perhaps Agnes had just observed them during the session, and had managed to see what he, at least, wanted to hear? She couldn't have missed how he had reacted when she had revealed – right in front of Vera – that he was attracted to intelligence.

He knew that the whole thing could have been taken from a chapter in *The Game*. *Cissi as his wingman introducing the chick crack astrology*. But he wasn't in on it, and why would Cissi do it? What could she possibly get out of it? It couldn't have been rigged, could it? Or had Cissi had a little word with Agnes in advance?

As he wiggled into his jacket he felt pain from the old injury in his left shoulder, and an achy stiffness brought on by several weeks of hard study radiated down his back.

42

Anyone who believes exponential growth can go on forever in a finite world is either a madman or an economist.

Kenneth Boulding, economist

'I feel the same way about astrology as I do about tarot cards!' said Vera as she helped Solveig clean out her refrigerator.

'Yes?' Solveig took the cheese Vera was holding out.

'I don't believe for a second that the cards magically wind up in a particular order for a specific person, or that they mysteriously "sense" that a person is thinking about a particular question when they're laid out on the table. But I had a colleague from Australia, one of the ones who disappeared in Colombia...' Vera's hands paused in their work; she felt a stab of loss thinking about gentle Eliza, who had occupied the bed next to hers in the dormitory of the old mission building. 'She wanted to do a tarot card reading for me once, and I said okay, and strangely enough, I got something out of it.'

Solveig looked at Vera from her wheelchair. 'Did she foresee something that happened?' she asked curiously as she tightened the lid on a tube of caviar.

'Well, that would have been something: "Here we have the Grim Reaper. Soon we will be faced with mortal danger,"' mumbled Vera with a shiver as she continued wiping out the little fridge with a clean dishcloth. 'No, it was more like the symbols on the cards inspired me.'

'I see. So they helped you to think in a new and useful way?' The old woman's eyes sparkled with interest.

'Yes, exactly. Eliza claimed it was because the tarot cards

magically arranged all universal archetypes, but to me it was more like how you described it – an emotional and mental exercise. And that's similar to how I understand astrology. Maybe 10 or 14 variables, all independent of each other, can exist in 12 different signs at 30 different degrees, and then on top of that something called houses, plus angles between heavenly bodies. If you were to do the math – how many unique horoscopes are possible?'

Solveig smiled and shrugged her shoulders.

'Also, she talked about how our different horoscopes are related to each other, and the relationship between our birth chart and the positions of the planets right now. It seems unbelievably complicated.' *Typical Cissi*, thought Vera with teasing affection. 'Anyway, what the astrologist said,' she continued, 'was strange, because she was uncannily correct about how my past year has been! And I keep thinking about it...' They had now finished cleaning the fridge and were putting things back. Vera rinsed out the rag, washed and dried her hands, and leaned against the kitchen counter.

'Do you think I should forgive Adam?' she asked.

Solveig seemed to think through her answer carefully. Then she said, 'Yes, I think so. Because forgiving is not about accepting the behavior, it is about letting go of it. Forgiveness is about letting the past be the past – about putting it to rest.'

'But how can *I* do that? It's in him, not in me. Whether or not the misery lives on is up to him. I'm completely helpless!' Vera's voice broke and tears welled up in her eyes.

'But what I mean is that the forgiveness isn't really about him. You should do it primarily for your own sake. Let go of what pains you and move on. So forgiving is something you should do regardless of everything else. The difficult question is whether you should move on with him or alone.'

'But that's what I'm asking! That's what I mean!'

Solveig sighed pensively and rolled across to her geraniums on the windowsill. She began dead-heading the flowers, picking off the withered ones. Vera handed her a plastic container from the dish drainer to put them in.

'Life is a mix of the good and the bad,' said Solveig. 'Closeness means that your partner's problems are yours too. Sometimes you have to take the bad with the good, but sometimes it's better to give up the good with the bad. What you should do in this case is something that only you can decide.'

She looked searchingly at Vera, who averted her eyes and stared down at the floor. Vera had hinted at what it was about Adam that had hurt her so badly. She had tried to explain, but couldn't. And Solveig didn't insist on knowing more; she simply moved on to the next beloved geranium.

'But then, of course, there is the dream about heaven,' she said carefully, as she returned to her dead-heading.

'Heaven?' A shiver ran through Vera. *Shangri-La*?

'Yes, the most difficult thing about life is how often the good and bad are connected. So we dream that at least after death things sort themselves out, so that all the bad is in hell, and heaven is unstained happiness. But sometimes, when people communicate well with each other, they can get close to heaven by separating the two – by protecting what is good for us from what causes harm. Naturally it's never problem-free, but it can be so much better!'

Vera thought about their chapter. Despite Sturesson's ill-concealed threat, they had now sent 'Structural Integrity' to the printer. And wasn't that exactly what they had tried to do? Distinguish between the two, to separate the bad from the good? Wasn't that exactly the question they had posed? *How can we protect the benefits of the free market while also limiting the damage it causes?* She made a mental note to remember this for the press conference, because she felt that what Solveig had said was a key insight. They would try to communicate it well, so as to ensure that the powers of the market worked for the common good. For the solution to *Koyaanisqatsi: what are you doing, little brothers and sisters?* was to identify and scrap the rules of the game that incorrectly assumed the planet's resources were infinite and indestructible, and to replace them with new ones that worked. Vera couldn't see any other way to bring an end to what was wrong – the exploitative, degenerate species of market forces that created this destructive shortsightedness.

✖

Kalle, the guy who had loaned Vera his room, unexpectedly showed up at the dorm on the last Thursday in May. He played on one of the top-ranking teams in the big annual rounders tournament, and he wasn't going to miss it. On meeting Vera, he quickly reassured her, 'You don't need to worry; Matt said I can stay with him over the weekend.'

Vera thought about the kind, bear-like man whose room she was renting as she biked across town under a clear blue sky. The breeze caressed her skin and she smiled when she caught sight of Umeå's signature sign of spring – hundreds of teams practising their batting, catching, throwing and base-running. There wasn't an empty patch of grass to be found. And when it came to team names, the stranger the better. When they had looked through the local paper's special rounders supplement, Vera had laughed at 'Lawn of inertia' and 'Roundheads'. Cissi's favorite team year after year was 'It's fine to make love with redheads', which had actually won back in 1985. On one field, Vera saw a practice session being interrupted by a big Bernese Mountain Dog that couldn't resist chasing the ball. Vera fondly remembered when she had played in the tournament, and the fun they'd had coming up with silly team names.

Everything she saw glowed in the warm sun; everywhere she looked she saw movement and happiness and ball-play. May had started out cold, but the snow had finally melted and yesterday the Russian warmth had arrived. Now it was 80 degrees in the shade, and, as if on cue, the trees had burst into leaf.

The bike path took her towards the woods, and she heard birds singing all around. Cissi wanted to do a final run-through at the lake. She had suggested that they meet at the China Bridge at two o'clock, and then walk from there to the beach with the polished flat rocks.

Vera was intentionally early. She parked her bike and eagerly walked down the trail that led her in among the trees. She wanted

388

to think in the woods. She had been mulling over what the astrologist had said... *'I think you two are good together.'* Yes, Vera had thought, she felt like that about some of her friends – that they were good together. Why couldn't she admit that Peter was such a person? Was it because she had realized that she felt they were *so* good together, that it might be interpreted as together with a capital *T*? Because that was completely different.

Suddenly she heard his voice close by.

'Is it always like this up here? You have winter, winter, winter... *bang!* Summer?' Peter appeared from the trail that came from the right to meet the one she was on. He was dressed in a light-blue t-shirt.

'Yes, it isn't so unusual.' Vera made an effort to regain her balance.

'I saw you, but you didn't see me. You just locked your bike and took off into the woods.'

'I like to be in among the trees.'

'I know.'

'It recharges my batteries, helps me think better. Researchers say that the hundreds of shades of green in the woods are good for us. They're healing, help relieve stress.'

They had reached the lake. Peter smiled. 'You seem to think like that a lot, all science-like.'

'Yeah, it's nerdy, I know.'

'No, it's good. It's like you know what's what. So what do you say about this?' He picked up a flat rock, bent down, and threw it smoothly so that it skipped repeatedly across the surface of the water.

Exquisite. Vera blinked mutely.

'Skipping stones. I've never been able to do that,' she admitted.

Seemingly without effort, Peter crouched down, picked up three stones, and stood up again. He held out his open palm to Vera. 'Pick the right stone!'

She looked at him hesitantly and then chose the flattest one, her heart pounding worryingly. He nodded in approval.

'Good. Now hold it flat and horizontal, and...'

Distracted, she tried throwing it like a Frisbee. It didn't go very far, landing in the water with a plopping sound and splashing Peter.

'Hey!' said Peter with a mischievous twinkle in his eye. He quickly threw a stone in the water in front of Vera, splashing her back. She laughed and escalated the game, throwing a bigger stone that splashed him even more. He smoothly jumped out of the way, and, giggling, pointed at a boulder that she realized he could pick up and throw into the water if he wanted to. She smiled and backed away from the water with her hands up.

He moved towards her again and, in a tone of reconciliation, said, 'No, seriously, throw with the inside... wrist first.'

He picked up another flat stone and showed her how to hold it. She did as he instructed, and let him touch her hand to adjust her fingers. She tried a few more times, and on the third try the stone actually skipped four times. He smiled.

'Good! You're a fast learner – in this too!'

Her fingers burned where he had touched her. Their bare arms brushed against each other, and she felt electricity. She saw from the corner of her eye that he was looking at her.

'So, what's going on?'

You are simply exquisite, was the answer that immediately popped up in her head. When he wasn't moving, or walked normally, she had no problem accepting that his beauty wasn't her business. But every smooth and softly co-ordinated throw awoke a deep longing that she couldn't control. Guardedly, Vera glanced at him. The sun made his turquoise eyes sparkle, despite the fact that he was squinting against the light.

'I mean, how do you explain the magic?' he went on.

She couldn't control her thoughts as she tried to concentrate on what he was saying.

'You know, why can the stone walk on water?'

She tried harder to focus. 'Hmm, maybe because the friction of the kinetic energy against the surface tension overpowers gravity for a few seconds?'

What kind of nonsense was that? she thought. The unspoken truth filled her head. *Physical attraction overpowers my self-*

390

control for a few seconds. It was just a brief moment. All she had to do was wait patiently and it would pass. Or would it? Vera felt anxious. This riotous attraction was growing increasingly unmanageable. *What is this?* She had seen plenty of beautiful men before, as well as beautiful men who moved beautifully. But this was something else. The question really was: what on earth is going on?

It was just after two, so they returned to the bridge where they were supposed to meet Cissi. They waited in the octagonal pavilion in the middle of the bridge and looked out over the water. Vera was intensely aware that he was standing behind her. He took out his expensive new phone and took a picture of the view. She noticed that he wasn't holding it as carefully as he had held her old, worn phone. He looked at the picture on the screen.

'The day before the baptism of fire. I want to remember it. Can I take a picture of both of us?'

'Sure,' she managed to say.

He moved closer to her and supported himself by putting his left hand against the post directly behind her hair. He stretched his arm out in front of her, pointed the mobile phone directly at them and snapped a picture. They looked at the result. It was crooked, showing only Vera and Peter's left hand against the pole – an open and relaxed, slightly angular hand. The squarish nail on his thumb was short and neatly cut. The capable hand of a man. And now she sensed what this increasingly unmanageable feeling was all about.

'Whoops! "Vera with hand". We need to redo it.' He reached out and took another picture, this time at a better angle.

'You have beautiful hands.' *Did I say that out loud?* She blushed, looked down at the water, and thought about what she had said. It had mostly sounded like a statement of fact. It was true; no big deal, right?

'Thanks.' He looked at her in surprise as he showed her the new picture. *This one was good, wasn't it? Maybe a little dark?* He looked at his left hand and held it out to her.

'But what about this nasty scar across the thumb?'

'I don't think it's nasty at all. When I see it I think about...'

391

She stopped, interrupted by her memory of taking care of him, her heartfelt desire to nurse him back to health, to protect him from what he was so afraid of, to dry his tears.

'What do you think about?'

Vera gathered her courage and met his eyes. 'I think that if you ever decide to have children, you'll be a good father.' She went quiet, swallowed the last part of the sentence... *and husband.*

The insight had come into focus: that was the reason. She went weak-kneed when his physical flexibility reminded her of his disposition. Of all human strengths, the power to change had to be the most important one. *You can change yourself.* He had shown her that it was possible. You could stop having endless hook-ups and become a one-woman man – for months she had seen only Linda, and she hadn't heard a peep from the other side of the wall. You could have a rich, upper-class background with strong ties to finance, and still have the courage to question that world. He had the ability to take in the truth and think about what could be done to bring about positive change.

We need to redo it.

Since childhood, her father's personality had been her anchor and touchstone. But Peter's way of being felt like an improved version of her father's. Yes, she was increasingly sure that he was Sven-Erik 2.0 in this most important respect. He wouldn't repeat his own father's mistakes, and he wouldn't let his wife be like Gunilla either. He wouldn't let his children grow up in a home with a substance abuser.

Love doesn't mean letting someone hurt you.

Her admiration seemed to know no bounds, and she felt like he was cast in one piece, complete. He gave her a sense of hope and optimism. She remembered Agnes' advice: *You need to become more alike.* Well, she had nothing against that. *I also want to be as good as I can be.* If the world were full of people like Peter, then the future of humanity would be bright. She could sense that he was still standing just a few inches behind her, but she resisted the impulse to lean back a little and let her back touch his blue shirt. The very thought of it was strictly forbidden.

Remember who you are and who he is!

'Sorry I'm late!' breathed Cissi as she rushed toward them, almost running. 'It was the press release. Journalists have already started calling. I promise you, our chapter is the first one they read! Anyway, I'm here now, let's go. What will they criticize us for?'

They followed her over the wooden bridge.

'Yes, that's the question,' said Peter after a pause.

It took Vera about 10 steps before she could focus on the task at hand, but then she said: 'Will they say we're communists?'

'Yes!' grinned Cissi, 'and then they'll say that everybody who has tried communism has wound up creating more poverty, wasting more resources and creating more environmental destruction than the market economy.'

'Yeah, and it's true!' said Peter.

'Yes, really, who wants to move to North Korea and starve to death?' wondered Vera.

'But it's not like that everywhere, is it? Nobody starves in Cuba, do they? Although, on the other hand, we also have Kamchatka and nuclear waste...' grimaced Cissi.

Peter turned to Vera.

'Just because Marxism has failed, that doesn't prove that capitalism is flawless and doesn't need to be improved.'

Vera was filled with a glow of recognition.

'That's exactly what we should say!' smiled Cissi. 'I was right, wasn't I? It was *so* worth it to come out here. You think best when there's good *chi*!'

Peter continued looking at Vera. 'I just remembered something a wise person once said, that we must surely be able to think of more than two ways to organize the world?'

The warm glow spread through her. Smiling, she looked directly into his eyes. She wasn't exactly sure what she communicated, because the smile she got in return made her feel light-headed.

They went through everything that might come up at the press conference for two hours, then headed home. When Vera's phone rang she answered without checking to see who was calling. It was Adam, and she stopped and spoke quietly with him, agreeing to his suggestion that they meet at the weekend to talk.

The others had slowed their pace, and when she caught up with them Cissi asked curiously, 'Adam?'

'Yes, he's coming up. He'll be at his parents', and he wants to see me.'

Cissi looked at her searchingly and asked neutrally: 'Are you leaning towards forgiving him? I mean, do you want to get back together?'

Vera's heart pounded. *Together with a capital T.* For some reason, it felt strange to be talking about it, and her reply was almost inaudible, 'We're married on paper, so it requires deliberate action to...'

'To get divorced?' asked Cissi.

Ugh! That word! 'Yes, to change the situation. At the same time, what we have now doesn't feel stable at all,' she admitted honestly.

Peter looked at her with a steely expression. 'I think you should beware of spallers.'

Vera suddenly felt dizzy and she tripped on the edge of the wooden bridge. Peter took her arm lightly to steady her.

'Are you okay?'

'Yes, I'm fine, no problem.' Blushing with embarrassment and with something else that felt unfamiliar, she was sure she was lying. Because whatever it was that she was irresistibly being drawn into, it was definitely not unproblematic.

✖

The murmuring in the packed auditorium emphasized the importance of the event. Vera took a deep breath as she waited nervously behind the thick stage curtains. The preparation was over. Now it was show time.

Peter turned towards her in the half-darkness. Two fingers touched the outside of her hand, and he said in a thick, soft voice, 'Put Dopey on the kick-sled.'

He looked at her and the unexpected message took her by

surprise, forced its way through all her defensive barriers. It was as if he had picked up on who she really was, tuned into *her* wavelength out of all the billions out there. Vera's heart pounded wildly in the face of the new, dizzying possibility that suddenly opened before her.

The moderator began to talk and it was time to go out onto the stage and into the glaring light. Vera started when she saw the crowd. Almost every seat was filled. Curious students hung over the balcony railing. TV crews had set up cameras, and microphones had been placed on the lectern and beside the nameplates on the long, covered table. Vera and the other chapter authors took their seats. Seven men and one woman. The lectern, decorated with a large arrangement of flowers, was to the far left. Behind them, the back of the stage was lit up with a projection of the project's title – 'Wealth and Welfare in the 21st Century – Challenges, Risks and Opportunities.'

Vera saw Sturesson confidently grasp the sides of the lectern.

'The Wealth and Welfare of the 21st Century…'

For some reason, Vera and Cissi had been placed farthest away from the lectern, while Peter sat on the other end of the long table, closest to it. Vera's gaze slid over to Peter. Her ears were buzzing. He looked back at her with a serious expression. The surroundings felt blurred, and Sturesson's introductory comments seemed to be coming from very far away. Unaccustomed thoughts spun around in her head and she looked down at her hands. After a while, she was roused into the present by the sound of applause, and she realized that she hadn't even noticed that Sturesson had switched languages. *Get a grip, Vera!*

'… leading experts. Professor emeritus Lars-Göran Sparre from Lund.'

Vera saw that everyone sitting in the front of the sloping auditorium had been given a copy of the expensive publication, and her stomach flipped over when she thought about how people she didn't know would read what she had written. She suddenly had an unrealistic desire to talk to every one of them, to ask, 'so what do you think about this?'

The ceremonial introduction was followed by a slow hour

during which Sturesson and Sparre lectured with the help of 40 PowerPoint slides. Vera could tell from all the squinting in the audience that the text on the slides was far too small. Finally, Sturesson stopped talking and invited the audience to ask questions.

The first questions were about growth theories and demographic developments in the West. The older people on the panel seemed to agree that freedom from regulation was the best way to encourage necessary growth.

'But in practice,' said Cissi, 'the market only works when it is regulated.'

Professor Sparre looked dismissively at her. 'Regulated how? Five-year plans, perhaps?'

Several panel members smiled indulgently. As expected. Cissi had said *one* sentence, and that was enough to be accused of having communist tendencies. Vera looked encouragingly at her. *We expected this. You know what to say!* Sturesson looked to the audience in search of a new question, but Cissi responded.

'For example, contract law, laws about competition, patent law. Does anyone here think that these regulations are unnecessary and that we should just get rid of them?'

Vera looked appreciatively at Cissi and felt energized to get into the discussion. Without hesitation she looked at Sparre. His opinions had been quite clear in the parts that he had written.

'But you base your conclusions on a different set of values. You favor more deregulation, correct?' Vera heard her own voice projected out into the auditorium, and noted that it felt strangely unfamiliar.

'No, you misunderstand. It has nothing to do with me. It's a fact that in today's globalized world, barriers to the free market are more harmful than helpful.'

Sturesson pointed to a light-haired journalist in a tweed jacket, signalling that he should ask a new question.

'But based on the perspective in the chapter "Structural Integrity"...'

'Excuse me, what chapter did you say?' Sturesson thumbed awkwardly through his stiff copy.

'Structural Integrity: New Perspectives for Sustainable Wealth and Welfare,' read the blond man from his book. 'Page 180. The obvious follow-up question is harmful for whom?'

Sturesson bent the book open, cracking its spine, and flipped clumsily through it looking for the right page. His neck turned pink, reminding Vera of strawberry sorbet against the porcelain white of his shirt collar. Suddenly it hit her: *he hasn't read our chapter!* Vera's pulse quickened. This wasn't good!

'Excuse me, you'll have to clarify your question.' Lars-Göran Sparre looked worried.

'He wonders if it wouldn't be good for the majority of humanity if we regulated global capitalism's often shortsighted behavior,' explained Vera. She looked at the blond man, who smiled crookedly and nodded.

'But now you are obviously talking about values, which is hardly science!' Sparre's voice sounded controlled, but the hardness under the surface was unmistakeable. *This is outrageous!* Vera thought she heard.

Sturesson anxiously straightened his tie and pointed to a new questioner, a woman farther back in the room.

'I just want to say something about the same chapter. Finally, an economist who knows something about the situation for people working in healthcare!'

Sparre looked darkly at Vera. 'But, unfortunately, that is also an example of a personal opinion. These young people don't have any real knowledge about the care sector.'

'I have to disagree with you there.' *As I told you last fall*, she thought as she continued, 'I have worked as a nurse for five years.'

She saw that Sparre was at a loss, that he probably remembered now, and Vera felt that he was suddenly even more dangerous, like a wounded bear backed into a corner. Vera remembered the first piece of advice she had got from Lilian, so experienced in the strange wonderland of academia. *Never embarrass a professor.* But now it was too late. Sparre was redder than Sturesson, and he raised his voice authoritatively.

'So you three think that you can understand a system as complex as the global economy, and that you...' He turned so as to include Peter in his comments, 'three students with very little economic expertise, can come up with solutions to global problems?'

She looked over at Sturesson behind the lectern. He looked pleased – he was eager to hear them answer the question. Vera felt herself shrinking in her chair. *How can we answer that? Yes, maybe we can come up with a little bit of the solution?* Or perhaps, *At least we're trying, because we think somebody should?* No, that was even more provocative. *What can you actually say in this situation?* She was scared.

'I'm not really sure I understand the question,' said Peter, with an unexpected calmness. 'Do you mean, who do we think we are? That what we write or say, by definition, can't be of any value because we're not, or at least not *yet*...' He looked at Cissi before continuing, 'professors?'

Vera was flooded with affectionate warmth. *How well I recognize you!* She looked at Peter. *Thank you!* The energy in his eyes filled her as his question to Sparre hung unanswered in the air. Sturesson cleared his throat and looked stiffly out at the audience.

'We have a... vigorous debate here. Does anyone have a question about something else, perhaps? Ah, yes, here is *Dagens Industri* with a question.'

'Regarding Chapter 6, on what grounds do you think you have the right to call into question the well-established Black-Sholes price-setting mechanism?' wondered the man in the dark-blue suit.

'That's an important example of how we use equations from natural science to try to predict human behavior, and trillions of dollars of trades in derivatives are based on it,' answered Cissi. 'But economists are reluctant to use natural-science equations on subjects in which they have much greater validity; that is, with regard to natural resources and the environment. We thought that was odd.'

'But nature is not the subject of Economics, and we need an instrument to price options!' said the thin man sitting next to Peter.

Nature isn't the subject of Economics? That's where we get everything that keeps us alive, all energy and all raw materials! thought Vera, dumbfounded, though she dared not say it out loud.

'Yes, if the instrument leads to correct price setting.' Cissi's cheeks turned red. 'But don't we also need to know the limits of nature?'

'What if our actions are based on wishful thinking rather than reality?' Vera couldn't remain silent any longer. 'We want to believe that physics equations are good at describing human behavior and that wishful thinking gives us a good picture of our physical condition. But that's the wrong way round. We can negotiate with each other, with people. We can't negotiate with nature!'

'We've had 10 years of enormous growth in the financial sector, but our material foundation, which is based on real resources, is weaker. So we've created a tough situation for ourselves,' continued Peter, putting his hand over the book in front of him. 'Even before that, the quantity of money increased faster than the goods and services we expect to get for it. We think the problem has become worse, and in a dangerous way too.'

Sturesson grabbed the edges of the lectern and seemed to be making an effort to sound mildly deprecating.

'Yes, this chapter, Chapter 6, is – of course – normative, and we all must read it with that in mind. Next question?'

Normative. There was that word again. The word that had been written in red ink on her draft. She looked at Peter and took a deep breath. It is best to confront recurring problems. *It isn't loving to let someone hurt you.*

'But hold on, Åke Sturesson. When you say normative, what do you mean?'

It was surely also breaking the rules to ask the moderator a question during a press conference. But she didn't care.

'That it's based on values and not facts,' was the immediate response from the lectern. Sturesson was obviously surprised at the question.

'But all human activity is based on values,' said Vera. 'The person who doesn't value anything doesn't get up in the morning, and ought to be indifferent to continuing to breathe.'

'But, my dear,' said Sparre sharply, holding the book up at her, 'what he means is that what you have written is too normative to be considered scientific.'

'If so, then that's true of the entire discipline of Economics, surely?' Vera was surprised at the sharpness of her response. 'The task of finding the best possible way to use scarce resources has *everything* to do with values. The truth is that it doesn't matter how many formulas we use; it makes no difference, because the discipline couldn't be more normative!'

'I think it's also worth remembering,' said Peter, 'that the discipline's founding father, Adam Smith, was actually a moral philosopher.'

Cissi leaned towards the microphone and spoke softly. 'If what you are saying is that the discipline should take facts more seriously, then we applaud the effort, because that is exactly what we think. And we also think that we should pay more attention to our values, that we should be more aware of them.'

'What do you mean?' The question came from the woman on the panel.

'Well, since norms influence people and people form the world through their behavior, norms are constantly shaping economic facts,' said Vera eagerly, warmed by the first sign of real interest from one of the others on the project.

'Give me *one* example of economic facts created by norms!' said Sparre incredulously.

'Over 150 million women are missing in the world, mainly in Asia. Why is that?' asked Vera. When he didn't answer she continued. 'Because millions of families act in their own interest, given existing norms, so they kill female fetuses in the hope of getting a boy next time. Because when they have sons, they benefit from the dominant economic and social rules of the day. But what happens when everybody does the same thing? What happens when we have too many men? 150 million too many, who can never get wives?'

'Aha!' Sturesson's effort to laugh sounded nervous. 'That is unfortunate, but it is hardly relevant, is it?'

'You're completely wrong,' said Vera, feeling unexpectedly

combative, as she had at that appointment with the chief orthopedic physician. She enjoyed the intoxicating feeling of being fully capable of defending her position. 'It has everything to do with future wealth and welfare. Today we rush full speed ahead despite serious problems with the steering mechanism. We have rules of the game, for example rewards and obligations, that don't promote farsightedness, but instead encourage behavior that will lead to resource scarcity and suffering in the future.'

Peter looked at her; she felt all the strength he had given her. *Do you recognize yourself in my daring?* she asked with her eyes, as he took up her line of thought without missing a beat.

'Yes, today we act in ways that reduce our future choices. We misallocate resources we need for better things. Another example. If you earn more betting other people's money than trying to solve problems and meet needs, then too many people are going to bet and too few are going to focus on problems and needs. In 2007, over 40 per cent of company profits in the US came in the financial sector! If, in addition to that, you don't need to take responsibility for your own losses when you bet incorrectly, because someone steps in and bails you out, then of course people will continue to take unreasonable risks.'

'All of this is abstract,' objected a ruddy man on the panel. 'Explain a concrete so-called "rule of the game" that would make the world better if we adopted it.'

'We would need to analyze it, of course, but I think we should forbid the sale of naked Credit Default Swaps in order to reduce the share of pure speculative trade in the financial market,' said Peter. Vera noted that even he was surprised at how quickly he had answered. 'Because when you study financial growth it's obvious that we have huge, unmanaged problems with moral hazard, where the market economy doesn't function as it should.' Peter looked directly out at the audience, and appeared not to notice Sturesson's expression.

'Such a statement from a Stavenius makes me think of that old saying about "those who live in glass houses",' said Sparre tartly.

Peter's gaze seemed stuck on the first row of the audience. Vera saw something in him freeze up; he turned red and stiffened, fell silent. Vera's heart pounded; she recognized the reaction and understood how it felt to shrink. Now it was her turn to help.

'I would say that it's a temptation that we've all fallen for. We're all involved.' She turned to face the audience. 'Do you know that when Sweden established public pensions in 1913, the retirement age was set at 67, even though average life expectancy was 55? But now we all think it's reasonable that others support us during a long period of education and training when we are young, and then 20 more years after we retire. For over half of our lives, we expect to be supported by someone else's labor. Today there are 29 retired people for every 100 people working. When I'm 80, if we don't change the retirement age, the number will be over 50 retired people. That is a demographic fact, but the only answer we seem to have to the problem is a belief that money will grow – and grow a lot – if we save it, regardless of how that actually happens.'

'I agree,' said Cissi. 'We all have strong incentives to believe in what George Soros calls "finance alchemy", and if you want to believe strongly enough, then you allow yourself to be fooled.'

'What are you saying?' asked the man in the dark-blue suit. 'Are you warning us about financial growth?'

'Yes, we have to warn about financial growth, because a lot of what we think of as savings and investments that will produce a yield and increase in value are actually loans for consumption, and it's extremely doubtful that people will be able to pay them back. And then we won't just wind up with no yield, we will also have used up the original sum invested too,' said Peter.

'If your claim is true, how serious is this problem?' The woman on the panel looked at Peter worriedly.

'We don't know exactly how serious it is. It depends on how much of people's savings are,' Peter made quotation marks in the air, '"invested" like this. The financial sector's percentage of GDP ought to be one clue, the degree of indebtedness another. In terms of relative size of the financial sector, Iceland is in the worst position, but it's also bad in Great Britain. As for indebtedness, it's bad in Ireland and the US...'

'Great Britain and the US? This is ridiculous!' interrupted Sparre.

'But the financial sector's share of GDP is a rough measure – it only measures quantity,' continued Peter. 'It is clearly a question of quality. Of course, there is also more sensible, realistic financial activity – old-school bankers who loan money to projects that will increase productivity, loans that can therefore be repaid with the expected interest.'

'Remember what Adam Smith wrote as early as the 1700s,' said Cissi. 'Welfare exists where work efficiently creates goods and services that people need and can purchase, nowhere else.'

'And we can loan money to each other as much as we want, convince ourselves that they're investments and maybe delay the moment of truth, but it's like the emperor's new clothes. We can pretend as much as we want, but if there isn't any cloth, then there isn't any cloth,' said Vera.

'And if complicated "financial products" that nobody really understands promise extremely good returns, then warning lights should start flashing!' said Peter.

'What evidence do you claim to have to support all this?' Vera noticed that Sturesson's forehead was shiny as he poked at the pages in the middle of the book.

'We have data on the finite and increasingly hard-to-reach world oil reserves, and on the slowing of real productivity growth in large parts of the world, especially the West,' said Cissi.

'But growth in the industrialized world is good!' Sparre slammed his hand down on the table in front of him.

'Maybe on paper, but how much of it is the financial sector's empty numerical growth? Loan-financed consumption?' Cissi looked at Peter. 'That is, pseudo-growth? And how much is real, long-term, value-creating growth?'

'I think the key question is this,' said Vera, who suddenly realized that the energy in her spine had returned, that her antenna was alive and well and was now glowing powerfully. She understood the lopsidedness of the whole notion. *Those who say that we should continue on with business as usual claim that everything they think is based exclusively on fact, while those of us who want change are accused of having unscientific 'values'.*

'What we are really wondering is, what is most credible?

403

That growth in the exploitation of resources can continue as we have got used to? Or that the last 200 years are an unsustainable parenthesis in the planet's history? Because our entire economic system is based on the belief that the economy can always grow, and therefore, money can grow over time, can accumulate. The system demands continuous growth, otherwise it will collapse, but what if we can't have continuous growth? What happens if, or when, growth in real assets comes to an end and the economy begins to shrink?'

Peter looked at her and leaned forward towards his own microphone. 'If there are defaults, that is, suspensions of payment, then the prosperity that we were sure we had will disappear.'

'But this is an absurd way of thinking,' snorted Sparre. 'Irresponsible!'

'Why do you think that?' asked Vera, and there was an oppressive silence before the professor answered.

'Because it is as if you're blind to the gigantic improvements in wealth that innovation-driven industrialization produces and will continue to produce!'

'Yes, why should all the conditions of the modern world suddenly change, as you seem to be suggesting?' asked Sturesson.

'Previous growth was possible because we exploited a larger and larger share of the planet's raw materials, first through colonialism and slavery, and then more recently by industrialization driven by cheap oil,' said Cissi. 'Today everyone agrees that the supply of easily accessible fossil fuels is declining.'

'But you completely ignore man's capacity to innovate!' said the thin man near Peter.

'No, not at all,' said Peter as he turned towards his neighbor. 'Innovations often enable us to do things smarter and more efficiently, and we need new innovations. And there is absolutely real growth in the world, just look at Asia. All we're saying is that the point of a free market is the mutually beneficial exchange of goods and services. And that we need rules and frameworks for such exchange that take into consideration what we really need, over the long term, to survive. But what incentives do we have today? What do they promote?'

Deadly fucking chicken racers, thought Vera, looking at Peter.

'I agree with you,' he said, looking back at her as if they were the only two in the room. 'We don't need to talk so much about us.' Peter looked over at Professor Sparre. 'Prove that we *don't* need to establish new rules of the game to protect future wealth and welfare.'

'Yes.' Cissi was flushed by the importance of what she wanted to say. 'And to those who say that we don't need to put a price on emissions, travel less or eat less meat because we lack proof of humanity's impact on climate change, we say the same. Prove that we *don't* create unacceptable damage to the climate and ecosystem with our current emissions.'

'Now we *must* allow someone to ask a question,' said Sturesson. He dabbed his forehead with his handkerchief and pointed at the blond in the tweed, who had been waving his arm for some time.

'I just want to ask a control question. Do you mean that you think GDP growth is bad?'

'No, not necessarily,' said Vera after briefly considering the question. 'But we object to the dominant view that a high and growing GDP is by definition good, and that everything that prevents it is by definition bad. That leads to rules of the game that encourage short-termism and that value quantity over quality. Because imagine what happens if growth consumes more and creates more expensive problems than the value it creates?'

Then the tragic result is that the greater the growth, the greater the poverty, continued Vera in her head.

Cissi sent a silent query to Vera. *Yes, say it!* responded Vera silently. Cissi turned towards the microphone. 'Is it not possible that GDP often measures the speed at which we transform raw materials into trash and oil reserves into greenhouse gases?'

The ripple of laughter that swept through the room contrasted with the frightening image that came to Vera's mind of a senseless, blind rush towards great impoverishment.

'But what solutions can you offer?' asked the man in tweed.

'We need rules that reward a different kind of behavior than what's rewarded today. We should strive to meet human needs using the fewest possible resources,' said Peter.

'Because,' Vera added, 'we don't inhabit an infinite pioneer world where we can use more and more resources all the time, and simply move on when we've depleted them. We are on a spaceship together, and we need smart solutions; we need to waste less.'

'And that's why GDP is misleading, because it doesn't measure resource efficiency,' said Cissi.

'A measure of the greatest possible benefit using as few resources as possible – what might that look like?' asked the woman on the panel.

'A society where people's basic needs are met – food, clean water, shelter, health, security – without consuming too many natural resources is a good society. And development that takes us in that direction will genuinely encourage prosperity,' said Peter.

'And the opposite is also true. A type of development which requires us to use more and more of our limited resources in order to secure our basic needs is negative development, even if it increases GDP enormously when more people purchase alarms for their homes, expensive medicines, private water-purification systems and armored cars,' said Cissi.

'You aren't answering the question,' insisted Sturesson. 'What does an alternative to GDP look like?'

How much is it reasonable to demand of us, thought Vera, *when there are several thousand economists in the world?* She looked out over the audience and then back at Sturesson's distrustful expression.

'There must be alternatives, right? Otherwise we thought that those of you who devote your whole lives to studying how we can use our scarce resources wisely might perhaps come up with one. Isn't that what economists usually say is the point of their work?'

A dark-haired woman from the local newspaper had been given the microphone. 'But it's an enormous task to reform the global economy.' She flipped worriedly through the book and nodded at the panel. 'It's much harder than the measures the others have proposed to secure future wealth.'

'Yes, exactly,' interrupted Sparre, directing a look of controlled aggression at Vera. 'Or, to speak plainly, these normative proposals are out of place here, and in practice it is impossible to implement them. Surely even a nurse can understand that?'

Vera felt torn between different versions of herself. The old Vera would never even have got this far, and if, against all odds, she had, she would have remained silent during the whole press conference, overwhelmed by the loud, negative feelings radiating from Sturesson and Sparre. *They are angry and afraid. They think that we've carried out a brazen coup against their beloved baby, which they saw as the foundation for their future brilliant success in academia. They're worried that we've destroyed it.* Vera observed the telling looks that passed between the two colleagues who were hosting the event, and the almost apologetic way they were looking at Morley and his international gang, who occupied the middle of the first row.

They're ashamed of us!

But the new Vera... She was reconnected to her life's purpose, warmed by a sense of direction, the desire to change the world for the better. And she was stronger than ever. It wasn't her fault that they were incapable of seeing anything other than their own perspective, unwilling even to discuss alternatives to *business as usual*. Nothing would get better if she also stopped questioning. The insight was a source of power equal to Peter's gaze. It was not her responsibility to protect their feelings. Her responsibility was to stand up for what she believed in!

'Do you mean that we should describe problems so that they fit the solutions we're prepared to accept?' she asked calmly. 'I thought that we would develop solutions once we understood the problems.'

The room fell silent. Sturesson moved the book to the side of the lectern and the sliding noise was amplified by the microphone. He looked at her. 'So tell me, what is the point of this... philosophical pirouette?'

'Do you mean that we should think: "This patient needs an operation, but since we don't want to do it, or because we don't think we can do it, we'll just *say* that it's only heart palpitations and they'll resolve themselves?"'

43

A civilization is defined not only by
what it creates, but also by what
it refuses to destroy.

Kogi Mama

The pounding bass from the dance floor was so loud that Peter
barely heard the water running when he washed his hands in
the men's room. On his way back to the bar he took out his
phone and looked at the picture of him and Vera in the pavilion.
Once again the picture reminded him of the New Radicals' line
'You're in harm's way, I'm right behind.' It had felt like that at
the press conference too. He knew that he had supported her,
and he had felt calm and strong, at least until…

It had been an unfortunate coincidence that, just when he
had been asked a personally difficult question he had noticed
the heavily pregnant Jeanette watching him from the first row
of the auditorium. The sight of a woman in the later stages of
pregnancy usually filled him with tender warmth; that kind of
beauty reminded him of love and new life. But evidence of the
unborn child and the guarded, appraising way Jeanette was
watching him was a painful reminder of what he had allowed to
happen – *or, fine, what he had done!* – and the feelings that the
memory awoke were anything but tender. Fuck! He had frozen.
Unflattering descriptions had rained down on him: *you are weak,
cheap, predictable, easily manipulated, a waster, an immoral
swine*. He had been paralyzed by a feeling that the whole world
was staring at him. With his heart pounding anxiously like a
caged animal's, he had sat there defenselessly – *what had Sparre
asked him?* At that moment, Vera had been there for him, steady

at his back, fiercely impressive and generous. Her answer had pulled him out of his funk and, from 15 feet away, her energy had liberated him. It had been nothing short of a miracle. He put his phone back in his pocket, filled with warmth as the song once again echoed in his head.

Now say you're mine.

He saw people from the dorm and Cissi over by the bar – Vera must be with them. Peter went over, said hello and caught the bartender's attention.

'She's had *"fyra glasar"*,' said Matt, nodding at an empty wine glass on the bar.

Cissi looked kindly at Matt. 'Four glasses is *"fyra glas"*. You know, it's an *ett* word that ends with a consonant, so the word is the same in the singular and plural.'

'There's a rule?' asked Matt as he turned towards Cissi. 'Okay! Explain!'

'*Ett hus* – a house. *Ett* and a noun ending with a consonant. So the plural is the same. *Flera hus* – several houses. Same with parasol – *Ett parasoll, flera parasoll*. And table – *Ett bord, flera bord*. Get it?'

'Okay, so how about, home? *One* hem, *several* hem?' tried Matt. Cissi smiled and nodded.

'Exactly!'

'I've been living here for two years and nobody has told me that. Thanks.' Matt rested his feet on the frame of barstool, turned towards the bar and took a big gulp of beer.

Peter ordered and then looked around restlessly, trying to find Vera. He sipped his beer in silence and waited. One of the foreigners whom Peter recognized from the press conference – he had been seated in the first row – was staring at Cissi. Now he pushed his way forward so that he was standing next to her.

'Hie-llo again, my beautiful.'

Right. He was Russian, recalled Peter.

'If you accept my hand in marriage, I will give you something few men can,' continued the tall, slender man.

Jesus, thought Peter, *he's coming on strong!* He looked at the guy. Thirty-ish, thick, sandy-colored hair that he constantly brushed out of his big eyes with pale, sensitive fingers. Definitely a guy that many girls would peg for a poet. Peter really liked Cissi. If this guy was playing The Game Russian-style, then he wanted to warn her before she got too involved. She looked at her suitor inscrutably.

'Oh, really?'

He lifted his gaze from Cissi's becoming purple dress to her face.

'Yes, absolutely. I am a Popov. In Russia, you are a woman, you get an an A. Your name would be the most beautiful in the world – Cecilia Popova!'

Cissi smiled. Peter couldn't be sure – maybe the guy was being serious? And what about Cissi? Was she a pick-up artist? Or genuinely interested? Or was she just being polite? When he was a player he had been able to recognize other players a mile away. Now he didn't have a clue. He realized that he had lost it. Or maybe he had assumed that everybody was playing, some more skilfully than others, because he had had no idea how you could want somebody with all your heart.

A wave of people from the right suddenly pushed forward and a somewhat drunk woman with dark, spiky hair fell into Matt's lap. She struggled anxiously to get up, but Matt smiled gently. Newly confident with his Swedish, he announced proudly:

'Du får gärna sätta *på* mig.'

She stared at him, and when she had managed to regain her balance on her four-inch heels she slapped Matt across the face before indignantly stumbling away. Matt rubbed his cheek in confusion, and turned accusingly to Peter.

'But I emphasized the small word like you said! The preposition!'

'What was it you wanted to say?' asked Cissi, struggling to keep herself from smiling.

'"No problem, you can sit on my lap",' mumbled Matt, blinking dejectedly.

'Okay. Then you want to say "*sitta* på mig",' corrected Cissi kindly.

'But isn't that what I said?'

'I'm afraid not. What you actually said was…' Cissi hesitated.

Toby had been listening, and he wasn't bothered about softening the blow. 'You said "I wouldn't mind you fucking me".'

'*What!* No way! Bloody language from hell, this is!' Matt buried his face in his hands, slumped over the bar and whined, 'I might as well just stop trying!'

The guys grinned, but Cissi tried to comfort him.

'No, don't give up. It's just a temporary setback!'

Peter couldn't wait any longer. 'Where's Vera?' he asked.

Toby shrugged his shoulders. 'She was just here, getting more wine.' He nodded towards the glass.

The girl who tripped out on magic markers? Peter looked at Cissi.

'Really? I didn't think Vera was big on drinking.'

'No, she doesn't usually drink. But she's celebrating tonight.' She nodded towards the dance floor. 'She's dancing.'

Peter went towards the pulsating dance floor, looking for the only person who mattered. It didn't take long for him to spot her, smiling in the glow from the colorful beams of light sweeping over the crowd. She was with Lotten. His heart pounded and he let the exciting music overtake him as he worked his way through the crowd towards them in the darkness.

She moved to the rhythm of the music with softly flowing movements. He could see the music pulsing in her; it was as if the sound that surrounded him came directly from her. He felt her pulse within him. She smiled and turned towards him, and they moved, dancing separately but together. They shared an unbridled life force of energy, freedom and joy, celebrating how far they had actually come. In the pulsating present, all that existed was the two of them, and in the fragment of lyrics that he heard, he thought he recognized his innermost thoughts being spoken aloud.

I'm releasing my heart and it's feeling amazing… Love me, and I won't let you fall, girl.

44

There you go, flashing fever from your eyes.
Hey babe, come over here and shut them tight.

'Show Me Heaven', McKee, Rackin & Rifkin, 1990

Vera couldn't recall ever having had so much fun. The music was joyous, and she remembered why she so loved to dance. And when Peter came over to her...

In the pulsating music, in the glimmering light of the warm darkness, she saw him mirroring her, and she was intensely aware of his presence. She smiled and mirrored him back, intoxicated by the feeling that she could match him and his exquisite agility. She was caught up in an exchange of energy, a communication flow of untold possibilities. She had never even imagined the array of positive feelings that four minutes on the dance floor could trigger. Appreciation, humor, intimacy, playfulness – together they added up to an immense attraction with limitless potential.

She heard them singing about *Forever*, and she really wanted the music to go on that long, but soon the dance floor was flooded with calm, slow, 1980s-style organ sounds punctuated by percussion that reminded her of her own racing pulse. The playfulness was replaced by a seriousness that was just as pleasurable but much more edgy. He smiled and said something, and she moved closer to him.

'What did you say?' She was careful not to speak too loudly.

'It's spring and you're dancing,' he replied, and she heard the smile in his voice.

Vera remembered their plane's descent through the clouds. It was strange how long ago it felt.

'Yes, thanks to you.'

'Maybe in part, but mainly thanks to you. You should be

proud of how hard you've fought.' He made a move as if he had something on his mind, but then stopped. His hand brushed against hers.

Limitless potential, but complete madness!

'Do you want to carry on dancing?' she asked. The opportunity was irresistible.

He nodded and she moved closer to him, putting her hands on his shoulders. When he wrapped his arms around her waist and carefully pulled her to him, she melted inside; to be in his arms felt surprisingly good. She felt his warmth radiating through his thin shirt. They had only danced to two bars of the song, yet already she felt weak at the knees and like she never wanted to leave his arms. He danced a careful foxtrot, and she followed him easily. She felt him slowly pull her closer, and he moved his hand a little higher, resting it lightly on her back under her hair.

Was it her imagination, or did he inhale deeply, shakily, against her head, as if breathing in her scent? She felt a swelling against her hipbone, and was filled with a fascinated pleasure, but also with a feeling of transgression. Her sense of discipline broke the spell and she reluctantly pulled herself away from him, forcing herself to ask:

'Isn't Linda here?'

'Huh?'

'Linda. Where is she?'

'I have no idea where she is,' he said in confusion. He stopped dancing, seemingly lost without her in his arms.

'But I thought, when I saw her...' *in your bed.* 'I assumed that you were, I mean, that you are... together?'

'No!' He stiffened and looked at her with alarm. 'We aren't! She had an old key; she just appeared. I couldn't get her out of there fast enough!'

He took her in his arms again and leaned down close to her ear. 'I told her, I'm a completely different person now, because I know what it means to be in love.'

The disobedient hope throbbed and spread through her – that same intoxicating feeling she had experienced before the press conference.

Can it be true? Can it be that he understands who I am and has found in me something he really wants?

The magical minutes ended, and she reluctantly left his arms. There was something about how he moved when he released her, a rigidity as he turned that she had never noticed before.

'Do you hurt somewhere?'

He took hold of his left shoulder. 'I have a bit of pain in my back; an old rib injury. I was up late yesterday and,' he smiled, 'I must have sat studying for too long. I never thought that was something that could happen to me!'

She looked at her watch and saw that it was only eleven o'clock.

'Well, today has been a long day. I feel pretty tired...' *and dizzy.* 'Shall we go home?'

They went home together. The evening was chilly, as if to remind them that although the sun warmed the days, they were still close to the North Pole, and traces of winter remained in the still-cold ground. She shivered in her summer clothes, and he stopped and turned towards her.

'Come here.' He opened his jacket.

She looked at him, trembling, and hesitated.

'I can see that you're freezing. I'm warm.'

Oh, God, I know that! Slowly and shyly she moved closer to him and wrapped her arms around his warm chest. And it was just as she had imagined. Her uncontrollable body found him so inviting that she felt like she was beyond rescue. He held her as if it were the most natural thing in the world.

We're acting like a couple. Together with a capital T.

She felt her cheeks turn warm and she looked down at the ground. When her phone rang, he let go of her and she backed away, feeling the cold return. It was Adam. Had he sensed that she was inexorably moving away from him? He asked where she was. When she answered that she was on her way home to the dorm, he asked if he should come over.

'No, don't. There's no need to come into town. I'm coming out there tomorrow; we can talk then!' she said. 'Yes, yes, I'm sure. Okay. Mmmm. Right. Bye. Yes, good night.'

Peter walked beside her silently.

'Adam has come up. He's at his parents', in Vindeln.'

'Oh, okay,' he said, glancing at her.

She knew that she was a bit drunk, and she felt free. Free in the sense of not knowing what might happen.

It wasn't a long walk home. They stood awkwardly in the empty hallway. The silence was oppressive, like the calm in the eye of a storm. She felt two strong, opposing forces pulling at her.

'If your back hurts, I can massage it, if you want?' she heard herself say.

'Are you sure you want to touch me? When we talked about massage before, you said that you...' He fell silent and looked down at his feet, an endearing uncertainty written all over him.

The magic had become too strong. Vera had already thrown caution to the wind.

'Yes, I want to touch you.'

Very much.

45

They were in his room. She was sitting on the edge of the bed, on her hands, and he was standing up. They agreed that it was too difficult to reach the area that hurt the most with his collar in the way, so he unbuttoned his shirt, noticing as he did so that she looked away.

You don't regret this, do you? I never want you to regret anything that has to do with me! The thought swept through him.

He took off his shirt and lay down on his stomach on the bed, a thin pillow under his chest. She carefully straddled his lower back. Still unable to bend her left leg as much as her right, she let it hang off the edge of the bed. His whole body felt electrified. He hadn't thought it possible to experience greater pleasure than he had felt with her in his arms, but now he felt his body begging for more.

'Is this okay?' she asked softly.

'Mmm,' was the only response he could manage. So she started. She rubbed her hands down the long muscles on both sides of his spine and squeezed around his neck and shoulders. She bent forward and let her weight increase the pressure. Her practised movements relaxed his muscles all the way to the bone. Warmth flowed from her gentle hands, and when her hair brushed his skin, it sent shivers of pleasure all the way down his arms. The aching and stiffness he had experienced earlier were dissolved by Vera's magic touch.

Peter lost track of time. He had no idea how long he had been in this heaven. When she suddenly bent forward, her dark curls falling in front of his face, he took in her scent. It was like melon and something else, a clean person, a baby, perhaps. She curled up and put her ear against his back, as if listening to his body. Then she whispered, 'I dreamed that I held your heart in my hand.'

He couldn't take it any longer. His pleasure was overshadowed

416

by a strong pressure in his crotch, and he couldn't remain on his stomach another second. As he rolled over, she slid off him, down onto the bed next to the wall. Though he hadn't planned to, he couldn't stop himself from reaching out his right hand to stroke her hair. Then he buried his face in her neck and took a deep breath, like a sob. In a tremulous voice, he said: 'You hold my heart in your hand!'

His heart was pounding and his ears were ringing. *Have I said too much?* He slowly controlled himself and pulled away from her. But she put her arms around him and turned her whole body towards him, searching for him. She pressed her hips against his, and, undaunted by his erection, buried her fingers in his hair and showered him slowly and carefully with soft, light kisses. She started at his jaw, moving towards his ear and then down his neck. Her lips were warm and silky. They rolled over so that he was on his back. She sat on him, and her hair fell like a tent around them. When she moved over his chest, he groaned with pleasure. From deep in her throat came a soft moan of reassurance.

The longing that had raged in him since the Thursday when he had seen her outside the changing room, the longing that had been strengthened by dreams of what she had done to him when he was sick, was finally relieved by her soft lips. Her hands on his skin had a healing power. But an even more forceful feeling arose in him in response to her touch; burning with desire, he lost himself in her. Could this be true? Was it really happening? Could he be the chosen one, the one she really wanted? Her hand moved down his left arm, towards his hand, as if she were answering him. She lifted his hand to her face and carefully touched her soft lips to the ragged scar on his thumb. That old, bitter sorrow that she, in just a few words, had transformed into a beautiful hope for the future. And now she was kissing it! He felt intoxicated, whole, and somehow grown up.

Yes! My answer is yes!

He opened his eyes and looked up into the dark green of Vera's. The most beautiful eye color he had ever seen.

'You are so beautiful,' he said thickly.

417

'So are you,' she answered with a smile.

He ran his hands through her hair and his left hand stroked her little pointed ear.

'My ears aren't normal,' she said, with what sounded like displeasure.

'No, they are particularly lovely.'

'They stick out too much!'

He smiled. 'That's because you're an Elf.'

And you should know how much that means to me!

She looked at him seriously and lay down gently on top of him. Slowly, hesitatingly, she moved her lips closer to his. Her fingers in his hair sent shivers down his spine. He waited patiently, with a pounding heart. When she finally kissed him, almost shyly, his passion grew, and when she parted her lips and he felt her tongue for the first time, the fire in him roared and he couldn't hold back any longer. His body reacted of its own volition. He rolled her off him and took her in his arms, one hand behind her neck and the other around her waist. He pulled her even closer and in the endless kissing, he felt her melt into him. Desire flooded through every fiber of his body. He felt dizzy and intoxicated, but also wide awake.

I'm so happy about you.

They exchanged small, fascinated smiles.

'Wait,' he whispered and brushed away her hair, eyes fixed on her left dimple.

'What?' The dimple deepened and he let his lips slide over this indentation that spoke of happiness. *Happy Vera in my arms!* They turned serious again, his mouth searched for hers, and they shared an exquisitely slow sharing kiss. Time disappeared; their soft fumbling grew inexorably in strength until her hot, jeans-clad leg was entwined in his.

He stopped himself and put his hand over her left knee. 'Be careful.'

She looked at him in wonder and sat up. Something had been decided and she was resolute. She unbuttoned the top buttons of her blouse, crossed her arms and pulled it off over her head.

He breathed in sharply when he saw her. Her long, dark hair

fell free from the blouse, framing a slender, lithe body. Her cheeks were rosy; her eyes serious and clear. She lay down gently on her side next to him, and, by the light of the Norrland night that shone in through the blinds, he saw the steep curve of her hip and the glow of her white bra.

So shatteringly beautiful... and how young she looks. Like a girl who has just become a woman, and who kissed a boy's scar and turned him into a man. He traced the curve from the highest point of her hip down to where his hand reached her jeans, his thumb brushing her navel. *How can someone so thin be so muscular?* he wondered. He had no power to resist – she was like a magnet, pulling him towards her, his lips towards her throat. Driven by months of longing, he stroked her collarbone with his lips and breath; he got so close that his bare chest rubbed against her naked skin. Her response made him lose himself even more and he knew that they were close to the point of no return.

Against his better judgment, he carefully pulled her bra strap off her shoulder and kissed his way downwards until he uncovered her girlish breasts with their surprisingly dark, small nipples. Without a thought for the consequences, he filled his hands and bent forward to taste them.

It was an unrestrained declaration of love. His body was eager to show what he hadn't dared to say. Her breasts were a bit like her – easily overlooked from a distance, because they didn't seek the limelight, but eminently desirable close up. Here, tonight, in his bed, was absolute beauty – in every sense of the word. He felt as if he had found a priceless, secret treasure. He was floating in dimensions that he had never experienced before, enjoying her with all his senses, how she felt, looked, tasted, smelled. He inhaled her incorruptible intelligence, let his tongue caressingly ask the Elf to come out and play. He hungrily partook of her good-hearted healing powers; he held her tenderly, wanting to protect the young woman who had been forced to struggle so much on her own. And how she responded! She gasped and whimpered with sensual pleasure; moving with slow, cat-like movements that flowed and surged through her lean, muscular body. She willingly accepted that which he didn't have the courage to say with words. And he witnessed her whole body answering *I love you too.*

It was an enchanted miracle – he was in a forest fire of desire, enclosed in a place where his mind was at peace, a place he had never imagined existed! When he was finally able to catch his breath and look at her, she opened her eyes. He was met with a wide-eyed seriousness; her veiled expression made him feel new and magically chosen. He was blown away – this was the sexiest thing he had ever experienced. And when she looked deep inside him, and rotated her hip slightly to ask for more, he was more than willing to go on. With his eyes locked on hers, once again he lost all sense of time and was filled with joyful, boundless excitement. She closed her eyes; he closed his too, enjoying the heightened sensation of not-seeing. The two thinking, feeling beings that had gradually connected over a period of months were now finally a single, sparkling energy source. It was an experience more intense and more alive than he could ever have imagined. And the sweet, endless exploration went on and on.

But when he kissed her soft mouth yet again and tasted something new, like clean water, he came back to reality. He looked up at her and saw something unspoken in her shining eyes. A heavy tear rolled down her face.

'What is it?' he whispered fearfully, lying completely still with his face next to hers.

Vera smiled a little and dried her cheek. She ran her tear-stained fingers slowly across his lips and cheek and then stroked the hair at his neck. She tried to say something, but couldn't.

What are you going to do now? He was sure that was what she wanted to know. A cold worry spread through him. Was he about to destroy everything by having sex with her when she was drunk for the first time in her life? He was suddenly aware of his throbbing erection, worryingly sticky against his stomach and aggressively struggling to push itself up and out of his jeans. He was almost disgusted with himself.

How was she going to believe that he had really become a different kind of person if he acted like this towards her the first chance he got? Supposing he just let his body get what it wanted – would she feel violated, like just another conquest? Worry grew into fear. What if she regretted it tomorrow and hated him for it? He couldn't let that happen.

I never want you to regret anything that has to do with me. He never wanted to let her go, which was precisely why he had to do so now.

46

When she was new in Kivu, Vera had cried so often that she'd been told she needed to have less empathy or she wouldn't have the strength to work for Basic Needs. At the time, she had felt it was a burden – that in addition to her own pain and setbacks, she deeply felt others' pain as well. Empathy wasn't a strength in battle, either. Awareness of the chief physician's discomfort when she was fighting for her knee operation had only been distracting and stressful. And today she had been forced to consciously ignore the feelings of Sparre and Sturesson in order to do her job.

But now she was lying here with Peter, in the bed where she had first seen her Prometheus, and the situation was completely different. She would never have thought that her empathy could bring her such pleasure. Empathizing so deeply with him now was heavenly. Her old cautiousness was overcome, and she succumbed to the powerful feeling of attraction growing inside her. She surrendered herself to the captivating journey of discovery over the landscape of pleasure that he embodied, and she felt him crave her touch like a dehydrated person thirsts for water. It was as if his soul spoke directly to hers: *Take me, I am yours.*

Could it be true?

It seemed unbelievable, and yet… The signs had been there for months. She had started to respect him after she stopped being afraid. She had looked beyond his heartbreaker good looks and focused on his personality and his thoughts. And she had been surprised to discover that she admired him. In the context of the project, it had seemed perfectly safe and impersonal. Her fear and ego had been overshadowed by the task at hand and the synchronization that had developed between them. So, without a thought of getting anything in return, she had allowed her gaze to let Peter know that she appreciated him. She had told herself that it was only right –she felt the appreciation belonged to him, because *he had created it.*

She hadn't asked for anything in return, but something unimaginable had happened. His eyes had devoured what she offered, doubled it, and immediately offered it back to her. He hadn't let her be an independent observer. He had pulled her into an intoxicating exchange and something huge had begun to grow between them. Suddenly, worryingly, it was no longer impersonal. And what was happening now was not, after all, an unreasonable progression. The magic had become too strong; it had simply continued to grow. What had previously seemed forbidden and unthinkable, tonight felt as natural as breathing, and now all she could think of was to keep breathing, drawn by the magnetic lure to take ever deeper breaths.

Are you mine to love? Can it be true? The thought gave her the courage to bend towards his lips, and when he responded with an incredible kiss, something new and spectacular arose in her as suddenly as birch leaves burst into leaf in the spring after a long, cold, northern winter. His taste, his skin against hers, his scent. His beautiful hands around her waist, up under her hair, caressing her shoulder and coming to rest on her neck... She shivered. She felt breathless when he undressed her – *such a dizzying pleasure* – and when he kissed her breasts she felt weightless. She was floating, suspended, higher than when she was on morphine, and the answer to the question about 'her charms' was suddenly obvious. It wasn't one person who was supposed to be charmed, it was a magical union. The hot, tender touch of his gentle hands spoke love. She felt his hot tongue on her hardened nipples, and with every movement they grew harder. When he quickly responded by passionately sucking the left one, desire shot through her body. She arched like a swimmer doing the butterfly stroke, and moaned audibly. He groaned in affirmation, a sound that made her insides quake, as he moved on to her right breast.

She was overwhelmed by a burning passion. She was a concentration of nerve endings, and all she could do was live the experience. Beyond all logic and science, she could have sworn that she was fully enveloped by him in all his beauty. She existed where he was; the rest of her was vapor. Her fingers caressed his neck, a sweet, rich part of their magical union. She fell headlong into his wide-open eyes and discovered capitulation. Lost, and without a thought for discipline or self-control, she pressed her thigh shamelessly up his leg and across his hip. And as she hungrily climbed onto him she felt him hard as wood inside his jeans with her concentrated nerve endings – *about 8,000 of them!* It was reckless; it was risky; but nothing could stop her. It was a raw, uncut, primordial force, a close encounter with the stranger who had become the person she wanted to be closest to. A potent mix of safety and thrill.

His attentiveness and excitement increased her own lust; she was turned on because he was turned on because she was turned on… *ad infinitum*. She wanted more; her desire for him was bottomless and as she closed her eyes, she cried tears of joy in response to the wonder of it all.

Not of this world.

His hand caressed her softly, from her neck to her cheek; he wrapped his fingers in her hair as he kissed her mouth. He pulled himself away from her and asked, breathlessly, *what is it?* She opened her eyes and saw the passion in his face, his sculptured features, his shoulders, collarbone, his beautiful nakedness. His loveliness made her ache, and the question in his eyes was beautiful too. She was unable to force the answer past her lips, but she was sure that he couldn't misunderstand it.

I want you more than anything.

But Peter looked at her sadly and pulled away as if he'd been burned. He sat up on the edge of the bed with his back towards her, rested his elbows on his knees and looked down at the floor with a sigh.

'Forgive me Vera. I didn't mean to. This isn't right. I want…'

He handed her blouse to her and kissed her quickly on the forehead.

'When do you think you'll get up tomorrow? Maybe we can get together and do something?'

She could barely find her voice. 'I… I'm… um… I'm going

to... Vindeln tomorrow, but I can come home in the evening.'

'Okay. I'll call and we can decide on something.' He stroked her lightly across the cheek and moved over to let her up.

He wants me to leave!

Her hot heart pounded as she numbly did as he asked, silently leaving the room, confused feelings ripping through her. The huge, unfamiliar force inside her made her restless. She didn't know what to do with it, and realized that she would never be able to sleep. Imagining that she needed to think things through, she decided to go out and clear her head.

In the woods, the fog hung like artfully draped veils just off the ground and the lightness of the night felt magical. She tried to understand what had happened. She knew that he liked her; she thought she knew that he liked her *a lot*, but... There was obviously a *but*. She thought frantically. What did he mean by *this isn't right*?

Then she went ice-cold. *His previous girlfriends. That was it!* She didn't look like the women he usually had sex with. Adam's preferences... was it the same with Peter? The thought cut into her and tears started to fall. It was a grim fate, yet she hadn't been able to stop herself from falling in love with him. *Out of the frying pan and into the fire.* Her common sense had tried to prevent it, but she had believed she could have Peter, have all of him, even though he was so ridiculously popular and good looking that she wasn't even in the running. The parallels she drew with her failed marriage were like a knife being twisted into her. *Not again!*

She reached the southern tip of the lake. Through a fog of tears she saw two mallards sleeping curled into each other for warmth against the chilly May night. She realized she was freezing, and dried her tears to look at her watch. *I should go back.*

Being in the woods hadn't helped; the confusion and conflict she felt hadn't disappeared. She realized how sad it was, that she had been married for almost eight years, and yet this evening's rejection was by far the most erotic experience she had ever had. She was 30 years old, and tonight was the first time she had really understood what sex was. It was certainly peculiar, exclusive and supremely enjoyable, but it was still a form of communication.

When people communicate well with each other, they can get close to heaven. She hadn't known that it could so literally be true! The sudden insight was unforgettable. *Peter in bed...* Desire surged through her again – *it was addictive!* If she could power herself with that, she would have the energy to save the world several times over!

So was that what it could be like? And that was just the beginning. By the time she was almost back home, she had come to a conclusion. She had convinced herself that her feelings for Peter were dangerous. They were too much, too soon. *I need to be more liberated.* She tried to think like Cissi. 'The world is full of attractive men to have fun with; it doesn't have to be serious all the time.' *Don't settle just because you want to feel safe. You'll only wind up creating a prison for yourself.*

She suddenly remembered the second most memorable exhibit from the class trip to the Louvre – the Venus de Milo, the armless marble statue of the goddess of love, the classic Greek ideal of female beauty. Vera mainly remembered that she was struck by the fact that this Aphrodite looked so normal, almost like herself. Or rather, how she would look when she was older, more motherly. *How I look now, at 30?* Yes, pretty close. *Although I'm still too thin.* She grinned at the thought. *Venus de Milo is nothing to aspire to anyway, because I'm quite fond of my arms!* And, for some reason, the curly, dark-haired Italian from the spa popped into her head. She comforted herself with the fact that *there are men who get turned on by me just as I am!*

The thought did her good and gave her a new feeling of independence.

47

Post-decision surprise, sometimes pleasant and sometimes unpleasant, is characteristic of decision making.

James March, 'A Primer on Decision Making: How Decisions Happen'

It wasn't a difference of degree; it was a difference of kind.

He had come to believe that engaging with Vera intellectually was better than sex, but he ought to have realized that it wasn't better than sex with *her*. Physical closeness to Vera was something new. His only experience that was even remotely similar was the perfect wave at Côte des Basques. Peter wasn't a surfer, but he'd tagged along anyway. After a full day of exhausting effort in the waves on the Atlantic coast of France – 'the world's best surf spot' – he had completely forgotten his hunger, the smarting abrasions and his burning muscles. Several tons of deep green ocean water had lifted him up and driven him forward forcefully. Time had stood still, leaving only the present. The water had been like a curved mirror; he had been one with nature, weightless and biddable in the power of the waves. It had been an adrenaline kick, euphoric, the experience of a lifetime, but it had lasted only a few seconds. Now something similar had been exploding in him for hours.

Peter had lost himself in thoughts of Vera many times since the fall, but this time it was different, because he could close his eyes and turn back the clock a few minutes and she was with him again. Her scent lingered, and his mind was drunk on sensory impressions: her taste, her sound, the feel of her in his hands, her incredibly smooth, soft roundness and the small, hard peaks against his tongue. Best of all, the wonderful seriousness in her face as her body responded to him, which made him feel like he might actually be the one for her, this thoroughly beautiful creature that was Vera. His love for her had not only been welcome, it had been like a key that opened her up. Her raw, powerful femaleness left them both wide-eyed and gave him a sense of his own masculinity that was different from anything he had ever felt before.

No thinking. No role-play. No performance. Just a magical meeting of love and instinct. When he took his erection in his hands he felt like he could burst with joy. His fantasies felt real, and the reality he had experienced with Vera had surpassed his dreams. He was sure that they had shared something entirely new. He had never experienced this magic before, and the same was true for her. That was just one of the things they had communicated wordlessly to each other.

The only thing he needed was greater patience. He had to wait until she wanted to come to him sober. It could only be a matter of time...

What do *you* want, for *you*?

Dizzily, he remembered how demandingly her climbing leg had pulled him closer, how she had stroked her pelvis against his erection, and he was sure of the wonderful message she was conveying: *I want to know you.*

He hung onto the memory as he tried to touch himself in just the way she had touched him, and imagined that kiss without clothes. *Yes. Come on. Feel it. Everything I am is for you.* His heart swelled, and tears welled in his eyes as he recalled her fingers running through his hair and bracing themselves against his neck... What a view he had had of her in that moment!

He held back, focusing his mind on what he wanted most of all. *I'm here... let yourself go!* Her eyes were as deep as the ocean. And finally, after long months of longing, of gradually getting closer to her, he allowed himself to believe that one day she would take him inside her curvaceous, slim, arching body. He let himself drown in the enchanting thought, his skin still warm from the memory of her raw desire. *Into the finest...*

wisest... loveliest – the most outstanding woman, because she wants me! He threw back his head as he came, releasing a passionate groan that arose from his core. An ecstatic yes to Vera, to the world, to life.

Afterwards, he looked at himself in the bathroom mirror. His chest heaved; he felt his racing pulse, his wildly pounding heart. His lips were red and swollen, and his cheeks bore traces of tears – reminders of his rapturous adventure. His trembling body spoke to him in a language he hadn't known he knew. *This is what it should be like!* It's called making love. He felt a sense of pride. Her uniqueness had called forth from within him a man who was solid, whole and grown up. *Because I have been chosen by you.*

He turned on the water and climbed into the warm shower. He had just got himself thoroughly wet and was regretfully thinking about how he was washing off her kisses, when he heard a knock on the door. Maybe she couldn't sleep either? Maybe she wanted to stay with him? *Oh, my love, come and sleep in my arms!* He was euphoric. *Or, why sleep... we can talk instead. I want to know where all your wonderfulness comes from.* She was a mystery; behind every veil he found something enticingly unknown, ideas and experiences he had never imagined. He had started to realize that she had depths that he would never fully understand, but he didn't ever want to stop trying. *What do you think? What do you feel?*

He dried himself with lightning speed. He knew that he had just disarmed his dangerously impatient lust, but thought it nonetheless wise to keep clothes between them. *If she starts to undress again, I'm not sure how I'll react.* He grinned in embarrassment at his insatiability, quickly pulled on shorts and a shirt and pulled open the door in expectation.

A dishevelled Matt stood there, his collarless shirt open over an unexpectedly hairy chest.

'How's it going?' said Matt, looking at him worriedly.

'Um, okay, thanks.' Peter focused on his body. He didn't even feel his back any more. He had never felt so good. 'Really great.'

'We, I mean I, heard you... sort of shout? Did you hurt yourself?'

'Ah, um.' Peter raised the towel in his hands, hiding his face as he dried his hair. 'I just… burned myself a little in the shower. I'm fine.'

'Are you sure?'

'Yes, go back to sleep.'

'Yeah, okay.'

Peter lay wide awake in bed. His heart seemed to have wings, flying in a clear blue sky of happiness. There was so much he wanted to do with Vera! He enjoyed the fantastic sense that he had found his way home, and that it was in heaven. The miracle of that night confirmed what he had felt for so long – Vera was the one he had longed for. With her he had found the extraordinary. Imagine if the astrologist had been right about their being an unusual match? Wasn't that what he'd felt? What he'd tried to say to Vera all winter? *Instant chemistry.* He smiled in embarrassment at the notion: *Well, imagine that! Astrology turned out to be 'guy crack' for you!* But if Vera's gaze could lift him up across the wide stage of the auditorium, was it so remarkable to believe that planetary harmony might somehow be involved?

His thoughts were suddenly interrupted by a noise from the other side of the wall. Someone was in Vera's room! He sat up hastily. *A man?* Of the two soft voices, one was clearly deep, like a man's. Peter couldn't hear what he was saying, but an ominous knot grew in his stomach. He recognized tenderness in the tone and rhythm, an affirmation that slowly transformed into the sound of physical contact, of sensual pleasure. *What is she doing?*

It wasn't that the noise they were making was particularly loud; they were actually being rather discreet. But it didn't take many decibels to knock him out of his wonderful heaven down into his worst hell. Because, in the end, there was no reasonable doubt that what was happening on the other side of the wall was intimate, joyous sex.

Had Adam come over after all? This is what happened when you were stupid enough to love a woman who was married to someone else. All rights adhered to the marriage. His body screamed in protest, but Peter knew that according to all the rules, what he and Vera had just done in his bed was wrong, and what he was hearing now was right. But wasn't she going to get a divorce?

Crushed, Peter realized what was happening. A couple that shared what he was hearing wouldn't divorce. *They weren't going to divorce!* Sick with despair, he hastily got out of bed. Had it sounded this loud when she had knocked on the wall? He heard the rising intensity, and her fruitless effort to keep her voice down signalled that they were nearing a genuine simultaneous climax. *Does that even exist in the real world?* As if paralyzed, he just stood there, wallowing in the painful truth like a mad flagellant. *She* was definitely close to coming – so maybe he was just turned on by that? *Who wouldn't be?* And then he heard the answer to his question. After she had been satisfied, there was a panting recovery, a little tender whispering, and then the bed started to creak. *He obviously knows rule number one – Ladies First!*

Peter covered his ears with his hands and fled the room, moving zombie-like towards the kitchen, screaming a silent *nooo!* His jealousy seemed to echo through the universe; the loathsome feeling that he had lost something priceless wouldn't leave him. Shaking, he decided to drink something, thinking that might calm his nausea. He searched randomly in the cupboard and found something called Evening Tranquillity – he really needed that – and took a bag. When he went to sit down at the table with his tea, he discovered that he wasn't alone. Kalle was sitting there in a worn-out t-shirt eating a sandwich. He looked at Peter and immediately stopped chewing.

'Shit, Peter. You look like hell! Did you have a nightmare?'

Peter stared at him with an empty expression. What could he say? If only it *had* been a nightmare.

'Did Matt wake you up, too? I'll be really glad to get my room back in August.'

'Are you coming back in August?' asked Peter, a slight horror in his voice.

'Yes. I'm only replacing someone this year; and I need to take pedagogy so that I can get my teaching degree. If I don't, I'll never get a permanent position anywhere.'

Vera won't be living here in the fall!

There was no logic to his reaction. The fact that she was Adam's wife – and had just had Reliably Good Sex with her husband – meant it couldn't make any difference. Yet his feeling of loss just grew stronger. What would the dorm be like without Vera?

It wouldn't feel like home any more.

He was tired, empty and aching. He felt like nothing mattered.

'I'm in love. I've just experienced three hours of heaven.'

'With whom?' asked Kalle, curious. 'With Vera?' He nodded, impressed. 'Congratulations!'

'But do you know what she did afterwards?' Peter's voice broke and he pointed towards her room. 'Now she's sleeping with her husband…'

'What?' Kalle looked confused. 'Did you have a fight?'

Peter shook his head.

'Did she change her mind and leave?'

Peter shook his head again.

Kalle looked at him suspiciously and took another bite of his sandwich. Finally, he took another guess.

'Did you get bored?'

'No!' He could never get tired of it, and from what he'd witnessed, the same was true for her. He whispered the only word he could think of, although it wasn't enough to really capture it.

'Hot. It was… hot!'

Kalle squinted in puzzlement. 'Okay. So why…?'

'I wanted to take things slowly.' Peter heard how pathetic he sounded.

'I haven't seen any Adam. And I haven't heard anybody come in, either,' said Kalle with concern. 'I think it's Matt. He came in with half his clothes off, turned the whole room upside down before he found his condoms, and left. I couldn't get back to sleep, and I felt hungry, so I got up. I don't usually eat at night.' He looked almost shamefully at his large, half-eaten sandwich.

'Think about it. You turned her on, left her unsatisfied, and

Matt saw the opportunity and took it. You know...' Kalle wiped two fingers over his forehead, 'Mister I-want-a-girlfriend.'

With a whimper, Peter covered his face with his hands. He realized that Matt must have come from Vera's room when he had knocked on the door. Good neighbor that he was, he came to check that Peter wasn't flat on his back in the bathtub or something, suffering a crippling muscle spasm. New, horrible details enriched the image that the noise behind the wall had all too clearly planted in his head. Peter could barely breathe as disappointment flooded through him. How could he have been so wrong about her? And what did it mean that not even Vera could be trusted? He had thought that the whole challenge had been to get Vera to trust him – it had never occurred to him that he couldn't trust her.

He suddenly felt both arrogant and naive. How many times had he reasoned in the same way? *'I never made any promises.'* Now he understood what it was about Vera that had made him feel so gloriously chosen. He had felt like he had been promised something priceless, certainly from the point when they had enjoyed each other's nakedness. Everything she had done and everything she had welcomed from him, he had interpreted as words of honor, wondrous promises that there would be more of the same in the future, and that it was reserved for him. And he had given her as many promises as he had thought she had given him.

He looked at his right hand, and the bittersweet memory of such reciprocity flooded through him, seemingly insignificant, but in reality deeply imprinted on his soul. He remembered the curve of her hip under his hand, her warm, surprisingly strong, supple waist, his shaking thumb finding her middle as she bent towards him like a gift offered gladly. And he remembered other things he thought she had given him... Her dimple against his lips. A sweet dream come true.

That and everything else that had unfolded in paradise. To object afterwards that nothing had been promised with *words* – such measly small things in comparison – felt irrelevant, absurd. He didn't imagine that she had promised to stay no matter what.

433

It was more that he had felt that she wanted a life with him, and that she, in all her loveliness, wanted to help make it happen. It had been his life's most precious opportunity – he was sure of it. Together he and Vera would wholeheartedly try to do as much good for one another as they could, and harm each other as little as was humanly possible. A dangerous trapeze act that he would only dare to try with someone like... like the person he had thought Vera was.

I won't let you fall. It was the belief in that promise that had released his boundless hope, the fantastic love and the forest fire that was so much larger than he.

He suddenly understood Linda as never before. *If she had felt that she had been promised the same...* He felt a knot in his stomach. Would he ever deserve someone who took him seriously, who kept her promises to him? Was The Game the only option left open for him, wandering in and out of shallow hook-ups, never risking his heart? Was the only other option, if he wanted to avoid becoming a bucket full of holes, to live alone, avoiding women and every chance of love? The knot in his stomach shifted and lodged itself painfully in his throat. Agonizingly, the brave hope inside him continued to ask what had happened. He had experienced sky-high flames of desire in total safety. *Had it really been just an illusion?* He violently wiped away a tear that defied his efforts to maintain control.

Kalle was looking at him with concern. 'Ah, Peter. Just remember what you always say: don't take everything so seriously. Talk to Vera. She's human too, you know. Think about it! She got married young; for the first time in her life she's grown up and single. Maybe she just wants to sow her wild oats.'

Sow her wild oats? Maybe it wasn't so serious, then? Did she really want Peter? *If so, could I forgive her?* Could he accept women acting in the same way that he did? Could he accept it in The One? Would he have to wait for her to sleep with 50 other people before she caught up with his tally?

'You just need to decide.' That was what Kalle had said about humans – the species that was distinguished by its large frontal lobe. But the problem was that faithfulness wasn't a house he

434

could build himself. It was always dependent on someone else. It was always a risk. With Vera he had dared to stretch himself, had allowed himself to become attached, because he had been sure he would be safe. The loss of what he had taken for granted dripped from his heart like blood. *Integrity. That was what I first loved about you!*

Peter thought about when they had discussed the prospects for the climate conference. He had thought it was simple: everybody ought to reduce emissions equally. Vera had said that China and India and all the other economies that were developing now would hardly be willing to forgo development just because the West had already damaged the environment. She had said that we probably needed to do more, because we were responsible for most of the emissions that had already occurred. But Peter had objected, said that *the difference was that we didn't know then what we know now.*

That's exactly how he felt. Now he knew – and surely she did, too? – that what they had was worth holding on to. Before, in a different and alien life, when he had had sex on the other side of Vera's wall, he hadn't known. Peter felt strongly that Vera couldn't behave now as he had done then without destroying something irreplaceable. She had made him realize that quality was worth more than quantity. And quality was what he thought he had found in her. He was so sure that they had something unusual, something exceptional. He thought that she was The One. But could somebody be The One and still behave like that? Self-critically, he asked himself the counter-question: *Can I be The One after the way I've behaved? Or is the truth once a spaller, always a spaller?* Now that Vera had changed for the worse, could he forgive her? Could she change back? And if she did, could he trust her then?

Because what she's doing now is no small error.

48

Vera found it surprisingly easy to rekindle the feelings that had been building up inside her and her night had ended with a powerful, jubilant leap from a high summit into an ocean of rhythmically inviting waves. Afterwards, she likened the feeling to a vertiginous flight down from the snow-capped Sierra Nevada into the relaxing warmth of the Caribbean Sea and hadn't she been aware of colors exploding in her head like fireworks?

When she woke up the next morning she understood that she had crossed over into a new territory. She had entered a new life, a new world. Yesterday, that part of her which had previously been dry and brittle, rendering sex without the assistance of a lubricant painful, had become swollen and slippery. In her old life, it had at best been *kind of nice to be so close, but sex had felt overrated.* She was thrilled to discover the fantastic power that lived inside her.

Now she knew that the physical expression of love was a powerful experience and important to her. She realized what she had been missing, and her uncertainty about Adam no longer had anything to do with forgiveness. It was more *'how could I have...?'* Last night had been a healing experience, but it had also revealed the magnitude of what she had been missing out on – all those years without it, without anything even remotely close to it. She wanted to cry, yet also realized that she had been liberated. She could look forward, simply refuse to dwell on the past, because now she could see the problem clearly. The inability to combine love and lust was Adam's problem, not hers. But just as her mother's problem had harmed her father, Adam's had harmed her.

How much sickness did you have to take before the best course of action was to end it?

Vera nervously fidgeted with the papers in her bag as she rang the doorbell at the Henningssons'. She smiled self-consciously at her father-in-law, who stood behind his wife as she gave Vera a bear-hug.

'Um, is Adam home?'

'Yes, he's upstairs. Adam! Aaadam!' called Eva enthusiastically. 'Guess who's here?'

Vera felt uncomfortable when she glanced at the old tapestry on the wall on her way up to Adam's room. She had seen it so many times, the gold-embroidered wall-hanging with the merciful angels and the grandiose proclamation: 'The Son of God has come to seek and save those who are lost.'

Lost? Was that how Adam had been raised?

As Vera closed the door behind her, Adam turned off Eurosport and stood up. His arms hung passively by his sides, but his eyes were hopeful. They greeted each other awkwardly. Vera tried to swallow the lump in her throat, knowing it would only be cruel to delay what she had come to say. She pulled out the papers she had been keeping on her shelf for months.

'There are lots of things about you that I admire. You've actually been a good friend, and I hope we can remain friends.'

'What? What are you talking about?' Adam looked scared, and as he read he became increasingly agitated. 'Divorce? But why? I love you! And I'm much better. The therapy is helping!'

Vera looked at him. Her voice trembled, but only a little.

'Maybe you should try to look at things differently. Try to see the Madonna in the women who turn you on.'

Adam slumped onto the sofa and buried his face in his hands. 'It sounds so disgusting when you put it like that!'

'Why?' she shot back at him angrily. 'It's not like they're unrelated – sex, pregnancy, parenthood!' She went over to the window and looked out at the greenness of early summer. She lamented the fact that Adam's internal conflict had left everything tattered and torn. The cracks in him were breaking him apart too, and she knew that he needed to know.

'You have conflicting feelings about so many things. When you say your patients "aren't exactly reserves of talent with healthy self-esteem", you aren't respecting them. And if you don't respect them, then you can't respect what you do.' She was crying now. 'And if you're in conflict with yourself then you can never be happy, Adam. I wish, for your sake, that you could heal yourself and become whole.' She turned and looked at him pleadingly. Crying, Adam hung his head and buried his hands in his hair.

'What are you saying? Can't we work this out? Isn't there any way to save us?'

Vera sat down next to him on the sofa.

'Maybe if you had dealt with it straight away; if we had talked about it, maybe we could have solved it, but now... Ten lost years and who knows how much cheating...' The pain of it silenced her.

'It isn't "who knows how much" cheating. It was... four times, while you were abroad, never before that!'

'It doesn't matter.' She dried her tears and stood up. 'I don't want to do it any more. I'm finished crying over what we had. I want to move on.'

Hands still in his hair, Adam looked up at her in despair.

'Is it him? That guy in your dorm?'

'What?' said Vera, suddenly unsure.

'That young guy. He's called Peter, right?'

'What?'

Not bothering to dry his face, Adam looked at her searchingly. 'When I came to see you in the winter I felt like he was challenging me. Apparently he won.'

I'm not a prize to be won! I have a will of my own! The whole thing with Peter was confused and complicated, and she wasn't ready to talk about it. Particularly not with Adam.

'He brought you food rich in iron!' He sounded accusatory. 'That's what a husband does! That's what I used to do!'

She could think of quite a few things Adam had never done that she now knew she wanted a husband to do, *and that* she *wanted to do with him*! She felt herself turning red.

'I heard it when you paused, you know!' He hung his head again. 'You said that he was your closest... and then after a couple of seconds you said neighbor. Your closest!' he moaned.

Yes. He's already got closer to me than you ever have, she

438

thought. He had seen her true self; he had made her quake inside and released an uninhibited wildness that Adam had no idea existed. But she didn't want to rub salt into his wounds.

'Does it really matter? If it isn't Peter then it will be someone else. Because, Adam, think about what I – and you too – think about what we've missed out on! It's the same big problem with our whole civilization. We think you can separate everything, chop reality and life up into little pieces. We think we can separate the economy from the environment, what we do now from what happens later, how we live here in Sweden from what happens to people elsewhere. But everything is connected, and denying it is just a dangerous lie. I met some indigenous people in Colombia...'

It's unbelievable! I haven't even told him! What a complete breakdown in communication...

She started over, trying to bridge the months of silence.

'The Kogi people live in the mountains of northern Colombia, and they have a completely different view of the world, and of God, than the one we grew up with. For them, there's no border between the physical and the spiritual; they're two sides of the same coin. And now I'm sure they're right – that's the way it is and should be!'

She thought about what she had experienced just a few hours ago – the glorious sense that the body can love just as the soul can – or, more correctly, she thought about desire ad infinitum and felt the muscles in her loins respond – *the soul love that is also... We shall not want.* Desire ran along her spine.

'My decision is about me. I want a man who doesn't need therapy to want me or be faithful to me.'

The decision, like the glorious night that had helped her make it, was crystal clear. But the feelings that followed were clouded with contradictions. She checked her phone after she left the Henningssons'. She hadn't missed anything; he still hadn't called, not even sent a text. *What did Friday night really mean?* He said they would get together today! Was it just a line? An effort to make his rejection of her a little less cruel? If so, maybe she should just stay in the village with her Dad rather than go back to the dorm.

A feeling of terrible loss descended upon her.

49

Peter took the night train to Stockholm for Monday's board meeting, not because it was cheaper, but because he felt like it. He wanted to stay on the ground, to travel sustainably. He wanted to experience the distance; see the forests, fields, bogs and villages appear and disappear in the golden light from the northern night sun shining through the train window. *Vännäs, Anundsjö, Mellansel, Långsele.* Perhaps most importantly, he couldn't spend another night alone in his bed.

The astrologer had said that he and Vera needed to become more alike. He had felt that it was true and that they should meet happily in the middle. Instead, it was as if they had changed places – she had become how he used to be, and he was like her. If so, it was a sad irony. Yet he also took comfort in the fact that, if it were true, at least he was the winner. He had turned into the sort of person he admired. He had wanted to be worthy of an Elf, and if he had started to be like Vera had been… Didn't that mean that *he* could be an Elf?

As the train rolled into Stockholm's central station early on Monday morning and he prepared to disembark, Peter promised himself that at today's board meeting he would act in a way that he could admire.

✼

Lennart was standing under the crystal chandelier hanging from the vaulted ceiling in Great Escape's office when Peter came in. The first thing he said when he saw Peter was, 'I saw you at that press conference.'

'Really?' Peter was surprised.

'It was broadcast live on the public service station.'

'Oh.'

'What did you say about Iceland? Why are things precarious?'

'Because the Icelandic banks have assets that are close to 10 times bigger than Iceland's GDP. They attract capital from the whole world by promising a good interest rate on deposits. They've managed to create a dangerously large and risky finance sector.'

Uncle Ernst, impeccably dressed in a dark suit and red tie, looked at his nephew with interest as he poured himself a cup of black coffee.

'Yes, and as I've said before, the population of Iceland is about the same as Norrbotten's.' He looked at his younger brother. 'Perhaps your son has answered your question about the tulip bulbs.'

'But a Nordic bank has to have a stable deposit insurance guarantee, doesn't it?' said Lennart sternly.

'How much money do you actually have in Iceland?' asked Ernst, although he didn't seem surprised when Lennart ignored the question.

Elegant bone china coffee cups in hand, the successful Stavenius brothers crossed the expensive carpet on their way to the boardroom. Peter knew that Barbro didn't approve; coffee stains on the light-blue carpet always ended up being her problem, but today she was off sick.

Lennart put his cup down beside his papers on the dark oak table. He looked at his son critically and said: 'But what the hell was that about forbidding naked CDSs? Don't you know that's your cousin's bread and butter?'

'Yes, I know,' answered Peter, who actually regretted not going further at the press conference. *Why not forbid all CDSs? Why not at least simplify the derivatives market, regulate and supervise it like the stock market?* But he knew that now was not the time to pose such questions.

'Are you so damned envious?' sniffed Lennart, turning towards his brother. 'I have to apologize for him; I tried to raise him to earn his own money, but he seems to spend most of his time trying to undermine others who have actually succeeded. Speaking of which, is Charlie coming?'

'Yes, he's on his way.'

The room filled up with the other board members, all of whom were eager to greet Lennart and Ernst, so Peter clenched his teeth and took his seat. He had always known that it would be a thankless task. He nodded at his cousin, who arrived last and shut the door before taking his seat.

As the meeting proceeded, Peter let his eyes scan the gold-framed awards that decorated the room. Great Escape had received considerable recognition and distinction over the years. He noticed a magazine on the sideboard. It was open to the page with the watch ad featuring Lennart and his Cessna in the Himalayas. It gave Peter sudden inspiration.

Look for similarities that illustrate what's important!

He wrote a few words on one of his papers and decided to reorganize his whole presentation. He wasn't going to do an ordinary SWOT analysis. He would start by proposing a new travel destination!

When they reached agenda item number 9, *Revision of Risk Analysis*, the chair looked at Peter and nodded. Peter picked up the magazine and held it up for all to see. 'I'm not sure how many times I've seen this. Imagine seeing your father in various quality magazines under the heading: "People do not decide to become extraordinary. They decide to accomplish extraordinary things."' He paused so that the men around the table had time to absorb the challenging words.

'I've been very privileged; not everyone is fortunate enough to be able to feel such pride,' he added, noting that Lennart had straightened up a bit, both surprised and flattered, but also a bit wary.

'All of us can be proud of the innovative thinking that has characterized Great Escape over the years; we've been pioneers and trailblazers. We've been ahead of our time, creating trends rather than following them. This has allowed us to develop a feel for the future, for what will be in demand in the years ahead. In this spirit, I ask all of you to imagine a new Great Escape. The journey starts in Chile: a fully rigged sailboat heads straight out to sea. We're following in the footsteps of the Dutch explorer

Jacob Roggeveen. It took him 17 days to make the trip, but with our modern sailboat we can make it in… maybe 2 weeks?'

The men in the room glanced at each other incredulously and Lennart frowned.

'Two weeks! Before you even reach the destination? Impossible.'

'Hold on. I said imagine,' said Peter calmly. 'Our destination is far out at sea. A small, triangle-shaped volcanic island sheltering a mystery that has inspired the most unbelievable stories. Because when we get there, we see a sandy, beige, windblown speck of land where a couple of thousand inhabitants support themselves by fishing near the shore in leaky canoes.'

'So what's so special about the place?' wondered Birger, the oldest board member. 'An impoverished pile of sand in the middle of the Pacific Ocean?'

'Well. It's a pile of sand in the middle of the Pacific that's decorated with 393 artfully carved, carefully arranged stone statues, most of them about 16 feet high and weighing 10 tons, but many significantly higher and heavier. And the biggest stone platform weighs 9,000 tons.'

'Who put them there?' asked Charlie.

'Quite! Not the Museum of Modern Art, that's for sure!' smiled Peter. 'That was the mystery when the Europeans discovered the island on Easter Day 1722. In the language of Easter Island's people, the statues are called Moai. The Moai mystery has given rise to all kinds of explanations, from Heyerdal's Kon-Tiki theory that a civilization of South American tribal people made them, to Von Däniken's assertion that the gigantic figures with their huge heads could only have been made and placed around the island by stranded aliens, who were subsequently rescued from the barren Pacific island and taken back to outer space.'

Amused chuckling spread around the polished oak table.

'Von Däniken, remember?' whispered Birger to Ernst. 'Everybody had pyramids in their basements, and razorblades stored in them supposedly miraculously sharpened themselves?'

'But archeologists did their job. They asked the people living on the island what had happened, and it turned out to be pretty easy to figure out the truth,' said Peter. 'If you follow the transportation routes that still exist, up towards the crater of the volcano, you can see the trail for yourself. Here's a statue left on the road, and then, further along, up in the quarry... Imagine a factory that was suddenly abandoned. You find almost 400 other statues at various stages of construction. The biggest is 70 feet tall and weighs close to 300 tons. On the ground you discover hammers, pickaxes, drills and trash. Even a bone from a finger was found crushed under a statue that had fallen.'

There was silence around the table. Peter walked over to the window and looked out on the traffic below before turning his attention back to the dark-suited men.

'It wasn't the Incas. It definitely wasn't aliens from outer space. It was Polynesians who had successfully colonized the island from the west. They had found a leafy green oasis where they could raise chickens and find food in the wild. There was a rich forest with the world's largest palm trees, and it provided them with both food and materials for building ocean-worthy canoes that enabled them to fish far away from land. It was home to Polynesia's greatest variety of bird species. Quite simply, it was something of a paradise.' Peter looked at the faces around the table. 'They used the limited amount of fresh water available on the island to grow crops in the soil that volcanic eruptions had made fertile, and they succeeded in producing a surplus of food. The population increased to almost 20,000, and not everyone was needed in agriculture. They divided into different clans, each of whom owned a little slice of the island. They were industrious and hard working. For 300 years, a quarter of the island's food went to the people who worked on the statues. They carved, transported and – with the help of timber and ropes made of bark – erected increasingly grandiose images of their progenitors in a competition to determine which clan had the highest status and greatest piety.'

Ernst looked uncomfortable, cleared his throat and took a sip of water, but he let him continue.

'The statues appear as they do today because Westerners brought cranes to the island and erected them again. When

Roggeveen found them, they had been toppled and vandalized,' said Peter as he returned to his seat.

'Why?' wondered Sigurd Holm, the grey-haired accountant who had been stuck with the unpopular task of keeping the minutes in Barbro's absence.

'What would you do if you had struggled year after year to erect the highest and finest statue because that's what everyone else was doing, because that was what everybody said you should do, only to discover that it led to catastrophe?' Peter looked directly at his father. The silence was oppressive and Peter turned back to the pallid Mr Holm.

'Sometime during the 17th century, the inhabitants rose up in revolt and toppled all the statues. But it wasn't particularly constructive and they reacted too late. When the forest was gone, the island couldn't support them, and they didn't have any lumber left to construct new ocean-worthy canoes capable of crossing long distances. So they starved. They couldn't stay warm at night. They were vulnerable to disease. They waged war on each other. In only a few decades, they had almost died out. Only a remnant of a people remained to greet Roggeveen and his crew when they arrived on the island.'

'Yes, well,' said Lennart after a pause. 'And why are you telling us all this?'

'Don't you think it would be a very instructive journey for our customers?' asked Peter. 'Unsettling, unforgettable. Like our adventures usually are, but more so. You could see it as a risk analysis for the whole planet. What can happen if you engage in…' He looked at his well-dressed cousin. 'A short-sighted and false game to earn status and glory, completely unrelated to what we really need.' Charlie looked as though he had been struck; Ernst was fiddling with his gavel. Peter knew he was hanging by a thread; he needed to get to the point. He got up again, suddenly enthusiastic.

'My point is that we can be part of the solution! What's happening under the surface determines the future. The rules of the game are going to change; they have to change. We can be prepared for a world without *externalities*, I mean, when the price

445

of everything, all goods and services, reflects their true cost. And in that situation, the solution is to meet people's needs using the smallest possible amount of resources. It's our moral obligation, but also critical for success in the future. It won't be painless, but it's better than what will happen if we don't change!'

'What, exactly, are you talking about? In concrete terms?' Birger asked, looking at him from under his bushy, old-man eyebrows.

'In concrete terms? When things cost what they actually cost, we're going to have to live in smartly planned cities, where we walk and bike more and drive less. We'll transport ourselves in electric vehicles or ones that run on biofuels. We'll travel more by train. We'll have better cars and boats. We'll fly less, but air travel will be more efficient. We'll eat more vegetarian food. Much less beef. We'll minimize waste, insulate our homes better. We simply can't afford to ruin the planet and renewable energy will replace finite and polluting...'

'But none of that has anything to do with us, this board of directors!' interrupted Lennart in irritation.

'Well, of course, it's comforting to think so, but it isn't true. It has to do with everybody and with what everybody does!' Peter turned towards the whiteboard and drew a circle at the top. 'Why are we in business? What's our vision? What do we want to give our customers? And when we have answered those questions...' He drew an arrow pointing at the circle. 'How can we create it using as few resources as possible?' He pointed to the circle and wrote an 'R' inside it. 'We sell recreation, memorable escapes from the routines of everyday life. What are the Great Escapes of the future?' He looked at the picture of Indiana-Jones-Lennart in the magazine again, and then at his audience. 'That's what we need to aim for. What are the extraordinary accomplishments of the future?'

'The future Great Escape is to the moon. Do you have any idea how much we have invested in spectacular journeys?' Lennart had raised his voice. '*Travel*, Peter. You say that people have to travel less, shorter distances, non-extravagantly. The whole point is that it requires *lots* of resources; it's extravagant;

it's something only the richest can afford!'

Peter pulled out his chair, but remained standing.

'But what about the example you always use, about the consumer-appliance giants? The one that thought it was in the ice business went bankrupt, but the one that realized it was selling coldness prospered. I think that we sell new experiences, unusual recreation, and we can continue to do that in a resource-efficient economy!'

'You know perfectly well that we sell status!' Lennart shot back.

'Okay,' said Peter willingly, holding up his hands. 'We sell status. What gives status in the future? What kind of people will we admire? We just need to be creative, think in new ways. Because we can't escape the truth that the most important commandment in the future is going to be: "Thou shall not waste!"'

Peter sat down. He felt his adrenaline rush dip. Uncle Ernst looked at his expensive watch and announced it was time to break for lunch. Peter felt as though he had sworn in church. The men rose from their chairs hastily, obviously relieved to flee the uncomfortable atmosphere in the boardroom.

Lennart was the last one out. He looked at his son with an ominously dark expression.

'Escape is my company, and after what just came out of your mouth, the only conclusion I can draw is that it will *never* be yours!'

The look Lennart gave him was like a slap in the face, and the ominous pronouncement startled him. He felt like he was falling, swirling around in a broth of mixed feelings. The first was worry. *How the hell is it possible?* There are so many obvious signs that we're moving in the wrong direction. *How can he choose not to see? 'The future Great Escape is to the moon'!* He thought about the captain of the Titanic, standing there with the warning about the iceberg in his hand, but still ordering the crew to continue full speed ahead. He also felt disappointment spiced with the old sense of being rejected, a good-for-nothing. *Father doesn't think I'm a suitable heir.* So who gets my share? It ought to be Vicky and Sofia. Half each?

And yet at the same time he felt a sense of freedom; a large part of him was strangely untroubled by the great loss his father had just announced. Peter had done what he could. He had said what was in his heart and the rest was up to those with power.

On the way to the restaurant for lunch, the two cousins walked together side by side, slightly behind the other board members.

Charlie looked at him. 'What the hell is up with you? What were you going on about back there?'

'Well, the story about Rapa Nui…'

'Rapper who?' grinned Charlie.

'I don't know how the hell you pronounce it, but whatever. The island is called something like that in Polynesian. Easter Island is what Europeans call it. The whole lesson from Rapa Nui is about striving after the wrong goals. The risks of doing so.' *Pseudo*, thought Peter and looked at his cousin questioningly. 'For example, we can earn tons of money, but will it make us happy?'

Charlie kicked at a stone on the sidewalk and Peter grabbed him by the shoulder, forcing him to stop and look at him.

'If you hang out with thrill-seekers in the City, play with other people's money all day, snort cocaine and visit prostitutes all night, does it make you happy? Does it give you what you *really* want? What you really need?'

Charlie looked at his cousin solemnly. He seemed to restrain himself and then blinked and looked down at the ground. They resumed walking in order to catch up with the others.

When they were alone in the restaurant's subdued, dusky coatroom Charlie looked at Peter. White-faced, he asked him, 'How do you know?'

'What?' asked Peter.

'That it's all just fake, that I'm just playing.' Charlie sighed in frustration, and spat, 'All I'm doing is trying to keep the mask in place!'

'But you told me!'

'I told you?' Charlie looked at him skeptically.

'Yes.' *Hadn't he basically come right out with it? 'Forget*

448

productivity. Sell unrealistic promises in a pyramid scheme so you can earn 70 million in a year.'

'Was it when we got drunk? Did I also say it's my boss?' groaned Charlie in despair.

'Huh?'

'That it's my boss. I'm hopelessly in love with my boss.'

'Uh, no, you didn't say that. Are you... unhappily in love?' In the scenario he conjured up in his mind, he recognized himself more than Charlie could imagine and grinned wryly. 'Is she a happily married mother of three or what?'

Charlie winced and rubbed his hands over his face in humiliation.

'No, no. Not married. So I ... I didn't say anything then.'

'What?'

Charlie looked warily at Peter. 'We don't have any female bosses at the firm.'

It was quiet for a second, and Peter felt like an idiot when he finally understood.

'It's a *him*?' Peter heard that his tone was all wrong, and Charlie seemed to shrink as if he had been punched in the stomach.

'Fuck! Yeah, you get it. I can't even accept it myself. So I can't do anything about it except try to... repress it. Forget. Stop feeling. Play hard, indifferent. Psychopath, that's me. But he's so damned good, a good person right in the middle of the hysterical insanity.'

He looked pleadingly at Peter, who nodded awkwardly.

'And I've always known, really,' continued Charlie. 'With girls, things have never exactly taken off. I've never really felt engaged. Except as friends. They can be great friends. Really great.' Charlie crossed his arms over his chest, closed his eyes and pressed them hard with his left thumb and finger.

Peter took a deep breath and tried to get control of his feelings before continuing. He didn't want to make his cousin any sadder.

'If you're gay, then you have to just allow yourself to be gay. And if you love him – maybe you should just tell him. The most important thing is to be true to yourself, because otherwise you

449

dry up, or die inside, and then you just crumble. You become like dead wood,' said Peter, thinking about Ivar and how he had rested his powerful arm on Peter's shoulder. The human warmth of the men in Vera's family. *Someone who's good enough.*

'Damn it! I know!' said Charlie, head hanging and arms still crossed protectively in front of him. 'I've been really successful, and it was fun for a while, but now I'm just exhausted and basically feel like... "Yeah? So? What now?" I can buy whatever I want, but I've realized that what I really want isn't for sale. Like David. Like time. More time, more sleep, more rest.'

Peter put his arm around the man who, over the years, had been the closest thing to a big brother he'd ever had. *More time?* He thought about the ice floe gliding silently, the old man he had met in the winter garden. 'You're right about that. Life itself is passing all the time...' He hugged Charlie encouragingly. 'We're all allowed to be ourselves as long as we don't hurt anyone else. That goes for you too!'

Charlie gave a small smile and straightened up, as if to shake off the embarrassing gesture of closeness that was so uncharacteristic of the Stavenius family.

'To think you're the one who gets me,' he mumbled.

I don't get you at all! thought Peter. *How can you seriously promise 12-per-cent risk-free interest on US mortgages?*

Peter squeezed his cousin's neck, a playful gesture from their youth, and asked, 'In your job, do you have any idea about the quality of the ingredients in the mix that you repackage and sell? Given the demand for your "product" it seems like they've started to turn green and stink.'

Charlie looked at him, silent and unreadable. Peter went on.

'The "ingredients" in your product are US mortgages, and credit-worthy borrowers dried up a long time ago. So what do the sellers do? They go out and pick up any sap they can find who is willing and able to sign on the dotted line. "Want to borrow a million dollars, live in a luxury condo we're building in the middle of nowhere? If things don't work out, you can just leave the keys with the bank and take off." I mean, damn it, Charlie, the whole system is full of sick incentives!' *And that includes yours!*

Peter felt an unusually strong sense of outrage and tried to calm himself before continuing.

'I've come to realize that I don't understand you at all. What are you really all about?'

Charlie looked away, but Peter couldn't let it go.

'It just doesn't make sense, because I find it hard to believe that you're some kind of machine without a conscience! Are you like a kid, trusting the grown-ups and doing what they say in the hope that you'll be rewarded with candy?' Peter took hold of his cousin's shoulders as if he were going to shake him to wake him up.

'Charlie, *we're* the grown-ups now! You have every right to be gay, to live happily with David if that's what you two want. But the game you're playing with the future hurts other people. You know that you guys are making promises you can't keep; talk about overselling and underdelivering! In the long run, what you're doing has implications for the maintenance of humanity. Damn it, Charlie! That's just not okay!'

He forced himself to stop. Charlie suddenly looked so exhausted that Peter almost regretted his words. He lowered his voice and looked pleadingly at his cousin.

'What I really mean is that we need you. People like you have knowledge that can help close the gigantic casino. *Deadly fucking chicken racers,* Charlie!'

He let his cousin go, took a deep breath and paced up and down to release the surplus energy his outburst had created in him. Charlie headed towards the room where lunch was being served. He walked stiffly, like an old man. Peter whispered as they walked.

'You know what money and love have in common, don't you?'

Charlie shook his head, eyes wandering timidly around the dining room they were walking through. Today he didn't want any heads to turn towards them.

'They're both built on trust,' said Peter calmly, as Charlie turned to look at him. 'If trust is well founded then the economy, or the relationship, can grow and blossom stably. If it isn't well founded, then sooner or later a crisis will erupt, a crisis of confidence. And if it is really bad, then the whole thing will break apart.'

Charlie clenched his teeth, avoided Peter's gaze and opened the door to the separate room where the other board members were already sitting, linen napkins on their laps.

And destroy everything around it too, realized Peter as he watched his cousin dejectedly take his seat.

Peter had felt strong all morning, but now a painful thought returned. *Destroy everything.* Once again he was deeply conscious of the fact that he was suffering from a Vera-shaped hole in his body.

✖

When Peter got back to the dorm, Vera still wasn't there.

'I don't think she's back from Vindeln,' said Lotten, who was in the middle of packing.

'Do you know what karma is?' asked Peter on impulse.

'I think it's something Asian, like, from Buddhism or Hinduism,' she said.

'Yeah, but what does it mean?'

Matt's door opened, and Peter saw tall, blond Lotten cast an appreciative look at the dishevelled Englishman with the bronze-colored stubble. And Peter also noticed that Matt seemed different. He tried to figure out what it was. Did he usually go around unshaven? Peter noticed something else. Matt's shirtsleeves were rolled up and he was wearing dark brown leather bracelets around his wrist. Did he usually wear them?

'Do *you* know what karma is?' asked Lotten, looking at Matt with her light eyes.

'Karma? That what you do influences your future, what goes around comes around,' said Matt and looked at Peter. 'It's poetic justice, like in the song you're always playing. "You only get what you give!"'

Peter realized that Matt did look different, but it didn't have anything to do with what he was wearing. It came from within. He was relaxed but imperturbable, surrounded by an aura of secret, happy knowledge. *So damned much a man*, Peter thought, feeling a sense of inferiority.

Toby came in from outside, and he also seemed to notice a change in Matt.

'How's it going?' asked the police candidate from Skellefteå.

Matt thrust his leather-adorned hand into the pocket of his jeans and looked steadily at Toby. 'Sweet.'

Peter was suddenly filled with a feeling that was overwhelming and unbearable. He fled the dorm, jumped onto his bike and took off, away from Ålidhem. It was only now that he fully realized what he had invested, the risk he had only dared to take because he had believed that if Vera was anything, she was reliable. What he had wanted the whole time was a woman that you stayed with because she made you feel good. He had thought she was one, like an Elf, and that's why he had dared to start loving her. And he still did – no matter how foolish and masochistic it was.

Obviously he had known that there would always be other guys who would want to be with her, the prettiest, smartest girl in any room. The Elf with the dimples. But he had expected that she would turn them down in favor of a chosen one. He had taken it as a given. It was devastating to realize that he had been wrong. And he kept returning to the unpleasant ethical dilemma. Could he accept that Vera had done what he used to do? Could he leave it and move on?

Without thinking about it he had cycled to the lake. He parked and walked down the path he had shared with Vera, remembering the wonderful summer day last Thursday. Today the weather was grey, windier. *It can definitely be called poetic justice.* Peter understood that he was experiencing the same feelings he had caused in many others, perhaps Linda in particular. Yet there was something about that line of thinking that felt wrong. Full of frustrated energy, he threw a flat rock and watched it sink rather than skip across the surface of the water. That's when he realized the flaw in his thinking. Yes, she had had alcohol in her system, and yes, she was probably filled with unsatisfied physical desire. But would Vera really hop into bed with the first guy she happened to see, just because she could?

Peter had reached the pavilion. That had been his destination, because he thought it might make him feel better. But the happy memory of her here, right in front of him – talking about his scar in a way that would forever change how he thought about it – was brutally overshadowed by the images flashing through his mind. Peter saw Matt in front of him, Matt as he had looked today, with his hairy chest now private behind his buttoned-up shirt, and he suddenly remembered words from another time.

'Not all of them prefer you, you know.'

With rising dread Peter thought about what he knew about Vera and Matt, how they laughed and cooked together, sat up late at night, how he had noticed her, helped her, how she had stroked his hair – *how he instinctively seemed to have understood Rule Number One!* – and an even more terrible thought came to him. Maybe it was the drunken hours with Peter that represented Vera's little adventure into his old life? Because, of course, Matt wasn't just the first guy she happened to bump into. Maybe what Vera had done with *Peter* had been – the idea was physically painful – *just a meaningless drunken fling before she realized that it was Matt she wanted.*

It didn't matter that Peter had top-notch head-turn quotient, or that he was actually a little older and quite a bit bigger than Matt. He'd been out-Alphaed just the same. *'Very manly, I think.'*

Pained, Peter remembered that there was something deeply enviable about how Matt had stood there in the dorm. Something about his posture, the look in his eye. And the word he had said, which burned through Peter like an instrument of torture.

Sweet.

One word. Matt said nothing more about the obviously life-changing secret he was keeping. He just stood there, brandishing his radiant happiness and integrity like a shield. Had Matt now become an Elf? Peter heard thunder in the distance and his legs gave out. He sat down on the wooden bench in the pavilion, immersed in the heartbreaking, but all too plausible, possibility that Matt was her chosen one.

Both Peter and Matt had shared the delusion that Peter and the guys in *The Game* had something to teach Matt about love, but in reality it had been the other way around. Because why wouldn't she choose him? He had done the right thing from the beginning, been kind and considerate, waited for her and not attracted crap karma.

Poetic justice. Peter bent over, buried his face in his hands and sobbed.

I have to get away from here.

Jaws clenched tight, struggling against the sorrow, he forced himself to return to his bike and ride home. He didn't notice the falling temperature or that it had started to drizzle. He had only one thought in his head. *I have to shut myself in my room and be alone.*

Relieved that nobody saw him return, he retreated to his room and locked the door. But the sight of the bed where Vera, in all her beauty, had lain on Friday hit him like a punch in the stomach. The rain was loud against the windowpane. He fell weakly onto the bed; rolled over and grabbed the sheet. He pulled it to his face and breathed deeply, trying unsuccessfully to capture a hint of her scent. He gave in to his feelings and let the tears flow.

For some reason, he came to think about the difference between the top drawers of the desks in his two boyhood bedrooms. At his mother's house he had a handmade sable-hair brush, an inkstone, ink and elegant rice paper. The drawer at his father's was overflowing with stuff. Some of it was probably okay, but most of it was cheap junk that he had got at McDonald's when he was little, broken plastic things with poisonous, dead batteries in them.

Hazardous waste.

The calligraphy drawer was like Vera, and the drawer at his father's was like all the other women he'd had sex with. Not that there had been anything wrong with them; the basic problem was that his 'why not' attitude to all of it now felt like a 'no' to everything precious. If he could turn back the clock, knowing what he knew now, he would willingly avoid the junk. But what was done couldn't be undone.

And Friday night couldn't be undone either.

The precious hours during which he had held her close were

now a cruel memory – a heartbreaking glimpse of what he had lost. The pain was unbearable. His feelings for Vera were not a game. It was as if his nerves and blood vessels had reached out to her, entwined themselves in her, and now she had been ripped away, leaving deep, open wounds. He no longer had what he needed most. He had been mutilated. Torn in half. He had given her his heart, and she had crushed it, and perhaps it was all his fault.

He remembered the only time he had seen hardness in her green eyes. *If people deserve it, then others trust them.*

Lightning lit up the grey sky and the rumble of thunder was powerful. His body shook with spasms of despair. He remembered how he had wanted nothing more than to be sensitive to Vera, and he still felt unable to suppress his strong desire to be everything she wanted and needed. But no matter what he did, he could never be Matt – brown-eyed, shaggy, and with an innocent past that was a stable platform for his newly won integrity. Peter rolled over on his back and warm rivers of tears ran down his face as he thought that Matt was a better choice. To stay with him would make her feel good.

He is a good man.

50

A stupid person is someone who causes damage to another person, or a group of people, without any advantage accruing to himself (or herself) – or even with some resultant self-damage.

The Third Basic Law of Human Stupidity, Carlo M Cipolla

When Vera arrived at Cissi's brightly colored attic apartment, she discovered that Freddie was visiting. He was leaning over Cissi, jacket open, reading along with her from a paper on the little kitchen table.

'Hi Freddie,' smiled Vera. 'How's it going?'

The lanky teenager stood up straight, smiled back at Vera and said, 'Hi, yeah, great!'

'His Gandhi essay was a hit!' said Cissi proudly, holding it up to show Vera what they had been reading. 'Look here! A+! "Interesting thesis – nonviolence as love."'

'Really?' said Vera, and immediately realized that she sounded surprised. 'I mean, well done! Nobody can say you didn't work hard for it.' She looked through the essay. *But Gandhi?* That was unexpected. She read further. *Satyagraha – insistence on truth. The unbreakable spirit of love. Soul force.*

Freddie looked at Vera proudly as he collected his essay. 'There is no path to peace. Peace is the path!' he called, his voice echoing in the hallway before he slammed the door on his way out.

A tall, slim vase containing a large red rose with a card tied to the stem decorated the table. The flower cheered Vera. Ever since Cissi had told her about Joakim, Vera had thought it was a real shame that they had split up. She of all people knew that such a relationship should not be taken for granted. What an unnecessary waste!

'Is it from Jocke?' asked Vera curiously.

'Huh? No,' said Cissi.

'You know, don't you, that what he said was wrong?'

'What?'

'It doesn't matter... how slim, how thin you are. Natural breasts don't point upwards if you're on your back, they flatten out and hang down sideways. I know, because Adam says that you can always tell if breasts are fake by feeling them, but you shouldn't be able to tell by looking at them. I mean, if the surgeon is good, there's only one tell-tale sign they're fake – they don't move, no matter what. They point straight up even when the woman is on her back. So either Jocke had been with someone who'd had plastic surgery or he watched silicone porn.' Feeling a need finally to let go of her painful secret, she continued: 'Or maybe he was like Adam, both at the same time...'

'What are you talking about?' asked Cissi incredulously.

'You know, when I was here in the fall, and you said that you can't fool your body...'

Cissi nodded and Vera told her about catching Adam on the coffee table with an unfamiliar, silicone blonde; loud, strangely choreographed group sex visible on the screen in front of them.

'That's the worst thing I've ever heard!' said Cissi.

'Do you remember when I told you about sitting on the bus with Adam in the fall, when I started to feel so sick that I threw up in a bin for dog shit?'

'Yes, I remember...'

'I tried not to, but it was impossible. The song playing on the bus made me think of that woman on the table and everything. It was that "Don't you wish your girlfriend was hot like me" song.'

'Right,' said Cissi grimly.

Vera stood with her arms crossed and looked sorrowfully out at the playground, which was full of children. Cissi came closer and looked at her kindly.

'You know what they say – "it's no surprise I felt sick; my stomach was full of vomit".'

Vera laughed. 'No, I've never heard that one before!'

458

Cissi continued. 'You can also say, "it's no surprise you threw up, if you put your head in..."' She paused and looked at Vera. 'Don't do it.'

'I promise. Never again!' Vera smiled wryly and they stood quietly, observing the activity in the playground. Then Vera said, 'And maybe you should tell Jocke how things really were?'

'You mean I should have spoken Giraffe?'

'What?'

'I just read about it in Freddie's essay. An American psychologist who teaches people to communicate in a nonviolent way, with big ears and eyes and a soft muzzle – like a giraffe. So you say: "When you say that, then I feel sad because I think you mean that..." And then you say what you think. And then at the end you say – "I would like you to..." And you say how you wish things were instead.'

'Yes! Exactly! You could say, "I wish you appreciated my breasts as they are". And Jocke needs to hear that too. I mean, it's just like with the Titanic and the global economy – as big as possible isn't the same thing as good.'

'Yes, I know. I'm not completely stupid. I understand what happened now. He said something stupid, and I got scared. I thought it signalled some kind of irrevocable loss, and so I said things that made it so. An irrevocable end.' Cissi sighed.

Vera winced at Cissi's words, but also felt her brain working, searching for something. She looked meditatively out of the window until she realized why Cissi's words sounded familiar. It was like her mother being afraid that Adam's family didn't think the Lundbergs were respectable enough. So she went to their house and acted in a way that probably turned her fear into reality. And all of it was caused by a fear that, as far as Vera knew, was completely unfounded.

'Yeah, there's some truth in that. Sometimes we create what we are most afraid of,' said Vera with a sense of discovery.

Cissi smiled sadly. 'You know what I think Peter would say, if he were here?'

'No.' *Peter...* Those two syllables were sufficient to awaken an anxious longing in her. *If he were here.*

'He would say that because we're afraid of being poor in the future, we let the finance guys create pseudo-growth now in an effort to avoid it. But since pseudo-growth borrows from the future and uses finite resources, it will actually make us poorer in the future.'

Vera was captivated by what Cissi said. 'That's exactly right!'

She was filled with a sense of exploratory playfulness and felt relieved to be experiencing a kind of happiness that didn't remind her too much of Peter. *Yes! Let's play 'find the pattern!'* She let her thoughts roam free, and they raced like a thoroughbred over green, wide-open spaces. It was fascinating. She saw patterns in everything, even in the apparently unrelated.

'Do you remember what I said about resistance? We're afraid of disease, so we overuse antibiotics. The result is that we have even greater reason to fear infectious diseases.' *Infectious diseases. My feverish Prometheus. Apparently she couldn't keep herself from bringing him into it!* The shining memory of Peter's caressing hand around her unusual ear – and the joy she had felt when he said that her ears were particularly lovely – gave Vera even more evidence for her theory.

'How many people get plastic surgery because they're afraid that they won't be considered attractive as they are? So they have an operation and turn their fear into reality. I mean, after they've had the operation, there's no "as they are" left to consider attractive.'

It was a censored and abstract way to put it, but Cissi understood. 'Like Michael Jackson? Who went from healthy-looking black man to looking like a sickly, chalk-white woman?'

'Yes, exactly.' Vera also thought about Adam and what Cissi said she wanted to say to Woody Allen. *It's basically a matter of how they've practised.* Was the root of Adam's problem that the boy who had grown up 'lost' feared that sex was sinful? It started with a fear, and then he thought it was a fact, so he snuck away guiltily with his desire, away from the person he wanted to live with, and imprinted it on another object. *And so behaved in such a way that he became lost.*

To me, anyway.

She felt a sharp relapse of the old pain – *but it was him; and it was then; I have the rest of my life ahead of me*. She forced herself to stop dwelling on it, climbed out of the abyss of regret and let her thoughts run free again, striving for a bird's eye view. She sensed that this wasn't a trivial problem for humanity.

'We could sit here all day coming up with examples of destructive, self-fulfilling prophecies.' That was it! The essence of the pattern, the least common denominator. *Destructive, self-fulfilling prophecies*. Having reached the finishing line, the thoroughbred slowed down and lowered its frisky, swishing tail to rest. Despite the glorious feeling of letting her thoughts run wild, Vera suddenly felt like something had been missing.

'We have a lot to work with when we think together.'

She had always loved to think long and hard, to solve problems, but it never used to elevate her pulse. Cissi was no mean thoroughbred either. But it was *his* gaze that had created a private universe. She no longer corralled her thoughts, staying within the boundaries of the logic defined by 'these are the given conditions, make the diagnosis and solve the problem'. She was no longer the submissive nurse who knew her place and bit her tongue rather than question authority. When Peter had rushed along beside her, it had spurred her to reach further, dare more and see more clearly than ever before. It was as if he thought that they were capable of comprehending the incomprehensible – and so they did!

She also realized why she had never dared to liberate herself fully before. It could actually be unpleasant to be herself, and not just because she provoked people. What they had discovered was a heavy burden, a weighty responsibility. If the ability to understand the world was a gift, how were you supposed to have the strength to bear it? She realized that Peter – outspoken, open and gloriously willing to change – had influenced her to aim high, to dare to strive to reach her potential. Secure in the knowledge that a wholehearted effort was good enough, she had blossomed. She no longer censored herself through fear of what others would think or feel.

She had dared to develop her ideas fully. Peter had been at least as brave in his effort to glean answers from the top of the economic hierarchy, the elite in the world of finance. Cissi had successfully challenged her employer. They had drawn their conclusions, written them down and defended them. And it had felt fantastic! Vera decided that she would write to Basic Needs in northern Colombia, and ask the organization for an important favor. She wanted to contact Kogi Mama and thank him for the task he had given her. She had only just begun, but her antenna was back, she was re-anchored to her inner compass, the nerve of energy at her core. Everything was meaningful in the most fundamental way – whatever happened, there was meaning in her having lived.

She thought about what she had said to Adam – that he was limping along, an incoherent patchwork quilt of contradictions – and realized that she could just as easily have said it about herself. How could the world ever be better if those who really wanted to bring about change refused to risk hurting someone or exposing themselves to criticism? It was only now that she was a coherent whole that she dared to devote herself fully to the task of making the world better. Gone was the gnawing frustration that she hadn't quite found her way, the feeling that she wasn't devoting herself to the right things.

She remembered something she had read a long time ago about how Western aid workers could be seen to be standing beside a rapidly flowing river, trying to rescue drowning babies without asking themselves what or who was upstream throwing in the babies *in the first place*. At the time, she had felt insulted, as if it were an attack, but after she had met Kogi Mama she understood the criticism much better. And she, Peter and Cissi had looked upstream – *Koyaanisqatsi* – and tried to do something about it. Vera had no idea if what they had written and said would have any impact on the world, but she felt the potential, the pay-off in terms of a better future that could come about if enough people understood and did things in new, more far-sighted ways.

She was pulled back to the present by Cissi speaking to her from the kitchenette. 'Jocke and me... did I create what I was afraid of?' Her expression was thoughtful but grim. 'Well, in that case I would say it was a co-production. I contributed, but I didn't start it. Yes, I know I sound like a little kid, but it felt crap! It wasn't like we were at the store and he said that I ought to give up pizza and sausage in favor of Weightwatchers. We were… in an intimate situation and in a single breath he said that there was something wrong with…' Cissi's voice broke and she looked at Vera silently, her eyes shiny.

'I understand,' said Vera. An image of the Titanic popped up in her head – a sudden screeching rip through five watertight bulkheads. *Integrity breach.*

Cissi took a shaky breath and dried her hands on a dishtowel before continuing. 'And I was so completely unprepared; it came out of nowhere, without warning.' She smiled crookedly. 'Do you remember Cipolla? Those who hurt others in the pursuit of their own interest are bandits, but you can protect yourself against them because at least they're predictable. Stupidity, on the other hand… "the stupid person is the most dangerous…"' Cissi broke off sorrowfully.

'Idiocy strikes completely randomly, so you can't defend yourself against it, can you?' asked Vera.

'Exactly. And I was so crushed that I responded in a way that made things even worse. Super-stupid. But that's life. And I'll tell you one thing – at least *I'll* never do it again!'

'But you don't think it could happen again, do you? That someone else will say the same thing?' protested Vera.

Cissi's eyes were shiny again. She looked down and shrugged her shoulders. 'At least I'll never be unprepared again.'

Sadness for her friend coursed through Vera, and she recognized herself in Cissi's comment. *Never be unprepared again.* The price was as high as the one the Little Mermaid had paid for her human legs. Every step would hurt. And it was a mute pain, without a tongue with which to speak. Wouldn't it have been better to remain a mermaid? It was a matter of trust, and Cissi had lost trust. Jocke had, too. Their entire fate was nothing more than a super-stupid destruction of something valuable. She also thought about Adam's boss and what he often said about how they 'create happy people'.

'But what if Jocke never understands what really happened, and he feels so bad that he goes and does something completely unnecessary and stupid, like getting plastic surgery?'

Cissi shook her head. 'When I saw how crushed he was... Of course I told him that I hadn't meant it, that he was exactly right for me as he was.'

'Ah, okay. But even Viagra didn't help?'

'No. He just said, "where there's smoke there's fire", and why would I even think it unless there was a reason?'

'Okay, and the reason, the real cause, it...'

'Damn it! He should have been able to figure it out himself!' Anger flashed in Cissi's big eyes before her voice dropped to a sad whisper. 'It was just as well the pill didn't help; I didn't feel like it either. I tried to make amends, but he didn't. I guess what he said to me wasn't as without foundation for him.' Cissi's tears overflowed and she turned away to dry them.

Everything human is fragile. A couple of sentences and everything was destroyed. Vera felt like crying herself. She patted Cissi's arm awkwardly.

'In any case, there is absolutely nothing wrong with you; it was Jocke who was wrong. I mean, not just his opinion but the whole trend, and what it creates, a world where millions get plastic surgery, where the unreal ends up being what people think of as normal.'

Cissi took a deep breath and gave a jerky sigh, as if she were blowing out a candle. 'Environmental damage. You need to let it go.'

'Yes,' admitted Vera, looking at her friend. 'But I'm not the only one.'

They fell silent and Vera looked around the room. She caught sight of the rose again.

'So if Jocke didn't send it, who is it from?'

She suddenly realized that the young assistant, the promising economics graduate student who had been with Morley, was from Russia. Surely it was too unlikely to be a coincidence. It must have been the same Russian that Cissi had met in Switzerland, the one she had turned down because she was with Jocke, *Mr You-look-like-my-ideal-woman?*

'Can I see?' Vera reached out, looked questioningly at Cissi, and then turned over the card without waiting for an answer. Someone had drawn a heart and exclamation mark.

Cissi's entire posture changed; it was as if the sun had broken out from behind heavy rainclouds. But the rays of sun were shy and Cissi seemed uncertain. Finally, she said, 'Just a guy... kind of an impulse... I don't know.' She suddenly seemed eager. 'But he's so likeable, so sweet and...' She stopped talking, glanced at the rose and looked away with a smile, a blush spreading across her cheeks.

'You're in love!' Vera grinned in surprise.

'I don't think that would be such a good idea. He's way too young for me.' Cissi shook her head dismissively.

Vera thought about the Russian with the ash-blond hair that kept falling into his eyes. *He wasn't that young, was he?* She guessed he was maybe five years younger than Cissi. That was nothing! Vera smiled to herself. It was funny how you could change your mind. She used to think she and Peter belonged to two completely different generations. Now her heart suddenly told her that a difference of five or six years was unimportant. And besides, she had a feeling that in some ways Peter was more of an adult than she was... For example, better at dealing with setbacks.

Vera looked at Cissi and said, 'Whether or not he's younger doesn't matter; that's what you said about the Italian guy.'

Cissi's blush appeared instantly. 'Yes, it's not so complicated if it's a temporary thing; but if you think that...'

...that it might be more long-term? sensed Vera, but remained silent.

'Well, we'll see,' sighed Cissi, as if struck by stage fright. Then she looked at Vera. 'But, listen, this stuff that Adam is involved in, that's his problem, not yours!'

'I know. And now I'm separating myself from it; I went to see Adam and I gave him the divorce papers.'

'Because of you and Peter...?' Cissi saw through her. Vera trembled and looked down at the floor. *You hold my heart in*

465

your hand. She had believed Peter. She thought she probably still believed him. But Adam's despair came to mind; it's true for Adam too. Yet it's clearly not enough, *if the heart isn't attached to the rest*. She thought about the deeply troubling fact that Peter hadn't called in several days. *Why?*

'I really don't know what to think,' she said out loud.

'Yes, well, it's been pretty obvious for quite a while,' said Cissi.

'What?'

'The way you guys look at each other.'

'Really?' blushed Vera. 'How?'

'How?' teased Cissi. 'Hmmm, just like best thing in the whole world is right in front of you.'

'Ah,' said Vera, looking down again.

'Yes, I've clearly been our chapter's third wheel. But I'm really happy for you guys. It seems like real love.'

'You think?'

'I can't lie. I was pretty doubtful in the beginning. You know, I didn't want you to get hurt or anything. But I think Peter's different now; he's completely sold on you. It's probably been like that for a while, but it was obvious when we were at Agnes'.'

'Did you tell her anything about us?' wondered Vera.

'What I told her was that the three of us were facing a difficult task, that there was some tough opposition and we needed some team-building to get to know each other better, our strengths and weaknesses…'

If she was lying, she was hiding it well.

Vera went to use the bathroom. She noticed the little bathtub and recalled scrubbing it to get rid of the hair dye. If Cissi hadn't been on her way to becoming a brilliant academic in environmental economics, she could have been a psychologist or therapist. Vera smiled and heard Cissi's phone ring.

When Vera returned to the living room Cissi looked up and said, 'Professor Överlind.'

'Personally? Not Lilian? What did he want?'

'To sort things out. Monday. The entire executive board.' Cissi paled slightly. 'I knew exactly what I was getting into.'

Seeing how worried Cissi looked, Vera found it easy to say: 'I'm going with you.'

They were in the same bright room where they had interrogated Vera in the fall. Cissi and Vera sat around the same wooden table with Professor Överlind, Department Chair Lange and Åke Sturesson. A copy of *Future Wealth and Welfare*, with its dark blue cover, lay on the table in front of Sturesson.

Vera had understood the first time she met the diminutive Marianne Lange that she was someone to be reckoned with, unsentimental and tough. The Department Chair addressed Sturesson: 'So you're saying that you no longer want to be Åström's thesis advisor? Is that correct?'

What? Vera looked at Cissi, who was taking the news with remarkable equanimity.

'Yes. Exactly. That's correct. In my view she has difficulty co-operating, I mean, being a team player,' said Professor Sturesson emotionlessly.

Överlind scratched his head and turned towards Cissi. 'Well. What do you think happened?'

'I'm not sure I understand. What do you mean, what happened?' she asked.

Överlind gestured at the book and took a breath, as if preparing to answer, but Sturesson turned towards Cissi in irritation. 'You said that you were going to write the chapter, but you failed to mention that it wouldn't be a revision of your first draft! It's hardly a coincidence that your chapter includes…' he nodded towards Vera, 'not just that nurse's unconventional ideas, but also more advanced criticism of growth.'

Cissi remained silent and the Professor turned towards Överlind. 'In my view, Ågren is responsible!'

'Åström,' said Cissi coldly. 'My name is Åström!'

Sturesson leaned back and slammed his palm down on the table. He looked directly at Överlind. 'It is impossible for the Department to keep a graduate student who is so disloyal!'

'She isn't disloyal!' protested Vera. 'Although maybe she's

too fearless for this place.'

The silence that filled the room was so tense that Vera felt as if even the men in the portraits hanging on the wall were shocked. Marianne Lange glanced from one colleague to another, but seemed to realize that none of them was prepared to take charge.

'Well,' she said. 'Let's start again from the beginning. How did all this actually come about?'

Vera finally broke the silence. 'I had started to write about the undervaluation of reprodu…'

'Right!' interrupted Sturesson. 'And we agreed that it wasn't suitable for this project!'

Överlind leaned his lanky frame in the direction of his colleague. 'Åke, I must ask you…'

'No, you didn't think it was suitable,' said Vera. 'Then we started to wonder if this was how things always worked in academia, that controversial subjects were cut.' She glanced at Lange and Överlind. 'Whether that was why the majority of full-time economists the world over seem to want to avoid the hardest and most important questions – because if you ask them, you get kicked out?'

The people around the table had become almost as glassy-eyed as the figures in the portraits.

'We were told that due to printing costs, instead of three chapters from us, there would only be one,' explained Cissi. 'So we simply decided to solve the problem by writing one chapter together.'

'And it wasn't a coup,' said Vera. *Except perhaps that we truthfully answered Lilian's question about what would get the most media attention,* thought Vera. 'We turned the chapter in on time, so if you had read it then you wouldn't have had to stand there…' Vera stopped herself, recalling Sturesson on the stage, shiny with sweat, dumbfoundedly cracking open his new book.

Cissi took over. '… with your pants down, to put it bluntly.'

An image of the Professor with his trousers around his ankles, baggy boxers and knobbly knees exposed to the world, suddenly came to Vera's mind. She thought that Överlind looked mildly

468

amused too, but told herself she must be mistaken, because he suddenly leaned grimly towards Marianne Lange and said something inaudible. When he communicated his decision to Sturesson, Överlind acted as if Cissi weren't even in the room.

'We aren't going to force you to keep advising a graduate student you don't want. We agree that there appears to be a problem of co-operation.'

Cissi was in her office packing her personal effects into removal boxes. Her expression was hard and defiant. Vera looked at her sympathetically.

'I'm just so sorry. You've devoted years to it. And you're the best teacher they have; it's such a loss!' *Again! What a meaningless waste!*

'But the whole point of being here is that I want to say it like it is!' said Cissi. 'Our chapter is the most sensible thing I've done in this place.'

They heard a knock and Professor Överlind opened the door and came in.

Cissi straightened up slowly, turned away from the boxes and looked directly at him. 'Yes?'

'We've heard that you've questioned the house gods and are a bad influence on our youth.'

Vera noticed that Cissi was bracing herself for another unpleasant shock.

'That's what they said about Socrates too,' grinned the professor. 'And I'm just wondering who Socrates wants to have as a new advisor?'

'What?'

'Yes, well… there are several possibilities. For example, I'm interested. If you want. What do you say?'

Cissi stood still, expressionless. Then she continued slowly to pack the boxes.

'Maybe we should also recruit Plato here,' smiled Överlind and nodded at Vera. 'What do you say?'

'Thank you for the offer, but I think I'll decline,' said Cissi.

What? thought Vera, but then she thought she understood.

469

Don't settle just because you want to feel safe. You'll only wind up creating a prison for yourself.

'Well,' said the grey-haired man in puzzlement. 'I think that's a pity. Can you please think about it?'

Överlind seemed disappointed when he left. Then he turned around and stuck his head back into the room. 'Another idea I had, regarding "Structural Integrity". Perhaps the three of you would like to go to Copenhagen next fall? To the Climate Conference?'

He left again, and Vera and Cissi looked at each other.

51

We must be the change we want to see.

Mohandas Karamchand Gandhi

Peter couldn't sleep. Desperate questions danced around in his head. What had happened? Should he have done something differently? Would things have taken a different turn if he had told Vera that it was *his* unspoken wish, not Matt's, to be a good man, *a man you stay with because he makes you feel good*? He tossed and turned in torment; it hadn't been that easy. Just like in *The Game*, talk is all well and good, but *it's what you do that counts*.

He felt terrible; frighteningly so. Never before had he been unable to sleep for several nights in a row. He knew he needed to do something. If he didn't talk to someone soon he would fall apart completely.

But who?

He was forced to admit that his gut reaction was to talk to Vera; she had saved him from sleepless nights of worry before. But it seemed impossible this time. He realized that he didn't have any close friends.

Kalle? No. And anyway, Kalle had already made his view clear. His mother had enough to worry about; he didn't want to burden her with something this similar to depression. He missed his grandmother. Her secure presence had helped him a lot over the years. If only she were still alive!

Since the alternative was another night of agony alone in bed with unanswerable questions, the decision was, in the end, simple and once it was made he finally dozed off for almost four hours. When he awoke it was morning, and the mission he had given himself forced his tired body to get up. He showered

471

quickly, thinking that it was enough that he had shaved yesterday, and perfunctorily ran his toothbrush over his teeth. He ignored the fact that his hair was sticking out all over the place, drank a mug of water, hid his eyes behind sunglasses and cycled through Sofiehem towards the path along the river. The water was sparkling in the sun, floating jetties were bobbing in the water and cocky gulls were soaring and diving overhead. The bird-cherry trees were blossoming. Peter thought about the last time he had taken this route – the ice floe, the darkness of winter, the relentless march of time.

He looked at his watch as he knocked. Twenty past eight. *Old people were always awake by this time, weren't they?* Solveig opened the door expectantly, dressed in a light-blue robe, reading glasses and curlers. He entered her little apartment and tremblingly breathed in the comforting scent of geraniums. She looked at him with alarm when he removed his sunglasses.

'Darling boy, what in the world is wrong?'

What should he say? That he would gratefully turn the clock back a month – just to be able to enjoy walking beside Vera, distracted by a strong desire to hold her hand? That he missed her? Her beautiful soul, her brilliant insight into how to save the vulnerable, blind maniacs of the world. Vera – the backbone in the madhouse? *And, God, what a backbone!* Should he admit that since Friday it was also to do with her – the only word that popped into his head felt ancient – her maidenly, magically overflowing aura? How she made life seem brand new, crystal clear and powerful?

He let Solveig guide him to the sofa, and after he exhaustedly collapsed onto it, he began talking.

'I had been longing for the opportunity for months, so when I finally got the chance to chase the perfect wave, I took it. I ran into some hard-core guys at the bar who used to tear off to the beach as soon as the wind blew hard enough from the southeast. I had told them that I surfed at Biarritz, and they lent me some gear. We went out to Torö, outside Stockholm. It was just as tough, although the water was colder. It was only April, but we had wetsuits on, so it was okay.'

'Are you talking about surfing?' asked Solveig kindly.

'Yes. It's fantastic when everything clicks, indescribable. But the Baltic Sea didn't want to...' He took an uneven breath and tiredly rubbed his eyes. 'I was terrified and disappointed. It was a close call. It was like I was in a washing machine; I was helpless and thought I was going to die. I was thrown against the bottom, on my back, into a large, sharp rock that ripped through my wetsuit and broke two ribs.' He weakly lifted his left arm and pointed to his back. 'I was incredibly lucky. If it had been a foot higher my life would have been over at 21.'

He had never been this close to admitting to anyone that he had been conquered. Deep in his soul, he would always be a devoted surfer. *It was just that...* He still remembered his disappointment, fighting back the tears on the ride back into town, acute pain radiating from his back.

'So I never did it again.' His voice was a defeated whisper.

'Surfed?'

'No. I haven't dared.'

And now, with Vera, he had experienced the intensity of living fully in the moment not just for a matter of seconds, as he had while surfing, but for hours. How would he be able to *live with that memory...* 'That one time, never again!' He slumped over on Solveig's sofa and hid his head in an embroidered pillow.

He didn't want to know what that would be like.

She rolled over to him in her wheelchair and stroked his back with her warm hand. 'But that was a long time ago, wasn't it? So what has happened now?'

What has happened now?

He had been on a path – the expected path, the same as his Stureplan acquaintances, his old school friends. Like his father and Charlie, except he wasn't as successful yet. But then...

So why is this a good idea? Seen through.

He sat up heavily, looked at Solveig and tried to explain.

'I'm *not* a finance yuppie. I actually don't like to pour champagne down the drain; I don't want to devote my life to superficialities, to mindlessly chasing money and status.' He had raised his voice, and now he tried to control himself. 'Sorry if

473

I sound so angry,' he said, shamefaced. 'It isn't directed at you. It's my father and people like him I'm mad at.'

Solveig smiled and shook her head slightly, as if to say that it was okay, and he continued.

'I don't want to live like only the richest of the rich can. I want to solve problems, not create them. I would have been unhappy and in any case never as successful as my father and cousin.' He looked at her. 'I have a cousin who's made it big in the City of London. He made 70 million kronor last year, and for a long time I thought that I ought to move there and try it too. But now I know that I would be a poor imitation of him; it isn't me. And most important of all, I want a family that I'm a part of, that I want to spend time with, and a wife who's happy!' Restless, he got up and looked out of Solveig's window. 'It's only now that I finally understand what I really am.'

'And what are you?'

It was a fundamental question. He thought about it, because the answer ought to be the foundation of everything he did for the rest of his life. He realized that it wasn't just Vera and her infectious energy – it was something deep inside him, actually independent of her, but something she had recognized and encouraged. His innate nature, his real disposition, regardless of the environment he happened to have been born into. It felt difficult to explain, but Solveig was waiting patiently, so he tried.

'I'm a seeker. A curious detective in the face of the world's mysteries. I want to know, to find out. I want to change, to improve!'

'So.' The old clock on the wall ticked loudly. 'It seems like a lot has happened!' Solveig looked at him warmly.

'An incredible amount has happened. Because she sees so much; she says what she thinks, and she has made me wake up. I would probably have woken up eventually, but it's obviously very different if you only realize what life you really want when you're 60.'

'Yes, although of course 60 is nothing!' smiled Solveig mischievously.

'Of course... but I meant family and everything.'

'I understand what you meant. Of course you're right. Time is all we have.'

'Exactly. That's why I've realized that who you choose to be with is so important; it determines your whole life!'

'Yes, it's one of life's most important decisions, especially if you have children. But there is something that is more important, that determines your life even more,' said Solveig.

What can possibly be more important? thought Peter, bewildered.

'How you behave towards the person you choose,' continued the old woman. 'There was another man who wanted to be with me, and he wasn't bad at all. His name was Karl. I chose Gustav, but that doesn't mean a life with Karl wouldn't have been good, although in a different way. What would have been similar for me, regardless of which man I lived my life with, is how I was myself, what I brought to our life together. That's also the most important thing. You can never get everything, but you can join in and make what you have something wonderful.'

What did Vera bring to a life together? Sense and comfort. Intelligence, integrity and empathy. Energy. Absolute beauty. Hours of the perfect wave. He smiled to himself almost incredulously and shook his head slightly.

'What is it?' asked Solveig, looking at him with curiosity.

'She was with me on Friday. I mean, in my room, in my bed.' Peter blushed.

'I understand.'

Peter looked down. 'Yes, but we didn't do it, I mean, we didn't...' He looked up again, because he wanted to try to describe it. 'But it was magical, as if what she wanted, desired and needed was exactly what I wanted, desired and needed. It was fantastic with her; to give was to get and to get was to give. There was no difference, just... paradise.' He looked at his hands, and knew that there was only one thing they wanted to do.

'The more I give to thee, the more I have,' smiled Solveig, looking at him over her reading glasses.

'What?'

'History's most sensual and erotic wordsmith expressed 400

475

years ago what you are describing now – William Shakespeare.'

'Is it from *Romeo and Juliet*?' he asked.

'Yes.'

'But that didn't end well, did it?'

'No, it was a tragedy.'

Peter was filled with an ominous feeling. He remembered Linda's words and feared that the curse had become reality. *Things are going to go fucking badly for you!*

'This has also ended badly for me, because…' his voice broke and he seemed to shrink into himself. Vera was frustratingly headstrong. She could just give up, cramp up in an unconstructive way. She made herself unhappy because she wasn't perfect. From what he'd seen, she was a terrible cook. And she was more than a little strange when it came to her mother. Nonetheless, not even the old cut-and-paste ideal had a chance against the reality of Vera. She had advantages that he hadn't even realized existed, magic and strengths that he had never been close to before! Peter wondered if he was thinking in such strange words because he was talking to an old person. *Had he been swindled? Or spurned?* He realized he was deeply understood and yet not chosen. And that was worse, much more painful, than being misunderstood and rejected. Because he knew that Vera knew him better than anyone else. She knew what she was saying no to! A terrible sorrow seized him and he buried his face in his hands.

'What ended badly, Peter?'

Solveig's worried voice sounded as distant as if it were coming from another room. He wasn't contactable, lost in the grim conviction that his irrepressible love for Vera had been degraded into something inappropriate, a shameful abomination. He should drag it into a godforsaken cave; cut it out of his body, drive it out of his soul. Solveig rolled forward and bent over, putting her shoulder under his drooping head and her arms around him. She reminded him so much of his grandmother that he let all his feelings out. His tears flowed, and with them came the horrible truth.

'I could look for the rest of my life, but I'll never find anybody like her!'

She stroked his back gently and after a moment said: 'There is always an alternative, even if you can't see it right now. That's what I was trying to say before, about Karl. Things are good in different ways; people, too. When you meet somebody new, she will be good in new, different ways!'

He knew Solveig was trying to comfort him. What she couldn't know was that she had just filled his head with all the ways in which Vera could think that Matt was the better man. Involuntarily, Peter thought about every detail of Vera, the magic they had experienced. What did it mean that she had still chosen Matt?

She has an even stronger connection with him. Can there even be a stronger connection?

He reminded himself that what he felt wasn't necessarily what it was like for her. Maybe he was wrong about them sharing a unique communication. *Maybe she simply felt that magic whenever...* The sounds he remembered from the other side of the wall confirmed the thought, and he whimpered in pain.

'Please, Peter! Can't you tell me what's happened?'

'It was on Friday. Right after she had been with me... she had sex with...' His voice broke and the rest was barely audible, 'someone else.' He took a breath and got the rest of it out. 'And she hasn't called. No explanation, nothing!'

Solveig stiffened, pulled away from him and studied his face. 'Oh. And imagine. I thought...' She backed away slightly.

'What did you think?' He looked up at her.

'I thought I knew who we were talking about.' She looked embarrassed. 'I thought it was Vera!'

'But it is Vera!'

Solveig looked perplexed. She rolled away a bit more and then turned back towards him. She seemed to choose her words carefully, speaking slowly, hesitantly.

'She went back to her husband right after she was with you?'

'No. She was with Matt, a British guy who lives in the dorm.'

Solveig frowned even more. 'No, I can't believe she'd do that. Are you sure?'

'Yes. There isn't a chance in the world that what I heard was something other than...'

'But have you spoken to her? Told her how you feel?'

Why? What good would that do?

'No, but, she knows – I can't believe she doesn't know.' He thought again about Friday night. Not everything he had said had been wordless. *'You hold my heart in your hand.' How much clearer could I have been?* 'And I know. They're probably more alike. I *understand* what she can get from Matt that I don't have. I don't have the strength to hear it from her too.'

It isn't her fault that Matt is made of the stuff of Elves, and I'm not.

He wanted to cry again, but realized the absurdity of the situation. He had already bawled and sniffled on an old woman's shoulder. He wasn't a child at his grandmother's house; he was an adult and Solveig just a woman who reminded him of her. He got up and pretended that he needed to use the bathroom. He locked the door and splashed cold water on his tired face and red-rimmed eyes until he looked a little more like his normal self.

When he finally came out again, Solveig had taken out her curlers and made sandwiches. He sat down at the table and ate gratefully. He was surprised at how hungry he suddenly was, and realized that he hadn't eaten properly for several days. The bread was the same type of round, grainy roll that he had given Vera that night last winter. *Lights will guide you home, and ignite your bones, and I will try to fix you.*

He heard the guitar riff in his head. He had thought the music had helped him sleep, but it had actually woken him up, woken him to his real life.

'Did Vera buy this bread for you?' *Maybe she remembers that night, too?*

'Yes. She keeps me full between meals.'

'You and Vera are very tight, aren't you?' He heard the embarrassment in his voice.

'Tight?'

'Um, yeah, close... close to each other.'

'Of course. Why?' He didn't answer, but she looked at him

kindly, her voice mildly teasing. 'Don't worry. If she doesn't ask, I won't say anything.'

'But what will you say if she does ask?' replied Peter, recognizing that he was exposing himself. *The truth, of course. 'He came here and cried like an inconsolable child because you chose to make Matt your Elf.'* He looked down at his lap in humiliation. Hell had just got a new circle – shame.

Solveig looked at him mildly. 'Then I guess I will have to say that if Peter Stavenius says that he loves her, she should believe him.'

He smiled at Solveig, but realized that he shouldn't be surprised. *That is also true.* If there was anything he had learned this spring, it was that. The truth looks different depending on the angle, and the truth that one sees often says more about one's self than reality. As with the proverbial glass, the same reality could be interpreted as half-empty or half-full. And if you couldn't sleep and were starving and your heart was broken and you needed to cry on someone's shoulder – well, Solveig was a good choice. You could live with her truths.

If I say I love her...

He looked at Solveig. 'It doesn't matter what I feel, because she has made her choice. She's done what she's done.'

'But what you say she's done sounds very strange, because the best thing about Vera is that she is so heart-friendly.'

Heart-friendly. He smiled sadly. It was a good description.

'And what you say she's done,' continued Solveig skeptically, 'doesn't sound friendly at all.'

Her words hit him. *She's right!* Because even if the most beautiful thing he'd ever experienced was to her just a meaningless, drunken one-night-stand, he wasn't so worthless that she could just ignore him, was he? Regardless of how head-over-heels in love with Matt she was, she could at least have had the decency to talk to him and tell him what had happened. Otherwise she was heartless. He thought about films he'd seen where people's bodies had been possessed by spirits, or taken over by aliens from outer space. *Edgar the Bug.* It was as if something like that had happened – he actually didn't recognize

Vera at all.

'You're right. There's something strange about this.'

'Think about the journey you've taken. Do you regret it?'

'Do you mean do I wish I hadn't met her?' He thought about it. He shook his head. It was as if he had been wobbling around on two lopsided wheels, and was now left with only one, but it was straight. Regardless of what she had done, he had already transformed himself. Because he had met her, he had a better chance to create the future he knew he wanted. So he would just have to try to learn to get around on a unicycle.

'Could you have grown as you have – as you've told me – if it were only you who loves? Don't you think she loves you?'

He looked at the scar on his thumb. It used to be a symbol of vulnerability and terror to him, but now he wore it proudly, the mark of his rite of passage. It was the finest compliment he had ever received, and he felt that it was true, that he would be a good father if he had the chance. Even if he had misunderstood her soft kiss last Friday, when she had seemed to lay claim to him and his future fatherhood.

Solveig cocked her head and looked at him. She was wearing a necklace and she pulled its long chain out of her blue robe. A small antique ring decorated with colored gems and oriental ornaments was dangling from it.

'Can you believe that I used to have such small fingers?' she asked, smiling. 'Gustav and I got engaged when we were travelling in northern India in 1946, when it was the first colony getting ready to liberate itself from the British Empire. We were at the Savoy in Mussoorie, with a majestic view of the world's mightiest mountain range...'

The world's mightiest mountain range; everyone in the Stavenius family knew what that was. 'The Himalayas.'

'Yes. That's where this came from, and it came complete with a story, or perhaps a legend.'

Peter looked at her curiously. 'A legend?'

'Yes. Let me see if I can remember it.' She sank into thought as she carefully lifted the necklace over her newly curled hair. 'There was a fight over the kingdom, and if the crown prince could be disposed of, then another clan would be able to claim the throne. The enemy came, and the young prince was only a little boy, so his servant fled with him to a fast-flowing river. When they had to cross it, the servant carried him. Imagine, the clever antique dealer said to us, that pitch-black Indian night hundreds of years ago, the pursuit on horseback, maybe with dogs, how they used bamboo sticks to beat down the grass along the riverbank, how the servant sought protection for the boy in the darkness and the fast-flowing water.'

'A clever antique dealer?' asked Peter.

'Yes, because we weren't allowed to hear the rest of the story unless we decided to buy the ring, even though it was very expensive. He probably had a whole storeroom full of them and told the same story to every gullible tourist,' Solveig smiled.

'Right. But you did buy it,' said Peter, looking at the semi-precious gems. 'So what happened in the story?'

'They got away and the dogs lost the scent thanks to the river, or maybe the pursuers gave up, thinking that they would drown in the river anyway. In any case, the prince had a pointed pendant on a chain around his neck, and it ripped through his servant's shirt and scratched his chest as they fled across the river. When they got to the other side, the servant opened his shirt and showed the prince his bleeding wound.'

'He didn't say anything?'

'No, he probably wasn't allowed to address the prince freely. The young boy belonged to a high caste and reacted as if insulted. "Do you show me your wound to embarrass me, or because you no longer wish to serve me?" he asked.'

Solveig laid the ring carefully in her palm, looking at it nostalgically. '"No," said the servant. "I do it because I want to carry you over the next river, too."'

Peter was reluctant to disturb Solveig's thoughts, but he was still curious. 'So did the prince take the sharp thing off?'

'Yes, he did. Later he had it turned into a ring. And he gave the ring to the brave servant!'

Peter nodded.

Solveig looked him in the eyes. 'So my advice is: tell it like it is, even if you bleed! Perhaps especially when you're bleeding. Do you know what the longest journey is that a person can take?'

'To the moon?' guessed Peter, thinking of Lennart's vision for Great Escape.

'No, no!' said Solveig, shaking her head and smiling. 'You can go to the moon and come back home and be the same person you were when you left. The longest journey a person can take is from stranger to life-partner.'

Peter looked at her and thought about his parents, about Lennart's inexhaustible hunt for heaven on earth, and how it had cost him his wife and left him with a fractured, part-time family.

'And the longest journey has its scary parts,' continued Solveig, looking at him. 'You said that it ended badly. But has it really ended? If she hasn't said anything, then she hasn't ended it with you.'

'But I don't even know where she is!'

'She's at home with her father, at the cottage on the Vindel River. She marked it on my map, you can look at it.'

Right. He knew what he had to do. There was a big risk that hearing her decision would crush him, but at least he would know. Knowledge and experience would be his return on investment. It was cruel and meager compared with what he had thought he could get, but he knew that it was better than nothing.

They stood in the hallway saying their goodbyes. He realized how much better he felt, in spite of everything. He had arrived feeling completely empty. Two hours with Solveig had strengthened him in many ways.

'Thank you so much for the food and everything, Solveig.'

When she smiled and gave him a hug, he spontaneously blurted out: 'You know, you remind me so much of my grandmother, but she died. Can I adopt you instead? I mean, like a bonus grandmother?'

Solveig looked surprised. She thought for a second and then said, 'Of course you can! What fun!' She patted his arm. 'Good luck! And whatever happens, let's talk. Sometimes I'm away at the swimming pool, and sometimes I'm in the common room, but

482

I'm almost always on the premises somewhere. There aren't too many people who take me out to Chinese restaurants, you know!'

'We must do that again some time!'

When he was on his way down the hall, Solveig opened the door again. 'Wait! An important thing, on the long journey...'

'Yes?'

She held out her hand and he met it with his own, looking at her quizzically. She put the old ring in his hand, closed his fingers around it and patted his fist.

'It's going to take courage.'

52

Call it the angels' meadow or heavenly earth if
you so wish.

Evert Taube, 1971

Peter walked up the ridge through the verdant early summer.
The noise of the river grew louder. He saw her from a distance –
exactly where Sven-Erik had guessed she would be. She sat with
her back to him, braiding her hair.

He remembered how she had climbed out of his bed at 2:19
on Saturday morning, her curves clad in jeans that ended just
under the waist. How captivatingly her womanly muscles had
moved under her soft skin when she pulled up her bra strap and
stretched for her blouse!

A Stradivarius.

He relived his desire to stop her, pull her back to him. *Not
now, but in an oh-so-wonderful future encounter* he had
promised himself. He hadn't had any idea that there wouldn't
be such an encounter. He hadn't had any idea that there would
be no such future.

2:19 a.m. on Saturday. When time had restarted.

His eyes burned.

Vera sat on her favorite place on the rock, looked at the river,
fastened her hair tie around the end of her braid and wondered
if there might in fact be a reasonable explanation for why Peter
hadn't called – a reason other than the one she most feared.
Over the noise of the water and the soft murmuring of the
aspen leaves she suddenly heard a cracking sound behind her,
someone stepping on dry twigs. She turned around to look, and

saw him. He was wearing a white t-shirt and denim jacket, his wavy hair was sticking out all over the place and he looked worn out, almost haunted. Her heart beat hard in her chest. She had never seen anything so beautiful, but her joy was clouded by discouragement.

Why does he have to look so much like James Dean – only taller? She stood up, wiping little pieces of lichen from the stone off her flowery dress.

'It's nice here,' he said hesitantly.

'Yes. Evert Taube wrote a song about the Vindel River,' she said. '"Let the last river keep roaring freely from the mountains through the woods."'

'How are you?' His expression was serious.

Strong feelings struggled inside her. *Where have you been? I've missed you every minute!* She swallowed and gave the standard answer to the question.

'I'm fine. How are you?'

It must be obvious a mile away!

'I'm okay, nothing to complain about,' he heard himself say. 'I've been in Stockholm, at Great Escape. I tried to get the board to realize the times we live in, the responsibility we need to take. You know, satisfying our needs using as few resources as possible. So we don't turn the whole planet into Easter Island.'

She nodded. 'No, because then there's no Great Escape for anybody.'

'Exactly.'

'How did they respond?'

'Not well. I was disinherited on the spot, you could say.' Peter was suddenly filled with fear. Here was a risk that hadn't occurred to him. He'd lost an inheritance worth hundreds of millions and turned down Charlie's invitation to try to make as much as he had in London. Sandra would have thought he was crazy and left him for less. *But if you don't think I did the right thing, then I love the wrong woman.*

'Have you ever heard of Prometheus in Greek mythology? You remind me of him.' Vera looked at the ground. 'Before

485

Prometheus, humans lived miserably in the cold. He wanted them to develop and live better, so he suggested that the gods teach them about fire. Zeus didn't agree, and when Prometheus defied him and brought fire to humanity, Zeus punished him hard.' She looked at him, 'Just because you're punished by those who have power, it doesn't mean you're wrong.'

He smiled at her answer. 'Prometheus, that means... promise, right?'

'Maybe... I think Prometheus means foresight. You know, like looking forward, into the future. Maybe you should do Future Studies?'

He smiled and remembered the respect and handshake he had got from the chair of the board. 'My uncle Ernst actually said something similar.'

'It seems like a good idea. You're capable of doing a lot of good with all your assets – you have assets in the true sense of the word, real ones.' She met his eyes calmly.

Peter's heart pounded. He was surer than ever that he would be happiest sharing his life with her. His emotions shifted from elation to despair and back again. *Why does she have to be with Matt?*

'On the subject of people with power to punish,' said Vera, 'I went with Cissi to a meeting with the Department's executive board. It turns out that Sturesson was so angry about our chapter that he wanted to kick her out of graduate school. And at the meeting that's what appeared to happen. But then Överlind came by her office and offered to take over as her advisor. He even talked about us, all three of us, going to the Climate Conference next fall.'

'But why didn't anybody tell me there was going to be a meeting?' asked Peter. 'It's my chapter too!'

'Of course it is!' She crossed her arms defensively and her voice became weak. 'But you were gone, and you didn't call, not even after... after Friday.'

Friday. Heaven and hell!

The contradictions tore at him, and he knew that he sounded almost defiant as he retorted, 'Why should I have called?'

Because it's... complicated, still not carved in stone. Because I have feelings for you, he silently willed her to answer.

But she just turned around and walked off. He followed her a bit, but then stopped, anxiously wondering what she was thinking.

He was desperate and she had fled. *Maybe I should just go and leave her in peace?*

His cold expression, asking that question! It was like a punch in the stomach, and Vera turned away, eyes filling with tears.

Why should he have called?

She walked away from him, downstream along the ridge. Vera remembered the last second before she had lost consciousness, the cracking feeling in her knee and the sharp stab of pain that told her something had suddenly gone very wrong. In contrast to a regular broken bone, the kind of knee injury she suffered wasn't something that would mend on its own.

'If the cruciate ligament breaks, it breaks – snap!' That's what the orthopedic specialist had said, snapping his fingers.

What would happen if she went snowboarding, which she loved, and she caught an edge? Or if she was just clumsy, maybe tried to move too quickly on an icy November day? Would she be able to heal next time? The riverbank got steeper and steeper, and she looked down the rocky slope towards the river.

With her heart still wounded after Adam, why had she closed her eyes and taken the plunge? She had thought she'd been received so readily... But it couldn't be helped. She knew that no matter what happened now, she would always remember him. Nothing would change that, not even that *he'd asked her to go, and now wondered why he should have called.* Her heart pounded and tears ran down her face. The loveliness all around her was no comfort, because the beauty only made her more aware of her pain. Her feet followed the path automatically, while something inside her fought back, struggled against the chaos.

Without warning, a question popped into her head and brought her to an abrupt stop. *Is it possible that I was so fundamentally wrong about you? If so, what the hell were you doing?*

She turned around and screamed at him. 'You made that up about wanting to see me the next day, and then you didn't call!'

When she turned around, Peter finally felt as though he could start breathing again. He was relieved by her rage, but couldn't understand it. He went closer. When he spoke, he realized that he sounded angry too.

'What do you mean, "made that up"? I would have called, but... after what *you* did!' An unpleasant image of Jeanette flashed in his head as he continued. 'I know what you're going to say, "I didn't do anything you hadn't done", but I think there's a huge difference. We didn't know each other in the fall, but now... I thought that you at least felt *something* for me! And then, on Friday. I know that I'm probably the last person who should expect it... But I thought that you and I... That you were at least a little attached to me?'

Her furious breathing calmed down slightly when she heard his question.

What is he talking about?

'I am attached to you,' she said before fear shut her up. *But I don't want to wind up at another dead-end!* She raised her eyes. 'What do you mean, "what I did?" What did I do that was so wrong that you don't even want to talk to me?'

Peter saw the tears in her eyes and felt his own despair overflow.

'You know what I mean!'

'No, I don't! I have no idea!'

It was painful, but he had to say it. *I show you my wound, because I want to carry you over the next river too. Or up the stairs the next time you need it.*

His heart was pounding so hard that he could hear it as he forced the difficult words out of his mouth, the question that exposed him to the coup de grace.

'Explain it to me. How could you leave my bed, after what we had shared, and then go and have sex with Matt?'

488

And far too good sex with Matt, at that.

What he had heard through the wall echoed painfully in him; it had destroyed his dream of rightfully claiming her. It hadn't bothered him when other men had stared at Sandra's generous décolletage; maybe he had even felt a bit cocky – *Yeah! And she's with me!* But this was different. The feeling was new and strange. He understood it was unavoidable, but still. The very thought that some other man would see Vera like that and want to get close to the secret paradise that he had discovered felt unbearable, not to mention the possibility that she might consider the offer! He glanced bashfully at her youthful female form under her dress, and the mental image of her with Matt threatened to paralyze him. He noticed a tree close to the edge of the cliff, with branches stretching out over it. He felt as though he were clutching one of the branches, feet dangling, and that what Vera was about to say would sever it and send him falling to his death on the rocks below.

But she just stared at him, blinking away her tears. 'What?'

'How could you? I'm a complete wreck. If you wanted to get revenge, you definitely succeeded.'

'I didn't want revenge!' Vera thought about it. 'That night, when you wanted me to leave, I felt so restless…' *and confused and unsatisfied.* 'I needed to think; I wanted to go to the woods – when did I go? About 2.30? And I saw a whole group out in the yard, including Matt.'

Now Peter had to ask.

'And he stood there and you thought he was…' He pictured Matt with his open shirt, and his voice broke as he once again thought about the painful possibilities as to why she would choose Matt over him:

Unconventionally, ruggedly handsome?
A God-given, instinctive artistic talent?
As heart-friendly as you?
A faithful catch? Charming, romantic innocent?
A real man (who doesn't need to lie and put on an act)?
He cleared his throat and forced out the question.

'And you thought he was irresistible?'

Vera looked at him blankly. 'No. I said hello to him, and then I talked to some of the others for a few minutes.'

Are you going to stand here and pretend nothing happened?

'Don't try it on. I know what I heard. I had a strong urge to knock on the wall!' His effort to laugh sounded horrible – choked and witchlike. 'It would have been funny, if it hadn't been so terrible.'

A knock on the wall? Vera finally understood. Peter hadn't called because he had heard people having sex in her room that night! A comforting sense of order started to drive out the painful, incomprehensible chaos and a huge tenderness filled her. *I understand. You poor thing! But how could you think that…?*

She took a step towards him, sensed for the first time that the tortured expression, weariness and dark circles under his eyes might actually have something to do with her. She resisted the impulse to touch him; his pain was still too hostile. This needed to be resolved with words. *Truthful words.* But what did he think he knew?

'Okay. You know what you heard. But I know what I did. You think that Matt had sex in my room?'

'I *know* that Matt had sex in your room,' he said in a pained voice.

'Yes, Kalle was sleeping in Matt's room, so it was occupied,' she said thoughtfully. Suddenly, things became clear. 'Ah! Yes!' Her dimples deepened.

'What?' Peter looked at her strangely.

'They stood there talking about Swedish grammar, and when I was leaving Cissi asked if she could borrow my computer. She was going to show him something, so I gave her my keys. And now she's in love with some new guy who she thinks is too young for her.'

Well, that makes sense – there must be 11 or 12 years between them.

'*In religion, an anomaly is a miracle.*'

'*So likeable and sweet.*'

A heart with an exclamation mark.
Vera smiled. *Of course, it was Matt!*

Anguish released its cold grip on Peter. Slightly dazed, he tried to think.

How could I have missed that? He realized with a growing sense of relief that he had probably even witnessed the decisive moment. Cecilia Åström had said that she didn't think Matt Donnelly should give up, and the dishevelled Englishman had looked at her as if transformed, from humiliation to complete focus on the present. If Peter had been paying attention he would have been able to read it in their faces – the second when the perspective shifted.

Peter's sense of relief was indescribable.

She isn't Matt's! I don't need to move on!

The dissonance about Vera that had tortured him for four days was gone. Nothing contradicted his vision of what she was or his hope that she shared his feelings. The thoughts bounced around happily in his head before he acknowledged out loud the critical detail that changed everything.

'So it was Cissi?'

'They must have been pretty quick,' said Vera, 'because nobody was there when I got back, just the keys in the lock. How long was I gone?' She blushed at the answer that popped into her head. *Long enough for my crotch to start freezing.* In her inexperience, she hadn't realized that she should have changed her underwear before going out into the chilly evening air. She remembered how surprised she'd been. *How did I get so wet?*

'Forty…' She was distracted by the curve of his upper lip. *Not of this world.* 'Forty minutes maybe?'

Peter smiled to himself.

'What?' she dared.

'Have you thought about the fact that Cissi looks a little like Rose in *Titanic*?'

'Now that you say it… yeah, she does.'

'He thinks she's gorgeous,' smiled Peter.

Vera thought about how radiant Cissi had been. *It might be more long-term.* She smiled back. 'Yes. Never say never.'

A wave of joy swept through Peter at the sight of Vera's lovely dimpled smile, and he fought a strong desire to take her in his arms and never let her go. Solveig's ring was in his wallet, in his back pocket, and he longed to show it to her. Yet he hesitated, toeing the ground restlessly, realizing that something must still be wrong. *He* hadn't called her – but *she* could have called him! Why the silence?

Maybe she really doesn't feel like I do? Maybe she still doesn't want me now that she's sober?

Although unintentional, his next words sounded like an apology.

'I know that I hardly…' He swallowed the rest of the sentence: …*can be called a dream prince.* 'I know I've spent most of my adult life behaving… idiotically.' *It would kill me if you behaved the same way.* 'But you've said it yourself. People change. And I won't behave like that any more.'

'Yes, I noticed. "You can't change other people, but you can change yourself." And you have.' She looked calmly at him. 'I believe you.'

Thank God! 'So why didn't you call?'

It had been easy for her to encourage Cissi to tell Jocke the truth, but now it was her turn. On the one hand, she remembered how Peter had first been attracted to her when she was dressed up to look like something she never thought she could be – like his other women, like Sandra, and creepily similar to the women Adam preferred to have sex with. On the other hand, she thought about how good she felt Peter was for her, and the intoxicating feeling of perfection awoken by being in his arms. In that moment, love triumphed and she was able to admit the truth.

'I'm afraid.'

'What? What do you have to be afraid of?' He looked uncomprehendingly at her, but doubts now kept her quiet.

'I'm afraid, too,' he admitted after a short silence.

'Why?'

'Why haven't you come to me when you're sober?' *If you feel like I feel after Friday, why aren't you with me all the time?* 'Why have you changed your mind?'

'I haven't changed my mind. And I wasn't so drunk,' she said.

'You drank four glasses of wine, according to Matt!' It had been a pretty small wine glass, but still. *Four glasses. In that little body.*

'So you were keeping tabs? I drank wine; I drank water; I danced until I was really thirsty. And I felt like *you* had changed your mind.'

'Why did you think that?'

'Because you didn't call either, and you said you would!'

'Yes, but you know why!'

'Now I do, yes, but then... I started to have doubts.' She looked down at the ground.

'Why?' Worry squeezed at his heart. *What is there to have doubts about?*

Vera searched for a credible explanation that didn't leave her exposed. If she assumed that Peter was like Adam – incapable of physically appreciating her as she was – then it would be best for both of them to just let it go now, not say any more. What was it that Black Swan-Taleb had said?

That which is shaky should be allowed to fall apart when it's small, before a collapse can cause too much damage.

Exactly. It would hurt, but that pain now would be nothing compared to how it would feel to discover later that they lacked structural integrity. If so, the heartbreaking truth was that she ought to forgo the good in order to avoid the bad. She should just take her sparkling memories and go. The problem was that there were so many, and they were powerfully, indelibly etched into her – ever since she saw herself in his eyes and the rest of the world had receded. She thought about all the different kinds of happiness she had experienced with Peter that spring. If she were to hide them all in her heart, it would fill it up – there would be no room for anything else!

Her mind raced, frightened and confused because there was

so much at stake. How long would she be filled with fruitless longing and loss? What was the half-life of the magical warmth that being with Peter had spread through her body?

This was life on earth – the planet was ruthlessly exploited for short-term gains, war victimized the weakest, volunteer workers were murdered, people suffered injuries, became gravely ill, parted in bitterness, got drunk and violent, misunderstood each other, were super-stupid. This was definitely no neat, well-ordered heaven. *All this endless uncertainly.*

And yet, at the same time, there were solutions, hope, help, consideration, humor, healing, happiness and love. She remembered how she had been lifted out of the dilemma of wanting so much yet daring so little. Only then was she able to be whole. And not all of the life-changing steps she had taken with him were on that level. *There were also experiences I had no idea life could offer.* She looked at him.

It was as if the very act of being in his presence had finally allowed her to become what she was meant to be. Tears came to her eyes as she faced the truth – to forgo the good of being with Peter would not just be unbearable, but also limiting. Because how could she know how much more potential was inside herself? It was a powerful insight, but not one for the weak, because it forced her to ask: how grim would it be, this bad that she would have to take with the good? In the larger scheme of things, perhaps it was an insignificant problem. She braced herself and spoke.

'You know when I told you that Adam was unfaithful?'

'Yes, he has a hole in the head, that guy,' Peter answered immediately.

That's actually a pretty good description, she thought. 'Yes, he has a problem. But not with, uh, someone else… completely different from me.' *Who looked like Sandra.*

But she couldn't get her next words out; it was as if there was a blockage. She blushed, feeling that it wasn't an insignificant problem at all. It was a significant barrier to the life she wanted. *I'm size 32B. I don't have 'maximum height, full projection'.* Vera suddenly understood Cissi's stubborn opposition. *I wish you appreciated…* She had wondered why it was so impossible

494

to just tell the truth. Now she understood; it was more than just a matter of pride. She wanted him – altogether enchantingly and of his own accord – to appreciate her as she was. It was that feeling that had healed her wounds like nothing else. How could it ever be the same if she needed to ask for it?

So, instead, she just said, 'Well, you could interpret what happened on Friday along those lines.' Humiliated, she stopped talking and looked down at the ground. *You're such an irritatingly conceited Miss Try-to-Fix-Everything – you can't even bring yourself to follow your own naïve, glib advice!*

Peter had been listening carefully, but he was having difficulty understanding – *along what lines?* But he could make an unpleasant guess, and he realized that this was a case of adultery that his body had definitely not said no to.

'What? Did you feel you were being unfaithful?'

Unfaithful? The thought hadn't even occurred to her. Sure, legally, on paper, and absolutely in the eyes of the Church and her mother, Friday night was definitely a case of unfaithfulness, *big time*. But emotionally? No. What she and Adam had once had died long ago. She just hadn't had the strength to bury it. She glanced at Peter. His shape under his clothes, his profile, his beautiful hands. Her heart belonged to nobody else – *and with you I feel more alive than I have in 30 years of living.*

He looked straight at her, eyebrows drawn together in a frown.

'I thought you had decided to leave him.'

'Yes, I talked to him about it, and I signed the divorce application on Saturday. "Sometimes you have to break a promise," remember?'

Peter smiled with relief. 'Okay. So what's the problem?'

Vera clenched her fists so hard that her nails dug into her palms.

'I was afraid that it would be the same thing again. I can't do it. If I'm going to be with a man, I want... all of him!'

God, to be that man! The thought came spontaneously, and he realized that the irrepressible desire was as close to a prayer as he had ever come.

'What do you mean, the same thing? I still don't get it. What is it you're afraid of?'

She felt as though she were walking on thin ice and being forced to take another step. Her voice barely held as she tried to talk about the fracture that she had lived with for so long that it had penetrated deeply into her as well.

'I'm afraid that you'll think that I'm a fantastic nurse, a good friend, smart and fun to be with, and maybe you'll even think I would be a good mother, but you won't think that... all of me is good enough.'

The relief he felt made his whole body relax. He smiled teasingly. 'You mean you have a problem with not being perfect?'

His words stung her. *I want you to think I'm perfect.* It was a lot to ask, she knew, but she couldn't help it, because now that she had tasted the heavenly pleasure that it offered, she didn't want to live without it. *Ad infinitum*, the missing piece – the most valuable memory of them all. Tears rose in her eyes.

It's a memory that will shine for my whole life if you just leave it be. We shall not want. Please don't say I misunderstood!

It didn't need to be perfection in the sense of couldn't-be-any-other-way. But since Friday night she was transformed. It was his own doing and nothing could undo it. Never again would she settle for a life without that irresistible lust that left nothing more to desire. She knew it, but she didn't say anything, because talking about it felt like destroying its novel pricelessness. She pressed her lips together tightly and hoped that the wetness that blurred her field of vision would not spill over into tears.

Peter looked out over the enchanting view. 'Can I ask you something? What do you think about beards?'

'Huh?'

In his head he saw an image of Adam with his dark beard, and shaggy, bronze-colored Matt. 'Hairy, bearded men, full beards. What do you think about them?'

What kind of question is that? Vera thought first about the stable, good-hearted men of Västerbotten, like her father and grandfather. They had had beards when she was a child. Then she thought about Adam, who seemed to want to hide something from his wife, and she shuddered in discomfort.

'It depends entirely on the man,' she said.

Here's another wound that requires courage to show, he thought, and he leapt in, saying: 'Ever since I started getting attached to you, I've been ridiculously worried about what you think of me. I know why you said it, and I agree that Sturesson's behavior was completely weird. But that *word*. Shit! It hurt! Because it makes no difference how old I get, I'm never going to grow a decent beard. I don't give a damn what other people think, but what *you* think...' He tapped himself in the chest and bent over, as if he had taken a powerful hit.

What? He took it like that? She glanced shyly at his broad chin, which was a little angular towards his jawbone. *But what are you now, if not unshaven?* It was obviously not what he thought a stubble beard should look like, or more correctly, what he was afraid *she* thought. And all because of stupid, unjustified words.

'Sorry, that's something I've never really thought about. In fact, I think you're...' She looked at him uncomfortably. *Prometheus at the Louvre, a frightening fact. Insanely beautiful, the apple of every woman's eye.* '...to be honest, unnecessarily good-looking.'

He seemed worried. 'What?'

'It's actually a bit scary. So many women find you attractive.' *Women who want you. I feel unoriginal, superfluous, without a chance.* 'And there have been quite a lot of women to compare me to,' she said dejectedly.

This was exactly what her common sense had tried to warn her about for months. *Don't play with that fire, because you're going to get badly burned!* But had she listened? Not really. And now she wanted it so badly that it ached, despite the unanswered key question.

Would it be for keeps? *Realistically, what were the odds of that?*

Wouldn't there always be a hoard of admirers between them? Even if he miraculously wanted her today, when would he lose sight of her, distracted by one of the many others?

This was something he understood! How he had suffered by comparing himself to Matt! It had been like torture, imagining every difference between them as yet another reason for her to prefer Matt. Multiply it by 50 or more – deadly! But it was also completely unnecessary. How could he get her to see that? He glanced at her. *Do you have any idea how you could triumph in The Game if you wanted to?*

He thought about Vera in the red dress, with less than half the effort that Sandra put into it. Or at the banquet, the exquisite Elf. Imagine if she chose to use her mental powers to hunt and manipulate. He shivered.

'I really regret behaving like that. But we got to know each other at a particular point in time. There's a before and after. And think about me; you went and got married when I had just finished ninth grade! It's just stuff you've got to live with. And are you going to compare me to Adam? How will I look then?' *I'm not a dark-bearded top surgeon who makes tons of money. I've never built a kitchen; I don't even know if I can make lasagne.*

She pulled a leaf off a tree and started shredding it.

'I don't think I would, but if I did…' She thought about everything she already knew about him. 'You would come out looking really good.'

'Good! Because it's the same here. Now that I know you, I only want you.'

She cocked her head skeptically and looked at him searchingly. 'Why?'

Okay. This is important. He could sense it. He thought carefully about his response.

Because you are the most admirable person in the world, and I am completely attracted to you, because you see me for who I am; you give me direction; you make me want to be a better man. It didn't matter that it was true; it sounded clichéd. *She doesn't like clichés!*

So what about: *Because I have trust in you on the trapeze, and I never want to lose the most magical…* Right, as if anyone could understand that!

Because you are fiercely impressive at press conferences and shatteringly beautiful and sexy and I want you in my bed all the time. No. A bit vulgar and not exactly Shakespeare. He blushed, smiled crookedly and shrugged his shoulders a little.

'What you think about me is also ridiculously important,' said Vera impulsively.

'Okay, what about this,' he said, heart beating faster. 'I'm pretty critical of your behavior over the past few days. What would have happened if I hadn't dared to come out here and ask you what's going on?'

She stared down at the lovely green moss as he went on.

'Do you know why *Romeo and Juliet* was a tragedy?'

'Wasn't it some family feud?'

'Forget the families. They could just have run away together. It was a tragedy because people were missing vital pieces of information! Romeo killed himself because he thought Juliet was dead. And when she woke up and found him dead beside her, she took her own life for real.'

A destructive, self-fulfilling prophecy! An image popped into her head, the life-threatening encounter. *Never stare at the truck that's thundering down the road towards you!* The insight was chilling. How Romeo had behaved when he *thought...*

How would she have reacted if she'd thought Peter had had sex with someone else that night? The mere thought of it made her feel like she was at the edge of an abyss. To have put him through something she herself found unbearable to contemplate was not exactly flattering. If the situation had been reversed, in that decisive moment, she would desperately have needed to hear from him – *vital pieces of information*. She thought ruefully about her most important lodestar. *Do unto others.*

It had been an unfortunate misunderstanding, but she hadn't done anything to help him out of it, so he had gone around for several days thinking *it was me in that room, not Cissi!*

She recalled Cissi's shy glance at Matt's rose – and how the enthusiastic Sivan's down-to-earth pupil, who knew her own body so well, had blushed so fiercely – and imagined how they must have sounded through the wall. *And despite that, he came to me!* Filled with a strange mix of admiration and fear she looked him in the eye.

It's thanks to you that we didn't create that which we are most afraid of. She suddenly remembered his gaze outside the changing room. It had been so ill timed and unlikely that she had interpreted it as a threateningly well-played move – *all the things I would do for you!*

What if it had been neither a move nor a threat – what if it had been a promise? A promise not to the clothes or the make-up, but – *maybe even without him realizing it* – to her. And what she had thought impossible then had now occurred. She was infinitely grateful for it, because what if that had decided the outcome – his promise in that instant the only margin between safety and catastrophe? *The unbreakable spirit of love. Soul force. Thank you my love, my brave one!* She never wanted to subject him to something so difficult again. But the only words that came out were: 'I understand. It can't just be your responsibility.'

'Exactly! Because the last few days have been horrible. Talk about keeping me on tenterhooks! So don't kid yourself that you're perfect.' *Nobody's perfect; not even you.* Peter looked at her, and the vulnerability he saw in her eyes spread a warm feeling of tenderness through his body.

'But if you're wondering...' The memory of her in his bed made his voice break. '... about your... uh, physical attributes, well, I think that you're...' He swallowed. 'Exactly as you should be.'

Although she still felt scared, she said, 'For me, Friday was completely....' She hesitated because *there are no words that are sufficient!* 'Indescribable, but when you wanted me to leave in the middle of everything – it felt bad. I thought that you maybe felt... like I didn't do it for you!' She blushed agitatedly, quickly dried a tear from her eye and looked down at the ground. *Kryptonite.*

'You thought you didn't turn me on?' *What an absurd pseudo-problem!* 'No! That wasn't it at all!' *I must be the only person on earth who gets an erection just thinking about crisp flat-bread and lingonberry jelly.* He stepped closer to her and stroked her arm. 'How in the world can you even think such a thing?'

Well, where should she start? With the strange feeling that Venus de Milo looked too ordinary to count as beautiful today? Or maybe Cissi's subdued posture when she said that she would never be unprepared again? Vera felt like a pathetic Don Quixote, insignificant in the face of overwhelming forces, but no other alternative was possible. Her pride was uncompromising and the thought painful: *This is what I am, and I'm not changing it. So take it or leave it!*

She was silent. The cat-like Amazon he had discovered in his bed stood before him, blushing indignantly, teeth clenched hard, hollows in her cheeks that weren't dimples at all. Her eyes were shiny and fierce when she looked up, locked eyes with him and refused to look away. He suddenly found it difficult to breathe. *Who wouldn't be turned on by her?*

He remembered her in his arms, her wide-eyed seriousness, how she had shared his solemn fascination with her abundant womanliness. And suddenly he realized what she had been trying, with great difficulty, to talk about.

Her husband. She had only been with Adam before him, and he had said it himself; Adam had had a completely outstanding wife, but *he hadn't...*

Peter looked away as a feeling of euphoria overwhelmed him. It meant that what he had experienced wasn't just lovesick wishful thinking. The conclusion made his heart race. Heaven *was* new for her too!

He turned away from her and focused all his energy on hiding the inappropriate joy he felt. He never wanted her to know how happy he was that Adam shared Charlie's inclinations! He felt a shameful gratitude towards Vera's ex-husband – the perfect parenthesis, the bridge over the gap. She got married when he had just finished ninth grade; he had been a pseudo-idiot for years. And yet there it was – paradise had waited for them! He suddenly realized that if Adam had been a normal man – *okay, wrong word, sorry, cousin* – a regular guy, then he and Vera would have had no chance. It was a sobering thought.

Would she have asked, 'Why is this a good idea?' during the

summer course? Absolutely.

Would she have yelled at her idiot neighbor? Probably.

Energized her colleague? Maybe.

Taken care of him when he was sick? Possibly.

Given him the most fantastic dance-floor moments in his life? Not *completely* impossible.

But several hours of the perfect wave... Not a chance. Not when that magic was already bestowed upon another charmed man. She would already have been caught by other open arms on the trapeze, busy with someone who would never let her fall. And letting go herself, unprovoked – that was something she would never have done. A done deal, gates to paradise locked. And that was no small thing. It was what he had first loved her for!

Imagine if she had just left him smoldering on the dance floor? The very thought of it was painful. He shook off the feeling of loss, reminded himself that in reality there was a chance, because as things stood now, half of the kingdom was his.

I want it to remain so. We'll keep it so. That's what integrity is for – he knew that, that's why it was so fantastic. The opportunity he saw before him was priceless. The gates would be locked with him on the inside, and all of her intoxicating magic, everything behind all the veils, would be and remain his, his Stradivarius to explore for eternity!

But the wave of hope that rolled over him was in sharp contrast to how she seemed to feel, because she was still defensively biding her time, seemingly impervious to his comforting hand. And he understood.

Of course she doesn't want to go through the same thing again!

'I think it was obvious on Friday, I mean, you don't need to be worried that I... I mean, I'm not inclined in another direction than... yours, you could say.'

Holy shit! He looked longingly at her, his feelings bouncing around inside him like a marble in a pinball machine.

'I can't imagine anything better. Quite simply, you are exactly to my taste.'

502

To put it mildly. So Matt and other strangers needn't bother, *because I belong to her and I plan to deserve her!*

She sat down on a log and thought about the ramifications of what he had said. It was as if he had opened his door and welcomed her into a cozy home, and now, for the first time, she had come in from the cold. Now she realized that she had lived her entire adult life in a miserable tent – a cold and uninviting place where heavenly experiences were impossible.

I can't imagine anything better!

She hung her head, hid her face in her hands; she was moved to tears.

'Vera! What's wrong?' He crouched down, trying to get her to look at him.

She slowly straightened up, took a breath to collect herself and looked at him. 'But then, why did you want me to leave?'

The memory swept through her like a rush of cold air from a door that was still open behind her. *A true 'I want you,'* and the response; *the sudden withdrawal, the blouse back in her hands, the reserved peck on the forehead. 'Forgive me Vera, this isn't right...'*

Was it so strange if that message – after four days of silence – had started to sound like only one thing – *'On second thoughts, no thanks.'* Or even worse – *'I really tried, but sorry, this isn't working!'*

He got up and looked out over the river. He really didn't want to talk about why he had forced himself to leave paradise.

Because I haven't been like Matt.

He turned pleadingly towards her. But he saw that she needed to know. He took a deep breath.

'You must never believe that I... I mean, it's the exact opposite – it worked spectacularly for me! There was nothing I wanted more than to be with you...' *I was just so incredibly turned on that I didn't trust myself. And when you...* He sighed, releasing a whimper. *Fuck my old reputation and my damned crap karma!*

'The last thing I wanted was you waking up the next day with

503

regrets, thinking I was still like I used to be and that I had...' He fell silent, ashamed of the ugly words.

No. Forget about Koyaanisqatsi. I'm playing to my strengths.

'I want you to trust me – I mean, trust me 100 per cent. That's why I wanted to wait for you. I want you to understand how special you are to me, and for you to come to me when you're sober.' He took a deep breath. 'So that I can be sure that you really want to, and will stay with me.'

Again, he imagined himself hanging from the branch over the edge of the cliff. Everything was in her hands now, and his heart beat so hard that he was sure she could see it. He glanced anxiously at her face.

Maybe the odds aren't so bad? A glimmer of hope awoke as she slowly got to her feet. It had nothing to do with her! The door closed behind her for good, and she was now completely enveloped, protected in the cozy home he offered her. And she knew that she could offer the same to him.

She remembered what Solveig had said about not always having to take so much bad with the good, about separating the two. *It's never problem-free, but it can be so much better.* She put her arms around him and sobbed against his throat. *You want me to stay with you? So much the better!*

His arms felt shaky when he put them around her, because a fearful uncertainty swept through him. *What is this?* Was his demand too much to ask – his uncontrollable need that she honor the promises he had understood her to make in his bed? An unbearable thought – was Kalle right? *Is this a goodbye?* He wished he could see her face; he needed to know what she was feeling.

'Vera, what is it?'

'Of course we should wait,' she answered thickly, head buried against him.

When he heard her voice, Peter realized with a jolt of relief that she was moved, not at all regretful about, his pitiful fate – the former serial heart-breaker who, when it suited him, suddenly thought he deserved immediate, magnificent faithfulness.

'What did you say?'

'Of course I'll wait for you.' She finished the thought in silence. *But preferably the waiting can be like it was on Friday...* She longed for this defiance of the laws of physics; it would be a sweet hunger to wait. She pulled herself away from him slightly and looked quietly up at his face.

I won't touch a button on your jeans. I promise! She bit her bottom lip and buried her face in the white shirt, pushed the association aside and looked up again.

'But why wouldn't I stay with you? Can't you see how good I feel when I'm with you?'

He hugged her, dried a tear on her hair and ached with longing to let her know that *you are the finest of women.*

'I have missed you so much!' she continued. 'I had a terrible dream last night. But then I dreamed that you came and that helped.'

Her words were healing him, just as her hands had when he had been feverish. In her words he also recognized the most precise answer to the question she had asked him before – why she had her own place in his world that was so superior to all the others.

He pulled her closer, felt her curves against him, the soft fabric of her dress, warm and silky under his fingers. He buried his face in her hair, and with a thick voice he whispered into her Elf ear.

'Vera, it is exactly like that for me too. You never need to compare yourself to anyone else, because I have everything I want and need when I am with you.' He took a deep breath, filled himself with her scent. 'You are the one who eases my nightmares.' *And do I help you with yours? Is that what you said?* An enormous happiness filled him. *The more I give to thee, the more I have.*

Taking in their verdant surroundings, Vera felt great joy. A new, marvellous, shining memory had been created. Suddenly it was less important how many others would continue to try to push their way forward to Prometheus; she no longer thought that he would lose sight of her. Her sense of trust had returned and she was neither afraid nor alone. She was not easy prey. She had finally let her feelings for Peter flow freely, and they rang strongly in her. Everything new and heavenly had come to her like a gift; all that was needed was the courage to believe in it. She stood on tiptoe and breathed in his scent from the hollow under his ear, ran her fingers through his hair, fumbling for the familiar bumps on his head.

When she finally pulled herself away from him and they began walking, he asked: 'You're on vacation from the middle of July, right? I want to show you something. Will you take the train to Biarritz with me, to the world's best surf spot?' He looked in her eyes, deep green like the rolling Atlantic waves.

'Why not?' *I would follow you anywhere.* 'I love snow-boarding, so I'm sure I'll like surfing too. I just have to take it easy.'

'You're probably better than me. I'm a beginner. I've only managed to get it to work once. Just once, but I'm completely sold – addicted for life. That says something about the quality of the experience.'

He glanced at her and squeezed her hand. She nodded and looked down at the ground. They walked in silence a while, listening to the soft murmur of the river, their steps, the rustling of the aspen leaves and the birds.

'Is it very hard?'

'What?'

'Do you fall a lot, when you're surfing?' She looked at him.

'Yeah, I think so. In the beginning, anyway.' He suddenly realized that he had spent a whole day falling in different ways. 'It's actually a bit strange. When I couldn't do it, it was exhausting and I ended up with all kinds of grazes and bruises, yet every time I fell, I just thought, "up and at it again!" But the time I was in the Baltic – I made one error and I almost killed myself!'

'Oh yes, the Baltic. I've heard it's really hard to surf there.'

'Yes, it is.'

'But it isn't so strange, really.'

'What?'

'I mean, it's not exactly soft sand there, is it?'

'No.' *Dangerously rocky, in fact.*

'And the water's brackish. The mix of salt and fresh water

means it has lower density, so you don't float as well. You have to be really skilled to manage it.'

His whole body smiled. *Really skilled. Maybe I can be that, with practice.*

'The science nerd has spoken,' she said.

'Yes, my beloved know-all.'

'The question is, how will you put up with it long term?'

'Well, it won't be easy. The question is whether I prefer to live in ignorance.'

They smiled at each other.

'No, seriously, Vera. Trying to understand and solve problems – isn't that what we do? And you're fantastically good at it. Usually. When you aren't completely wrong, of course.'

She stopped. She felt like this was important. 'And then it's *your* job to object.'

'Yes, like you did when I was completely lost, and you said, "Your biggest problem is yourself." Do you remember?'

'Yes, but you seem to have solved it now.'

He looked away, down at the path. Yes, he was a lot better, more interested in other people's feelings in general, and Vera's in particular. *But don't think too highly of me*, he thought. He knew that if he had been able to control Vera's fate, he wouldn't have changed anything. Adam and the hell she must have lived through was what had brought her to him.

He suddenly saw something he'd never seen before in the moist ground beside the path. 'What are these, all these small roses?' Peter pointed at the tender flowers.

'*Rubus arcticus*,' smiled Vera.

'What's that?'

'They bear fruit, small berries, like little rubies when they mature in August.' *As exquisite as you.*

'It's a tiny plant.' He crouched down and carefully touched the petal.

'Yes, if you don't know what you're looking for they're difficult to see. To find them you have to look a long time and have a bit of luck. But it's worth the effort. Just for the scent alone.'

He stood up, looked at her and realized that she had no idea that he felt as though she were talking about herself. They walked on in silence.

Vera glanced at him. He had seemed uncomfortable when she complimented him, even though she had spoken the truth. Yet she was determined to say something more.

'You're so open and flexible.' *Such hope and potential.* She looked at him, remembering how he had pulled her to him – *the strips of muscle fibres on those shoulders!* A wave of desire surprised her as she briefly relived being in his bed. She supported herself against the trunk of a tree and concentrated on what she wanted to say.

'I'll have to work a little harder on my biggest problem.'

'What's that?'

'Trying to be perfect.'

'Okay, but don't work on it *too* hard, because you're seriously good the way you are. I just don't want you to be so hard on yourself that you feel bad or tie yourself up in knots and close in on yourself.' He suddenly looked worried. 'Not communicating is bad! It's like your nerves die. Worst-case scenario – you can injure people without even realizing it; it's like leprosy.' *Shit! It can be like what happened between my parents!*

Yes, Vera realized – that's what should have been written in the autopsy report about the sudden demise of Cissi and Jocke's life together. She winced. *How many of the world's problems are like this?* We chug along mindlessly because the nerves that connect our actions to an understanding of their consequences are dead.

Peter looked at her. 'Really bad things can happen if you don't communicate.' His turquoise eyes radiated a pure-hearted desire to connect. Attraction and great devotion flowed powerfully through her again, as she thought about the beautiful, impressive courage in the person she had so fruitlessly tried not to love. That courage that had decided the outcome – safety instead of catastrophe, the cure for leprosy.

'Yes, I know, you can even go around thinking that *I* seduced poor Matt.'

At first he reacted with a sting of discomfort, but then he looked into her eyes. Her energy spoke to him: *A stress test I know we can take. A figment of your imagination that you can forget about.*

Flattered that she already dared to joke about it, he grinned appreciatively. He felt so much a man that he didn't need to compete with anyone. And he felt a mild happiness for Matt.

'There's no such thing as "poor" Matt. And I wonder exactly who seduced whom. It sounded pretty mutual to me.'

'Yes, she's completely charmed by him,' admitted Vera with a smile.

'It's not hard to see why!'

'Ah, you think so?' Her eyes sparkled mischievously.

'Yeah, you know, a Game Changer – dark and good-looking, a bit on the short side, talented and the kindest person in the world, although not wimpy, the integrity of an Elf. Then you're addicted for life.'

And now I've said it twice. Fear flickered in him. But she laughed and looked happy, linking her arm with his and threading her fingers into his. Then she squeezed his hand.

'I like it when you laugh,' he said, squeezing back. 'You seem to feel a lot better now than in the winter.'

'Yes, I do.' *That's an understatement*, she thought. 'I'm a completely different person.'

'I am too.' She smiled at him, and he saw her reply. *I know.*

Bare wrists touching, pulse to pulse, hands clasped together as if in joint prayer, they descended the hill. Sensitive, flexible and strong, with happy expectation in every cell. *Everything we no longer need to be and everything we can become. Shangri-La?*

Acknowledgements

The journey towards *Integrity* has been aided by many, including the jury that awarded an early draft first place in an anonymous screenplay contest. The development of the story while in script form was, thanks to this, aided by producer Göran Lindström and film dramatists Kirsten Bonnén Rask and Jimmy Karlsson.

I also want to thank John Truby, who for years accompanied me to the gym: his was the voice in my headphones, telling me about masterpieces, love, comedy and detective stories.

Thanks to the Kogi, Alan Ereira and the rest of the BBC team behind *The Heart of the World* for a mysterious coincidence, to Doctors Without Borders for providing hope and rescue every day (some golden karma you guys are building!) and to everyone else, near and far, who has dared to tell me things, some very personal, that have allowed me to understand.

Many thanks to my colleagues at Polarbröd, The Natural Step and all other doers out there who are busy reconstructing the ways we provide for ourselves on the urgent journey towards a sustainable livelihood for all. I am honored to be working with you.

I am grateful for support and contributions from Cajsa, Petra, Jonas, Peter, Annika E, Marcus, Lena, Maria, Martin, Annika Å, Karin L, Solveig, Berith, Börje, Jonathan, Pär, Linus, Ida, Mats, Catharina, Gracia and many more.

Thanks to Rickard for being a writer's best lawyer, to Johan for your unfailing eye and to all Swedish followers sharing your insights and reading experiences on the *Tunna väggar* Facebook wall.

Many thanks to Chris for intuitively getting it, professionally editing it and naming it *Integrity*. I am thankful to Jo, able to read Swedish, for her recommendations and keen eye on the text. Thanks to everyone at New Internationalist who voted to take on this genre-breaking novelty. I am grateful to Cindy for intelligent viewpoints and for diligently translating it into English, while keeping it true to itself.

Finally, thanks to Roger for structural integrity and everything we can still become, to my aunt Elisabet for development, to my parents Kjell and Margareta for your appreciation and everything you have taught me, to my uncle Anders for adorning our lives with your endlessly creative *Västerbotten* humor, and to my late great-aunt Edith for inspiration. Thanks to my one and only sister Karin for putting up with 'Being in the head of Anna Borgeryd' and, as usual, emerging with support and good suggestions for improvement.